Blessed Are
the Cheesemakers

Blessed Are the Cheesemakers

Sarah-Kate Lynch

WARNER BOOKS

An AOL Time Warner Company

Copyright © 2002 by Sarah-Kate Lynch
All rights reserved.

This Warner Books edition is published by arrangement with Black Swan, Random House New Zealand, 18 Poland Road, Glenfield, Auckland, New Zealand.

Warner Books, Inc., 1271 Avenue of the Americas, New York, NY 10020
Visit our Web site at www.twbookmark.com.

 An AOL Time Warner Company

Printed in the United States of America
First U.S. Printing: July 2003
10 9 8 7 6 5 4 3 2 1

Library of Congress Cataloging-in-Publication Data

Lynch, Sarah-Kate.
    Blessed are the cheesemakers / Sarah-Kate Lynch.
        p. cm.
        ISBN 0-446-53128-6
            1. Grandparent and child—Fiction. 2. Dairy farmers—Fiction.
    3. Cheesemakers—Fiction. 4. Farm life—Fiction. 5. Aged men—Fiction.
    6. Ireland—Fiction. I. Title.

PR9639.4.L96 B58 2003
823'.92—dc21

                                                                2002031127

Book design by Giorgetta Bell McRee

For Sandy Lynch and Mark Robins
with all my love

Blessed Are
the Cheesemakers

"What's so special about the cheesemakers?"

Monty Python's *Life of Brian*
Handmade Films (1979)

CHAPTER ONE

*"You can't hurry cheese. It happens in its own time
and if that bothers you, you can just feck off."*

Joseph Feehan, from *The Cheese Diaries*,
Radio Telefis Eireann (RTE) Radio Archives

The Princess Grace Memorial Blue sat on the table in front of Abbey, screaming to be eaten.

Abbey, as always, was smiling her dreamy smile, her eyes half closed and her head slightly thrown back, as though she were preparing to blow out a candle and make a wish. Well, it was her twenty-ninth birthday, after all, and there would have been candles, too, had not the Princess Grace been a particularly fussy cheese, inclined to expel a pungent foul-smelling aroma if fiddled with in any fashion. Actually, this pernicketiness was what made her so special. She was made with fresh Coolarney milk hand-expressed at daybreak every April 19 and she was treated like royalty from the first tweak of the first teat to the last crumb on the last tongue. She insisted on it. She was that sort of a cheese.

Her creators, Joseph Corrigan and Joseph Feehan, better known as Corrie and Fee, could not take their eyes off her. They'd been making the Memorial Blues just one day a year ever since Grace Kelly (with whom they were both in love at the time) broke their hearts by marrying Prince Rainier of Monaco on April 19 in 1956. The resulting cheeses were wildly sought after and cherished through-out the world, but nowhere as much as at home.

"She's a fine feckin' thing," Fee said, licking his lips in a mildly lascivious manner, his cheeks rosy with anticipation as his fat round bottom bounced in its seat.

"She's all right," agreed Corrie, raising his eyebrows in a show of appreciation. Abbey looked on, smiling.

Princess Grace stood taller than the average Coolarney Blue. Her flesh was palest blond, the exact shade of her namesake's hair in her heyday, and her veins were a perfect mixture of sky blue and sea green, silvery in some lights, black in others, depending on her mood.

Her fans had been sitting in the smoking room for nearly two hours, just watching and waiting for her to reach the perfect temperature. The room was their favorite and, unlike almost every other in the rambling, gracious home, was out of bounds to the many Coolarney House comers and goers. It needed little sun, which was just as well because little sun was what it got. Two whole walls were devoted to shelves, overflowing with magazines and books, some of them over one hundred years old. The other walls were painted a rich dark green and the wood-work, too, was varnished extra dark, giving a somber, hunting lodge sort of appeal.

Corrie was in his brown leather La-Z-Boy rocker recliner, Fee in his overstuffed patched brocade armchair. Between them, on a little round table with unmistakable altar overtones, as befitted this and every cheese-eating occasion, sat the glorious Grace and, of course, Abbey.

At seventy-three Corrie bore the same uncanny resemblance to Jimmy Stewart that he had as a younger man (although the girls commented on this less now that Jimmy was mostly a memory, long since replaced by Mels and Harrisons and Brads). His eyes were sparkling blue, his gray hair thick and slicked back with some ancient odor-free hair cream. He'd been six feet two once upon a time, but admitted now to a stoop that he blamed on the years spent bending over the cheese vat, which had shortened him by a couple of inches. Always impeccably dressed, he was wearing a pale blue woolen sweater over a crisp white cotton shirt and a dark brown pair of '50s-style high-waisted trousers.

Fee, on the other hand, was wearing a desperate pair of pond-scum green corduroy pants, belted around his not insubstantial middle with an old piece of twine. His checked brown shirt and gray cardigan matched only in the number of holes that happened in the same spot, giving the impression that at some stage, many years earlier, he had perhaps been poked all over with a giant sharpened pencil.

Fee was as short and stout as Corrie was tall and lean, and should they be standing close together, as they often were, from a distance they looked for all the world like the letters *d* or *b*—depending on which side Fee was standing.

"Twenty-nine," Fee said, shaking his head in Abbey's direction, his voice tinged with a peculiar sort of amazement. "You wouldn't credit it."

Corrie nodded in agreement, and looked from Abbey to the Princess and back again. God knew he loved his cheeses, but what he felt for Abbey at that precise moment, or any moment she occupied his thoughts, no dairy product of any kind, even an impeccably flawless gem like Princess Grace, could ever hope to match. Yet still he felt sad. He poked at the fire's glowing embers and concentrated on the loud tick-tocking of his grandfather's clock as they waited in companionable silence.

"It's time, Joseph," Fee said finally, when he knew that it was, and he sat forward in his chair and reached for his cheese knife.

"For Grace?" Corrie asked, surprised. He'd have thought it another while away yet, but Fee was the expert, there'd be no argument there.

"For a lot of things," Fee said cryptically, sucking a wedge of the Princess off the blade of his bone-handled knife and forcing it up against the roof of his mouth. He pushed his tongue against it, soaking up its perfect texture and exquisite flavor.

"Right so," said Corrie, gently moving in to slice a chunk out of Grace with his own stainless-steel knife. He'd known Joseph Feehan for seventy-three years and for the first sixty-five had tried to make sense of what he said. More recently he had given up, realizing that it made no difference to the outcome and anyway it was part of Fee's charm. And Fee needed all the charm he could get.

Corrie raised his knife, sporting its perfectly balanced creamy blue wedge, in the direction of Abbey and toasted her.

"Happy birthday, Abbey," he said. "I hope you're enjoying it and please God you'll be with us for the next one."

Abbey kept smiling her dreamy smile, eyes half closed, head slightly thrown back.

Corrie tucked his melancholy away and surrendered his senses to the touch and taste of Princess Grace. How she lingered on his lips! How she sang to his saliva! How she tap-danced on his taste buds! When the last tingle of the first taste had melted away to nothing, Corrie turned to his granddaughter, reached across the table and picked her up, planting a kiss on her smile. He looked at the photo awhile, tracing with his smooth cheesemaker's finger the lip-shaped smudge his kiss had left on the glass in the frame, then he sighed and put Abbey back on the table.

It's time all right, Fee thought quietly to himself as he reached for another wedge.

CHAPTER TWO

"Once upon a time, before the world was run by men in fancy suits, 'grass roots' meant just that. Grass roots. With cheese, that's where it all begins. You can't make good cheese with bad grass."

Joseph Feehan, from *The Cheese Diaries*,
RTE Radio Archives

A month or two later, across the Atlantic in New York City, another Princess Grace was living a far less fêted existence. Sure, she was sitting in a state-of-the-art refrigerator in a $7,000-a-month loft apartment in fashionable SoHo, but her only companions were two bottles of Budweiser and half a pizza that had gnarled and twisted almost beyond recognition.

The Princess oozed annoyance. She emanated anger. She fumed. Literally. She *fumed*. And when a good Princess turned bad, it was an eye-watering experience. She'd been sitting there in her waxed wrapper inside a brown paper bag from Murray's Cheese for nearly three months now, and it had taken this long to permeate all the layers. Now, her time for being tasty was over. Now she was just plain evil.

In the bedroom down the hallway Kit Stephens, oblivious to this, opened his eyes and felt the bashing of a thousand tiny hammers against his skull.

"Go away," he growled to himself. "Leave me alone."

The banging continued. It was still dark in his room, but then that was what three walls of mind-bogglingly expensive blinds straight out of the pages of *Wallpaper* bought you in Manhattan. It meant nothing. It could have been midday for all he knew (although he hoped it was not). The mere thought of moving his arm to look for his watch, however, made him heave.

Searching the bits of his brain that weren't being hacked at by pickaxes, he tried to recall the events of the previous night. There'd been martinis, a lot of them, after work at China Grill, he could remember that. Then there had been some inedible muck at one of the ethnic restaurants that Manhattan was full of these days. He could vaguely remember crashing through a Korean place to the secret bar at the back and, Jesus, had someone been doing lines there?

Kit moved his head ever so slightly and looked at the other side of the bed. Someone was in it. And it wasn't Jacey. Jacey had long blond hair, a model's body and the face of an angel. Whoever this was had short black hair, a model's body and a face he couldn't see because she was lying on her stomach, turned away from him. Actually, thought Kit, almost raising his head off the pillow despite its condition, her shoulder blades were exquisite and the back of her neck . . . Ouch. The back of her neck just ached to be nuzzled and kissed.

A lump rose in his throat as he thought about the back of Jacey's neck. He closed his eyes again and stopped almost raising his head. Would he ever get used to waking up without her? Or worse, waking up with a complete stranger and wondering how the hell she got into his bed? It hadn't happened often, but it had happened. He looked over at the beautiful back of whoever she was and felt nothing but an overwhelming sadness tinged with shame. He was feeling a lot of that lately.

Kit took a deep breath, rolled onto his side and swung his legs out of the bed, his head spinning with the movement, despite trying, as he was, to sit up in slow motion. Carefully he stood up, waiting to see how the contents of his stomach would cope. Almost immediately he felt rebellion from down below and, staggering to the bathroom, he fell to his knees on the tiled floor, clutched the toilet bowl like an old friend and horked up half of Ethiopia's annual food supply.

Classy, Kit thought to himself as the retching started to subside. Real classy. With a groan he let himself slide down to the floor until his face hit the tiles and, comforted by their coldness and hardness, the room spinning slowly around him, he passed out.

"Hey, buddy. You. Buddy. Wake up!"

Coming to sometime later was hardly a more enjoyable experience. The girl who had been in his bed was now standing over him, nudging his shoulder with her foot. She wore metallic purple nail polish and had a silver ring on her second toe.

"Jesus, I thought you were dead," she said, standing naked with her hands on her snakelike hips, looking down at him. "You got any cigarettes? Beer? Blow? Anything?"

Kit slowly pulled himself up to a sitting position and leaned back against the wall beside the toilet, suddenly irrationally embarrassed by being naked in front of this strange woman.

"Yeah, right." The strange woman snorted derisively at his modesty, then turned around and sat on the toilet.

Kit rested his head on his knees and listened to the tinkling sound of her bladder being emptied.

"Don't worry," she said in a bored tone, her hand flailing around beside him looking for the toilet paper. "We didn't do it or anything. Just talked about your dead wife for two hours." She wiped herself, sniffed, stood up and flushed the toilet as what she had said sunk into Kit's addled brain.

Jacey was dead? The little hammers had stopped banging but Kit was suddenly being deafened by another sound: his heart beating louder and louder and louder inside his chest. Jacey was dead. Jacey was dead. Jacey was dead. If he said it enough times, maybe . . . He threw on the brakes. The little men with hammers were easier to bear than memories of Jacey. He hugged his knees even closer to his body, and although he really, really didn't want to—especially in front of this girl, whoever she was—he started to cry.

"Jesus," said the girl, by now washing her hands. She looked at him in mild disgust, then snatched a towel from the heated rail and threw it at his feet before turning to inspect her pretty face in the mirror. "Hey, where did you get that coke anyway?" she said, zooming in on an imaginary spot on her flawless skin and inserting a casual tone to the question that was far from genuine. "It was pretty good."

Kit picked up the soft, warm towel she'd thrown at him and buried his head in it, soaking up the comforting clean smell and rubbing the velvety fabric up and down against his cheeks, sobbing as noiselessly as he could.

"So, would it be okay if I, like, helped myself to your stash before I go?" the girl said. Kit looked up and saw she was twisting her hips at him like a little girl asking for candy. Her pubic hair was waxed into a tiny little Brazilian runway, which for some reason depressed him even further. He felt disgusting. Disgusted. With himself.

"Okay," the girl said, after he collapsed into his towel again. "*What*ever."

She padded out of the bathroom. Sometime later, Kit had no idea whether it was five minutes or fifty-five minutes, he heard the door to his apartment open and close and he knew she was gone.

What's happening to me? he bawled into his towel, but he couldn't bear to answer himself. Instead he thought about his breathing, then, when he had controlled the sobbing, he crawled into the shower where he let the hot water deal with his hangover and his tears.

Half an hour later he was dressed and shaved. It was past eight o'clock and he had already missed the seven o'clock trading meeting, not for the first time in recent weeks. He would have hundreds of messages waiting from clients and e-mails mounting by the moment. George would be pissed.

Kit looked at himself in the hallway mirror. Apart from the dark circles under his eyes, he thought he looked okay. The square, handsome face looking back at him showed little sign of a late night binge or, worse, he cringed, a crying jag. But as he stared at the green-eyed image of himself, Kit felt the thoughts he hadn't wanted earlier attempt another ambush on his brain, and the weird feeling he'd been having so often started to creep from his groin through his gut and up to his chest.

He was sure he saw his face grow pale in the mirror and, unless his imagination was playing tricks on him, each breath was more shallow and coming quicker than the last. Panicked, he gripped the hall table, his knuckles white with the effort. Then he saw it. Sitting in the silver tray with his keys and his wallet was a little plastic bag containing a dusting of white powder. So that's what the girl had been talking about. The blow. But why hadn't she taken it? Kit thought to himself as he stood, trembling, in his hallway. It wasn't his. He didn't do drugs. He never had and he never would. Especially not now, after . . .

A vague dreamlike image of money changing hands in a busy bar started to cloud his thoughts like an incoming storm, and panic grabbed again at his stomach. He tried to get his breathing under control but still it raced away from him, dread lurching from his heart to his guts and back again. If he was going to be able to cope with the next few moments, let alone the rest of the day, he needed to ease whatever was gnawing away at him.

Grabbing the little plastic bag from the hall table, he stumbled into the kitchen and emptied what little remained of its contents into the sink and washed it down the drain. He rinsed out the bag and threw it in the trash.

His stomach was still revolting. He needed to calm down. He needed peace and tranquility. Kit looked at the refrigerator for less than a heartbeat before opening the door. The smell hit him like a tsunami but, blind to the Princess and her fury, he had eyes only for the Grey Goose in the freezer.

He poured the contents of the bottle down his throat, his chaotic innards falling into line as they were massaged by the smooth satiny vodka. Relieved and much calmer, he easily took a deep, long breath and headed for the door, looking again in the mirror as he walked by with a confident smile. Now he could face the day.

Outside his apartment, the Peterson girls were giggling in the hallway, waiting for the elevator. Or him. Giggling and the Peterson girls went hand in hand where Kit was concerned, although he had not noticed this until Jacey pointed it out and started a relentless campaign of teasing him about it. Since then, he'd tried as hard as he could to avoid them, avoid the whole family, in fact. It had been their mother, Sasha, who had found Jacey and—Kit pulled nervously at his tie. He closed his eyes and tried not to think about it again. About her.

Inside the elevator, the two girls continued to whisper and giggle, getting louder and louder until finally the elder one, Charlotte, pushed the younger one, Jessica, so that she fell into him. She jumped away and stood up straight, blushing and glaring at her sister.

"Ask him," dared Charlotte. "Go on. Ask him."

Kit turned to look at Jessica, as though he had only just noticed her.

"Ask me what?" he said as coolly as he could without being unfriendly.

Jessica shook her head and hugged her schoolbag close to her chest.

"Ask him," insisted Charlotte, eyeballing her sister ferociously.

"Ask me what?" said Kit, now directing his question at Charlotte.

"Ask you what Coco Lloyd was doing coming out of your apartment at 7:30 this morning," said Charlotte boldly.

Kit's confidence in his ability to handle the day vanished. He felt sick, but tried not to look it. So he'd been right. She was a model. Trust one of those Prada-conscious Peterson girls to be lurking around at just the wrong time. (He hadn't done anything wrong but that didn't mean he didn't feel like he had done something wrong. He considered offering up a prayer that the girls wouldn't tell their mother but doubted he'd get a lot of sympathy.) It was less than three months since he'd lost Jacey, and he didn't want Sasha Peterson to think he was that sort of guy because he wasn't.

"I'm doing some work on her stock portfolio and she was dropping off some papers, if you must know," he said, acting far more nonchalant than he felt. Picking up strange women in bars was really not his thing, even if it had happened a couple of times lately. Not to mention that it was too soon. He thought so and everybody else would too. "She's one beautiful woman, though, I'll give you that," he added.

Charlotte and Jess exploded with laughter.

"'She's one beautiful woman,'" Charlotte mimicked, amid snorts and guffaws.

"What's wrong with that? What's funny about that? She is a beautiful woman," Kit said, vaguely annoyed, as the elevator arrived at the ground floor and the door opened.

"She's a beautiful *girl,* jerk-off," said Charlotte as she pushed past him. "She's in Jessie's grade at school."

Kit felt the familiar frenzy clawing at his innards again. Barely able to move, he watched Charlotte and Jessica wave at the doorman before disappearing into the street in their school uniforms. In Jessie's grade at school? But Jess was only in eleventh grade. How old did that make her? Sixteen? Fifteen?

"Oh, Jesus," groaned Kit.

"All right there, Mr. Stephens?" Benny the doorman called, stepping out from behind his desk with a worried look on his face as he came to Kit's aid. "You'd better sit down. You look all done in."

He guided the shaking Kit over to the leather sofa in the reception area and eased him down onto it. "Can I get you anything? A glass of water?"

Kit nodded his head and Benny disappeared into his office just as Kit's cell phone started to ring. The feeling of dread doubled, then tripled, then multiplied itself by a thousand.

"Kit Stephens," he said, without much enthusiasm, into the phone.

"Where the hell are you, Christopher?" George's voice boomed out of the earpiece. "We've got the Chemocorp deal going through this morning, the AsiaBank report—as if I need to remind you—out at eleven and your assistant is starting to put your calls through to me because some of your clients are ringing back for the third time today. Did I mention we missed you at the meeting this morning? Christ, that's the second time this week, Kit."

There was silence.

"Kit, are you there?"

"Yes, George, I'm on my way. Something came up and I—"

"Spare me the details. Just get here." George hung up in his ear.

"Sounds like what you might call a shit of a morning, huh, Mr. Stephens?" Benny said cheerfully, appearing at his side with a glass of water, which Kit glugged down greedily before getting to his feet and checking to see if his legs were working properly.

"You could say that, Benny. God, what's the matter with me?" He felt his pockets just to reassure himself he was still inside his suit, then exhaled sharply and collected his wits. "Hey, thanks for the water, pal," he said. "I was just, uh, surprised by something the Peterson girls sprung on me, that's all."

He offered the doorman a weak smile and patted him on the shoulder in a friendly show of appreciation.

"They'll have a few more surprises in store for the likes of us, them two, huh?" said Benny as he watched Kit's back retreat through the doors and out into the street in search of a cab.

For once, Kit didn't stop to take in the breathtaking view from the twenty-seventh floor of the glass and stainless building they called the Toast Rack when he arrived at work.

His assistant, Niamh, stood up from behind her desk when she saw him and intercepted him at the door to his office. "George wants to see you," she said, looking at him closely. "And I don't think he wants to swap recipes."

Kit closed his eyes and tried to straighten his head. Niamh strode back to her desk and opened her top drawer, returning with some breath-freshening mints.

"Don't blow it now, Kit," she said, staring at him with her earnest eyes. "You've come too far."

For a moment Kit thought about asking her to hold him and let him cry for a while on her shoulder. But even through the jelly in his head he realized now was probably not the time. Now was the time to get yelled at by George, his friend and boss, a guy famous for having very little patience and a lot of sarcasm. He turned and walked past the rows of trading desks where eighty of his colleagues were shouting into headsets and bashing at their telephones and keyboards. Nobody was looking at him but he couldn't remember if that was normal or not. He passed Eddie's office but the door was shut. Maybe Ed hadn't made it into work this morning either. God, thought Kit, it would be great to not be the only one in the shit.

George's assistant, Pearl, a gorgeous Asian woman with legs that raised the temperature of water coolers the whole floor over, indicated that he should go straight in.

George was behind his desk, on the phone. "I'll call you

right back," he said into the receiver and placed it carefully in its cradle.

"Kit," he said, motioning for him to sit down. "So nice of you to join us."

George's eyes were as cold as Christmas yet his lips were smiling and the sunlight glinting off his shiny bald head cast a certain jauntiness on the scenario. Kit suddenly wondered if he was dreaming and started to smile as well. Maybe the not-really-happening-to-him feeling that had been plaguing him these past few weeks was justified. Maybe it wasn't really happening to him.

"I'm glad to see you have retained your sense of humor, Christopher," George said, the smile slipping off his face like mud in a landslide. "That the seriousness of the situation is not dampening your spirits in any way."

Kit cleared his throat. The chances of it all being a dream, he supposed, were really quite slim but that was okay. He wasn't naturally a dreamer, he had his feet on the ground, everyone said so.

"God, George," he said. "I'm real sorry about this morning. It's just that, ah, I got held up back at the apartment with the neighbors. One of their girls had taken the dog for a walk and lost it in the park and Sasha Peterson—remember her? I think you met her last Thanksgiving. Anyway, she came and asked if I could—"

George, unable to listen to another syllable of Kit's labored excuse, suddenly thumped his fist on his desk with a rage of which Kit had heard but never dreamed he would bear the brunt.

"Don't. Fuck. With. Me. Kit," he said in a voice so cold and hard Kit couldn't believe he wasn't shouting. "I've had enough. I've heard enough. You are messing up big time, buddy, and you are not going to do it on my shift any longer."

"Your shift?" Kit laughed, albeit nervously. "Come on, George, what is this, *Hill Street Blues*?"

George took a deep breath. "Kit, you don't seem to understand. You seem to have forgotten that there are kids out there on that trading desk who would do your job for free, just to prove that they can. There are kids out on the streets who would do the jobs of the kids on the trading desk, just to prove that they can. The places left empty on the streets? They would be filled like that"—he snapped his fingers—"with other kids also willing to do anything, *anything*, for nothing, no money, nothing, just to prove that they can. Are you with me?"

Kit was bewildered.

"What I am saying, Christopher, is that you are no longer an indispensable part of the broking team here at Fitch, Wright and Ray. As of 8:30 this morning your clients were transferred to Ed Lipman, and your office is to be occupied by Tom Foster from the desk. We will pay you a month's notice and your stock options can be cashed in with no penalty for choosing not to remain employed here for the required ten years, although you will have to wait until the ten years is up. I believe that will be, luckily for you, in just a couple of weeks' time. In the meantime, good-bye."

The sun still glinted off of George's bald pate as Kit sat stunned in his seat.

"Jesus, George," he said, trying to laugh and failing miserably. "You're firing me?"

"No, Kit, you are resigning."

George paused, then looked at his friend and shook his head, thawing slightly now that the worst part was over. "Jesus, man, look at yourself," he said more softly. "You've been a mess since Jacey—"

"This is *not* about Jacey," Kit broke in, his voice shaky but determined nonetheless. "Do *not* talk about Jacey."

"Kit, you've got to accept the facts," said George, exasperated. "Without her, you have been a disaster area. Jesus, and I thought *with* her you were a disaster area. You can't do a decent day's work anymore, Kit. You don't sleep. You can't concentrate. Your drinking is way out of control. I can't trust you anymore. Your clients can't trust you anymore. You're a mess, my friend. You are an embarrassment."

"But, George," Kit said, feeling the words starting in his throat strong and sure before stumbling over his tongue, tripping on his lips to end up weak and pathetic and whining, "we're buddies. I'm your daughter's godfather, for chrissakes. I made a speech at your wedding. Jesus, we go back. Way back. I'm your top guy. We built this firm up together, you and Eddie and me, from almost nothing. The money I've made you, made us. God, doesn't that count for something?"

George looked at him sadly. "Kit, the day you met Jacey Grey was the day you stopped being my top guy. It was bad enough when she was here but since she's been gone you have turned into someone I don't even know anymore. Look at you! I can smell the booze from here, Kit. When did you have your last drink? Did you even get any sleep last night? Can you even remember where you were, what you did?"

Smell the booze? What was he talking about? Kit started to feel the panic rising in his stomach again.

"Remember what I did? Sure," he said, uncertainly. "Had a few drinks with the guys at the Grill and then, uh, hung out a bit, I guess. What does it matter?"

"It matters to me," said George, once again cold and

unfriendly. "It particularly matters to me that you downed half a dozen tequila shots in some swanky bankers' joint then shouted for Cristal for your companions before snorting a line of coke on the bar in front of two of our biggest clients. You then tried to pay the bill with your company credit card, which, by the way, is maxed out. It's not the nineties anymore, Kit. Nobody wants to see money being spent like that. It's disgusting."

Kit was speechless. George had his facts wrong. What the hell was he going on about? Snorting coke in a bar? Someone had been but it wasn't him. The panicky feeling had reached the insides of his face by now. A drink would be great, he thought. He realized he was sweating.

"You're not the smart, great-looking guy from Burlington, Vermont, who'll do anything to prove himself to the world anymore, Kit," continued George, his anger building again. "You're just another Wall Street burnout with a drinking problem and I don't want to know you anymore. I don't know you anymore. Now, get out."

George dismissed Kit by picking up his phone and punching in a number. "I said, get out," he repeated as he waited for his call to go through. "Straighten out. Clean up your act, Kit. Maybe you can start again someplace else."

By the time Kit had stood up and made it to the door, George was already explaining to Neil Ryan, formerly one of Kit's A-list clients, that Ed would be taking him to lunch next week to discuss future initiatives. Standing outside George's office, Kit looked around the trading floor. Not one single dealer could meet his eye. The noise in the room seemed wrong. Too quiet. Or too loud. He wasn't sure, couldn't remember. They all knew, Kit suddenly thought, feeling the sweat running down his spine under his shirt. They all knew.

Attempting to pull himself together, he walked down the hall to Eddie's office and opened the door without knocking. Eddie was sitting on the edge of his desk laughing, his back to the view. Tom Foster was sitting opposite him.

"Kit, hello," Eddie said, standing up as the smile dropped from his face. "Tom, would you excuse us for a moment? Thank you."

Tom snuck a look at Kit before snatching a bunch of files off Ed's desk and leaving the room.

"Did you know about this?" Kit demanded, trying to sound angry but only half getting there. "Did you know George was going to fire me?"

Eddie slunk around behind his desk and sat down. For the first time ever, Kit noticed how smarmy he looked. That slicked-back blond hair, those glasses. The lips already too moist that he kept licking. Was this really his best friend? The firm's other hotshot managing director? He and Eddie had been George's natural choices as right-hand men and had helped him build the firm up to the level and significant status it enjoyed in the banking industry today. They had worked and played together side by side for years now, yet suddenly he felt as if he'd never really looked at Eddie before.

"Listen, Kit," his friend said soothingly, picking his words carefully, "this has been coming for a while, you must know that. Christ, you can't even make it to lunch without a drink these days; you're not paying your way, your clients are nervous. What did you think would happen?"

Kit slumped into the chair left warm by Foster's butt. The butt that was replacing his.

"God, doesn't a guy get a second chance around here?" he tried to joke. "Couldn't you have said something to me? Warned me?"

Eddie looked pained. "Kit, you have had all the second chances and warnings you were ever going to get. Jesus, it's not as though we didn't try to help you. There was the weekend up at Mary's family place when we tried to sober you up for two days. There was the counseling George organized. We had an intervention at your apartment, for chrissakes. What else could we have done?"

Kit was stunned. Not for the first time he felt as though he had slipped into the shoes of some nightmare-ish stranger. Counseling? Sobering up? Intervention? Was it possible they were talking about him?

"Christ, Ed. You talk as though I have some sort of terrible problem. I mean, it's not like I go out drinking on my own. You're usually there, for one. I mean, you were there last night. You're always there."

"The difference is, Kit, that I stop and I go home. And I get up and come to work in the morning." Eddie paused and looked him in the eye. "Tell me, Kit, what time did I go home last night?"

Kit stared at him. Had Eddie been at the restaurant? The secret Korean bar? Jesus, was George's story about the coke true? Had Eddie seen that? And why hadn't he stopped it? He cleared his throat. "You came to the Tibetan place," he said, without great certainty. "And then Mary called and you left."

The pity—or was it disgust—was plain on Ed's face.

"I had one martini at the Grill and advised you to do the same," Ed said, "then I went home. I don't even know those guys you were with, Kit, did you? They were assholes. Hey, we all feel bad about Jacey and the baby, buddy. But when it comes down to it she's gone. You're still here, and you're fucking things up, man, just like she did."

The brick wall Kit had built in his mind to block out the pain of what happened to Jacey started to crumble. The baby. He couldn't bear it. With all his might, he put the bricks back in place. Then, sitting in Ed's office, looking out across the buildings and cranes to the glimpses of green from Central Park beyond, he suddenly caught flashes of Ed and Mary and George and Julia searching his apartment. For what? Something round and silver flashed in his memory. Something jammed in the S-bend of the basin in his bathroom. The top of a bottle? Jesus.

"We all wanted to help you, Kit, but nothing we do seems to make any difference. You can't expect the company to pay the price for the fallout from Jacey."

Kit shut his eyes. Flashes of Jacey lying on the floor invaded his thoughts. Jacey, her face pale and blank, their unborn baby already dead inside her. His heart started beating its terrified tattoo. Jacey was gone. Jacey was gone. Jacey was gone.

"I just need more time, Ed," he beseeched. "More time. That's all."

"Kit," said Ed. "It has been almost three months. You've had all the time we can afford to give you. Anybody else would've been out weeks ago. It's only because George thought so much of you that he hasn't done it already. I tried to tell him a month ago that we should—" Ed checked himself. "I'm sorry, man, but that's the way it is. Now, I'm calling Niamh to take you home. Go on vacation. For chrissakes, get your shit together."

He picked up the phone, and as he punched in the numbers, a dangerous crack formed in Kit's wall of resolve. As he sat in his best friend's office, the bricks came down, slowly at first, then in a great gushing, thundering heap, and for the second time that day, he wept.

CHAPTER THREE

"Of course the grass is only part of it. Without the sun, the rain, a slightly salty sea breeze and whatever you're having yourself, your milk will taste like shite and so will your cheese."

Joseph Feehan, from *The Cheese Diaries*,
RTE Radio Archives

*A*nother Princess Grace was alive and well, as it happened, and living on the other side of the world in the remote Sulivan Islands. This Princess was occupying the imagination of Abbey Corrigan, who was mud-bathing on the squishy banks of the Ate'ate Stream.

Actually, Abbey thought she was imagining Gorgonzola but the Princess didn't mind. She was more miffed at having to share Abbey's daydream with an automatic washing machine.

Lying on her back in the warm mud, eyes closed, Abbey's smile soaked up the sun. In her head she did loads of clothes with one press of a button while creamy wedges latticed with bluish-green stripes floated in the air around her.

The mud always reminded her of cheese, it was just one of those things. It didn't make sense but then neither did anything else so she didn't worry about it. As for washing machines, she thought about those because she spent hour after infernal hour on the banks of the Ate'ate Stream, soaping and dipping and rubbing and rinsing and wringing out her and Martin's dirty laundry by hand. That didn't make much sense either, she thought idly as she lay in the mud, as they had a perfectly adequate supply of running water in their hut. But Martin wouldn't hear of using this water for washing their clothes—it was a precious resource not to be wasted, he was always telling her, and while this was not, in fact, the case, she knew he didn't like to be reminded of that. All in all it seemed easier to do the laundry the hard way.

She opened one eye and squinted up at the stunning blue sky above her: not so much as a whisper of tattletale cloud left behind after the morning's rain. Abbey flattened her palms against the soft ground and squelched the silky mud between her fingers, imagining it was the innards of a thousand overripened Camemberts and wondering if the push-up bra really pushed up. She thought about bras a lot these days too—underwear generally but bras in particular. They were the only thing that really made her wish she could jump in a cab and whip up to Harvey Nichols with her mother; in fact, apart from that, she didn't miss Harvey Nicks or her mother at all.

"Is it normal," she asked the sky, "to lie in the mud and think about bosoms?" She barely recognized her own voice these days with its funny English base, Irish inflection and hint of Sulivanese pidgin. It sounded like it belonged to someone else.

"Well," she spoke aloud again. "Is it?"

The sky didn't answer her but Abbey thought she knew the answer anyway and it was no. It was not normal to lie in the mud and think about bosoms. It was not normal to lie in the mud, period. But it seemed that the longer she lived in the islands, the less normal she became; and the less normal she became, the less she knew what normal was anyway. She wondered if that evened things out a bit, somehow, and decided that it probably didn't, but she couldn't be sure. She couldn't be sure about anything these days. It drove Martin to distraction but then so did everything, everything to do with her anyway.

She'd arrived in the Sulivan Islands eleven years ago with two pristine white B-cup bras; perfect for the rosebud breasts she had at the time. Within a year, however, she'd been bursting out all over. Her mother had always told her that she would blossom "overnight" but then her mother had also told her that Santa Claus was a child molester and that it was good luck to have nobody remember your birthday, so she hadn't been holding her breath. Typical that just when she had least access to department stores, her boobs decided to show up. She didn't think she'd grown any taller than the five feet five she had been when she arrived. Her hair was still reddish brown, her eyes hazel, her waist small and her thighs firm. Okay, so she probably had a few more freckles (after all, she was an Irishwoman in the sun) but otherwise the package was pretty similar—apart from her bosoms. They'd grown big for someone her size but were perfectly round and quite pert, and after her initial shock at their tardy appearance she had become quite attached to them.

Abbey turned her head to one side, not so far that she would get mud in her ear, but far enough to see the overflowing basket of laundry plopped next to her on the bank. She sighed and awarded herself a few more minutes' daydreaming. Really, what was the hurry? Closing her eyes again she indulged herself in one of her favorite lingerie fantasies. In real life she'd been making do with the same three Elle Macpherson sports bras for the past six years, but in her dreams her corsetry was far saucier. This morning she was imagining a full, milky-white breast bursting out of a scarlet Yves St. Laurent cup, maybe just a hint of nipple threatening to expose itself at any minute. Eyes scrunched closed to keep out the daylight, she followed an imaginary finger, a man's finger, smooth and pale and strong, as it traced its way across one rising bosom, down into the sacred valley of the cleavage, then up the sloping hillside of the second breast before tenderly coming to a stop, then tracing its way, unbearably slowly, toward—

"Abbey!" Martin's voice at such close quarters jerked her out of her daydream with a gasp. "What on earth do you think you're doing?"

She sat bolt upright, her body making a large "ploop" as it rose out of the mud, and turned around, into the sun, to see the dark form of Martin surrounded by golden rays, wearing his uniform of Akubra hat, open-neck shirt, bandanna, khaki shorts and sandals. He looked like a summer version of the Marlboro Man, even in silhouette.

"You're covered in mud," Martin said, his posh English accent surprising her as it often did. "What happened? Did you fall over? Are you all right?" He picked his way down the bank, frowning and staring pointedly at the basket of laundry, and stopped at Abbey's feet, taking off his hat and wiping the sweat on his forehead with his arm.

Abbey rubbed the back of her head, gooey with riverbank, and tried not to act as stupid as she felt. "I had a bit of a headache," she lied, fairly feebly, "so I just lay down for a bit. I'm fine, really."

She looked up at her husband and smiled, thinking for

the millionth time how handsome he was. His hair got blonder with every year, and she loved it long and roughly cut. Eleven years in the sun had weathered his skin but that just made his eyes look bluer, his teeth whiter, his smile all the more radiant when he chose to shine it on her. Is it any wonder, she thought, that she had followed this gorgeous man to the ends of the earth as a dreamy teenager?

"You look completely mad," said Martin. "What on earth is the matter with you? Get up." He held out his hand and pulled her abruptly to her feet. They stood there, achingly close to each other for just a heartbeat, and Abbey felt, in that moment, a glimmer of hope. Dashed, of course, almost immediately.

"You'd better get on with the washing," Martin said, putting his hat back on and turning away from her, making his way along the bank toward Irrigation Central, the "project" with which he had become more and more obsessed over the past decade.

Abbey watched him go, then waded into the water to thigh level. She crouched, facing downstream, so that the water flowed around her shoulders and neck. The noise of it rushing by with such determination made her feel excited, like she was going somewhere or something was about to happen, something that nobody could stop.

Drying out later on the river stones as she knelt and got on with the laundry, Abbey picked up a pair of murky gray Y-fronts and held them up in front of her. Had she known as a wide-eyed teenage bride that hand-rinsing her husband's briefs in an island river would be the highlight of her day, would she have been quite so quick to run to the end of the world with him? Abbey shook her head as if to rid it of dangerous thoughts and scrubbed at the Y-fronts a second time. She loved him, he was all she had, and that was what counted.

"Abbey! Abbey!" She was distracted from her thoughts by the urgent calling of her friend Pepa, standing at the top of the riverbank waving at her. "Jeez, Abbey," Pepa called with much dramatic wringing of her hands. "Plenty hoo-ha! Please! Come quick. Hurry!"

Abbey threw the washing in the basket and scrambled up the stone path, running after Pepa, who was scurrying toward the meetinghouse-cum-schoolhouse-cum-church that formed the central nucleus of the village.

From the stand of coconut palms to the left of the meetinghouse, Abbey could hear a great ruckus going on and it was toward the ruckus that Pepa was heading. As she got closer she saw that Oba, another friend of Pepa's, was kneeling by a tree, wringing her hands, obviously distressed, comforting her sister Nan, from whence the ruckus was erupting.

Abbey realized with astonishment that the noise was actually that of Nan crying—astonishing because the Sulivanese never cried. Not even when a limb was accidentally amputated, a labor spine-splittingly long and hard or a loved one snatched forever by an unforgiving sea. They mourned and felt grief, deeply and loudly, but tears they did not understand.

Today, though, huddled outside the meetinghouse, clutching her knees and burying her face in her skirt, there was no doubt that Nan was crying real tears, lots of them.

"What's the matter, Nan?" Abbey asked as she knelt down next to her, but Nan turned her face and waved Abbey off.

"What's the matter with her, Oba?" Abbey asked her sister.

Oba shook her head dramatically. "Ah-ah. Ah-ah, Abbey," she said, shooting Nan a warning look that only made the distraught woman wail even louder as she rocked backward and forward against the tree trunk.

"What's the matter with her, Oba?" Abbey asked again, perplexed. "I don't understand."

Oba leaned over and whispered sharply into her sister's ear. All Abbey could pick up was "Fafi," the name of Nan's eldest daughter, a well-developed seventeen-year-old who had eschewed further schooling on the main islands in favor of staying to help her mother with her four younger brothers and sisters.

"Is something wrong with Fafi? Is she all right?" Abbey asked. "Oba, you have to tell me what is going on or I can't help."

"Abbey no much help mos' likely anyway, hey," Oba said, studiously avoiding her gaze and turning her attention to Pepa, who stood behind Abbey nervously biting her fingernails.

"What is it, Nan?" Abbey asked again, ignoring the others and rubbing Nan's back with one hand. "You're frightening me. What is it?"

The woman's sobbing slowed to a hiccup, and Nan lifted her head and looked Abbey in the eyes.

"Abbey take Waraman away, hey?" she asked hesitantly, sniffing miserably in between each word.

Waraman, or Water Man, was what the islanders had rather facetiously christened Martin when his obsession with irrigation first became apparent. God in Heaven, thought Abbey, what was going on here? She laughed, in what she hoped was a reassuring way, and gave her a hug.

"Don't be mad," she said. "I will *never* make Water Man go away. Never! Sshhh, there's nothing to worry about."

But Nan had started sobbing again and nothing Abbey could say would stop her. Oba just sat by looking unhelpful, while Pepa fidgeted and tried not to meet Abbey's eye. Eventually, confused and feeling useless, she gave up trying to console Nan or get any sense out of Pepa and Oba and headed home. But the woman's tears unnerved her—why would anybody think she would take Martin away? Why would anybody think she would make Martin do anything? Could make Martin do anything?

After hanging up the washing on the clothesline behind the house, Abbey sat in the shade on the porch with the latest *Australian Women's Weekly* and tried to interest herself in an unknown TV star's table settings. Through the shrubs she could hear the sound of her next-door neighbor Imi having loud and athletic sex. Imi's husband, Nunu, had been away for more than a week on a buying trip and the strain of going without had obviously been more than she could stand. Nunu wasn't back yet but there was no mistaking Imi's cries of ecstasy.

The Sulivanese were a highly sexed crowd who enjoyed nothing more than a good seeing-to, as long as nobody involved was related. They specialized in a complicated arrangement of sleeping with each other's husbands, and wives, depending on which island their ancestors came from, and were great believers in the more the merrier. More than once Abbey and Martin had been invited to join in. Martin, of course, was quite opposed. Not that Abbey fancied the idea much herself, but sex of some description would be nice. She closed her eyes again and leaned back against the outside wall of her home, attempting to conjure up the little lacy bra and strong, pale finger that had captivated her during her morning mud wallow.

This time, the finger was tracing one of the delicate blue veins in the by now rapidly rising and falling milky-white breast. Down the finger slid, down, down, down, until it slipped ever so gently inside the cup of the bra and sought out the almost bursting nipple, feeling it harden and—

"Jesus Christ, Abbey, what are you doing now?" The sound of Martin's voice jolted Abbey out of her dreams for the second time that day, this time causing her to bang her head against the doorjamb.

Martin was standing over her, looking dirty and sweaty and more than a little grumpy.

"Haven't you got anything better to do than day-dream?" As he threw his hat on the rickety bench next to the door, for the first time in a while Abbey noticed his hands. The nails, half-bitten and chewed, were black and brown and torn in places, the fingers thick with calluses and scar tissue, the result of his endless toiling in the "proj-ect" behind the village. They were the fingers of a hard-working outdoorsman. They were not, thought Abbey, the fingers that had been trespassing on the bosom of her dreams, a bosom she had imagined to be her own. So whose fingers had those been? she wondered, with a nasty thrill that left her with guilty goose bumps.

"You haven't forgotten that the Fullers are flying in today, have you?" Martin's voice was reminding her from inside the house. Abbey opened her mouth in silent horror and rolled her eyes heavenward. How could she have for-gotten? Jim Fuller, who flew his Hercules in once a month with provisions from Queensland in Australia, had told them last month that he would bring Shirley, his wife, with him next visit. Abbey had stayed with Jim and Shirl six years before on an emergency trip to Brisbane and counted Shirl as just about her closest friend on the planet. How could it have slipped her mind?

Of course, I've got better things to do than daydream,

she thought, scrambling to her feet. Jim and Shirl were going to stay on the island overnight, and she was going to cook a meal, God help them, and she and Shirl were going to stay up all night just talking and talking and talking. She'd been looking forward to it for a month. How could she have forgotten?

She raced into the kitchen, cheeks flushed, to find Martin gazing around with a sour look on his face at the sad lack of preparation. Their breakfast dishes were stacked higgledy-piggledy in the battered old stainless-steel sink and the wooden floor hadn't seen the business end of a broom all week.

"Abbey, are you all right?" Martin said, looking at her, his grumpiness replaced by something else. "Is everything okay?" As she searched her mind for something sensible to say, he put his hardworking outdoorsman's hand on her back and steered her toward the kitchen table, then pushed her down into a chair.

"I am really terribly worried about you," he said, leaning toward her and looking into her face. "You're not yourself."

Abbey had to agree. She wasn't herself. She was someone quite like herself, but a bit madder. She couldn't explain it really. Well, not to Martin anyway, but she gave it a try.

"Do you ever feel like you're not attached to your life?" she asked her husband. "Like you're floating along beside it or on top of it and it's just getting on with things without ever really involving you? Like you could even drop off to sleep for a couple of years or go to Mars or something and when you came back your life might not have even noticed you were gone?"

Martin stared at her, thin lines of impatience quivering on his brow.

"Goddamn it, Abigail," he said, trying to contain his annoyance. "Why do you always have to make such a bloody fuss about everything? Women all over the world, wives all over the world, would kill to have your life. Lying in the sun all day on a desert island with nothing more than cooking a simple meal to worry about. What is the matter with you?"

Abbey was right, she hadn't been able to explain it. She gave up. "I'm just nervous I think," she said brightly instead, making it up as she went along. "It's so long since we had anyone here, Mart, and you know that I can't cook to save myself. I don't suppose there's any chance you told Jim it was pot luck?"

Martin ignored her attempt at humor, sighed and rubbed the bridge of his nose, a sure sign he was irritated. "How hard can it be to cook a chicken and make a salad?" he said, his exasperation giving the question its own little sea of peaks and troughs.

"Not that hard at all. I don't know what's got into me," she answered in a conciliatory tone, watching Martin retreat behind the curtain to the bedroom area to change his filthy clothes for freshly laundered ones. Did women all over the world, wives all over the world, feel lonely and empty and unloved? she wondered. Or was it just her? Abbey checked herself. Of course she was not unloved. Martin loved her. They were meant to be together. They had known that from the moment they first laid eyes on each other, across the dusty gloom of a Wimbledon church hall at an introductory meeting of Voluntary Aid Workers Abroad. Just when Abbey had needed rescuing from loneliness and heartache and betrayal, Martin had ridden in, her knight in shining armor, full of courage and strength and certainty.

A week before that miracle of timing, Abbey had been chugging along in her final year at St. Ignatius Catholic boarding school in Knightsbridge, without so much as a clue as to what she was going to do with her life. She'd been a good student, mainly because she loved reading, but her grades were average and she hadn't really fancied college anyway (but nor did she fancy being a hairdresser, which was where her mother felt her skills lay). That her mother had low expectations of her came as no surprise, because they were still higher than Abbey's expectations of herself.

She had nothing against hair, she liked it, felt it was necessary on a head, in fact, but she had no desire to make it her life's work. She wanted her life's work to be something special, something that would matter, something that would make her heart beat quickly and have people look up to her. The trouble was, she couldn't quite put her finger on what it was. She thought for a while it might have been writing. Poetry even.

"You must be feckin' joking," her mother had said to her, "or at least more of an eejit than you look."

When she was about fourteen she'd dreamed once—literally dreamed, asleep in her bed at night—of going back to her grandfather's farm. But when she woke up she realized she didn't even know where it was, as she hadn't been there since she was five. It was somewhere in Ireland. Somewhere green, but near the sea. She knew better than to discuss this prospect with her mother, though, who was long estranged from her father and hated to be reminded of anything to do with him so she trashed that idea along with the poetry.

So it was that at seventeen, without benefit of a clear plan for the future and in possession of a dreamy, sweet, old-fashioned sort of a disposition, she became an obvious target for recruitment into the convent.

"You're special, Abbey, you know you are," Sister Clematis had whispered to her during an early career counseling session. "If our Lord comes knocking at your door, make sure not to turn him away, Abbey. Let him in. Then the glory of God will be yours forever."

Quite pleased with this prospect, if only because it stopped her worrying about what else she should be doing, Abbey waited patiently for the vocational tap on her shoulder. Hormones, however, beat Our Lord to it.

One month into her final year, it was Jasper Miles from the neighboring St. Patrick's First Fifteen who came knocking at her door and Abbey let him in, all right, a finger at a time. She knew who he was, had for years, all the St. Ignatius girls did—he was gorgeous. Tall, blond, handsome, rich, the son of a business magnate and a former fashion model. But Abbey had never considered herself his type. She was small and quiet, bookish, not unpopular but not popular either. Her report cards said "could try harder" and "always dreaming" and her mother had once accused her of having the personality of an empty jug. Abbey felt like background, and Jasper was pure limelight. So no one was more surprised than she when, at an after-match function she had gone to with a trusted selection of senior girls, she had found herself kissing Jasper Miles passionately in the hallway leading to the girls toilets after fewer than a dozen words had passed between them.

For the first time in her life, Abbey had felt special. For the first time, real life was better than fantasy and it was a sensation like no other. She felt blessed. As though she had discovered every delicious secret in the universe and was seeing the whole world through entirely different eyes. Yes, Jasper Miles had unlocked something in Abbey Corrigan: pure unadulterated lust and lashings of it.

Pressed up between the chocolate vending machine and the fire extinguisher, the feel of Jasper's tongue on her lips, of his hands on her body, the hardness of his teenage boy parts pressing against her school uniform, Abbey had felt her resolve, her Catholic guilt, her good intentions, melt away. She had wanted Jasper Miles, just as much as he had wanted her. And two weeks later, after he had secured his school the Cardinal O'Keefe Cup, she had allowed him to lift her up against the damp brick wall behind the rugby pavilion and go as far as he wanted. And she had gone with him.

For the next few months they'd been at it like mad things: at her mother's place; his parents'; the bike sheds at his school; the science lab at hers; once in the chapel while the dead body of Sister Euphemia lay, for once not giving out about false modesty, just a few yards away. Anywhere, any time, Jasper was up for it and Abbey with him.

To this day, she couldn't remember a single conversation with him. Just the fireworks he had awoken in her. Until Jasper, Abbey hadn't realized she could be anything other than the solemn, silent type she'd always been. Yet, that big, sweaty, slightly pimply, upper crust teenage boy six days her junior had unleashed a noisiness she didn't know she possessed. A screaming and shouting and yodeling of senses, that she'd assumed was magic and had never happened to anyone else. And because in her dreamy, funny, old-fashioned way, she had expected to be with him forever and ever, despite never having even discussed plans for the following weekend, she hadn't hesitated to tell him, when her period failed to show up (for the second time in a row), that she thought she might be pregnant. That had been the last of Jasper Miles. She never saw him again.

The same night her mother, ice clinking angrily in her glass, had had a heated exchange over the phone with Mrs. Miles. It became clear that Jasper's mother didn't want anything to do with Abbey or her little problem and neither did Jasper, who had been dispatched already to his aunt and uncle in America.

"She has a smell of herself that one," Rose had railed and cursed after slamming the phone down in Mrs. Miles's ear. "The way she spoke to me! Nobody speaks to me like that, like I was some bog-Irish little floozy. Well, Margaret Miles might have a brand-new pair of diddies but her husband still prefers Pamela Harrington's and if you think I am letting her son's bastard into my house you can think again, Abigail Corrigan, because I'm not."

Instead, she insisted, she would be accompanying her daughter to an abortion clinic in Richmond, after which the name Jasper Miles would never be mentioned again.

Abbey refused to believe that the love of her life had abandoned her but after a week of having his mother hang up in her ear she finally tracked down his best friend, Grayson Smythe, who confirmed that Jasper had indeed flown the coop. It was over, Grayson said, he was very sorry and so probably was Jasper, although it was hard to tell. He'd been quite excited about going to America, apparently.

Stunned by this, Abbey agreed reluctantly to go along with her mother's plan. Rose made it clear that she would not allow her daughter to repeat her own mistake: bringing an unwanted baby into the world when her own life was just beginning. This depressed Abbey on so many levels she had no will to resist.

In the absence of Jasper to kiss away her tears and tell her everything would be all right, she felt she had no choice but to climb into a cab with her pinched-faced parent and count telegraph poles all the way to Richmond.

Rose, incensed and inconvenienced by her daughter's stupidity, took out her rage on a bar tab at Quaglino's and, after being waylaid in the back of a family sedan by an insurance salesman called Warren, was nearly three hours late to pick up her daughter.

It was sitting, post-termination, in the waiting room during those three hours, as the kindly receptionist tried hard not to look too sorry for the teenager sniffling quietly in the corner, that Abbey had picked up a local newspaper and seen the advertisement for Voluntary Aid Workers Abroad. Three days later, sad and lonely and overwhelmed with what she eventually realized must be anger, she found herself walking into a church hall in Wimbledon and there found Martin, a strong, handsome, earnest twenty-six-year-old looking for an adventure and someone to take on it, and her fate had been sealed.

Martin Kenderdine had been born in Kent, eight years before Abbey, the youngest of five siblings and the only one to suffer from acute dyslexia. His father was a doctor and his mother a teacher, and he was the only member of his wealthy, middle-class family not to go to a university and emerge with a degree, a fact he could never quite get over.

On leaving school he worked on a farm for a year, before traveling to Kenya to become a guide for a safari company. After Voluntary Aid Workers Abroad in Guatemala, he wound up in Western Australia, where he worked in an opal mine for three years. He had only recently returned home when Abbey met him. His brothers and sisters, he had just discovered, were now all wealthy professionals, with families and big homes and nice cars. This stuck in Martin's craw, as he knew he would never be one of them, and fueled his passion to aid those less fortunate than himself. By concentrating on Third World missions and operating in a different arena altogether, he could not be accused of failing to compete with his siblings. As he hadn't accumulated any wealth of his own, he chose to eschew wealth altogether, thereby convincing himself he hadn't failed at anything.

All he needed was a wife.

Martin had always taken on women as projects. He pursued them, often became fixated by them and was usually dumped by them because of his intensity and mildly unstable temperament. But he was nice-looking and charming and wasn't a bad person, just a vaguely scared and disappointed one.

When he saw Abbey he knew that she was the perfect mate. He saw in her a lack of armor, never mind chinks, that he knew would allow him to guide her into the sort of life he wanted to live. Plus, Abbey was beautiful. Small and soft and sad and needy in a way that made him want to take care of her. The timing had been perfect. They fell in love and within a month they were married; within two they were in the Sulivan Islands, right plonk in the middle of the Pacific, with nothing but a headful of dreams about doing something good, something great, something special for the planet.

Martin had chosen the Sulivans especially for their isolation: The group was made up of a string of different islands, mostly coral atolls, many uninhabited, in the middle of the Pacific. Before moving there, Abbey had never heard of them. The Sulivans' closest neighbors were the Solomon Islands. She had never heard of them either.

The Sulivans had a population of around 3,000 people, mostly Melanesians, with the majority living on the three main islands of Ika, Oma and Afo, Ate'ate's closest neighbor. Ate'ate was about two miles long and one mile across, with a tropical sandy beach running the length of the northern side and the village nestled on the southern side. Its deep natural harbor was protected to the east by Turtle Rock, at the foot of which the Ate'ate Stream formed the freshwater inlet where Abbey did her laundry. In the '60s, the island had been used by the Americans as a refueling base, which explained why for an island with a population of only around a hundred, it had a runway that could land, at a pinch, a Boeing 737. Not that that was ever likely to happen. Despite the idyllic beauty of the island it was largely bypassed by tourists. Even advertising men who had given up the rat race and spent their days sailing the Pacific in luxury yachts gave Ate'ate the swerve, heading instead for the bright lights of Afo and its tiny string of restaurants and bars.

Electricity and running water were commonplace on the three main islands, but in the outlying islands life continued in a fairly primitive fashion. In a 1980s United Nations study, the Sulivans had been classified as one of the world's least developed countries. This, of course, was what had attracted Martin, the UN report forming the basis of his case to VAWA to send he and Abbey there for aid and development purposes. Unluckily for them, at exactly the same time, a tiny atoll at the far east of the island group was discovered to be so rich in mineral deposits that the Sulivanese were told they could name their price for international mining rights.

No slouches in the fiscal department, the combined elders had worked out a foolproof trust and benefit deal that would see no man, woman or child want for anything until the year 2090, after which interest on their investments would continue to feed, clothe and educate the islanders in perpetuity.

Monthly supply drops from Brisbane in Australia were introduced, courtesy of Jim Fuller's Hercules, providing the villagers with everything from Heinz baked beans to hair gel. Generators were shipped to give the islands electricity and the appliances to go with it. Over the years the islanders had even given up drinking the fresh water on their doorstep in favor of Evian water imported directly from France. They wore clothes from the Gap and Country Road, often ordered over the Internet, and at least one hut on each island possessed a cappuccino machine.

Naturally, this was not quite what Martin had had in mind when he brought Abbey to the isolated island group. He had wanted to build bridges, clear jungles and get his hands dirty—and that was precisely what he had proceeded to do, despite there being absolutely no need for it. Voluntary Aid Workers Abroad had subsequently withdrawn its sponsorship when it became clear that the country could get along just fine without it. In fact, the Sulivanese Islands had loaned the organization a significant amount to go away and leave them alone. Martin, however, would not budge.

He and Abbey lived on the smell of an oily rag and the meager interest from Martin's savings, topped up once a year by his parents. Martin filled his days by working on a fantastically complicated irrigation scheme he had devised for a five-acre block in the middle of Ate'ate, which he said could one day grow all the produce the village needed to be self-sufficient.

That the villagers preferred John West Frozen Fish Fingers was of no import to him. He was a man obsessed.

He was also convinced that when the mining stopped at the end of the century, the Sulivanese would have no money and no clue how to return to subsistence living. That all the evidence pointed to them never needing to was a matter he chose to ignore. His arrogance in this and his other opinions won him few friends on the island, although the Sulivanese were a tolerant race, and they liked Abbey.

Her original plan to teach the island children to read and write had been somewhat overshadowed by the Sulivanese government's insistence on providing quite advanced and compulsory schooling for all children from six to fifteen without her. Still, she taught an English class every now and then, baby-sat at any opportunity, tried to keep house like a good wife, read whatever she could get her hands on, and daydreamed way more than was good for her.

It wasn't a bad life, but she wasn't entirely sure it was her life. She clung to her love of Martin like a drowning man to an inflatable life raft. But that afternoon as she sat at the kitchen table, her chin in her hands, her husband's disapproval still hanging in the air even though he had long gone, she felt truly troubled. She wasn't herself, Martin was right about that. But then who the hell was she? She didn't belong in this paradise, but she didn't belong anywhere else, either. She was nobody. Nowhere. That was what kept her daydreaming her life away.

That was what drowned out the steady *ppppfffffsssshhhh* of the air escaping the life raft.

CHAPTER FOUR

"On top of all the obvious old yoke, every good cheese-maker needs a secret ingredient. That's what makes your cheese better than the next bollocks's."

Joseph Feehan, from *The Cheese Diaries*,
RTE Radio Archives

*H*ow are you getting on with 'The Lonely Goatherd' then?" Fee asked, looking at the girl's fingernails.

She snapped the Discman headphones off her ears and flicked them lower around her neck, where they all but disappeared into her dirty-blond dreadlocks. "Do me a favor," she said, in a sweet little voice that belied her tough girl grubby ferret look, as she pulled her hands away. "I'm still puking my way through 'My Favorite Things.'"

"Will you look at that!" Fee said delightedly, ignoring her rudeness, his short fat cheesemaker's fingers now holding her by the jaw. "Here's another one of those tongue studs. Jesus, Mary and All The Saints, will you look at it!"

The three fat ginger cats sleeping in front of the fire raised their heads simultaneously and stared at him.

"Never mind, girls," said Corrie from the comfort of his recliner.

"Your cats are called Jesus, Mary and All The Saints?" said Lucy, a look of disbelief and disdain distorting her small pretty face.

Corrie looked at Fee and smiled. "We didn't do it on purpose, God bless us," he explained.

"Didn't the little gobshites take such a long time to get housetrained they were answering to Jesus, Mary and All The Saints before we'd thought of any names," added Fee. "And it could have been a lot feckin' worse!"

The two old men laughed.

Lucy looked from one to the other. It was possible they weren't quite right in the head. However, it was the only job advertisement she had ever seen for which she perfectly fitted all the criteria. "Must have short nails," the ad in the *Schillies Gazette*, pinned to the shop notice board, had read, "a good singing voice and enjoy a strict vegetarian diet."

"Right so," Corrie said, pulling the lever on his recliner and stretching his legs out as the footrest appeared in front of him. "When did you last eat meat, Lucy?"

"A lamb chop when I was five. And I remember because I stuck the bone in my brother's eye, the bollocks," Lucy said defiantly. "Oh, and some bastard poured meat juice on my vegetarian patties at a barbecue once, but I didn't know until afterward."

"What did they taste like?" asked Fee with interest.

"I dunno," answered Lucy. "I was bulimic at the time."

"You could be mad as a hatter and half the size and we wouldn't give a hoot," Fee said cheerfully. "We just want someone to milk our cows."

Lucy's heart sank down to the tips of her Doc Marten boots, via her torn kilt and holey fishnets. She should have known it was too good to be true. For nearly three hours she had sat here in this overheated, old man's library listening to *The Sound of Music* CD and drinking peppermint tea, and of all the possibilities she had considered none included the job she was applying for being that of a dairymaid. She knew that Corrie and Fee made cheese. In fact, her mother used to buy it to give to the snooty cows at her endless bloody bridge parties in Dublin. "Coolarney, the finest in all of Ireland, quite possibly the world," her mother would say, chipping off minuscule chunks and doling them out with expensive crackers and tiny glasses of sherry. But Lucy assumed that cheese was made with machines. In big vats. With milk from a factory.

"I thought cheese was made with machines. In big vats. With milk from a factory," she said. "What would you want with cows?"

"She's got that many holes in her head," sighed Fee, "the brains have fair seeped out of her."

"Our cheese, Lucy," said Corrie patiently, ignoring Fee, "is the finest in all of Ireland, possibly the world. It's made from our own cows' milk. Do you know, they've been grazing on these fields for hundreds of years?"

"So everything around here's ancient, then," Lucy said rudely, but Corrie continued.

"What we want, Lucy, is for the cows to produce the best milk so that we can make the best cheese." For generations, he explained, the Feehans and Corrigans had been in the business of making cheese together. The traditional deal had always been that the Corrigans provided the cows, the cows provided the milk and the Feehans provided the skills to make cheese—the profits, if any, were split down the middle.

"Thanks for the history lesson," Lucy said with a yawn.

Corrie plowed on. Coolarney Blues and Golds, in kilo

and dote sizes, he informed her, were now served at all official government functions ("and you know how that lot like to eat," chipped in Fee); the Blue had been a particular favorite of the late Princess Diana, between diets, and was served still at Buckingham Palace; and their precious Grace was the world's most award-winning cheese ever. It sold for £14 per one hundred grams, if you could get it on their side of the Atlantic, that was, Corrie said, most of it being exported directly to New York.

"Fascinating," Lucy drawled sarcastically. "What do you need me for then?"

"We need you," Corrie said, "because you're the special ingredient."

Lucy stopped looking bored. "Are you messing?" she asked suspiciously.

"Not at all," answered Corrie. "We need girls who can hold a tune and who don't eat meat to hand-milk the cows."

The milk, Corrie said, was sweeter that way. It was as simple as that. The cheese in turn aged more peacefully, which gave it the almost honey-flavored, lingering aftertaste that had those who sought it still drooling long after it had been smeared on the last cracker, served with the last grape, sampled with the last drop of wine.

Corrie and Fee ran a split herd of one hundred cows and milked fifty at a time. Each cow produced twenty-five liters of milk a day, in twice-daily milkings, morning and afternoon. They needed five singing vegetarians to deal with this schedule but were currently down to four, Mary-Anne's craving for sausage rolls having resulted in her return to her family in Donegal. It sometimes happened.

"You are messing," said Lucy, twisting a rancid-looking dreadlock in her hand, and scowling. "I didn't come up on the last load, you know."

Corrie and Fee looked at each other knowingly. Were the little ferrets ever any different?

"You lure me in here," declared Lucy, "make me listen to Julie bloody Andrews for hours on end, spin me some bullshit story about making stinky bloody cheese and expect me to accept a job 'milking'? I have seen perverts before, you know. I do know what they look like."

She jumped off the chair and started to extricate herself from the headphones, still tangled in her dreads. "I mean, what makes you think I would be interested?" she said. "You're both complete nutters, if you ask me."

One earphone remained planted somewhere around the side of her head. Corrie and Fee looked on with interest.

"I've never even seen a cow up close, let alone pulled its tits or whatever the hell you call them. I'm from the city," she said patronizingly, losing patience with her headphone extraction and perching on the edge of the chair as she systematically fingered her way through her dreadlocks, trying to find the one responsible for capturing the earphone. The truth was, of course, that she no longer wanted to be from the city. She wanted to be as far away from the city and her parents, her brother, her college tutors and that cheating bloody Eamon as she could, which was why she had sold her violin and bought a bus ticket to West Cork in the first place.

"And anyway, it's dangerous, isn't it? Don't cows, like, kick or bite or something?" She had both her hands behind her head now, marching their way from separate sides to find the source of the entanglement.

"We'll pay you £150 a week, board and feed you," said Corrie. "Meat-free, of course."

"You'll work a split shift, starting at five in the morning and finishing two to three hours later," Fee chipped in, "then the same hours in the evening. In between you can do what you like. Avis has the cottage set up so you can watch videos or paint or play board games with the other girls or you can earn a bit extra working in the curing room. And the pub's only five minutes down the road. The girls—the cows I mean—don't mind the smell of booze, in fact they seem to like it. Anyway, we've told Avis to get your room ready."

Lucy's fingers slowed and met at the errant dreadlock. Carefully, she untwisted the cable until the headphones came away in her hand.

"And what makes you dirty old bastards think I'm staying?" she asked.

There was a moment's silence. "Nobody listens to three hours of *The Sound of Music* unless they're fecked for a place to be," answered Fee, not unkindly, but nevertheless Lucy's face burned.

"Yeah, well, I am not so desperate for a job that I'll jump into whatever," she said, eyeing them both with deliberate mistrust as she threw the Discman onto the chair and picked up her bag again, getting ready to leave.

"Did you offer her the job yet?" Corrie asked Fee. "I don't think you should push her into it, Joseph. Why don't we just give her a place to stay while she thinks about it? We wouldn't want her rushing anything, now."

Lucy stopped what she was doing and stood still, hoping something would happen. Quickly. The fact of the matter was that she did find herself ever so slightly fecked for a place to be plus she was tired and hungry—£150 a week and all the food she could eat sounded like a pretty good deal.

Fee chuckled for no particular reason other than he'd been there a hundred times before and eased himself out of his chair. Slowly, he stood up and rubbed his back, his mouth squeezed into a silent "ow" of pain. "What's the bet Avis is here already?" he said, shuffling to the door and opening it.

"Talk about timing!" marveled a middle-aged matronly figure with ski slopes for breasts and a sparkle behind her spectacles as she bustled in the door. Her gray hair was twisted up on top of her head in a complicated arrangement that looked like something you'd buy in a French bakery, and she had crab-apple cheeks and an impossibly smiley countenance. She kissed Fee on the cheek.

"The state of you! Have you not had that back seen to yet, Joseph? I tell you, one of those osteopracters will sort it out in no time at all." As she spoke she grasped Fee by the shoulder and leaned around him to run her fingers up his spine like a piano player. The old man straightened to his full height, about level with her chin.

"And Joseph," she said, turning to Corrie. "How are you today?" She leaned down and gave him a quick peck, then turned to Lucy, who was still standing, stunned, next to her chair. "And this must be our new recruit. How are you there, girl? I'm Avis O'Regan. The cut of you! I'll have to get Jackie on to the nut roast again, I can see that. Did the old so-and-sos give you the full treatment? Take no notice, just come with me and I'll get you all settled in. Now, is there anyone I should ring to let them know you're in safe hands? You're not the first to arrive here in a state of confusion and still be in the exact same state four hours later, let me tell you . . ."

Without seeming to notice what was happening, Lucy was steered out the door by Avis, who paused, only momentarily, to tut-tut at the old men over her head.

Fee settled back in his chair and stared into the fire as Corrie leaned in to poke at the coals.

"Will she stay?" Corrie asked, when the fire was spitting and crackling again.

"She will," said Fee, smiling to himself, "and be all the better for it. She and the little one."

Corrie raised his eyebrows. How Fee knew these things, no one could figure, but know them he did. "I'm thinking of the very last of the Princess with a glass of something sweet and sticky," he finally said, after pondering the predicament Lucy possibly didn't yet know she was in.

"Is that right?" said Fee, closing his eyes and leaning back in his chair, a happy smile tripping across his face. "Are you thinking Australian Botrytis Semillon?" he asked.

"I could be."

"Are you thinking De Bortoli Noble One?"

"I could be."

"But are you?"

There was a silence while Corrie marveled at his old friend's gift. "I don't know how you do it," he said, standing to go and get the bottle.

Outside the smoking room, Avis had hold of Lucy's rucksack and was marching through the house. With Lucy almost running to keep up, she strode down the hallway and through a huge cluttered kitchen, then into an anteroom choked with Wellingtons and raincoats and out into a concrete courtyard. Wine-barrel halves singing with red geraniums flanked the back door; their other halves, exploding with giant purple poppies, rimmed a stone building opposite.

"The cheese factory," Avis said almost reverentially, stopping momentarily and nodding in its direction. To the left of the stone building was the top of the sycamore-lined driveway up which Lucy had walked some hours earlier; to the right was a tall, thick hedge with an archway in the middle, over which was threaded a thick covering of sweet-scented, tiny pink roses.

Avis turned through the archway. Following her, Lucy breathed in the cool country air and for a second almost forgot how unhappy she was. The afternoon's summer light cast a kaleidoscope of green and gold on the ground in front of her tatty boots as she followed Avis up the narrow pathway, blooming on either side with wild purple rhododendrons.

As soon as she realized she felt happy she wondered what she was doing there, following Mrs. Doubtfire or whoever the hell she was through the undergrowth to God knew where. Her footsteps slowed and she felt an imaginary cloud block out the sun and leave her feeling chilled and shivery. Perhaps she should run out to the road, flag down a car and hitch back to Dublin. Perhaps there would be no car. Or worse, perhaps there would be, it would stop and give her a ride, she would get back to Dublin—and then what? Nobody would give a shit either way so what did it really matter what she did? She just felt so incredibly tired. And angry. But mostly tired. And alone.

Lucy stopped on the pathway. She couldn't seem to help the single tear that made its way uninvited down her cheek. Shaking, her head bowed in shame, she sniffed and wiped the tear with the too-long sleeve of her scuffed leather jacket. But another followed, and another, and then her nose started to stream, and before she knew it, weeks, or maybe months, years, of tears were making a boisterous bid for freedom. Unable to control her distress, she seemed equally incapable of avoiding the enormous bosom of Avis O'Regan as it came bearing down upon her, sweeping her up in its ample embrace. On the narrow pathway in the middle of the purple forest of flowers, she howled with inexplicable pain and let Avis clutch her tightly and rock her gently, all the while murmuring into her hair that everything would turn out all right, no matter how she felt about it all now.

"Your heart might be full of anger or hate or emptiness, Lucy, but the thing is that you're among friends here," Avis almost whispered in a soothing singsong voice. "There's not one of us who hasn't come here looking for something; love usually, my darling, as the girls you're about to meet will surely tell you, and I'm not talking about the sort of love that can be found inside a farm lad's trousers either, in case you were wondering. I'm talking about the sort of love that makes you feel warm all over when you're just about to drop off to sleep at night or when you've just opened your eyes in the morning and have worked out it's not a dream you're having, it's real life. I'm talking about the feeling that if you hadn't woken up, you know, ever, that there would be people who would notice. People who would cry. People whose lives would be worse because you're not there anymore. You've already got more of those people than you know, did you know that? And now you've got people like Corrie and Fee. Yes, already! And me. And you're about to get Jack and Wilhimina and Tessie and May. What do you say to that?"

Lucy had calmed down enough to pull herself out of Avis's cleavage. She looked up into the friendly bespectacled eyes and sniffed.

"I thought you were going to bloody well suffocate me!" she said, her tears left behind in Avis's substantial brassiere but her voice shaky with an emotion that couldn't altogether be described as her usual anger. She wiped her nose on her sleeve again, then looked beyond Avis at the cottage behind her. "What is this?"

She was looking at a small, two-story, gray stone cottage, not unlike the cheese factory but with a red corrugated-iron roof and red window boxes brimming with a mixture of the poppies and geraniums she had seen back at the main house.

"This is your new home," Avis said, opening the wrought-iron gate that enclosed a messy cottage garden and motioning to Lucy to walk up the path through the wild lavender to the front door. "This is the dairymaids' cottage."

Avis gave a polite knock before opening the door and showing Lucy in. The ground floor seemed to be an all-in-one kitchen, dining and sitting room. It was small but beautifully sunny and at the rear, straight ahead of them, French doors opened out to a garden patio. On the right were two doors, and the wall that housed the kitchen appliances hid a staircase that led to the next floor.

"There are four bedrooms for the five of you girls, with the twins quite happy to share," Avis was explaining. "You can always call on me in the main house but out here you have, you know, your own space." She emphasized the word "space" proudly, as though it was a new term she had only just learned, then opened the first door on the right and led Lucy in.

"This is your room," she said, putting the rucksack on the dressing table. "Wardrobe over there, dressing table here obviously, writing desk, nice view of the woods and garden, radiator, extra linen in the chest at the end of the bed. Bathroom's through here—you share that with Jack. What do you think of it, then?"

The same dappled light Lucy had walked through earlier shimmied on the pink-and-white striped bedspread.

"It's a bit Laura Ashley but it will do," she said, sitting on the edge of the bed and testing its bounce.

"I'll leave you to take a rest, then," said Avis, ignoring the jibe. "The girls are milking so I'll be over in the dairy if you need me. It's out the kitchen door and around the side of the hill, about a five-minute walk. We'll be back after seven and the girls usually have something to eat then. But if you're starving and can't wait, there's Wilhie's bean casserole in the refrigerator. Delicious! Can you cook?"

"Toast," said Lucy, starting to take her boots off. A rest was indeed required.

Back at the main house, glowing from the benefit of said sticky Semillon on a summer afternoon, Corrie and Fee were heading for the cheese factory. They crossed the courtyard and stopped in the lobby just inside the factory door. On their left was the door into the shop, and on their right the little office where they tried not to spend any time at all but kept their cheesemaking clothes. Corrie pulled on his white overalls and Fee slipped into a white coat. The overalls, he had long complained, pulled on his paunch and gave him indigestion but the coat made him feel important. They stepped into white Wellingtons, dipped their feet in the in-tray and pushed open the door into the factory proper.

As always, they took a moment to soak up the smells and the sounds of the big white room where they worked their magic. To the left of them was Old Fart Arse, the pasteurizer; to the right, a vat, teak on the outside like a wine barrel, stainless and gleaming on the inside. It stood chest high, to Fee anyway, and was where their precious milk began its journey to cheese.

Beyond the cheese vat were two long stainless-steel benches, another big half-pipe-shaped vat filled with cleaning solution and equipment, and a stainless salting bin, packed with yesterday's cheeses. The concrete floor was painted yellow, with drainage at regular intervals, and stacked above the benches in slatted steel racks hanging from the ceiling were row upon row of gleaming molds, glittering in the late sun that filtered through the long, shallow windows at the top of the factory walls.

At the back of the room were two staircases heading down in opposite directions to the curing rooms, or "caves" as they were known. At the top of the stairs, mirroring each other on the side walls, were twin dumbwaiter arrangements, which took racks of cheeses down to the caves below.

If Coolarney was a religion, the factory was the chapel in which Corrie and Fee worshipped. It had changed immeasurably over the years. The pasteurizer was relatively new; the myriad cleaning facilities hadn't always been there; and the racks and benches and in fact the vat itself had once been made of wood, not steel. Corrie, who didn't feel the need to resist modernization, embraced the changes, but Fee was not as easily convinced. He still missed the wooden benches disposed of in the interest of hygiene more than a decade before.

"She's probably right about that back of yours," Corrie said, as he watched Fee move stiffly down the factory. "You should think about the osteopracter."

"When did I fall off the ladder turning the top shelf, Corrie? After the Alsace Riesling. Was it 1971?"

Fee's gift worked very well in forward gear, but was hopeless in reverse.

"No," said Corrie. "It was the year Abbey was born. Remember, she was teething and the two of you were making a racket fit to bring the house down." He sighed a sad little sigh. "Twenty-nine years ago."

"Well," said Fee, ignoring the melancholy, "I'll tell you what. If it's still giving me a pain in me arse in another twenty-nine years' time I'll go to the feckin' osteopath. Now get over here and down these stairs. There's work to be done."

"What do you think she's doing now, Fee?" Corrie asked as he moved in front of his friend to descend the blue stairs. It was nearly twenty-four years since he had seen his only grandchild and he felt her absence like a one-armed man feels a tickle in the hand he no longer has. He stalled for a moment and felt the warmth of his old friend's hand on his back.

"It's not too late," said Fee in his characteristically cryptic fashion. "It's never too late. Don't worry. How many times do I have to tell you not to worry? Now get your old bones down the feckin' stairs before I give you a push."

Corrie opened the Blue room door, soaking up the smell of a thousand cheeses and relishing the darkness that spared him the shame of letting Fee see his eyes, crinkled with tears. He turned on the dim lighting, his heart giving a little jump at the sight of rack after rack of salty Blue cheese. Listening to the sound of 90 percent humidity, he pushed his sadness aside and surrendered to his Blues, the mindless chore of turning them soothing his broken heart.

Not far away in the dairymaids' cottage, Lucy had been asleep for some time. When she woke up, Jesus, Mary and All The Saints had made themselves at home, one of them on her pillow, nestled in her dreadlocks. Lucy wrenched her head away, dislodging the ginger cat, who merely stretched her paws, opened one eye and went back to sleep where she fell. As Lucy sat up, there was a knock on the door.

"Can I come in?" asked a loud voice in a strange accent.

"Um, 'spose," Lucy answered, sitting up. The door opened and a large, pale-faced freckly girl with ginger hair plaited and beaded in dozens of unlikely braids stumbled into the room. "Hiya, Lucy, isn't it? I'm Jack. How're ya?"

She pulled the stool out from Lucy's dressing table and sat on it, facing the bed. " 'Spose you're a bit freaked out, eh? Don't worry, we all are when we first arrive. Hey, you guys!" she yelled in the direction of the door in a voice that made Lucy's toes scrunch up. "She's awake!"

Another braided head peeked around the corner. Its face was black and unspeakably beautiful.

"All right?" she asked Lucy coolly as she brought the rest of her body into the room. "Cat got 'er tongue?" she asked Jack.

"Oh, bugger off, Wilhie, she's only been here five minutes. Don't worry about her," Jack said to Lucy. "Doesn't take much to get her tits in a tangle. She's a hairdresser after all. And this is Tessie and May."

The last two girls to come into Lucy's room were identical twins. They wore their hair in the same style, in little coiled bunches that seemed at odds with their far less funky thick spectacles and protruding front teeth. They looked at Lucy, then at each other, and giggled.

"You'd better get used to that," advised Jack. "They're at it all the time, aren't you, girls?" The twins, on cue, looked at each other and giggled again. Jack rolled her eyes.

"All right?" Wilhie said again.

Lucy sat stock-still on her bed, unable to speak as her eyes flicked from one girl to the other and back again. Their hair. Their faces. Their big googly eyes. She clutched a pillow and pulled it over her midriff. Something was wrong. Horribly wrong. Their bellies! Each of the four girls crowded in here staring at her was undeniably, completely and utterly, without shadow of a doubt, 100 percent pregnant.

"Jesus H. Chrrrist," Wilhie said, rolling her eyes as she took in Lucy's expression. "She don't know!"

The twins looked at each other and bit their lips.

"Know what?" said Lucy, frowning and doing her best to look tough, even though her insides were heaving with terror.

"Know that you don't end up here unless you've got a bun in the oven and no bastard to help you cook it," said Jack.

CHAPTER FIVE

"Your raw material needs to be pure and good. It doesn't need to be perfect. Between the jigs and the reels you can always sort it out, as long as it's pure and good in the first place."

Joseph Feehan, from *The Cheese Diaries*,
RTE Radio Archives

*E*d did the decent thing and vacated his office so that Kit could blub like a baby in private. Every time he tried to pull himself together, a crack of a thought would appear in the dam of his mind and he'd lose it again. Jacey. The baby. His mother. His brother, Flynn. George. Ed. So, he'd let them all down. He'd let himself down, too. That old chestnut.

As he sat on Tom Foster's warm patch, his shoulders shaking with shame, Kit realized he couldn't even muster up any anger toward the so-called friends who were ruining his career. He deserved it. He had blown it big time and he had nobody to blame but himself. This was all the more incredible because he, more than anyone else, knew that without his career he was nothing. A nobody. Just some great-looking guy from Burlington, Vermont, as

George had so rightly put it. Just another Wall Street burnout with a drinking problem.

He laughed, or half-laughed, despite himself. At least he was great looking. "Do not joke," he said out loud, his voice thick with tears as he wiped his eyes with his jacket sleeve. "This is so not funny." Looks were accidental, he knew that. He'd had nothing to do with that. But there'd been nothing accidental about his career. It had been years of deliberate, carefully planned hard work. All for nothing.

As this desolate realization hit him, the door behind him opened and closed again with a soft thump. Turning in his chair, he was relieved to see it was Niamh, standing inside the office door looking as though she too were about to burst into tears, holding a cardboard box which he could only imagine contained the personal effects from his office.

"They really do that, huh?" he said, sniffing and wiping his eyes again.

Niamh raised her eyebrows quizzically.

"Put your photos and favorite pens and old school football in a cardboard box?" Kit smiled wetly. "I thought that only happened in *Jerry Maguire*."

Niamh laughed and silently thanked Kit for making it easy for her. She moved toward him and plonked the box on the corner of Ed's desk. "It's gas, isn't it?" she said, leaning her pert little rear on a pile of paperwork and facing Kit. "Only I couldn't find any photos or an old school football, and to be honest the box was looking a bit empty so I put a few of my own things in to flesh it out a bit. Oh, and a paperweight I filched off Tom Foster's old desk. You know, so you'll have something heavy to throw at his head while you're being escorted from the building."

Kit laughed. "I was just telling myself before you came in that this is really not that funny."

"Well, you've got that right," said Niamh. "You've got no one to blame but yourself though, Kit."

He sighed and looked at his Italian leather shoes. "I was just telling myself that, too," he said, his voice wavering before he checked it. He really couldn't afford to be any more pathetic. He leaned forward, forearms on his thighs, and tried to get his wits together.

Niamh, sensing his despair, gave him a sisterly rub on the back. "Have you thought about what you're going to do now?" she asked, the kindness and worry plain in her voice.

"Getting to a bar would seem to be in order," Kit said, wondering if he was joking again.

Niamh's soothing back rub finished abruptly with a sharp slap to the back of his head.

"Ouch! What did you do that for?" he said almost angrily, sitting up straight and rubbing where she had hit him. He'd forgotten she took boxing lessons twice a week.

"Is there not an ounce of sense in that head of yours, Christopher Stephens?" Niamh snapped, almost incredulously. "A bar is the last place you should be going to. A bar is where you got yourself into this mess in the first place. Jaysus, man, what's happened to you?"

Kit sighed, his shoulders slumping even further. He was getting tired of that question. But only because he was asking it himself and he didn't know the answer. He couldn't understand where it had all gone wrong. He never used to drink at all. A couple of beers in a night was about the limit. A glass of champagne when they clinched a big client or scored an important deal. What had happened?

Jacey had happened.

Kit closed his eyes.

"And don't give me that Jacey bollocks, either," Niamh said, poking him in the ribs.

Whatever happened to good old-fashioned respect, Kit thought to himself. Why was everybody sticking the boot into Jacey now that she was no longer here to defend herself? Niamh, in all fairness, had been sticking the boot in since Jacey first arrived on the scene. Always frank and upfront (often to a fault, he'd joked more than once), she'd made it plain she never liked Jacey.

"Jaysus, Kit," she was saying now. "Don't throw your whole life away over Jacey. She's not worth it. Nobody's worth it. You've worked so hard to get where you are—or were," she corrected herself. "I can't believe you'd give it all up like this. You're not setting much of an example to the rest of the wrong-side-of-the-tracks brigade, now are you?"

Her attempt to lighten the atmosphere only reminded him how true it was. Niamh was the daughter of Irish immigrants who had settled in the blue-collar suburbs of Chicago, and she had wriggled her way into Wall Street with two well-made suits, great legs and a determination to be better at what she was doing than anyone else who had ever done it. Long, shiny black hair, a stunning pair of green eyes and great curves had obviously helped her along the way, but mostly Niamh had gotten where she was with plain, old-fashioned hard work. Just as Kit, a natural salesman, had gotten where he was with two well-made suits and a line in genuine charm that had even the existing experts gaping in awe.

"Maybe once on the wrong side of the tracks, always on the wrong side of the tracks," he said gloomily.

"And the Oscar for best dramatic performance in a tragedy goes to . . ." Niamh said, rolling her eyes. "Come on, Kit, you can't sit here feeling sorry for yourself all day. Fast Eddie will be wanting his office back. I'll take you home."

"You don't have to," Kit said, slowly getting to his feet.

"Yes, I do," said Niamh. "George thinks you might try to do him a mischief on the way out so I've been ordered to escort you."

Kit didn't know which he'd rather believe: that George was fearful for his safety or that Niamh didn't think he could be trusted to get home in one piece. Or without drowning his sorrows.

As they got to the door of Ed's office, Niamh stopped and handed Kit the cardboard box containing his paltry belongings. "Hold this, would you?" she said, shrugging off her tailored jacket and draping it over the carton.

Kit looked down at the box. She hadn't been joking about putting her own things in there, he could see. There were two unopened packets of stockings and an ugly green troll that someone had given her as a joke in the Christmas gift pool. Niamh undid a couple more buttons on her blouse and rolled her skirt up at the waistband until it barely covered her butt.

"What are you doing?" Kit said, taking in her long legs in their sheer stockings and Jimmy Choo shoes.

"I'm making sure that everybody looks at me while we wait for the elevator," said Niamh, grabbing the carton and holding it under her breasts so that they rested dangerously on top of it.

"If I ever go into battle," said Kit, forgetting his misery just long enough to admire his assistant's strategic planning, "I am taking you with me."

"Puh-leeze," Niamh said in her best New York accent, "you've been there, done that and you did take me with you, you eejit."

She opened the door of Ed's office and sashayed into the open-plan trading area, Kit trailing behind her, transfixed himself by the rear in front.

"Hey, anybody seen my paperweight?" he heard Tom Foster calling from his new corner office.

Niamh turned to Kit as they waited for the elevator, every moment feeling like forever, and winked. As he stood with his back to the place he had called home for more than nine years, Kit felt his heart beating the Edinburgh Tattoo again as eighty pairs of eyes burned a hole in the back of his suit. Stepping into the elevator and turning, he looked at the view that had lifted his spirits every minute of every day he had spent here. It was the last time he would ever see it.

The cloud of doom that had been hovering over his head while he was fired and ejected followed them down twenty-seven floors, through the foyer and out into the street, where it suddenly burst and poured rain down upon them, thereby keeping them from getting a cab for nearly twenty minutes. Niamh put her jacket back on and rolled her skirt down to a more modest level, which Kit suggested was perhaps a bit premature in the circumstances.

"I don't see you getting your legs out to get a taxi," Niamh said sniffily. "Given that this is Manhattan, we might have more luck if you did."

By the time they finally hailed the most broken-down taxi on the island, complete with toothless, foul-smelling driver, the city was in the throes of its lunchtime bustle. The driver pulled out, oblivious to all other traffic, and Kit felt an ache as they pulled away from the building. As angry horns tooted and blared around them, he looked over at Niamh just in time to catch a tear falling from her cheek onto her lap. At that point it occurred to him that she must have been fired, too. Because of him, no doubt. Because of loyalty to him. He and Niamh had been a team for eight years and her devotion had been beyond extraordinary. He didn't deserve her. And she certainly didn't deserve him. The need for a drink washed over him again. God, when had he turned into this guy? This guy who woke up with strange women and had a stash of coke on his hall table that he couldn't remember anything about? This guy who craved a drink from the moment his eyes opened? This guy who was not the Kit Stephens he thought he knew.

"Jesus, I need help," he murmured, more to himself than anyone else, as he stared out the window at the Manhattanites dodging the rain.

"I know," he heard Niamh say and, for a moment, he felt safe. He felt maybe everything would be okay after all. But his happiness was short-lived. It was that kind of a day.

Benny looked at him sadly when he walked through the door of his apartment building. "You'd better check your mailbox, Mr. Stephens," he said balefully, cheering up only at the sight of Niamh and her legs.

Kit did as he was told. The box held one envelope. It was from the building co-op and it had a Day-Glo orange sticker on it that read URGENT. He stuck it in his pocket and headed for the elevator, Niamh at his side.

"Don't tell me you haven't been paying the rent, either," she said. "What kind of eejit are you?"

"The kind of eejit who would get fired and evicted in the same day, I guess," he answered, unlocking the door to his apartment, dumping the carton of pathetic personal effects on the hall table and heading straight for the kitchen.

"Can I get you a drink?" he asked Niamh over his shoulder.

"You can certainly show me what you've got," Niamh

answered, looking around the kitchen's latest Gaggenau appliances, the Bang and Olufsen phone, the jars of Balducci's preserves lining the glistening white shelves, the near-empty bottle of Grey Goose on the spotless counter.

"Well, I've got vodka," said Kit opening the refrigerator. "Jesus!"

He might have forgotten Princess Grace but she had certainly not forgotten him, and showed her contempt by directing a wave of nauseating stench directly at his nostrils.

"What the feck is that?" Niamh moaned, her face contorted in horror as she fanned her hand in front of her nose. "Something has crawled in there and died. Kit, what is it? You haven't got a cat, have you?"

Kit shook his head in disgust.

"You never used to have one?" Niamh asked, only half-joking as she backed out of the kitchen.

Kit slammed the refrigerator door closed and leaned against it. The smell really was vile. Jacey had not eaten dairy, but she'd been a regular at Murray's on Bleecker Street. It was not the first time a cheese of the week had been left to abduct the atmosphere. This one, though, must have been there for all of three months.

Thinking of Jacey, he girded his loins as he dived again into the refrigerator for an unopened bottle of Grey Goose. "Never mind the cat, there's vodka," he said, his eyes watering as he spied another two bottles in the pantry, "and vodka."

"And in here?" Niamh had retreated to the open-plan living space, where Grace's toxic fumes couldn't reach her. She bent down to inspect the innards of a low-slung wall unit she assumed contained a cocktail cabinet.

"Vodka," said Kit, watching her as she ferreted around

in the cabinet and returned to the kitchen, vodka bottle in hand.

"I guess it'll be vodka, then," said Niamh, putting her bottle on the counter, then grabbing the two Kit had retrieved from the pantry and the one he was still holding from the fridge. He stood by, helpless and humiliated, as she unscrewed the tops off all four bottles and started to pour the contents down the sink. He really wanted to do something to stop her, like hit her on the back of the head with Jacey's cast-iron frying pan, but the thought that he was thinking that only made him feel more wretched.

"Come on, Niamh," he said, cringing at the pathetic catch to his voice. "Do you really have to go that far?"

"You're the one that's gone too far, buster," she said, viciously sloshing the liquor into the sink. "You know, I have got better things to be doing than cleaning up after you and your wreck of a life, Kit, but luckily when it comes to boozers I do have some prior experience, and because of that I will impart some advice for your benefit. Now, sit down."

Kit pulled out a bar stool and sat at the kitchen counter, resigning himself to a lecture, knowing he deserved it, hoping it would be over soon so he could go out and get a drink.

"I come from a long line of alcoholics," Niamh said, dumping the empty vodka bottles in the trash, then replacing the moldy coffee in his machine with a fresh supply and turning it on. "I am not going to bore you with the sordid details but the good news is you are not necessarily one yourself."

She paused to let this sink in, even though Kit was too busy wondering if she had left any dregs in any of the bottles to really hear what she was saying.

"Your drinking though, Kit, has got to stop." She pulled out the other bar stool and sat next to him. "Did you hear what I said?"

"Yeah, yeah," said Kit. "The drinking has got to stop."

"Right," agreed Niamh. "And why is that?"

"God, Niamh, don't make me go through the list," he answered, aggrieved. "I've been fired, I'm losing the apartment, my refrigerator smells like one of those dumps kids live on in Brazil. You know, I don't really need reminding that my life has suddenly turned to shit."

Niamh's eyes narrowed and a flush crept up her neck toward her face. "Your life hasn't suddenly turned to anything, you complete and utter eejit. You've been on a collision course with disaster ever since—" She stopped and regained control, taking a deep breath and sitting up straight. "Look, Kit," she said in a softer voice, "drinking has messed up your life and in case you haven't noticed, you're kind of short on people who give a damn. Now get a grip and help me out here. Help yourself, for God's sake. Can you do that?"

As her words sunk in, Kit realized how grateful he was that she was his friend, that she did give a damn. He didn't deserve her.

"Have you thought about going back to Burlington?" she asked gently.

He leaked out a sigh and shook his head. "There's nothing for me in Vermont," he said, feeling sick that he even had to contemplate the thought.

"Well, there's family," Niamh said. "Times like this they can come in dead handy, you know. Can't you at least think about going home?"

It had been five years since Kit had been back to Burlington and, in truth, he hadn't called it home for a long time. He'd always kept quiet on the subject of his family, surrounded as he was by people who were born into money and style. His own background had been plain in comparison. He wasn't ashamed of it at all, but he preferred to keep it to himself, to protect it from the scorn of his colleagues. His dad, Ben, had been assistant manager at one of Burlington's biggest hardware stores for more than twenty-five years before being laid off in the mid '90s, a blow from which his pride had had trouble recovering. Ben Stephens was a good man and Kit loved him deeply and dearly. Ben had never had big dreams for himself, all he had wanted was a happy and healthy family. But he was so proud of his oldest son and what he had achieved.

"My dad's kind of retired," he told Niamh, "and he doesn't have a lot of money. He thinks I am great, Niamh. He thinks I have really made it. If I go back like this? I just can't."

They sat in silence for a moment.

"What about your mother?"

Greta. A vision of his mother dancing with his dad outside on the grass at some long-forgotten barbecue flickered through Kit's head like an old home movie. Greta had been the most wonderful mom a kid could ask for. Gorgeous and glamorous and the kindest woman he knew, she'd made him the man he was—or the man he had been. He was glad she would never know about his downfall.

"My mom's in a home," Kit said, awkward with the words. "She has an early onset form of Alzheimer's disease, you know, dementia. She's been there for a while."

Kit had always sensed, despite her gregarious nature and even temper, a solitary sort of sadness in his mother. There were moments when he caught her in a dream world, a faraway look in her eyes and a secret smile on her lips. "Away with the fairies," she would laugh when he was little and interrupted her private dreams. "Away with the fairies again."

As she got older, the sadness, or the secrecy, seemed to grow darker and Kit could see that his mother was spending more and more time away with the fairies and less at home with her husband and two sons. Eventually the visits to her faraway world became permanent, and no one ever saw the real Greta again. She lived now in a home with locks on the doors because her wandering, combined with her confusion when found, made it impossible to guarantee her safety. She didn't know Ben, she didn't know Kit and she didn't know his brother, Flynn, either.

"I am so sorry," Niamh said when Kit told her all this. "I had no idea. Where's Flynn now?"

Kit's ache grew. "At law school, courtesy of yours truly," he said, cringing and banging his forehead with his closed fist. "He's a pretty bright kid, you know. He only just missed out on a scholarship but he is going to be a great lawyer one day. He really is. What am I going to do?" He was desperate now. "Jesus, how could I let this happen? They all rely on me."

"You pay for your mom's nursing home, too?"

"Yeah, and I kind of supplement my dad, although he doesn't know that. I have a deal worked out with the local tennis club where he does odd jobs. You know he visits her twice a day, even though she doesn't know who he is?"

He was crying again, unstoppable tears of anguish. Niamh, her own eyes shining with compassion, leaned over him and rubbed his back.

"Aren't there uncles or aunts or grandparents? Anyone else you could go and stay with for a while maybe?"

"Mom didn't speak with her folks," he said, wiping his

tears and cursing the headache that came with them. "They had some falling out before I was born and Dad wasn't real close to his brothers either, although I do know where they are. I just don't know if I could turn up on their doorstep saying 'Hi, you barely know me but I'm your messed up, boozehound nephew Christopher. Got a room?'"

Niamh laughed, despite the hopelessness of it all. "I can't believe you've been doing all this without saying anything," she said, jumping off her stool and heading for the coffee machine.

"What's to say?" said Kit. "It's no big deal. It's one of the good things about having money. I'm hardly Mother Teresa, I'm just trying to look after my folks because I always thought they'd done a pretty good job of looking after me."

"It's not the end of the world losing your job, Kit. You can sort yourself out and start somewhere new. You're basically one of the good guys, you've just come off the rails."

She plonked a steaming mug of coffee in front of him and he stared at it without much enthusiasm. He didn't feel good. He felt far from it.

"The question is," said Niamh, taking a sip of her own drink then blowing on it to cool it down, "how are you going to sort yourself out?"

The possibilities had been swimming around Kit's head along with all his other tortured thoughts, but so far nothing had risen to the surface. He pulled the co-op envelope out of his pocket and ripped it open. There were no surprises there: Unless he paid the last month's outstanding rent within eighteen hours he would be evicted. He sighed and handed it over to Niamh, who bit her bottom lip as she read it.

"I probably know the answer to this already," she said, slapping the letter down on the counter, "but do you have any money at all?"

Kit thought about his different accounts, both in the country and offshore, and his smorgasbord of stock options. The truth was the past few years had not been as good as he might have hoped. His company, like so many others, had still been hurting from the crises in Russia and Asia, when the World Trade Center tragedy shook them even further. On top of that, Jacey had been expensive to run. He had chewed through his cash entertaining her and had let his accounting slip even further in the past couple of months.

He could have paid the rent, should have, but had let it slide, like so much else. He had assumed that one day things would get better and then he would sort it out.

"I can get my hands on some," he admitted, "but enough to pay Flynn's fees, look after my mom and pay the rent on this place?" He looked around at the shrine to style in which he'd lived so happily for the past year and shook his head. "We're talking seven grand a month here."

Niamh looked at him, her face impossible to read. "I might have a solution," she said slowly, "but you're not going to like it."

Kit laughed. How could Niamh possibly help him? Her salary was a tenth of his, a twentieth even, a fact that had long embarrassed him given her devotion.

"Tom Foster could sublet the apartment," she said, flooring him.

"Tom Foster? What's he got to do with anything?" he spluttered.

"I talked about it with him earlier," said Niamh, squirming uncomfortably. "Ah, don't look at me like that,

Kit. It's not what you think. It's just that—" She looked around at the kitchen walls as she carefully picked out the right words. "It's just that, well, Tom and I have been seeing each other for a few months. You know, as in going out together."

She let that hang in the air for a moment.

"You're dating him?" Kit finally asked, incredulously. "And he fired you?"

"No, Kit. I'm just dating him. You're the one that got fired."

The trapdoor that had been threatening to open under Kit's feet all day finally swung down and swallowed him up. "But you were crying in the cab," he said, trying to figure out what was happening. "I thought you'd been— What was that all about?"

"Well, sue me, Kit, but I'm allowed to feel sorry for you. Everybody feels sorry for you. You were the golden boy, the great white hope, everybody's darling, and now it's all down the bleeding toilet. I'm allowed to feel something, you know. You mean a lot to me. You really do."

Suddenly, it all fell into place. Niamh, far from being the tireless supporter, was in fact here because she wanted to check out the place for her new boyfriend, Tom Foster. How could Kit have been so stupid as to think she would stick by him in his hour of need? He cursed his naiveté and the drained vodka and stood up.

"You can go now, Niamh," he said, trying not to sound as hurt as he felt. "And you can tell Tom Foster I will torch this place to the ground before I let him set one single, solitary foot in it."

To his surprise, Niamh got up and rammed the stool he had stepped away from into the back of his legs, forcing him to sit down again with a thud.

"Don't be so stupid," she said forcefully, still standing, her face flushed again with emotion. "It should come as no surprise to you what I want and how much I want it, because you wanted it all yourself once, too. I'd love to give you my undying support and throw in the towel just because Jacey screwed up your life but I have worked way too hard for that. Now, sit there and listen to me for a moment, will you?" She sat down again and regained her composure, her face returning to its normal color. "Think about it this way: Can you really afford to blow Tom off right now? I mean, it's not just about money. You need to get away for a while. Sublet the apartment to Tom, Kit. You know it makes sense. Jaysus, you can probably cream an extra few hundred dollars a month from the man, he'll be that thrilled with the address."

Kit gave her a long, hard look. She was so much tougher than she looked. Than he had ever realized. She left him for dead.

"And what about me?" he asked pitifully, cringing at how he sounded.

"There must be somewhere you can go, Kit," she said, blowing again on her still too-hot coffee. "Or there's rehab."

She let the suggestion hang in the air for a split second before she heard it clang to the ground where it lay on the kitchen floor in a crumpled heap.

"I'm going to have to put some milk in this coffee," she said, getting up off her stool and heading for the Princess's tomb, a sour look of apprehension on her face. "Is it safe?" She opened the door and gagged at the smell. "Jaysus, Kit. What the hell is that?" She pulled a twisted, tortured pizza toward her and risked a nostril-full before throwing it back on the shelf and grabbing the Princess's bag. She hurled it into the sink.

"Right," she said. "Out you go, whatever you are." She reached gingerly for the bag and picked it up, but its bottom had become weak and sodden in the vodka-sluiced sink. As Niamh swung the bag high away from her nose toward the trash, it split and the Princess plummeted to the floor, landing on the marble tiles with a wet slap.

"Jaysus!" shrieked Niamh. "It's alive! Will this never end?" She snatched a paper towel and crouched next to the Princess, her eyes watering with the cheese's angry stench. Not enough, though, to keep her from reading the label: *Coolarney Farmhouse Cheese, Schillies, Co Cork, Ireland.* Niamh sucked in her breath and blew it out again with a rush, as though she'd been surprised by a whack to the stomach. Staring at the cheese as it leaked onto Kit's floor, she slowly rose to her feet. "I don't bloody believe it!" she said.

"Believe what?" Kit said, agog at the foul-smelling mess still lying there.

"Believe that the horrible smell in your fridge is going to save your life," answered Niamh, suddenly and excitedly searching the room for her handbag.

"I hate to break this to you," said Kit morosely, "but somebody's already discovered penicillin."

"If you trust me with this," said Niamh, thumbing through her address book looking for the right page, "I will get your life back." Her perfectly manicured finger scrolled down the list of names and addresses until it found the right one. "You, my friend, are going to go somewhere far out of temptation's way that does not involve locked wards and group therapy."

Kit looked at her, mystified.

"Here we are. Avis O'Regan. I don't know why I didn't think of her before. She's dried out two uncles and a cousin twice removed—that I know of—and trust me, Kit, you will not be bumping into anyone you know where she is."

"Oh yeah?" said Kit. "And where is that?"

"A mile out of Schillies. County Cork," said Niamh, picking up the kitchen telephone and starting to dial. "What time do you think it is in Ireland?"

"Ireland?" Kit repeated dazedly.

"Ireland," Niamh confirmed with a thrill of certainty.

The Princess, splattered and reeking on the floor, burped an extra stream of steamy gray ooze, which was her way of smiling.

CHAPTER SIX

"Without starter, the milk would still turn into cheese but the wait could kill you. The starter gives it a shove—and we all need a shove now and then, God bless us."

Joseph Feehan, from *The Cheese Diaries*,
RTE Radio Archives

*A*bbey sat at Imi's kitchen table, scratching her head and trying to work out how many times 57 went into 3,970.62. This quite often happened when she wanted to make a special effort on the food front, although, of course, the numbers differed. She could pretty much guarantee, though, that it would be long division, and she hated it just as much as Imi's nephew Junior did—which was why he was plucking her chicken and she was doing his homework.

"So if 7 times 57 is 399, then—" she mumbled. "Oh, feck it, Imi. What is 6 times 57?"

Imi was reading *American Vogue* and paying little attention to the mental athletics going on across the table.

"You want chicken, you do hum-wok," she said witheringly, not even bothering to lift her eyes from the glossy pages.

"Yes, I know I want the chicken," said Abbey, "but the homework is too hard. Why can't he just use a calculator like everyone else?"

Imi shrugged her shoulders and lazily flicked another page. Abbey scratched out another doomed calculation on the notepad Junior had left her and swore loudly when it failed to help the final solution.

"'Scuse please!" Imi interjected. Usually, she swore like a trooper herself but reading *American Vogue* unleashed uncharacteristic ladylike behavior. "Junior be plenty cross if you bungle hum-wok," she warned unhelpfully, shaking her head as she perused the favored shades of lipstick for the American fall.

"I won't bungle it," Abbey said, bungling it. "Oh, why can't I help him with his English homework?"

"Junior big-time good at Englitch already!" Imi chortled. "Junior don' need help wid Englitch. Junior need help wid map."

The same could not be said for Imi herself, thought Abbey, but she had a point about Junior. He was perfectly good at English, it was his math that was crap. It was just a shame that hers was, too.

Imi, bored with the homework debacle, turned the magazine around to point out a page to her friend. "Cindy Crawford gain plenty kilos, hey Abbey? Check it out!"

Abbey looked up from her math and stared at the photo of the curvaceous supermodel, squinting to read the caption. "She's pregnant, Imi," she said, trying not to let her voice betray even a sliver of emotion. "She's allowed to put on weight. She's having a baby. You know," she continued, unnaturally brightly, "a pikinini."

Imi's face fell, leaving her features draped in a mortified expression. She flipped the magazine over, quickly turning the pages in a bid to escape the model's pregnant form. "'Scuse please, Abbey," she said, quietly and far more politely this time. "'Scuse please."

An embarrassed silence mushroomed between the two women. Abbey couldn't think of anything to say so she concentrated on Junior's homework, but Imi, worried that she had upset her friend, was doing some mathematical gymnastics of her own.

"Sixty-nine and something!" she suddenly crowed, a look of triumph lighting up her broad, brown face. "Abbey, 69.66. Check it out!"

Abbey never failed to be amazed by her next-door neighbor. Her calculation was exactly right: 57 times 69.66 was indeed 3,970.62, and no sooner had Abbey written down the wretched answer than Junior bounced in the door, holding up her naked chicken.

"Done my homework?" the eleven-year-old wanted to know, looking over Abbey's shoulder. "Cool! Did you get it right this time?"

Last time Abbey had required Junior's plucking duties, she had answered all but one of his math questions incorrectly and he had had to fake an epileptic seizure in the classroom to get out of trouble. Rumor was that Junior had suffered a real seizure in the first few months of his life, forming the basis of a lifelong tendency to fake them whenever the going got tough. He would go far, that boy, Abbey often thought. His mother had not produced any siblings for him until five years ago, so the first six years of Junior's life were charmed. After Imi's sister Geen had surprised everybody with a late run of three more little "pikininis" in quick succession, though, Junior's latter years had been lived far from the entanglement of his mother's apron strings. The combination of intense adulation as a little child with a free hand as an older one had produced a confident, mischievous boy with street smarts almost wasted on life in the middle of a large ocean.

"Imi helped me out this time so you won't need to swallow your tongue on my account," said Abbey, swapping the homework book and notepad for the plucked chicken.

"How's Bing?" she wanted to know. Bing was Junior's five-year-old brother, who had just started school and whom Abbey knew was having a hard time because of his pale eyes and fairish hair. This wasn't completely uncommon in the islands. "Genetic throwback" was the term Martin used to explain it. The traces of dalliances with early missionaries and settlers showing up generations later, he said. Nan, too, had a couple of little blondies and there were a few older ones dotted about the island, but Bing was probably the fairest of them all and a target for bullying because he was small for his age and something of a whiner.

"He ordered a Malibu Barbie on the Internet," said Junior. "He's in the crap."

"'Scuse please!" Imi scolded him.

"Bing knows how to use the Internet?" Abbey asked, amazed.

"Everybody knows how to use the Internet," Junior said, rolling his eyes as he headed for the door.

"God, Imi," Abbey said, collapsing back into her chair with a bewildered look on her face. "A five-year-old can use the Internet and I can't even work your microwave oven? What is the world coming to? I swear I will never be able to leave this island. What use would I be in the real world?"

Imi, still trying to make up for any hurt she might have caused over Cindy Crawford's pregnancy, ignored the question and nodded in the direction of the plucked chicken. "You quick-cook him here, den bone-bone cook him at you-place?"

Abbey sighed. Cooking had never been her strong point. Yes, she told her friend, she would cook the chicken first in Imi's microwave then finish it in the traditional bone-bone way. This involved wrapping the food in freshly cut bamboo and searing it over the fire. Martin thought she cooked all their food that way but it wasn't called bone-bone (burn-burn) for nothing. Getting the charred food off the fire without burning herself was a skill Abbey had yet to master. For their first two years on the island her hands had looked as though she were wearing skintight brown and beige camouflage gloves, such was the extent of her burns. Then, as Martin had started to pay less attention to her and more to his redundant waterworks project, she had cottoned on to Imi's modern appliances and now cooked most of their food over there. (In fact, Imi or Geen—who had been sponsored by the village on a six-week Cordon Bleu cooking course in Paris—often cooked the food for her.) By finishing the chicken off bone-bone Abbey knew that she could get their hut to smell like a meal had been home-cooked there without singeing her eyelashes, a disaster that had occurred twice before.

Imi swiped the chicken off the table next to Abbey and proceeded to stuff its skin with herbs. "My crikey!" she suddenly exclaimed, "Geen make yummily salad for you and Lady Missus Hercules Man!" She whirled over to the refrigerator and took out a beautiful-looking salad, expertly presented in a traditional wooden bowl, sealed for freshness with layer upon layer of plastic wrap, Geen's favorite thing in all the world.

"Check it out, Abbey!" She thrust it under Abbey's nose. The salad was made of beans and peppers with pawpaw and peanuts, and was no doubt dressed with Geen's special vinaigrette using 120-year-old balsamic vinegar. Abbey felt a lump rise in her throat. What would she do without her dear, sweet, loyal neighbors and friends? Geen must have remembered the Fullers were coming even though Abbey couldn't remember mentioning it, and had forgotten it herself.

As the chicken rotated in the microwave, Imi returned to her magazine to work out her autumn wardrobe. The fact that the Sulivans only had two seasons, wet and dry, and you got a bit of each every single day, did not deter her one bit. Like most Sulivan Islanders she was tall and slim-hipped with big firm breasts, a narrow waist and broad shoulders. Her hair grew in an irrepressible Afro and she spent a small fortune in mail-order straightening products, none of which had the slightest effect. Today she was wearing red faux-snakeskin hipsters and a skintight Britney Spears T-shirt, revealing her taut midriff and diamond-studded belly button. Abbey always felt the frumpy white woman in comparison, not helped by the fact that she relied solely on Imi's castoffs for her own sartorial elegance. This afternoon was no exception: It was last year's cargo pants and a white cotton shirt, both from Banana Republic. Actually, the hand-me-down system worked quite well for her, apart from the fact that Imi was six inches taller, so Abbey's pants were, as usual, rolled up and the shirt tied at her waist. She looked like someone who had started the day much bigger. Coincidentally, she often felt that way, too.

The microwave boinged just as the faint sound of the Fullers' Hercules C130 heralded its arrival on the island. Abbey jumped to her feet and grabbed the chicken out of the microwave. She would have just enough time to wrap it and stick it in the flames before the guests arrived, but she really should have been keeping a closer eye on the fire next door.

"Aaaargh!" she gurgled to Imi as a boiling glob of chicken fat sloshed out of the Tupperware container it was in and landed on her hand. "Can you get me the salad, Imi? What was I doing sitting here reading magazines? I need my head read!"

Imi passed over the salad, shaking her head at her friend's panic. "Go slow-time, Abbey. They jus' friends."

Abbey balanced the salad on her hip and headed for the door. There was no such thing as "just friends" where Martin was concerned. Having people to visit was a big deal for him and Abbey didn't want to let him down. She'd done enough of that already.

"Thank you, Imi," she called as she made her way next door. "You're a life saver."

"No worries," came the reply. It was something of an island motto and Abbey wished with all her heart she could embrace it. But there was too much of the Londoner left in her, or left in Martin anyway, which she supposed was the same thing. Abbey wrapped the chicken and threw it in the fire, then pricked up her ears at the unlikely sound of a car engine and the tooting of a horn, followed by great cheers and laughter. Out on the porch, she was flabbergasted to see Tomi Papara, the island chief, driving haphazardly through the village in a brand-new bright-red convertible. The top was down and the little car was crammed with local children, all hooting and shrieking at every kangaroo hop and honk of the horn. Tomi looked as though he had died and gone to heaven.

"Check it out, Abbey, Mazda motorcar!" he called as he bounced past her house, waving furiously, while seven little heads behind and around him jerked backward and forward in unison.

Abbey was aghast. Ate'ate had one road. It went from the airstrip to the village and was about 1,500 meters long. It only needed to be 300 meters long, but the villagers had extended it so that they could have more fun driving an ancient Jeep left behind by the Americans. Having one vehicle on Ate'ate had been ridiculous, but two? Martin would be outraged. Still, Tomi's enthusiasm was infectious and Abbey couldn't help laughing.

"What's next, eh? Bloody traffic lights? And here I was thinking you were stuck in the wop-wops."

Abbey spun around and into the arms of Shirley Fuller. She'd been so preoccupied with Tomi's wheels she hadn't even seen her friend approach but soaked up her embrace like a dried-up sponge would the first fat raindrops after a yearlong drought.

"It is so good to see you," she said, squeezing her friend with surprising ferocity.

"Hey, hey, you'll bring tears to my eyes," joked Shirl, pulling herself away and dabbing dramatically at her eyes. "And I wouldn't want to go wasting any water now, would I? It's a precious resource, after all."

Abbey laughed, embarrassed. "So, he's already given you the speech then?"

"Try stopping him," said Shirl. "I had to take to my scrapers or I'd still be there getting a bloody ear bashing."

Abbey grinned at her friend, delighted at the sound of her harsh and scratchy Queensland accent.

"Are you okay, darl?" Shirl asked. "You look kinda"—she scrutinized Abbey's features—"I don't know. Different, I 'spose. Smaller."

Abbey managed a laugh.

"Well, it has been six years, Shirl, perhaps I've shrunk. Anyway, I'm happy to report you still don't look a day over twenty-one yourself."

Shirl laughed her smoky laugh. "Point taken," she said good-humoredly. "Now, are you going to show me around the place or what?"

Shirl was wearing her everyday outfit of sleeveless cotton shirt, below-the-knee moleskin skirt and RM Williams boots. She wore the same outfit whether she was going to church, loading crates into the cargo hold or sipping champagne cocktails at a mayoral reception. She was a true-blue Aussie and Abbey adored her.

"Come in, come in," she said, leading the way into the hut, where the smell of home-cooked chicken was making a very good impression. Shirl stopped inside the door and looked around her, aghast. She knew that Abbey and Martin had been living a pretty lean existence but she hadn't imagined for a moment that it was this no-frills. The hut was one big room with woven matting walls and exposed beams, through which she could see the thatched roof and, in places where it met the walls, the blue late-afternoon sky. There were windows on each side covered with bamboo blinds, and beneath the one on the right, surrounded by a flimsy curtain, stood a rickety wooden double bed with a lumpy-looking mattress and a candle-wick bedspread.

At the back of the hut was a battered stainless-steel sink, held up on either side with two beer barrels; to the left, a mesh-covered safe and to the right, a sort of indoor/outdoor open fireplace in which the green-wrapped chicken smoldered happily. Other than a shaky-looking set of shelves and the table with its three nonmatching chairs, the only piece of furniture in the room was a steamer trunk in which she assumed Abbey kept her clothes. Shirl tried to rearrange her lined, leathery face into a shock-free expression but it didn't work.

"Bugger me, Abbey," she finally said, showing her usual diplomacy. "Where's the rest of it?"

"Well, the loo's outside with the freshwater shower," Abbey said falteringly. "Come on with you, Shirl. It's not that bad."

Shirl walked, slightly stunned, toward the table and threw herself into a chair that threatened to topple sideways on its uneven legs. She sat like she'd been riding a horse for a week.

"I knew you were on the bones of your arse, Abbey," she said, "but, Jeez, you should have said something."

"We're okay, Shirl, really," Abbey insisted. "It's not about money. We have plenty of that. Well, Martin does. This is the way he wants us to live and it's not that bad. Honestly, I'm used to it. It's been eleven years for goodness' sake, and for most of those we didn't even have the table and chairs!"

Shirl looked doubtfully around the room once more, as if to check that there wasn't a luxury suite she'd overlooked the first time. She scratched her wiry gray head. "Well, no offense, darl," she said. "But if you think me and the old cheese are going to bunk down on the floor we might as well crank up old Herc right now and hit the road."

Abbey laughed at the look on her friend's face. "And here I was thinking you were the rugged Ocker," she teased. "Where's your pioneering spirit?"

"I'm fifty-two years old and I live in a sixteen-room house with four bathrooms and climate-controlled air conditioning," said Shirl. "If I want to rough it I turn the heat-ing down in the swimming pool. Now tell me I'm not sleeping here, Ab."

"You're not sleeping here, Shirl," Abbey said, amused. "You're sleeping at my friend Pepa's house, three huts away. She's going to stay at her sister's place and she's leaving you and Jim her heart-shaped bed and her Jacuzzi."

"Now we're talking," said Shirl. "So where are those blokes? I could murder a beer."

Later, as she gnawed on a chicken bone and sipped at a glass of wine the Fullers had brought with them, Abbey congratulated herself on the meal, by her standards anyway, being a roaring success, despite the draining properties of her husband's apparent black mood.

"A bloody Mazda MX5 convertible?" he had railed. "On a Pacific island with one dirt track not even a mile long? He must be mad. And what about the emissions, eh? Did he ever stop to think about that? About the damage the carbon monoxide could do to a delicate ecosystem like Ate'ate's?"

Abbey felt obliged to keep chatting with Jim and Shirl in between Martin's outbursts, even though she knew it was better to stay silent when he was in this frame of mind. Ignoring his rancid commentary, she knew, only made him worse, but on the other hand the pleasure of normal conversation in familiar English was too delicious to forsake. She expected there would be "a moment," and was barely surprised when it came as she stood to clear the plates.

"Abbey," Martin growled, staring at her thigh and throwing his knife and fork onto his chipped plate. "What is that?"

He motioned for her to move closer and proceeded to pull from the side pocket in her cargo pants a thick wad of plastic wrap. The same plastic wrap Geen has used to preserve her beautiful salad and which Abbey had ripped off as Martin and Jim arrived home for dinner. There was nothing Martin hated more than nonbiodegradable materials, especially plastics, and here she was flaunting one of the worst examples in front of their guests. Abbey's heart sank as her husband held the plastic wrap up in the air like a badly soiled diaper and his blue eyes darkened and hardened.

"Are you stupid?" Martin spat.

Jim and Shirl Fuller had stopped chewing and were watching the scene unfold with matching horror.

"Do you think we came all this way," Martin said, his voice low and dangerous, "and worked this hard for this long, so that you can pollute these islands with your disgusting rubbish?"

Abbey, praying silently for him to shut up and not ruin the evening, said nothing.

"Well? Do you?" roared Martin. "Are you that stupid?"

"Steady on there, mate," Jim said, saving the situation by casually standing up next to Abbey and reaching for Martin's plate. "Not an arm or a leg, eh?"

Martin fumed silently as Jim clattered and banged the plates while Abbey stood, rooted to the spot, waiting to see what was going to happen.

"Well, don't just stand there, Abbey. Help the man," Martin said, which meant he had decided not to take his rage any further. She shook with relief as she scuttled to Jim's side and started stacking the dishes.

"How about you leave the blokes to tidy up and take Shirl for a walk?" said Jim, his eyes friendly and sad above his bushy gray beard. "You'd like that eh, darl?" he said, turning to his wife.

The look that Abbey saw pass between them made her heart bleed. It spoke a thousand words. It said, we understand. It said, we'll help. It said, aren't we lucky we're not like that. It said everything Abbey had ever wanted to hear in a look but hadn't for so long that she couldn't remember now if she ever had.

Eyes down so that she couldn't see Martin's face and tell what he was thinking, she whispered her thanks to Jim and headed outside, Shirl following. The full moon was shining its giant flashlight on the Pacific as they walked silently down to the water's edge and sat on the jetty, their legs swung over the edge, as for a moment they just listened to the singsong lapping of the low tide underneath.

Then Shirl scooted closer and put her arm around her friend, pulling her close.

"Why in God's name," she finally said, as gently as an outspoken Australian from good Queensland farming stock could, "are you still with that blithering idiot?"

Abbey said nothing. She didn't want to have this conversation. She didn't want to think about it.

"I thought he was going to clout you back there, Abbey," Shirl continued. "And over what? A bit of plastic wrap. The man's a bloody nightmare. He's unhinged. Is he always like that, Abbey? Does he try a bit of biffo?"

Abbey, horrified, pulled away, staring at Shirl aghast. "Of course not, Shirl. God, don't be ridiculous. You've got it all wrong. It's not that bad. He's not that bad. We're actually very happy here. Look at it, it's paradise!" She threw her arms up to emphasize their surroundings. "You have to give Martin a break. He's really a lovely, lovely man, he just gets frustrated with the way things work here." She'd had this conversation with herself many times over and found that out loud it sounded quite convincing. "But hit me? A bit of biffo? Oh no. No, Shirl, honestly! As if I would put up with that. No. He's never laid a finger on me." She paused for a fraction too long. "He won't lay a finger on me actually. That's more of a problem."

Shirl, not one to bite her tongue, didn't. "So, you're not getting any, then," she said.

Abbey cringed and shook her head. "I can't talk about it. Oh Shirl, don't make me talk about it."

Shirl rolled her eyes. "Listen, love, I can see that things aren't cooking in your kitchen and you are not a happy camper. Now, you can tell me to shut up and stuff off, or you can let old Auntie Shirley lend an ear and give some advice. I haven't given birth to four great fat useless bastards and fended off a horny husband for twenty-seven years without learning a thing or two along the way, you know."

Abbey sighed and leaned against the jetty post, watching the moonbeams flitter and flash across the waves. "He went off me when I got back from Queensland," she said eventually when she was sure she could get the words out without dissolving into the tears she had long since trained herself to keep at bay, "and I told him what the doctor said."

Martin had sent her to Brisbane six years earlier, when after five years of marriage and no contraception she had failed to conceive. A laparoscopy had revealed that Abbey only had one Fallopian tube and that the poor lonely thing was even more severely hampered by the existence of a large ovarian cyst. When this was removed, it proved to be the size of an orange. The gynecologist told Abbey that she had just one in a million chance of getting pregnant.

She had used that one in a million chance, of course, with Jasper Miles.

Abbey had been devastated, as Shirl had seen while she nursed her through her recuperation. But when Martin found out he had fallen apart completely.

"He just lost it totally," Abbey told her friend as they sat on the jetty. "I've never seen a man so sad. He just rolled up into a ball and cried for a week, and nothing I could do would bring him out of it. It was awful! Then he disappeared for two days and when he came back it was like he was a different person. He looked the same and he sounded the same, but it was like he wasn't really there or I wasn't really there or—oh, I don't know." Her voice petered out.

"He doesn't blame you, though, does he?" Shirl asked. "For not being able to have babies?"

Hearing it out loud really hurt, Abbey realized. "Well, it is my fault," she said. "He should blame me. I had one chance and I wasted it." She shuddered. "I've ruined his life and I'm not going to walk away and leave it in tatters. Besides, I've nowhere else to go."

Shirl, flabbergasted, sat up and cleared her throat. "For a start, Abbey, it is not your bloody fault and you're not to bloody blame for bloody anything. Second, Martin's life is not ruined but yours is—and if you want to enjoy the rest of it you need to bloody do something. Third, you have got somewhere to go. You've got our place."

Abbey smiled at her friend and tried to imagine living the rest of her days by the side of the pool in the palace in Brisbane. It wasn't a bad thought, but it wasn't a helpful one either. No, she had made her bed and would lie in it.

"Thank you, Shirl," she said, trying not to notice the pity in her friend's eyes. She could hear dance music playing in the distance and cursed Frankie's satellite dish: MTV sure had made a big impact on Ate'ate.

"It might not be my fault about the babies," she started softly, "but it is my fault that Martin is so unhappy and I couldn't leave him here, I really couldn't. The islanders think he's a joke. He's out there all hours of the day and night, irrigating a sandy plot of land that will only ever grow coconut and arrowroot when there is no shortage of either and everything else is readily available anyway. What would happen to him if I wasn't here?"

She felt a bleakness she didn't usually allow herself.

"But you're only twenty-eight, Abbey," Shirl argued. "You've got your whole life ahead of you. You shouldn't be wasting it on someone you don't even love. Crikey, it's hard enough wasting your life on someone you do love."

"I'm twenty-nine," Abbey whispered. "I'm twenty-nine now. And I do love him. I really do. I'm all he's got and he's all I've got, and I do love him."

As the words came out Abbey realized, not for the first time, how hard she had to work to make herself believe them. The emptiness of her life rang a bell inside her that echoed and clanged around all the sad, hollow pockets of her body. She couldn't bear to think about it anymore so rose to her feet and pulled Shirl to hers.

"Enough of all this," she said, her voice pleading. "Let me show madam to her boudoir."

Keeping Shirl's hand in hers she led her up the path past the meetinghouse toward Pepa's place. Shirl, disturbed and saddened but recognizing the difficulties her friend was facing, let herself be led.

"Oh, look, it's Geen," Abbey said, passing Imi's sister's house and catching a glimpse of her dancing around the room inside. "I should go and thank her for the salad. Come in and meet her. You'll love her. Everybody does. She's the life and soul of the island."

She dragged Shirl inside, where Geen proved to be dancing not on her own but with her three youngest children, the not-so-distant club music providing the beat. Without stopping her butt from swinging or her head from shaking, Geen waved to her visitors and nodded in the direction of Bing and his two blond little sisters, who were all standing in a row dancing wildly and vigorously without one of them moving a single foot. They looked like they were glued in place on wobbly springs. Abbey burst out laughing and turned around to Shirl, who was standing behind her, to introduce her. But Shirl was looking as though she had just been socked in the jaw. Her face was completely white and her eyes were huge and black as she stared disbelievingly at the three jiggling children.

"What's the matter, Shirl?" Abbey said. Shirl doubled over and gasped for air, all the while still looking at the children, who had by now stopped jiggling and were staring back.

"Abbey," said Shirl, clutching at her stomach, her face scrunched up in pain. "Jesus Christ, Abbey."

"What is it, Shirl?" Abbey cried, panicked, as Geen started to chatter hysterically at the children.

Shirl grabbed Abbey by her middle and twisted her around to face the little blond disco babies, thrusting an intervening Geen out of the way. "The kids, Abbey," said Shirl. "The kids. You can't be that blind. They're the spitting image of Martin."

CHAPTER SEVEN

"Remember, despite all the rules, there really are no rules. Some of the best cheeses in the world have only been discovered by the cheesemaker making a ballyhays of something else. Now they call it diversifying, but in the old days it was just trying not to get the blame for plain old fecking it up."

JOSEPH FEEHAN, from *The Cheese Diaries*,
RTE Radio Archives

*I*t was pitch-black and freezing cold when Jesus sat on Lucy's face. It was her third night in the big feather bed in the dairymaids' quarters, and so far she had done little since she arrived but lie in her room, sleeping and thinking dark thoughts. Jack had insisted on bringing her food, which she had done her best to eat, but the truth was she felt ill a lot of the time, especially during the first part of the day. Jesus, Mary and All The Saints, the three fat ginger cats she had met during her interview with Corrie and Fee, had seemingly sensed her despair and draped themselves supportively around her, only leaving the room, one at a time, through the window for their ablutions. That it was the sunniest room in the house was probably just a coincidence.

This morning, though, cracks were showing in Jesus's supportiveness.

"Get off me!" Lucy croaked into the cat's fur, giving her a good shove. Jesus stood on all fours by Lucy's neck and yowled meanly back at her, prompting Mary and All The Saints to lift their drowsy heads from either side of the bed. Jesus soon stopped her yowling but the cats' heads stayed up, their ears twitching as they watched the bedroom door. Just as Lucy was pulling herself up to a sitting position to see what the cats were looking at, her door burst open, flooding the room with warm yellow light from the hallway.

"Awake already?" Avis said, smiling delightedly. "How about that? Talk about meant to be! Ready to start work today then, Lucy? There's breakfast on the table and cocoa in the pot. Pull on your woolies, we'll wait for you. Come on, girls!"

The cats stretched and jumped languidly off the bed, padding lazily in single file toward Avis, who opened the door wider for them to walk out, each one brushing their back against her stout legs as they went past. Only Jesus stopped to look back snootily at Lucy, who was still sitting, speechless, in her bed. Avis shut the door again and Lucy stayed there in the darkness for a minute or two, furious at being bullied into working at such a despicable hour. Although, she supposed, it couldn't strictly be called bullying, as Avis had asked her if she was ready to come to work and she could have said no—but for some reason, probably the hour, had said absolutely nothing.

Angry at herself for being awake to listen to the question in the first place, she threw back the covers and jumped out of bed, gritting her teeth against the shock of the cold floorboards and the wave of nausea that washed

over her. At the breakfast table Wilhie, Jack and the twins
looked most unsurprised to see her; she concentrated on
her food and ignored their interested stares. Once the
plates and cups were stacked in the dishwasher, the girls
assembled themselves at the back door.

"Blimey," said Wilhie, catching Lucy's scowl. "You don't
have to look quite so miserable, you know. It can actually
be fun, this job. And you get paid and it's only for a while,
innit?" She winced and rubbed her protruding stomach.
"Whatcha put in the porridge? 'Imself is 'aving a right
knees up in 'ere this morning."

The girls were helping themselves to duffel coats hanging on a rack by the door. Lucy, her cheeks flaming with
anger and embarrassment, pulled on the last remaining
one and stomped out after them. It was still dark outside
and there was a chill in the air but this didn't seem to
deter anyone but Lucy as they chattered happily all the
way around the hill to the dairy. They were a funny sight
from behind, all walking in various stages of what could
only be called a waddle: Wilhie had one hand on the small
of her back as she delicately dodged the cowpats and Jack
walked from side to side like a very old cowboy.

Lucy wondered for a moment if she had been sucked in
by an evil cult. She doubted, though, that Corrie and Fee
had brainwashed her, just made her listen to gobshite music.
And they hadn't asked her for any money. In fact, they
were giving her some. When they rounded the corner to
the dairy her suspicious thoughts were interrupted as the
smell of a hundred cows' effluent hit her in the face like a
game show cream pie. She gagged and tripped at the same
time, falling into Jack, who turned around to steady her.

"Pretty gross, eh?" Jack said cheerfully. "You want to be
here when the spring grass kicks in. Talk about shit!"

"Does it always stink like this?" Lucy asked, trying to get her dry retching under control and still clutching desperately on to Jack as Avis and a tall ginger-haired boy herded the cows toward the milking shed. The cows were diverted at the front into five different walk-through bails, their heads leaning over wooden doors on the other side. Up closer, all Lucy could see was five bony cows' bums, covered in muck and smelling like shit. She was green with revulsion and fear, and Jack looked at her with sympathy.

"You are in a bad way, aren't you, Luce?" she said pityingly. "I have to say yes, it does always stink like this. But," she said quickly as Lucy made to leave, "you do get used to it. Wilhie's right, Lucy. It can be fun."

Lucy slapped her hands together for warmth inside the too-long sleeves of her duffel coat and looked deeply unconvinced. Jack peered over her shoulder to locate Avis, who was still making her way through the herd to the dairy pit-lanes, and pulled Lucy into a conspiratorial huddle.

"Look, you get £150 a week and you don't need to spend a single penny while you're here. You get a roof over your head, it's warm and you get good food. All you have to do is sing a few harmless songs, lay off the burgers and do a bit of milking. And nobody hassles you here, Lucy, that's the beauty of it all. Everybody leaves you alone. And where else are you going to get that? You know, in our condition."

Before Lucy could contemplate the matter of her condition any further, Avis arrived at her side with a stool and a pail and directed her to the closest bail, which contained a sad-eyed cow called Maria.

"Actually," Avis said sheepishly, "amn't they all called Maria for the purposes of ease and convenience. Now!" She pulled Lucy around to face her, then sat herself down on the little stool, rested her shoulder on Maria's under-carriage and reached for her udder. "Oooh, I nearly forgot!" she said, standing up again with surprising haste for some-one quite so top-heavy. "Have you got the remote, Tessie?"

"Yes, Avis," came the reply from down the shed.

"Then what are you waiting for, girl?" Avis called good-humoredly. "Hit it, why don't you!" The gentle sounds of *The Sound of Music* soundtrack permeated the fetid area. The cowshed, quiet up until then apart from the sound of scraping stools and shuffling hooves, suddenly hummed and reverberated to the swelling strains of Rodgers and Hammerstein. Lucy stared open-mouthed as the four pregnant milkmaids and Avis O'Regan began milking in time to the title track. Avis was beaming and pulling Maria's teats in accord with the swell of the music. The milk seemed to emphasize the beat as it hit the bottom of the pail, and the whole strange scenario seemed to swim around Lucy like a dream.

"You try, Lucy," Avis said over the music as she jumped spryly off the stool again.

Lucy, for want of any alternative opportunity present-ing itself, sat on the stool. Under Avis's instruction, she leaned her cheek against Maria's warm side and reached for her udder. Her small size, more often than not a short-coming, proved otherwise in this instance. Her shoulder fitted neatly under the cow's belly, her head into the soft curve of Maria's flank. Reaching the udder was a bit of a stretch, but once she curled her violin-player's hands around the teats, Lucy felt as though she was just the right size for the job. Slowly she squeezed with one hand. Noth-ing happened. She squeezed again. Still nothing. Maria shuffled uncomfortably and stamped a hoof in impatience, startling Lucy, who reared back, only just keeping her bal-ance on the stool. She looked at Avis, who was smiling patiently and miming in the air the gentle but firm massage required for milking. Lucy moved in once more, her angry scowl replaced by her concentrating scowl and, within ten minutes, the first eight of them completely exasperating, she was milking Maria for all she was worth. It was hard work but quite satisfying once she got the hang of it. She looked up to share her achievement with Avis, but her supervisor had moved on. Only then did Lucy realize she was the only person in the shed who was not singing about the hills and how alive they were. She thanked God she didn't know the words, and poked her tongue out at the ginger-haired boy who was watching her. He blushed and bobbed down behind another Maria.

Across in the factory, Corrie and Fee were cranking up the pasteurizing machine. Corrie loved the factory first thing in the morning, when it was just he and Fee. The smell of cheese just made and milk about to arrive seeped out of the factory walls and floorboards like a comfortable old blanket. And the quiet! How he loved the quiet. Once, when the demand for their product had been smaller, they had been the only ones who worked in the building, managing the packing and the orders themselves. As their reputation grew, however, they had been forced to bring in outside help. Fee had wanted Carmelite nuns, whom he thought would work quite hard and not say much. They proved to be a bit thin on the ground, however, so instead they ended up with Marie Lonegan from the village and her sister-in-law Ruby O'Toole. The pair arrived on the dot of 8:30 every morning and neither drew breath until they left again.

It drove Fee especially to distraction. "Do they never feckin' shut up?" he had asked after the first couple of years. "Either one of them?"

Ruby and Marie both had the extraordinary capacity to talk at the same time yet still hear what the other was saying.

"The poor man, God bless him, left here all on his own—"

"And so I says to Patrick, 'Well, it was only 40p last time I looked—'"

"And the little fat one never likely to—"

"And there's nothing wrong with my eyesight either if—"

"Of course some people would say—"

"I can see clearly, all right, that's why—"

"It's nobody's business but their own."

"That's right, Ruby, God love you, that's right."

They also knew that Ruby and Marie were responsible for fermenting the many rumors that circulated about them, the kindest, yet most robust, being that they had a small fortune in cheese money buried on the farm somewhere. Every now and then Fee would have to take a potshot at a local, spotted rummaging around the cheese factory in the dead of night with a shovel, usually with drink on board and a sniggering mate in tow. He knew for a fact that he'd never directly hit anybody but suspected that a ricocheted slug had cost Seamus O'Connor half an earlobe.

Still, Ruby and Marie were worth their not insubstantial weight when it came to running the shop and processing the orders. Their mindless blathering never interfered with their weighing, labeling, phoning, faxing and (in recent years) e-mailing, and this left Corrie and Fee free to weave their magic in the cheese factory. They didn't want to know about orders and invoices and delivery dates and schedules. They cared only for milk and curd and the sorcery of cheesemaking.

Apart from Grace and another private specialty or two, they produced just two types of cheese at Coolarney: Gold and Blue. The Gold was a washed-rind cheese, which meant that once it had been shaped and salted, it was smeared every two to three days with a special Coolarney yeast culture, giving it a sticky glistening rind. This provided the perfect conditions inside to turn the curd into a strong, meaty, smooth, supersucculent cheese-lovers' cheese, while the rind started out sticky pale yellow and moved on to gold, then orange, then deep tangerine.

On alternate weeks, Corrie and Fee made Coolarney Blue. The secret to this cheese was in Avis's legendary home-baked raisin bread. Once a year, in early September, she made two hundred of the fruity loaves, using her ancient family recipe. The loaves were then stored in the Blue curing room, where after three months they were covered in spores of blue mold. This mold was then sieved and added to the young curd to give Coolarney Blue the spicy, sharp taste and blue-green veins for which it was so well known (and which no one anywhere else on the globe could match, despite many attempts).

Princess Grace was a variation on this cheese. Her taste was quite different though, because of the milk produced in April with the new spring grass and because, unlike a regular Blue, she was not pierced to encourage her blue veins, but was made with a looser curd and developed the veins on her own. As a general rule the less the cheesemakers had to do with Grace, the better.

This week was a Gold week. Corrie and Fee stood ready to weave their magic, watching Old Fart Arse as he huffed and puffed his way up to the heat required to kill the allegedly life-threatening bugs in their milk. The sound of his clattering and banging usually riled Fee into a whole new face color. For generations, Coolarney cheese had been happily unpasteurized, but in recent years it had come to the attention of high-ranking health authorities that cheese contained bacteria and this evil, unnatural substance must be stomped out.

Corrie and Fee, like other artisan cheesemakers around them, had been forced to undergo inspections by pimply young men with thick spectacles and excessive dandruff who had tut-tutted a lot and written very tidy notes on gleaming clipboards. The results were always the same. New European Union restrictions required the cheese to be pasteurized. Through farm after farm, the pimply young men wove their web of red tape, and Coolarney had not escaped their scrutiny. Corrie and Fee's inspector was a particularly unattractive individual by the name of Roger Swoole, or R. Swoole, as Fee insisted on calling him.

As a result of this interference, they had been forced to install, at great expense, Old Fart Arse, which was clattering and banging this very morning but strangely, Corrie thought, was having little effect on Fee's complexion. If anything, Fee might be considered a little peaky, he thought, but then he was wearing an orange T-shirt and a purple vest and had a green and red scarf wrapped twice around his neck. No one could look a good color surrounded by quite such a palette, thought Corrie, noticing also that Fee had two different shoes on. Ah well, they matched his socks.

When the two old friends finally heard the rattle of Avis's tractor delivering the mother lode of milk to the vat outside the east door of the factory, they moved toward the noise in unison, the same smile playing across their different lips.

The cheesemaking was about to begin.

Corrie and Fee set about their separate routines: for Corrie it was cleaning and preparing the surfaces and molds, for Fee it was overseeing the delivery of the milk. Outside, Avis was sitting behind the wheel of the tractor twinkling at the little man.

"You were right, Joseph," she said, putting the tractor in neutral and climbing down to ground level. "Little Lucy's going to work out just fine. I've hardly seen anyone take to it so quick. Mind you, isn't it always the way when Jesus, Mary and All The Saints take such a shiner. Hardly a word at all this morning and the face on her! And don't tell Joseph, but Jamie spoke. Can you believe it? He asked what Lucy's name was. What a day!"

Jamie was Avis's cowherd and almost pathologically shy, thanks to a speech impediment that made his sibilants sound like the grinding of old tractor gears. She'd discovered him hiding in the hayshed when he was twelve, shaking like a leaf after a belting in the Schillies school playground, and he'd helped her with the Marias ever since, albeit most days without saying a single word. That he had come up with an entire question thrilled her to bits.

She and Fee each grabbed a side of one full milk urn and heaved its contents into the tank using a handmade copper funnel, continuing until they were all emptied and the tank nearly full. Within an hour the day's milk had been pumped through Old Fart Arse; had reached, according to the gauge, the required 72 degrees Celsius for the required fifteen seconds; and was pouring into the cheese vat, its sweet comforting smell slowly warming the whole factory. The room was coming to life.

Fee and Corrie worked silently and separately, weaving in and around the vat and surrounding counters like so many threads of wool following an intricate pattern. When the vat was full and the temperature a steady 35 degrees, Fee added his starter, the first part of the secret to ripening the milk and kick-starting the cheese's flavor.

Like most cheesemakers they used a commercial brand of freeze-dried starter, which came in sachet form. They had spent much of the '50s arguing over whether to make the switch to this commercial product, Fee initially being keen to stick with making his own even though it was labor intensive and slightly unreliable. By the '60s, though, he had come around. The rennet, the coagulating agent, they similarly bought in, having not enough calves' stomachs on hand for the making of it. Despite the fact that this had weighed on Fee's conscience heavily for decades, he had to admit that the cheese had never suffered. Quite the opposite, in fact. And the cheese was the thing. The cheese was always the thing.

Once the rennet was added, the magic of the cheesemaking began in earnest. Before their very eyes, the milk disappeared and the cheese began to emerge. In more than sixty years on the factory floor, there had not been one single day when this point in the cheesemaking had not given each man a tingle of excitement up his spine. As the minutes ticked by, the thick creamy milk dissipated into a watery whey, leaving a shiny, solid, beautiful mass floating in its wake. This was the curd. And the curd was their gold. Every blade of grass they grew for every Maria to chew for every vegetarian to milk for Avis to unload led to this moment.

The curd. The first taste of what was to come. An inkling of the cheese it would one day be. The promise of perfection.

The secret potential of every cheese was locked up in the warm, soft curd and it smelled glorious. When the time was right, Corrie and Fee picked up their blades and, starting at opposite sides of the vat, began to cut the curd. The blades, like enormous, long-toothed combs, had ancient wooden handles shaped like baseball bats, each worn away in different places to fit its own cheesemaker's hands, attached to a row of sharp steel blades.

Corrie and Fee wove their blades through the soft curd like synchronized ice skaters, cutting patterns in the shiny surfaces that to begin with looked like melted checkerboards. They stirred and sliced and twisted and turned, until the curd was finally broken into tiny even pieces. At this point they abandoned their blades, and Fee started to drain off some of the whey.

As the grate in the factory floor spat and hissed with the barrage of watery waste, the sweet smell of grass and passion filled the air. Corrie and Fee looked at each other with identical satisfaction. In every batch, this was the moment they waited for, the moment that kept them in love with Coolarney cheese.

It was tasting time.

Breathing in the warm sweet air, Corrie leaned over the vat and dipped his arm into the curd, savoring its soft silky squelch before bringing a handful to his lips. On the other side of the vat, Fee too was savoring his first mouthful, his head back and his eyes pointed at the factory ceiling in full concentration.

No sooner had the first microbe of the closest curd hit Corrie's lips, though, than he knew something was wrong. His heart beating in his chest, he looked across at Fee, who had turned to stare at him, open-mouthed, his own half-swallowed curd sitting sad and unwanted on his tongue.

Corrie threw the remaining curd in his palm at the drain and dipped his hand again into the vat, his fingers trembling. He brought a fresh handful to his nose, crumbling it softly to release the aroma. To his horror, sure enough, there it was: the faint scent of failure, not right in his face but nevertheless wafting over him like a long-forgotten scandal being whispered about in a distant corner. He pressed the curd to his lips again, regardless, and was stung for a third time by its betrayal. It wasn't bitter, or sour, or rancid. It wasn't even unpleasant. It was something he didn't even need to put his finger on. It just wasn't right. That was all. Just plain not right. Nobody else but Fee would even notice the difference most likely. But nobody else made Corrie and Fee's cheese. Perfection was their goal and they reached it each and every day. But not today.

Fee was still staring at Corrie, open-mouthed and stunned.

"Could it be the starter?" Corrie asked, already knowing the answer. "Did something contaminate the starter? Or the new girl," he said, almost excitedly. "Could it be the new girl?"

Fee slowly spat the errant curd into his hand and sat down on an upturned bucket.

"Is it the rennet? Or the milk itself, Fee? Perhaps the Marias are poorly. Foot and mouth!" Corrie said, almost wishing the deadly disease would prove present. Anything rather than the truth. Fee just looked sadly at the curd in his hand, then at his old friend. His blue eyes had lost their glimmer, his round face had collapsed into a new miserable shape. He opened his mouth to speak.

"It's fecked," he said.

With those words Corrie felt the temperature in the room drop 10 degrees. If Fee was never wrong about even the stupidest most inconsequential things, he thought, it was unlikely he would be wrong about this. Of course, it shouldn't be coming as such a surprise, they were both seventy-three after all, but in such rude good health, apart from Fee's back.

Corrie staggered backward and leaned against the draining bench, cheese molds clattering to the floor as his hands reached behind to steady him. Fee's back! He felt a hole open up in his chest and swallow his hope. Fee. In the many, many years that the Corrigans and Feehans had been making cheese together the curd had soured on just a handful of occasions, and not a week following each such incident, they'd been dressed in black and praising the dead.

The souring of Coolarney curd signaled a changing of the cheesemaking guard from one generation to the next, and Corrie knew in his heart of hearts that this was no exception. Fee's back. His refusal to seek medical treatment. His peaky condition. God help him. God help them both. Corrie stared at the little round man on the bucket and wondered how much time he had left.

"Don't give me the feckin' eye," said Fee, surprisingly robustly for someone in such poor health. "Wasn't it allus going to happen?"

Corrie stayed where he was, stunned at the turn a day could take. One minute, as good as any other day, the next, the worst a man could have.

"I wonder would Abbey come home," Fee said, looking craftily at Corrie. "I wonder would Abbey make the cheese?"

Fee never wondered things, thought Corrie. He was too busy already knowing them. "I could try writing and asking," he said, the calm tone belying the hammering in his chest. "But with Rose, you know . . ." He trailed off. "Are you sure, Fee?"

Fee looked at him with his beady blue eyes and said nothing.

"Well, I don't think we should rely on Abbey," Corrie said eventually. "It's been twenty-four years since we even laid eyes on her, and she's a million miles away and lactose intolerant for all we know. We're going to have to go outside."

They had talked about this before, of course. About the possibility of bringing non-Corrigans and non-Feehans on board for cheesemaking purposes in the event of a disaster such as this. It had never been done before and there was no telling whether it would work or not. But Fee had never married and neither had his only brother, a retired plastics engineer living in Florida; and Corrie's only daughter, Rose, had not spoken to him since she had run off with her daughter all those years ago. The closest she'd come to the family cheese in recent years was ignoring it in Harrods food hall.

Abbey would have been their only hope, but she had long since been dragged into her mother's complicated war and exile. Anyway, she was living on a desert island in the Pacific Ocean according to Ruby O'Toole, whose next-door neighbor's daughter, Pauline, kept in touch with Rose.

"Outsiders it is, then," said Fee, standing up. "Feck it."

CHAPTER EIGHT

"So, the starter gives it a shove and gets it going, then the rennet comes along and kicks the separation process up the arse."

JOSEPH FEEHAN, from *The Cheese Diaries,*
RTE Radio Archives

*A*s soon as Shirl pointed it out, Abbey saw it for herself, clear as day. Bing and his little sisters Georgie and Martha were dead ringers for Martin. He could almost be their father. She started to smile at this cheeky nudge of coincidence, but before her lips had reached even half-stretch she felt her bone-bone chicken "thunk" to the pit of her stomach. One little Martin lookalike would be a coincidence, she realized, as the color in her face drained southward, but three? She forced her mouth a little further toward a smile and half-snorted at the realization that was tugging at her brain as she looked at the three blond, blue-eyed children.

He could *almost* be their father?

Her lips abandoned their smile like a released rubber band and regrouped into a wonky *O* of disbelief as Abbey took a step closer to the children, still staring at them as if for the first time.

He could *actually* be their father.

Nobody moved. Nobody said anything. Abbey shook her head. Martin and Geen? It wasn't possible. Gorgeous Geen with her long brown legs and crazy hair? Fertile Geen with her greedy ovaries and her new second family? She looked at Geen and in that single moment knew the truth.

Geen was staring at her, her face twisted with guilt and fear, but as she met Abbey's horrified gaze there was a flicker of something else, too. As Abbey felt the cold, wet cloak of dread seep into her every pore she realized her eyes were truly open for the first time in years. Geen's late run on childbearing had begun almost as soon as Abbey had returned from Brisbane with her terrible news, the news that had hurt Martin so deeply he had withdrawn his affection from her. She'd always imagined that affection had stayed inside him, that it was her fault he was mean and unhappy. But now . . .

"How could I have been so stupid?" she whispered, as Geen, suddenly panic-stricken, hurriedly rounded up her stupefied children and herded them toward their beds.

Shirl had begun to regain her composure but was still frozen with shock and scrutinizing Abbey for signs of hysteria, trying to think what would be the best next move. She'd assumed Martin was a bully and an arsehole, that much had been blatantly obvious, but this? How could he do this to someone as sweet and innocent and idiotically devoted as Abbey? Shirl wanted to wring the bastard's neck.

"Right," said Abbey, snapping out of her daze and shrugging off the cloak of dread. "Let's go." She turned on her heel and walked out, Geen crying now and following her.

"So sorry, Abbey. So sorry. Pleeeeease!" she sobbed, but Abbey, her back straight and her head held high, kept going.

Outside the same night sky and carpet of stars twinkled above Abbey's world, yet she knew that in those few moments inside her friend's house, her life down on earth had changed and would never be the same again. She walked calmly down the track, wondering how she should feel, where she should go. She'd always imagined that in situations like this people knew exactly what to do next, but she didn't have a clue. Geen, of all people. They'd been friends. Or had they? With a shiver, she realized she knew what that look on Geen's face was. That little hint of something not quite horrified enough at being discovered. It was a look she'd seen a thousand times before, just not on Geen. But of course, she'd seen it countless times on the sun-beaten features of her handsome, faithless husband. After every petty insult, after every needless humiliation, after every pointless row, there was a moment where Martin mentally tallied up the score and congratulated himself on winning. The result was a look. The look was triumph.

"How could I have been so stupid?" Abbey repeated, half to herself and half to Shirl. Shirl, still stuck for words, stumbled along beside her friend, wondering when the tears, the anger, the emotion, would come.

"I can't have children," Abbey said calmly, "so he stops wanting to sleep with me, then Geen gives birth to three blond babies one after the other and we all, stupidly, I suppose, say what a miracle it is. It's all so obvi—"

She ground to a halt midsentence, at the side of the meetinghouse, her mouth still hanging open, and turned to Shirl. Slowly, her big brown eyes widened as she began to shake uncontrollably. "Oh, my God, Shirl," she said, her face crumpling like a screwed-up paper bag, as her hands flew to her mouth in horror. "Nan!"

Abbey collapsed against the side of the building and let herself sink to the ground, her back against the outside wall. Nan's tears over Fafi, her daughter? Maybe she hadn't been asking if Abbey was going to take the Water Man away. Maybe she had been asking if Abbey *would* take him away. Maybe Martin had been cooking up a family with seventeen-year-old Fafi as well.

"I don't think they're the only ones, Shirl," she said, all calm abandoned and replaced by mounting hysteria. "I think there are more. Or he wants there to be more. Oh-my-God-oh-my-God-oh-my-God."

At that moment it just seemed too much to bear. Shirl was kneeling at her side trying to comfort her, but Abbey was being ravaged by reality, her body racked with shudders as she gasped for air. What about Imi? Her best friend? Had Martin been bonking her too? And even if he hadn't, she must have known. Her best friend must have known all this time what was going on. Abbey pulled her knees as close as she could and let her hot tears explode onto Imi's hand-me-down cargo pants. All this time she had thought that the villagers were her friends and she was protecting Martin from their scorn, when really they were laughing at her. Poor dreamy Abbey with her baggy clothes and burned hands and irritating irrigating husband. How could she have been so stupid?

She gave in to the hysteria that was clawing at her and howled at the awful truth of such mass betrayal. Her ridiculous life had all been a lie, and what's more, she didn't have any other life to go to. The loneliness that she had kept at bay for years enveloped her. Scrunched up against the side of the meetinghouse, the landscape of her existence a charred, empty desert, she wished she were dead. It would be easier and nobody would care anyway.

Sobbing into her knees, Shirl holding her as best she could, she imagined herself floating down the river on her back, stone-cold dead and pale as a ghost with blood streaming from her wrists, leaving ribbons of pink trailing behind her, winding their way around the many cheeses bobbing up and down in the current.

Abbey's wailing slowed a fraction. Cheeses?

She dismissed the river idea and instead pictured her lifeless body hanging rag-doll style from the branch of a giant oak tree, its leaves rustling in a cold evil breeze as overripe cheeses thumped to the ground.

Cheeses? Abbey hiccupped. This was not the time for daydreaming. This was the end of her life.

"Everything will be all right," Shirl was saying in a voice so soft Abbey wondered what she usually used it for. "Everything will be all right."

Abbey let her breathing fall into the pattern of Shirl's massage.

"Everything will be all right," Shirl whispered again, and this time Abbey turned her tear-stained face to look at her friend.

"How?" she said, her voice hollow and hopeless. "How can everything be all right?"

Before Shirl could answer, Abbey heard the crunch of an encroaching footstep, then Junior's voice.

"Is everything okay?" he said. "Is Abbey okay?"

Abbey looked over Shirl's head at his worried little-boy face and felt the pain of a thousand spears in her heart. How was everything going to be all right, exactly?

"Do us a favor, would you, love?" Shirl said, suddenly efficient. "Run over to Abbey's house and grab the old bugger with the beard for me, will you? Tell him Shirl says it's a code red and I'll meet him at Old Herc."

Junior turned immediately to go but Shirl reached for his hand and pulled him back. "Hang on a minute, love," she said. "What's your name?"

"Junior."

"How fast can you run, Junior?"

"Faster than a speeding bullet," Junior answered proudly. "Faster than anyone else at my school, anyway—apart from Lula Fasado and she's slowed down heaps since she got periods."

Shirl blinked at this last piece of information and then turned to Abbey. "Where's your passport, darl?" she asked.

"My passport?" Abbey repeated stupidly.

"Come on, Abbey," Shirl urged. "Where is your passport?"

"It's in my old handbag inside my trunk," Abbey said, "but why—"

Shirl was leaning toward Junior now, her voice grown louder with urgency. "Tell the old bugger about the code red," she said. "Then get Abbey's bag from the trunk in their hut and run like a gun, like a son of a gun, like a— shit, what was it?"

"Speeding bullet," said Abbey emptily.

"Then run like a speeding bullet to the plane at the landing strip. Junior, are you listening to me? You have to get there before the old bugger, before Martin does. You have to give me the bag before anyone else arrives. Can you do that? Abbey needs you to do that."

Junior looked at Abbey and, nodding silently, turned on his heels and ran.

Shirl pulled Abbey to her feet. "Just do what I say, Ab. We can work it all out later on."

She put her arm around Abbey's shoulders and shuffled her out to the main track around the village. A mist in

Abbey's brain was making it hard for her to understand what was going on. She was still confused by thoughts of cheese and she didn't understand about the passport. Everything was too hard, so she surrendered to Shirl's navigation and let herself be hurried along, her eyes remaining just out of focus on the ground in front. Through her haze she thought she heard voices growing louder and louder, maybe Pepa and Oba, maybe even Imi, but Shirl clutched her close and hurried her forward.

The noise, however, got louder and closer, until Shirl exclaimed, "Jesus H. Christ!" Before she knew it, Abbey was being thrust into the passenger seat of Tomi's Mazda and Shirl was flooring it in the direction of the airstrip. It wasn't far to go but the car certainly made it faster than the villagers; word had spread quickly that Martin's little secret was out and the gossips were on the warpath. At the Hercules, Shirl squealed to a halt and abandoned the car, pulling open the crew door at the front of the plane and bundling Abbey inside the aircraft before heading to the cockpit and flicking on some interior lights and a bank of switches on the control panel.

"Come on, Bullet Boy," Shirl whispered as she pulled down a seat in the cargo hold for Abbey to sit on. She reached through the cargo net beside her to pull out a thick woolen blanket and wrapped it tightly around Abbey's shoulders.

"I'm a bit out of my league, love," she said in her normal gravelly voice, looking nervously out the door. "But I think you should come home with me."

Abbey rocked back and forward, her eyes focused on an invisible point in front of her.

"You can always come back here if you want to, darl," Shirl continued, still craning her neck toward the darkness, looking for Junior. "But I think you need to get away for a bit to see what's what." She turned to her friend, aching at the sight of her. "Leastways it's what I would be doing."

With that the thunder of Blundstone boots alerted them to Jim's pending arrival.

"Bugger," said Shirl. "Where's the kid?"

Looking red-faced and puffed but not particularly surprised or angry, Jim sprinted toward them, a flurry of villagers in his wake, and dived in the door. "What kid?"

"She's my wife," Abbey heard Martin roar close by. "She's my wife. Let her out. Give her back."

As Shirl pulled Jim across the floor and lurched over to pull the door closed, a red leather missile came flying through the air and landed on the back of Jim's neck.

"You beauty, Speeding Bullet," Shirl roared out the door before pulling it closed with an almighty thud and locking it.

"What the bloody hell is going on here?" Jim asked, breathing heavily and rubbing his neck where an angry welt had already formed. He had taken in the semicatatonic Abbey, rocking back and forward in the empty cargo hold, seemingly oblivious to the fact that her husband was banging on the cargo door outside, demanding in a rage that Jim open it and let Abbey out.

"Your friend out there is starting a new breed of little Martins behind his wife's back is what the bloody hell is going on here," said Shirl, pushing her husband toward the cockpit. "Now get this thing in the air."

"Steady on, darl. How do you know about this? Who told you?"

"I saw them with my own eyes," said Shirl. "Now get this thing in the air or I'll thrash you, you great galah. Come on!"

Jim slipped into the pilot's seat just as Martin appeared in front of the plane on the airstrip, his face bulging with rage and a string of expletives pouring from his angry, spitting lips.

Jim looked uncertainly at Shirl. "Jeez, darl, this doesn't seem right. Are you sure it's what Abbey wants?"

Shirl looked back at the wretched sight of Abbey shaking underneath her blanket in the cabin.

"Do you want to go back to Martin, Abbey," she called, "or do you want us to run the useless bastard over on our way out of here?"

Abbey rocked back and forward, back and forward, her teeth chattering despite the warm air and the woolen blanket.

"What's she saying?" asked Jim, flicking switches above his head to engage the propeller blades. "She's saying something. What's her answer?"

"Get this thing cranked up, will you?" Shirl commanded, as she picked her way back through the hold and leaned down to hear what Abbey was mumbling.

"She says Martin's not his real name," she called back to Jim, straightening up. "She says his real name is Bruce."

Jim's anxious frown eased instantly and he exploded with laughter as the Hercules' engines sputtered into life.

"What's so funny about that?" Shirl wanted to know.

"Jeez, they must have really taken the piss out of him when he first arrived here," he chortled, checking his flight plan and slipping on his earphones. "Round here a brus," he shouted as the noise of the plane got louder, "is what you might let rip after a pot full of beans, if you get my drift."

"What?" squawked Shirl. "What's that about beans?"

"A fart," roared Jim. "The silly bugger's named after a fart."

Shirl was astonished. "And you're going to run him over because of that?"

"Nah," Jim shouted. "I'm going to run him over because he's a boring bastard who's been cheating on his wife."

With that the Hercules shuddered into motion and lurched forward.

Martin, wanting his wife back but not willing to end up splattered on the Hercules' nose, moved out of the way at the last possible moment, throwing his hat to the ground and kicking the dust in fury. A weeping gaggle of villagers clutched each other behind him but Abbey was oblivious to their cries. As the plane rose higher and higher, she pulled the blanket closer around her shoulders and, despite her emptiness, her loneliness, her despair, felt the smallest weight lift off them.

She never wanted to see Ate'ate nor her cheating, hateful husband again.

CHAPTER NINE

"There's a bit of thinking time between adding the rennet and cutting the curd. Different cheesemakers use this in different ways. Personally I favor planning elevenses."

JOSEPH FEEHAN, from *The Cheese Diaries,*
RTE Radio Archives

*I*n the parlor of her little pink B&B in the West Cork town of Schillies, Maureen McCarthy was attempting to drive Kit back to drink. He'd arrived in the village after a hellish trip from New York, expecting to be able to fall into bed and escape reality courtesy of a handful of Halcion. This, however, was clearly not on Maureen McCarthy's agenda.

"From New York, are you?" Maureen had asked, snatching away his bags and pushing him into an armchair in her stuffy drawing room the moment he arrived. "It looks like a wonderful place, sure it does, despite the twin towers—what a tragedy, all those lives, God rest their souls—and didn't Pauline O'Brien just down the lane have an uncle who moved there a few years back?" she said, disappearing to make a cup of tea but eerily leaving her voice in the room with Kit. "Run over by a yellow taxicab and killed stone-dead the poor man was," the voice said, enthusiastically. "Then his poor broken body trampled by a horse and cart full of tourists. Do you take milk?"

"Yes, thanks," Kit answered, although she was already back in the room with a mug full of milky tea.

"In the street with all the theaters. Do you know it?"

"Broadway?" Kit offered.

"The very one. Fancy that." Maureen beamed. "Pauline went there herself a year or so ago but it was hard to tell the exact spot where it happened, so she went to Starbucks instead then took in the afternoon showing of *Cabaret*. Well, she was in the area, God bless her."

A small, wiry woman, with curls set in rows of military precision, she perched like a bird on an uncomfortable little stool by the fireplace and took in every detail of her guest with bright, beady little eyes that didn't miss a trick.

"He's not the only one from around here to end his days under the wheels of a fast-moving motor vehicle actually," she said, as if Kit had just announced he were doing a thesis on the subject and did she have any other data that might be useful?

"There was Patsy Mulligan who came from up the lane bowled over by a bus on her way to Mass over in Cork," Maureen said, shaking her head. "Of course, she'd been into the sherry and hadn't she got Sunday morning confused with Friday rush hour but she was bowled over, nonetheless. 'Twas a terrible tragedy for the family. What with her being ninety-nine and all their hopes pinned on a big hooley for her hundredth."

She stopped and looked mournful for a moment before adding rather brightly, "I ended up with her toilet-seat cover as it happens. It's purple. It looks like carpet."

Kit had no response to that.

"There's been a murder here too, you know," Maureen continued. "Out by the coast, last year. I'm surprised you didn't hear about it in New York. Germans with boatloads of money. Boatloads. They built a huge house with four bathrooms and the husband wore thick socks with his sandals, but his wife was young and pretty as a picture. Pretty as a picture! She came to stay in the house on her own one weekend, but by the time her husband turned up she had been attacked and stabbed twenty-four times in the chest. Twenty-four times, God bless her. Or was it twenty-five?"

Kit felt sick. The tea had gone cold and there was something oily floating on the top of it. Actually, he didn't really like tea. He liked vodka. And a lot of it, right now, would have made him feel a whole lot better.

"So," Maureen said brightly, "what brings you here? Touring? Sailing? The Ikebana Festival in the village hall this weekend?"

"Much as I like raw fish," Kit joked, "I'm actually going to stay at a farm. They make cheese there. It's called Coolarney, and it's run by a couple of old guys and this woman, Avis something, I can't quite remember. I have the details upstairs. I don't suppose you would happen to know where that is?"

Maureen's eyes darkened. "Don't we all know where that is," she said. "A fine old time you'll be in for up there, no doubt. A fine old time indeed. Applying for the cheese-maker's job there, are you? I wouldn't have picked it. Not at all. With your fancy luggage and your fruity cologne. Still, it wouldn't be the strangest thing to happen, a fancy fella like yourself turning up to make cheese at Coolarney House, that's for sure."

"You think my aftershave is fruity?" Kit asked, trying

not to feel hurt and wondering what was behind Maureen's change of mood.

"Oh, well, you know," she said airily, picking a bit of imaginary fluff off her skirt. "Some people like it that way." Her momentary silence made it clear she was not one of those people. "There was a lad from across the lane who wore a very similar cologne," she started.

"Don't tell me," interrupted Kit, with his most charming smile, "he ended his life under the wheels of a fast-moving motor vehicle."

Maureen looked surprised. "Well, he didn't end it but he certainly slowed it down a bit," she said. "And anyway, it wasn't my fault and it certainly wasn't fast moving. What sort of an eejit would go to sleep on the ground behind a Honda Civic? Nobody would have seen him. That's what was agreed."

Kit made a mental note to avoid, under any circumstances, falling asleep behind Maureen McCarthy's Honda Civic. But he was intrigued by her insinuations about Coolarney House.

"So what goes on up at this cheese farm, then?" he asked. "You make it sound kind of weird."

"Well, I really couldn't say," Maureen said, with pinched lips. "I'm not one to gossip but over the years the shenanigans up the road there would curl your hair."

"Shenanigans?" Kit asked, trying not to smile.

"Let's just say there's more people gone into Coolarney House than have come out again—unless it's babies you're talking about, in which case it is entirely the other way around."

"Babies?" Kit wanted to know. "What shenanigans happen with babies?"

"You'll find out soon enough, no doubt," Maureen

snipped. "Being as you are headed there yourself. Two old men with a houseful of expectant mothers, it's not right. And Mr. High-and-Mighty Corrigan's own daughter the first to turn her back on them. If you don't count his wife, that is, God Rest Her Soul, wherever it might be with only those two old devils and your man upstairs 100 percent certain."

Kit was confused. "So his wife what? Died?" he asked. He'd put money on there being an automobile involved.

"Just try asking him yourself," Maureen said, surprising him by remaining stingy with details. "And while you're there, see if you can find out where the bockety old borries have buried their treasure as well."

Kit pretended to sip his oily, cold tea and wondered what a bockety old borrie was. He assumed it wasn't something great, although it had quite a nice ring to it. On the whole, he had to admit his hostess was hardly giving Coolarney House a rave review.

"What about Avis O'Regan?" he asked. "Is she, you know—"

"What?" Maureen prompted unhelpfully. "Is she what?"

"Well, is she all right?" Kit continued, wishing he were dead or asleep or just somewhere else.

"As well as any married woman living with two single men and not a husband in sight would be. Oh, there's been no sign of Mr. O'Regan in more than thirty years. You might happen upon him while you're digging for treasure."

Kit couldn't help but laugh. "Well, you make it sound like a great place," he said, "and I can't wait to get there. But I'm telling you now I'm not interested in digging for treasure or making babies or whatever else goes on up there."

Maureen raised her eyebrows. "So you are going for an interview then, are you?" She answered her own question. "The old bollockses. Typical, just typical they'd draft a dirty blow-in rather than help out a local lad. Cheese-maker, my elbow!"

She pinched her lips even further and Kit suddenly felt very tired and very thirsty. The intensity of Maureen McCarthy's scrutiny was sucking the life right out of him, and he felt the need to go somewhere very quiet and dark.

"Would you mind if I went to my room now?" he asked Maureen, leaning forward in his chair. "It's been a long day and I am totally whacked."

"Better be in good shape for your big interview to-morrow I suppose," said Maureen caustically. "Never mind me sitting all on my own here in the dark with no one to talk to."

Kit rubbed his temples and sighed. He'd spotted a bottle of Bailey's Irish Cream on the cocktail cabinet and it was unnerving him. "I'm not going there for an inter-view," he said, struggling to come up with a plausible rea-son for why he was going there. "I don't know anything about any interview. I'm just going to be staying there awhile. I'm working on a, ah, on an investment project with—"

He could see Maureen leaning toward him to glean as much as she could.

"Avis has some, uh, financial issues that she—"

Maureen was in danger of toppling off her stool.

"You know what," Kit said suddenly, standing up. "I lost my wife a few months back. I've been drinking a lot since then and I got fired from my job, so a friend of mine sug-gested I come and stay with Avis for a while to get myself cleaned up, you know? So if I could just go and lie down for

a while and maybe get some sleep, I would really appreciate it, Maureen. I really would."

Maureen's eyes glistened with this newfound knowl-
edge.

"I'm so sorry for your troubles, Christopher," she said,
trying very hard to keep the glee out of her voice. "Come
upstairs and I'll show you to your room."

Kit picked up his luggage in the hallway and followed
her up the narrow stairway to a room with a door so low
he had to bend down to walk through it. His room con-
sisted of a single bed, a nightstand, a framed picture of
the Sacred Heart of Jesus and an even smaller door that
opened into a tiny bathroom, complete with a purple,
frighteningly carpetlike toilet-seat cover.

"Would you be after me waking you in the morning,
Christopher?" she asked kindly. "I'll be up anyway making
your breakfast and getting ready to launder your linen."

How, thought Kit, does one get ready to launder linen?

"Thank you, Maureen. If I'm not downstairs by 8:30
please rap on my door."

He guided her out into the hallway and retreated to his
tiny room, banging his head in both directions, then
stripped off down to his boxers and T-shirt and flopped
onto the bed, every fiber of his being crying out for sleep.
Unfortunately, the mattress appeared to be stuffed with
porcupine quills, every fiber of his being poked by a different one. Sleep, Kit realized, was to elude him for a while
longer yet.

He let his mind drift to the events of the past few days.
They seemed to have passed in a long, frightening blur,
and it hurt to think about it. His stomach lurched back
toward his spine as he lay on the bed and thought of the
humiliating scene that had unfolded at the office. He

could still feel the hollow rap of horror as George bawled him out. How could it be that his career had ended that way? He still felt as though George had him confused with somebody else, although he was nowhere near as convinced of that as he had been three days ago.

A tear slid down toward his ear as he relived the hot burn of shame he'd felt waiting at the elevator in the trading room with Niamh. Niamh. Without her, he thought, he would be sitting right now in some badly lit bar, crying into his pretzels and singing old Neil Diamond songs. God damn her. Lying on a prickly bed in a strange country in a funny pink house, he realized just how removed he had become from his life. He'd gotten along fine without Jacey for the first thirty-one years of his life, so why had his world come tumbling down once she was gone? How could he not have noticed that drinking had become his job and trading his hobby?

Another tear slid down as Kit contemplated the possibility that his reason for existing had disappeared down the drain with his vodka collection. There didn't really seem any point in anything, he thought miserably. He didn't have a home or a wife or a job, and without any of it, his job especially, he didn't know who he was. Hell, even with it he'd gotten confused. Kit moved his gaze from the ceiling to the Sacred Heart.

He knew now that the vodka had become a problem. He knew that when one minute after Niamh had left his apartment he had turned the whole place upside down looking for a secret stash. He knew it even more when she called half an hour later to see if that was what he had done. He knew it when she came back and slept on his sofa while he paced the floor, alternately wanting to kill her, kill himself, kill a drink.

Every time he thought of Jacey lying on the floor, the promise of their baby leaking out of her, his hand had wanted to fly out and grab something—and a drink seemed to make the most sense. His thirst only worsened every time he thought of his mother or father or Flynn.

Niamh had stayed with him at the apartment, booked his travel, arranged this place in Schillies, made all the necessary calls, even packed his bags. She'd come with him in the cab to the airport and waited until the last possible moment before waving him through the departure gate, urging him to be strong when it came to the duty-free liquor.

"It will be all right, Kit," she had whispered into his ear as she'd hugged him good-bye. "You'll be all right."

True, he had resisted all offers of drink during the eight-hour flight—in Economy, for chrissakes, where alcohol was practically compulsory—had managed to walk past the airport bar in Cork before getting on his bus and had ignored the shelf heaving with spirits at the Schillies village store. But lying there on that prickly bed, his pillow soaking up the tears, Kit felt a growing emptiness that he desperately needed to fill, and he wondered if he ever really would be all right again.

With the bleeding heart of Jesus on the wall his only company, he prayed with all his heart that Avis O'Regan could help him. Then he fell into a deep, deep sleep.

CHAPTER TEN

"Show me a man who doesn't eat cheese, and I'll show his arse my boot."

JOSEPH FEEHAN, from *The Cheese Diaries*,
RTE Radio Archives

*F*ee looked out the window of the upstairs den at the raggedy bunch of hopefuls lined up by the farmhouse, waiting for the cheesemaker interviews to begin. There were six in all and his instinct was that there was not a cheesemaker among them. Usually he would have pointed this out straightaway, but Corrie had been so dispirited since the curd turned that Fee was loath to shatter their hopes at such an early stage. Anyway, his instinct was telling him that all was not lost.

"I think Brian Clancy is still fluthered from last night," he said, stepping back behind the drapes and taking a sip of his tea. "He's got hiccups, and yesterday's drawers poking out the bottom of his trousers."

Corrie raised his eyebrows at this piece of information and dipped a bit of Avis's home-baked raisin bread into his teacup. "Does there look to be a cheesemaker among them, Joseph?" he asked.

"It's hard to tell," Fee answered, "from this distance. With the ivy and all that."

Corrie sighed. He'd thought as much. "Who've we got, then?" he asked. "Apart from Brian?"

Brian would not be their cheesemaker. He was a nice enough fellow and in fact knew quite a lot about cheese, having worked in the high-end hospitality industry for years up in Dublin. However, he was severely hampered by often being unsteady on his feet, uncommonly attached, as he was, to the drink. Reliability was one of the keys to being a good cheesemaker, but Brian was something of a stranger to reliability and nearly everybody in Schillies had a story to demonstrate this.

"Dermot McGrath, for a start," Fee intoned, peering through the glass, unimpressed.

Dermot was a big lump of a lad in his twenties, swollen with a lifetime of successful bullying and his doting mother's dedication to overfeeding him. He wore a sleeveless vest designed to show off muscular biceps, but his upper arms in fact resembled two uncooked hams. His eyes were small and black; his hair dark, stringy and thinning on top, a fact he disguised, not very well, by wearing a baseball cap two sizes too small perched on top of his head. He'd had a lot of hot dinners had Dermot, and almost as many jobs, most of which were lost to him after a display of the nasty temper he kept well hidden until asked to do something.

"He's teasing poor Jamie," Fee noted, "the nuisance."

"Our Jamie? Jamie Joyce?" Corrie asked. "What's he doing out there in the first place?" Corrie asked.

"It helps to have a man on the inside," Fee said knowingly.

"Ah, but poor Jamie?" Corrie was worried now. "That big lump of a boy will make a mess of him."

"He'll be all right," said Fee, exasperated. "The state of you, sitting there with a face like a plateful of mortal sins! It's not the end of the feckin' world, you know."

But for Corrie it was. A life without Fee looked dark and grim and altogether pretty hopeless.

"Anyway," said Fee, changing the subject, "you don't need to worry about Jamie. He can stand up for himself. He'll be grand." He peered through the window again, just in time to catch Dermot holding Jamie up against the factory wall by his chin.

"Say Ulysses," Dermot was demanding.

"Pardon me," Brian Clancy said, interrupting the taunting by belching loudly and sinking to a sitting position on the ground against one of the flower barrels.

"Say she sells seashells on the scheaschore." Dermot's jeering continued.

"Oh, feck off, would you." Michael Cullen poked at Dermot with his walking stick. "Leave the poor lad alone."

"What the feck!" Fee cried excitedly in the upstairs den. "There's old Mickey Cullen! Jaysus, I thought he was dead. He must be more than a hundred by now. What's he doing here?"

"Making a nuisance of himself with his stick, no doubt," said Corrie.

Polio had left a young Mickey with a gimpy leg and in the many decades since the offending limb had withered, he'd become a deft hand in the stick department. Rumor had it that he'd once removed a man's spleen through his belly button with the offending staff, and although nobody could actually back that up, there was many a man down at Blorrie Flatt's bar who had worn the stick around the back of his neck for drinking other men's pints or being slow to put his hand in his pocket.

Dermot was rubbing his pudgy arm and eyeballing Mickey's stick. Although he was thick in the head, he wasn't so thick that he'd mess with the stick.

"What are you here for anyway, Mickey?" asked Fergal Whelan, who was kicking stones carelessly around the courtyard. "What do you care about working?"

Spotting Fergal from above, Fee growled and narrowed his eyes.

Corrie looked up from his newspaper. "Who's got the face like a plateful of mortal sins, now?" he asked. "What's happening?"

"Fergal Whelan's out there," Fee said darkly, watching Fergal chat good-humoredly with Mickey. "That's what's happening."

Corrie watched his friend closely. He'd never understood why Fee had such a switch about Fergal. He was a good-looking boy just a year or so older than Rose, and he'd worked at Blorrie Flatt's since he left school. He had the air about him of someone who might have gone on to bigger and brighter things if only he'd bothered his arse. He was a bit of a dreamer but he could still look you in the eye and have a half-decent conversation, which is more than you could say for many. It was hard to suppose what there was to not like.

"It's not a matter of not liking him," said Fee, reading Corrie's mind as he stepped back behind the drapes again. "Oh, don't bother yourself about it."

"I'm not here for the work," Mickey answered Fergal down below. "I'm here to find the money."

"Pardon me?" Brian Clancy repeated after another heinous belch.

"What money?" Thomas Brennan asked quickly.

"G'wan!" barked Fee, squashing his nose against the

upstairs window for a better look. "If it isn't Thomas Brennan!"

Corrie got out of his seat and shuffled to the window, looking down below. "Will you look at that," he breathed.

"All fur coat and no drawers, that one," Fee announced almost admiringly. "The cut of him!"

Thomas was wearing a three-piece suit and tie and was carrying a briefcase.

"Does he think there's a job going in management?" Corrie wondered aloud as he retreated back to the comfort of his chair.

Still, it was hardly surprising that Thomas had turned up for the job—he was probably Schillies' best-known unemployed person. The poor galoot had gone to Dublin a few years before with a great hiss and a roar to be something dot-com, a fact his mother Gertie never stopped reminding everyone and anyone who didn't see her coming and manage to duck into a doorway first. The poor woman had been quite conspicuous in her absence since her golden boy came home in disgrace. Rumor had it that Thomas had been relieved of his employment months before anyone knew, pretending even to his live-in girlfriend that he was going off to work when really he was leaving their Temple Bar apartment to sit in Bewleys all day long drinking coffee.

Normally, a situation such as this would have inspired much sympathy among the good people of Schillies. But since his return Thomas had insisted on keeping up the pretense that he was running a major telecommunications empire from his mother's kitchen; even after he had dropped his laptop computer case on the forecourt outside the Schillies co-op only to have it spring open and reveal nothing but three *Playboy*s and a peanut butter sandwich, he maintained the façade, shouting into his cell phone (unconnected to any network) as he walked the village's single main street.

Down in the courtyard, "What money?" Thomas asked Mickey, as he snapped the offending phone shut and put it in his pocket.

"Don't listen to a word he says," Fergal warned him lazily. "He's just messing with you. It's none of it true."

"It's none of it proved," corrected Mickey. "That doesn't mean it's not true."

"What's not true? What's not proved?" Thomas implored.

"Well," started Mickey as Fergal rolled his eyes, "the story goes that somewhere not very far from where we all stand right here there is a small fortune buried."

Jamie started to chortle, then checked himself.

"Shut up, stupid," Dermot said, not loud enough for anyone else to hear, flicking one of his huge fat fingers and stinging Jamie's neck. "How do you know about this then, Mickey?" he asked, in his big slow voice.

Inside the back door, Avis was getting the gist of the conversation as she tipped a tray of fresh baked raspberry muffins onto a wire rack for cooling. The hidden treasure story got bigger and better every time she heard it.

"When they were building this place three hundred years ago it was Cullen hands that laid the brickwork," Mickey said. "We were allus a hardworking bunch, we Cullens, big as oxen and strong like Samson in the Bible."

Fergal Whelan took in Mickey's wizened stature and tried not to choke with derision. "You're out of your mind, Mickey. There's never been a Cullen could reach the top shelf of the pantry let alone throw bricks about the place."

"And you're the genealogical expert all of a sudden, are

you, Fergal?" Mickey threatened, waving his walking stick in the bartender's direction. Fergal just rolled his eyes again.

"What about this fortune then?" Thomas prompted.

"Pardon me," belched Brian. "Jaysus, me guts are killing me."

"So it was Cullens built this great big house," Mickey continued, "with all its bedrooms and sitting rooms and water closets and the rest of it, and even though they threw it up in record time, did the master of the place shout them so much as a single pint? Did he shite!"

Brian went six different shades of green before settling on a hue that exactly matched the foliage on which his head was slumped.

"Would a smoke bring you round, Brian?" Fergal asked, rolling him one anyway.

"He paid them their weekly insult did old Joey Corrigan, but when it came to putting his hand in his pocket for a man with a mouth on him, you can forget it," continued Mickey. Brian took a drag on the cigarette Fergal had rolled him and Jamie watched his face slip from leafy green to clammy gray then to an almost human shade of pinkish-white. His eyes opened properly for the first time all morning as he expelled a lung full of tobacco smoke.

"Still," Mickey continued, "when it came time to build the cheese factory, there wasn't much of anything else happening work-wise so the Cullens came back, despite the boss being so mangy with the gargle. For months they dug into the ground with just a single pickax between the lot of them, excavating two fancy underground 'caves' so Himself could cure his cheeses just like the French do, oh la feckin' la. Anyway, they finished, and were ready to start work on the rest of the building. When," continued

Mickey, thrilled with such an attentive audience, "who should appear out of this very back door here but old Joey Corrigan himself with three bottles of Irish Whisky and cheese and oatcakes for the lot of them. Well, naturally, the boys were thirsty, but the old devil had slipped something into the drink so strong that they all, one after the other, fell into a deep sleep. When they woke up the next morning, the caves had been sealed and the lads were given their marching orders. And that, my friends," he finished proudly, "is the story of the buried treasure. It's down there, all right," he said, shaking his stick at the factory, "and ripe for the picking."

There was a moment's silence.

Finally, Fergal spoke. "There are more holes in that story, Mickey," he said, "than I can poke your stick at."

"So what exactly was the bit about the treasure?" asked a greatly improved Brian.

"How do you know it's money?" asked Thomas. "How do you know that's what is down there?"

"Well, why else would you get your workers to dig a great big hole, then poison them and block off the thing?" demanded Mickey.

"It sounds to me like the Cullens all got totally jarred and the boss had to finish the job himself," said Fergal. "And it wouldn't be the first time that has happened either, would it, Mickey?"

"Leave him alone," demanded Dermot, keen to be on the right side should the treasure turn up.

"It's not true," Jamie said, shocking everyone else into silence by speaking. "The factory wasn't built until two hundred years after the house, in the 1930s, and the curing rooms were only dug in the 1960s." His face flushed a deeper red with every slushy sibilant. "They're called caves because they're dug out of rock and not lined—it's to do with moisture and humidity. It's nothing to do with the French. It was Corrie dug them out, with great big machines brought in from Bantry."

Fergal looked at him and burst out laughing. "How about that, now? Two hundred years after the house with machines, you say? Those great big Cullens were fierce heavy sleepers, wha', Mickey?"

Brian belched again. "I'm coming right, all the same," he said, blowing a pall of smoke up into the air.

"What would he know anyway?" Dermot said, pointing at Jamie.

"I know about the buildings," Jamie said robustly. "I know about the farm." He stared at the ground in front of him. He'd never said so much at one time in all his life.

"Do you know something about the money, then, Fergal?" asked Thomas, nervously fidgeting with the phone in his pocket. "Like, where it is, for example?"

"Well, what I heard," Fergal said, deflecting attention from the blushing Jamie and picking a bit of tobacco off his bottom lip, "from Seamus O'Connor was that there's a trapdoor in the field between the factory and the dairy, the exact coordinates of which are kept in an impenetrable box in young Joey Corrigan's sock drawer. Seamus crept in here one night with Paddy O'Toole keeping guard and made it as far as the sock drawer before a booby trap nearly blew off his head."

"If he spent so long staking it out," Jamie asked, bolder now, "why did he need the coordinates? Why didn't he just go straight to the trapdoor?"

Fergal looked at him with renewed respect. He knew there was no treasure. He just enjoyed the messing.

"What's the matter with you?" Dermot said, punching

Jamie viciously on the shoulder. "How could he open the trapdoor without the coordinates, you useless feck?" There was an unbelieving silence.

"The great lump doesn't know what a coordinate is." Brian grinned at Fergal.

"I do so," Dermot snapped, flustered. "It's the numbers you need to unlock a safe."

"That's a combination," said Jamie, rubbing his arm where the big brute had whacked him.

"That's what I said, a combination of numbers," Dermot taunted, sticking his tongue out in a duncelike imitation.

Fergal looked at Jamie and winked. "Sure, if he gets the cheese job the treasure will be safe for another few hundred years, you can be sure of that."

"You're barking mad, the lot of you," said Thomas, punching numbers into his phone.

"Tea, anybody?" Avis O'Regan appeared holding a tray heaving with a teapot, cups, milk, sugar and a bewitching-smelling pile of muffins.

"You are an angel sent from God himself, Miss O'Regan," Brian waxed, starting to stagger to his feet, then thinking better of it and lurching back instead into his sitting position.

"Now there's the sort of talk a girl could get used to," she said, smiling and passing the tray to Fergal. She disappeared back into the kitchen, then reappeared with a fold-out table, upon which Fergal set the tea things.

"Excuse me," said Thomas impatiently, "but what time will the interviews begin? Some of us have other appointments to go to, you know."

The other hopefuls all snorted with laughter.

"Appointments me arse," Mickey grumbled, moving

Dermot out of the way with his stick to give himself better access to the tea tray.

"Well," said Avis, wiping her hands on her apron, then making a fuss of looking at her watch. "It's nearly half-eleven now so I would imagine that by the time you've all had lunch and filled out the forms and been through the tests . . . Yes," she said brightly, "Mr. Corrigan and Mr. Feehan should get to see all of you today."

With that she whisked herself inside before anybody could say a word and shut the door behind her, moving immediately to the upstairs sitting room to report to Corrie and Fee.

"They're not what I would call the most promising bunch," she said, her heart sinking at the sight of Corrie's worried face. "And the rubbish they're talking about the buried treasure, you wouldn't credit it!"

"What are they saying?" Fee asked, cheered by the thought of rubbish being talked. He'd been doing his best to lip-read from his vantage point at the upstairs window but all the squinting had given him a headache.

Outside Dermot was still arguing with Fergal about the difference between coordinates and combinations. "One is a combination of numbers which when used in the right order will unlock a safe," Fergal was saying with exaggerated patience, "and the other is a series of numbers indicating, on a numbered grid, the exact location of something."

Dermot felt disinclined to back down. "Well, a series of numbers is a combination too, you feckin' know-it-all. I'm not that feckin' stupid."

Brian and Mickey both laughed while Jamie pushed himself flat against the factory wall. He'd seen Dermot explode on many occasions and he didn't want to be a victim when it happened today.

Dermot, realizing he had made a fool of himself, was insisting, "They're all feckin' numbers, what's the difference?"

"Now it's sentiments like that which we can blame for this country's grand tradition of gross fraudulence and corruption," Fergal said to Mickey.

"Well, here's another grand tradition, you filthy bollocks," roared Dermot, launching himself at Fergal and misfiring an ungainly punch, which shot past Fergal's jaw and landed squarely on Mickey Cullen's chest.

The old man staggered backward and tripped over Brian's outstretched feet. He fell into the waiting arms of Jamie Joyce, who had seen Dermot's work so many times before he knew how to be in the right place at the right time. Dermot was strong, no denying that, but he was not fast.

"You great gob-shite," Mickey shouted, propelling himself with speed toward Dermot, who was still trying to work out what had happened. Before he managed it, however, he felt a rain of blows from Mickey's stick about his head and shoulders that his own enormous arms could do little to fend off.

"That's right," Fergal encouraged from his position on the ground where he had fallen after dodging Dermot's blow. "Give the poxy whore's melt six of the best for me, would you, Mickey?"

The commotion reached the sitting room, where Corrie looked at Fee expectantly for an update. "Mickey Cullen's giving the fat one a grand old hiding," Fee said delightedly. "You'd never think there was anything wrong with him to see him move that stick, would you?"

"What's Jamie doing?" Corrie wanted to know.

"Laughing his head off," Fee answered. "You don't see that happening too often. I told you he'd be grand."

Outside, Mickey's stick split in two over Dermot's skull, freeing the younger man to escape out of the firing line—but not without a severe poke from the jagged end of the longest piece.

"I'll get you, you old bollocks," he shouted, as he backed out of the yard toward the driveway. "And you won't have your stick to help you either."

"I'll still have twice the brains and half the lard, you great girl, you," Mickey shouted after him. "Now run home to your mammy before I stick me boot into you as well."

Dermot, choking with rage and unable to speak, turned and lumbered down the driveway, where halfway down toward the lane he happened upon Kit, hot and sticky after lugging himself and his bags from Schillies.

"Pardon me," Kit said, smiling at the fat, sweaty lad, "could you tell me where I can find Avis O'Regan?"

Dermot took in the American's good looks, fine clothes, sleek build and slightly lost expression and knew immediately that he hated him.

"That I could," he said, wiping his brow and catching his breath. "Haven't I only just seen her? She says she wants you to wait for her on the garden bench through the gate there, first on your right in front of the main house."

"Oh," said Kit. "Wait for her? In the garden? Sure. If that's what she wants."

"It's a madhouse up there today," Dermot said, removing his tiny baseball cap and wiping the sweat off his dome. "I wouldn't get in her way if I were you, she's looking awful fierce."

Kit felt his heart sink in his chest. What had Niamh gotten him into? He was exhausted enough by Maureen McCarthy and she wasn't even particularly fierce. Just nosy. The strain of her not asking any more about his personal circumstances over breakfast had plum tuckered the two of them out. By the time he had reached the cheese farm after a mile-long walk, he was dreaming of a friendly face, a darkened room and a cool glass of water. He sighed and hitched up his bags.

"Thanks," he said to Dermot, whom he suddenly noticed was covered with red welts. "Hives, huh?"

Dermot looked confused before examining his arm to find marks in the shape of bits of Mickey's stick all over it. His eyes hardened. "Fleas," he spat, darkly, "the size of rats. Look out where you sit."

And with that he lumbered past Kit and down the driveway to the road.

CHAPTER ELEVEN

"Some people should never make cheese. Liars make bad cheesemakers: It looks good but tastes desperate. Cheats make bad cheesemakers too, and there's never as much of it as they say there's going to be."

JOSEPH FEEHAN, from *The Cheese Diaries*, RTE Radio Archives

*A*bbey looked up at the pillar-fronted white-stucco building and scrutinized it for signs of her mother but did not find any. She wasn't really sure what she expected. But the building was pretty much exactly as she remembered it, although the Kensington street, like much of London, seemed tidier. Smarter. Taking a deep breath, she hitched her bag higher on her shoulder and climbed the front steps, not completely surprised to see her hand shaking as she reached out to press the buzzer for apartment C.

As the brass button reverberated under the touch of her fingertip, she felt a moment of panic. This couldn't altogether be considered sudden, as she'd been suffering similar moments since kissing Shirl good-bye at Brisbane International the day before, or the day before that, or whenever it had been. Did she really want to subject herself to Rose's particular brand of nurturing and support?

Were eleven years without it enough? Abbey felt an over-whelming wave of emotion roar through her and for a moment she considered turning and fleeing. But turning to whom? Fleeing where? She took another deep breath and pressed the buzzer again. She was only on Rose's doorstep because she had absolutely nowhere else to go in the world, literally. It wasn't as though she was choosing Rose over anything. Or anybody. Rose was it.

There was her friend Virginia Barker from school but in her last letter, more than two years ago now, Virginia had been in the process of moving to Scotland with her husband and twin sons. Abbey didn't even know which bit of Scotland. Or if Virginia had changed her last name. Or if she'd had more babies since then.

Babies. Abbey buzzed forcefully a third time.

"You'd forget your balls if they weren't in a sack." Her mother's unmistakable voice crackled loudly out of the speaker as the door clicked unlocked. Abbey, unprepared for such a response, gaped wordlessly at the intercom before deciding to simply push open the door and proceed upstairs. Whose balls? she thought uncomfortably. What sack?

She approached her mother's third-floor apartment, the elevator door closing with a clatter behind her, her heart thumping in her chest. She was just about to rap on the door when it opened, her mother's rear end disappearing behind it again before she saw who was there.

". . . the useless bollocks has only lost his keys again," her mother was saying into the hall phone. "Didn't I just tell him he'd lose his balls if they weren't in a sack?" She laughed into the receiver.

Abbey moved slowly inside the door. This wasn't how she had imagined her homecoming.

"Well, just as well he's good at that then, isn't it now?" her mother tinkled into the phone, lifting one delicately manicured foot to push the door closed from her position on the padded chair next to the hall table. She looked casually at Abbey's feet, then her eyes traveled slowly up her calves, her expression changing in slow motion as she took in not the hips and torso of whoever she was expecting but the body of her only child. The body she assumed to be sitting in the sun on the other side of the world. Her eyes landed on Abbey's with a look that defied description.

"Jaysus," she said, her perfectly lipsticked mouth falling open in shock, a column of cigarette smoke wafting moodily out of it. "I'll ring you back." She dropped the phone back in its cradle, blindly stubbed out her cigarette and slowly rose, staring disbelievingly at Abbey all the while.

"Hi, Rose," said Abbey. "I've come home." She was struck by, had forgotten somehow, just how exquisitely beautiful her mother was. Her dark red hair was shoulder length and set like a movie star's from the 1940s, and her skin was the color of milk. The delicate bones around her mother's neck and shoulders that she remembered so clearly were still in prime position, every stitch of clothing worn to show this feature off to its maximum potential. The makeup was perhaps a layer or two thicker, but the eyes were still an incredible shade of spring-forest green and the lashes outrageously thick and long. Her mother, Abbey thought with a jolt, didn't look a day older than when she had last seen her eleven years ago.

"Jaysus!" her mother said again. She was wearing an off-white floaty negligee arrangement with impossibly wide, sheer long sleeves, feathered at the wrists. It was a strange getup for the late afternoon but just the romantic sort of Zsa Zsa Gabor outfit her mother had always favored.

"I think I'm in shock," Rose said.

Abbey moved cautiously half a step closer. "You do know who I am, don't you?" she said, only half-joking. She could see her mother performing mental gymnastics behind her foundation and for one terrible moment wondered if she had in fact forgotten about her. There was a terrible, frightening corridor of silence then the curtain was lifted and Rose the actress emerged.

"Darling," she said, suddenly dramatic, holding her arms out for Abbey to walk into them, her face rearranging itself into warm maternal repose. "It's so wonderful to see you, of course it is. Just such a shock, that's all. A terrible shock. Mind the hair."

She kissed the air on either side of Abbey's face and then pulled back, but Abbey didn't mind. She'd never really been comfortable in her mother's embrace and now was no exception.

"I just can't believe it's you, Abbey," Rose said in a strange tone, giving her daughter the once-over. "Just look at you. That's quite a body you have on you now, girl. Give us a spin."

Abbey dropped her bag and dutifully did as she was told. It came as no shock that her mother would check out her measurements before her mental health, marital status or plans for the future. Some things would never change.

"I've been in the air for twenty-seven hours," Abbey explained, picking her T-shirt away from her slightly sweating midriff. She doubted that the too-big hand-me-downs that she couldn't afford to ditch despite their awful memories were doing her justice.

"Come in and sit down, you must be exhausted," Rose said, reaching for her cigarettes on the telephone table and turning Abbey with the tip of her talon toward the tiny sitting room. "Have you been working out, have you?"

"I have been in the islands for more than eleven years, Rose," Abbey pointed out. "Gyms are kind of in short supply in that part of the world." Actually, there had been an entire Nautilus weights system, two treadmills and a running machine in Tomi Papara's back room but she'd never felt the urge to use them.

"Of course you were, darling," Rose said, arranging herself on the sofa and pretending to scoff at her own silliness. "The shock of it all. Did you get my letter?"

Abbey looked at her mother. "The letter you wrote me, what, eight years ago?" she said brightly. "Yes, Rose, I got it. Did you get the letters I wrote you, you know, every Christmas and birthday and most months in between?"

Her mother caught the tenor of her tone and looked momentarily chastised. "Ah, don't look at me like that, Abbey. You know I'm hopeless at corresponding. I'm an immediate sort of a person, you know that. I'm an 'in there, in your face' sort of a person. Don't give me a hard time. You know I was never much good at writing letters."

Abbey swallowed her response. She felt shaky and emotional and didn't want to be sitting here bickering about letter writing. She wanted to tell her mother what she had been through. She wanted to cry and be showered, if not with sympathy then at least with advice for how to get on with her life. Rose certainly had the experience when it came to men.

"Oh, Rose, you won't believe—" she started.

"You won't believe how much—" her mother said at the same time, ignoring the intrusion and continuing to talk over the top of her daughter, "has gone on here since you left, Abbey." She lit a cigarette and kept going. "I got a part in an ongoing tea-bag commercial not long after you went. It was huge. I was voted one of the top ten most popular TV stars. Can you believe it? From a tea commercial? Anyway, that led to a tiny role on *EastEnders* as one of Phil Mitchell's girlfriends. Well, I just blew the producers away, Abbey. Totally blew them away. Next thing you know I have a starring role in *What Am I Like?* Did you get that over in Bali Hai? It was a gas sitcom, Abbey, you'd have loved it. Four seasons it lasted. Four wonderful seasons. And now I am playing Marilyn Monroe's part in a West End production of *Bus Stop*. Me and Marilyn Monroe, the critics have said we could be sisters. What do you make of that?"

Her mother, Abbey slowly realized, seemed to be displaying all the symptoms of extreme nervousness, not a Rose-like condition by any stretch.

"Look," Rose twittered, fanning her hand around the sitting-room walls at the selection of fussily framed magazine covers all featuring her beautiful face. "*Radio Times, You* magazine, *Hello*, of course, two lots of *Woman's Own* and the *Sunday Times* magazine, can you believe it?"

"Rose," Abbey said, "are you not going to ask me what I'm doing here?" She examined herself for signs of being hurt by her mother's self-obsession and apparent lack of interest but nothing painful seemed to have penetrated her. She felt surprised, bewildered even. But there was nothing new about that. She supposed she must be immune to Rose, and this was, after all, vintage Rose.

"What you're doing here?" Rose repeated, stubbing out another cigarette, then plastering on an empty smile and looking at the fussy gold clock on the mantelpiece above the fussy marble fireplace. "Well, I think I know what you are doing here. Let me see," she said, unconsciously checking the time again, "yourself and the lovely Bruce are back for reprogramming or whatever it is you people go in for, you've dropped in for a visit to show me that you're still alive and haven't been cooked up in a big stew, and in a few minutes you'll be out the door back to Bula-Bula and then it'll be another ten years before I see you again." The empty smile froze as she looked at her daughter, then she launched a sad little frown across the wrinkle-free terrain of her brow and let her eyes fall mournfully to her hands, which sat in her lap as she fidgeted with her rings. "I've learned to live with the pain of your abandonment, Abbey," she said. "I've moved on. I've had to. I couldn't just sit here for year after year weeping and wailing and waiting for my only daughter to stop turning her back on me."

Abbey had actually forgotten what a brilliant actress her mother was. She could have sworn she even saw her bottom lip quivering. She wondered why she didn't find the woman's gall more offensive. Suddenly an image of herself, abandoned at school for yet another lonely weekend, crept into her mind. *Rule number one,* she remembered herself scratching into an exercise book, *don't get sucked in. Rule number two, don't get angry.* Her mother, she recalled, had rung her at school to say her best friend Jacinta Jolly (stage name) had taken seriously ill with meningitis and needed Rose at her hospital bed should the end come sometime soon. When Abbey had turned on the television that night to see the two of them tripping down the red carpet at a televised celebrity do, she had devised the two-rule system to save herself the agony of dealing with her mother's lies.

Don't get sucked in, she thought, sitting there staring at her. And don't get angry. "Actually, Bruce and I are not together anymore," she said as calmly and confidently as she could. "I've left him in the islands. I've come home, Rose."

Her mother's mournful look was instantly twisted into one of extreme panic. "You've come home?" she asked, appalled. "Home where? And what about Bruce? You can't leave the poor man alone on the other side of the world without his faithful companion to help him, you know, do the stuff, you know, whatever it is he does, Abbey." She was so irritated she was having trouble lighting another cigarette, even though the one she had been smoking still burned in the ashtray. "What about your marriage vows?"

"What do you care about marriage vows?" Abbey asked, suppressing the nugget of anger she felt over her mother's about-face on the subject of Bruce, a man she described on the only occasion she had met him (their wedding) as giving new definition to the expression "damp squib."

Rose opened her mouth as if to say something, then thought better of it. "I just want what's best for you, Abbey, you know that," she said in a sugary tone. "And you and Bruce were such a delightful couple, made for each other even. What could possibly have gone wrong with such a match made in heaven?"

"Bruce was cheating on me, Rose," Abbey said. "He was fathering children with another woman. Not me." Hearing herself say the words out loud, Abbey felt sure, for the first time really, that leaving Bruce behind had been absolutely the right thing to do. At the mention of children, however, her mother's eyes bulged and she choked on a lungful of smoke.

"And you?" she said, waving at the cloud in front of her face, her voice unable to hide her horror. "Are there grandchildren?" She tiptoed over the last word as if it were green slime about to swallow her mules.

Abbey dug her nails into the palms of her hand to help maintain her composure. "No," she said, trying to look at Rose but only managing a spot on the floor. "I can't have children. That was a one-in-a-million chance. You know. Before."

Rose was confused. "Before?" she asked. "Before what?"

"Before, when I was pregnant," Abbey said, the pain in her palms barely keeping her temperature from rising, "with Jasper's baby. You must remember that? Mum? The termination?"

Rose's face drained to match the color of her spotlessly cream calico couch. "Jaysus, Abbey," she said. "Jaysus feckin' Christ Almighty Amen."

Abbey misread her mother's anguish as remorse for what had happened all those years ago and felt her resolve start to crack, her confidence to slide. "I know," she said in a voice that suddenly sounded small. "When the doctor told me that my ovaries were all messed up I couldn't help but think maybe it was punishment for—"

"Stop!" her mother interrupted abruptly, holding her hand up in a halting maneuver. "Please, Abbey, just stop." She pressed her halting hand to her temple and Abbey saw that it was shaking. "That was a long time ago and there's no need to be dragging it up now," she said. "It's water under the bridge."

I got sucked in, Abbey thought. Now, don't get angry.

"I'm dragging it up now because it's affecting me now," she said carefully. "Jasper's baby was it, Rose, my one chance in a lifetime to be a mother."

Her mother shook her words away, turning her head to one side and holding up both hands to stop any more reaching her.

"For God's sake, Abbey, stop it," she said. "Being a mother isn't all it's cracked up to be, you know. You don't know the half of it." She stood up and straightened her gown before looking at the clock again, edgy and flustered. "You really should try to get over it."

"Get over it?" Abbey said in amazement, watching her mother suck up her panic and metamorphose into a perfect hostess again. She felt like she was riding a roller coaster.

"Would you like something to eat before you go?" Rose said, gesturing for Abbey to stand up and completely ignoring the point the previous exchange had reached. "You must be starving. Look at you, you're a stick figure, Abbey, apart from that bosom, you need feeding up. How did you get here again?"

Abbey chastised herself for thinking that the subject of her painful past could be talked about with the woman who had designed it. "I'm not hungry, Rose," she said. "I've come from Australia. I was staying with friends for a few days after I left Mar . . . after I left Bruce in the islands. I got the Heathrow Express to Paddington and a cab here. But what do you mean, before I go? I haven't got anywhere to go, Rose. I thought I would stay with you. Here in the flat. I've got nowhere else to go."

Her mother seemed to be battling a complete nervous collapse. Her face was positively alive with the effort of trying to settle on an acceptable emotion. It hovered on horror then switched to terror, then settled on something between the two and stayed that way.

"Jaysus feckin' Christ Almighty A-bloody-men," her mother cried, wringing her hands in exasperation. "I can't deal with it, Abbey. I just can't. Oh, what have I done to deserve this?"

With the clink and tinkle of the wringing hands, something clicked in Abbey's brain. The rings. Her mother was wearing rings. On her wedding finger. Quite a collection.

"You're married," she said stupidly.

"Oh, Abbey," her mother said, grabbing her cigarettes and lighter from the arm of the sofa, "we need to talk. We really need to talk." Lighting up yet again, hands still shaking, she swept past Abbey and into the kitchen, her daughter following just in time to catch her feverishly snatching something off the refrigerator door and shoving it in the trash can. Her mother whirled around in the little galley kitchen and gasped when she realized Abbey was right behind her.

"It'll be the end of me," she said. "You've no idea. The very end of me, Abbey."

For a moment Abbey thought she was actually crying. "Would you like a cup of tea?" Abbey asked calmly and politely, in the absence of knowing what else to do, and moved to fill the electric jug.

"Tea? Now? Yes," her mother said vehemently, as though it was the most brilliant suggestion ever made. "You make the tea. I've just got a quick phone call to take care of. Just one quick call."

She disappeared into the hall, slamming the door unnecessarily behind her, leaving Abbey to discover where things were kept in the claustrophobic kitchen. As she marveled at the enormous array of tea bags, Abbey worked out what was happening, barely needing to employ her brain in the process. It was pretty obvious. Her mother had always been hysterical about her age, claiming for many years, even at Abbey's sixteenth birthday party, to be just twenty-seven. She never for a moment considered that anyone else had a better grasp of math than she did. She had always been terrified of growing old and ugly, and had preferred to entertain men many years her junior.

Her new husband, Abbey assumed as she poured boiling water into the teacups, would no doubt be very young and no doubt very unaware that his wife had a daughter in her late twenties. This hardly bothered her. She'd spent half a lifetime being explained away as a niece or a neighbor or a complete stranger.

"How did she get in here?" her mother had once said to a gentleman caller as she shuffled Abbey out the back door of their old flat upon finding her up late at night. "Climb in the window," she'd whispered before closing the door and locking it.

Abbey had noticed at once that there were no photos of herself anywhere. Lord knew there wasn't space on the sitting-room walls. She smiled. "Answer your fecking phone, you great eejit!" she could hear her mother urging in desperation in the hallway. Abbey carried the used tea bags to the trash can and pressed the pedal with her foot to open the squeaky lid. The tea bags slid off the spoon and into the garbage, coming to rest on a scrunched-up photograph. Aha, thought Abbey, reaching for it. So that's what her mother hadn't wanted her to see. There had been a photograph on the refrigerator. The kitchen door opened just as her fingertips hovered at the brim of the can and her mother's scream gave her such a fright she remembered it had been some time since she'd been to the bathroom. She turned to see her mother puce with rage.

"Don't you feckin' dare!" she shrieked. "You little monster. You're going to ruin everything, Abbey. Everything. Everything I've worked so hard for all these years, you meddling little monster," and with that she burst into tears that Abbey knew were real because they streamed down her cheeks.

"Rose, Rose, calm down," she said as soothingly as she could in the circumstances, pushing a hot cup of tea into her mother's hands. "Drink this. Come on, let's go and sit down. It's all right, I understand. Don't worry. I understand." Her mother laughed through her tears and said, "I don't think you do," but nonetheless let her daughter push her back into the sitting room.

"He's young, isn't he?" Abbey asked, once she had settled her trembling mother back on the sofa. Rose laughed and nodded, then cried even harder.

"And he doesn't know about me?"

"It's not that," Rose sobbed. "It's just that he's due home any minute. Jaysus God, Abbey, I can't get hold of him on the phone. You've got to go."

Abbey felt her patience on the rule number two front seriously stretch. "I've told you, Rose," she said tightly, "I haven't got anywhere else to go. In case you've forgotten, you're it. It'll only be for a couple of days. You can tell him I'm the daughter of an old school friend or something, can't you? Lying to him obviously isn't a problem."

Her mother slammed her mug of tea down on the oak sidetable and let it erupt and overflow into the neighboring ashtray. "Abbey," she said, choosing a pitiful look over an angry one, her eyes dramatized and aged now by blackened mascara smudges, "you have got to go. You can't stay here. You just can't." She pushed herself off the sofa, suddenly looking every one of her forty-six years, and moved toward Abbey's bag, picking it up off the floor with shaking hands and holding it out toward her daughter.

"You're kicking me out?" Abbey asked, aghast. "But, Rose . . ."

"I'll give you money," Rose said, shaking the bag at her daughter. "I'll give you money to go somewhere else, to live somewhere else. Abbey, please, just—"

The sound of a key rattling on the other side of the flat's front door paralyzed Rose mid-sentence. So, thought Abbey, his balls didn't need to be in a sack after all.

"Don't come in," her mother whispered hoarsely, her back still to the door as she stared at her daughter. "Don't come in," she tried again, whatever was eating at her swallowing the words, as the fumbling of the keys stopped and the latch clicked. "Go away," Rose croaked as the door swung open and Abbey reeled at the shock of who it was stumbling through and slamming it behind him.

His hair was longer and slightly thinning, there were the beginnings of a business-lunch paunch lurking under his suit and he wore a chunky gold bracelet on the wrist that was twisting at his collar to release his tie. He looked so grown-up that Abbey barely recognized him, yet how could she ever forget him? It was Jasper Miles and he was wearing a wedding ring.

"I say," he said, shocked, as he registered just who it was gawking at him from the sitting room. "Goodness." He put his briefcase underneath the telephone table the way, no doubt, he always did.

"This could be embarrassing," he said awkwardly. "Rose? Darling?"

For a split second, Abbey felt a thrill at seeing him, this smudged version of her first, perhaps her only true love. She had imagined this moment many times over the years. The moment when the Jasper Miles of her dreams, young and handsome and pulsating with hormones, would see her, smiling and gorgeous and happy, and curse the day he let her slip away.

But here she was, none of those things, and here he was married to her mother. The quiver she felt in her stomach wasn't a thrill of joy, she suddenly realized, as it gathered momentum and started roaring through her body. It was white hot, pure and overwhelming rage.

"You complete and utter bastard," Abbey said in a voice

she didn't know she had the venom to produce. "You wanking, stinking, cutthroat, jerk-off, heartless *fucking* bastard!" Rage engulfed her, and pushing past her paralyzed mother, she found herself springing at Jasper and punching him hard in the throat.

"Jesus," he gurgled, clawing at his neck. "Help."

But Abbey hadn't finished. Bringing her knee up swiftly she planted it smack in the middle of his groin, then as he doubled over in pain, she brought it up again, catching him under the chin with a sickening crunch. Jasper staggered back onto the telephone chair, moaning, as Abbey stood in front of him, shaking like a leaf, and wondering how else she could hurt him. She drew back her arm and whacked him with a right hook to the side of the head that spun him off the chair and onto the floor.

It took a moment to realize that although she had stopped screaming, she was still being engulfed by noise and pain. Her mother was slapping her from behind and shrieking at her to leave Jasper alone.

"Get off him," Rose was howling. "Leave him alone! Leave my beautiful baby alone!"

As quickly as the despicable rage had swept Abbey up and claimed her as its own, it deserted her, leaving her huffing and puffing and staring in horror at the specter of her mother kneeling at Jasper's side, weeping as she kissed his balding head.

"Leave my beautiful baby alone," she sobbed again. The words clanged around the little hallway as Abbey tried to gather herself. They said it all. The father of Abbey's unborn child was now her mother's baby. Hello and welcome to painful reality number 6957, thought Abbey.

The flat was quiet apart from the soft sound of Rose weeping as she soothed Jasper, who was bleeding slightly from the mouth, and Abbey felt a sudden enormous sense of embarrassment at what had just gone on. Yet in the surreal aftermath of such a raw and exhausting scene, she felt compelled to dig deeper.

"How long," she asked, "has this been going on?"

Jasper gurgled something unintelligible from the floor and Rose, clutching him now with both her arms, kissed his face, her own still streaming with a flood of tears and makeup.

"How long?" Abbey repeated.

"He came to see me not long after you left for the islands," her mother said, weeping, holding Jasper's head and looking at her daughter. "It didn't work out in America. We consoled each other, Abbey," she said defiantly, trying despite her distress to regain a dramatic edge. "We were both damaged goods and we found support in each other's arms. Can you blame us for that? Is that such a crime?"

Abbey looked straight at her mother. "I think you know exactly what it is," she said, and in her mother's emerald-green irises she saw that she did.

Rose, just like Martin, had chosen betrayal over love without so much as a backward glance.

Jasper was coughing into his hands, Rose was still weeping softly, but Abbey was silent as she reconciled herself with her situation. Really, she realized, she had only one option left.

"Where is my grandfather?" she asked her mother. "Where is the farm?"

Rose stopped crying.

"I will not let you go to that wicked old man, I will not," she said. "We swore we would never go back."

"No, Rose," said Abbey, "you swore we would never go

back. I was only five and, from what I can remember, perfectly happy there."

"How can you say that when I told you what he did to my mother?"

"How can I believe anything you've ever told me? Especially after this? After him?" Abbey looked at the still-cowering Jasper. Rose stayed silent.

"Tell me how to find my grandfather or I will sell my story to *OK!* magazine along with your real age," Abbey continued. "I will tell them that you made me get rid of my boyfriend's baby and then you banished me to the other side of the world and ran off with him."

Her mother hiccupped as she calculated the fallout from Abbey doing what she was threatening to do.

"I'll tell them my father was a gypsy traveler who worked for a sideshow carnival. I'll tell them you didn't even know his name." The subject of Abbey's father had not been broached for many years and never, ever to her satisfaction. She'd long given up wanting to know the truth but suspected, rightly, that it was still a weak point in her mother's fabric.

Rose let go of Jasper and collapsed on the floor next to him, her back against the telephone table, her legs straight out in front of her like a broken puppet's. She opened and closed her mouth like a beached cod. "You little bitch," she said eventually.

Abbey hardened her heart. How could this woman still hurt her? "Tell me," she said.

"I'll never speak to you ever again," Rose said.

"I never want you to," answered Abbey. "Tell me."

"Coolarney House," Rose whispered. "Schillies. County Cork."

Abbey turned and picked her bag up from the sitting

room, then swept past Rose and Jasper and opened the front door of the flat.

"Go to your grandfather and that is it between you and me," her mother said in a cold, dead voice. "I mean it."

Abbey turned to look at her again, feeling a strange empty blackness inside. She supposed she should have felt strong and triumphant but she didn't. She felt sad and humiliated and dirty.

"What is there between you and me, anyway, Rose?" she said. "Apart from our two names on my birth certificate?" She looked at Jasper, still with his head hidden in his hands so he could avoid any involvement. "Oh, and him."

Her mother looked suddenly furious and, abandoning all question of glamour, scrambled undaintily to her feet. "Just ask that old bastard what happened to your grandmother," she spat from the entrance to her flat as Abbey walked toward the lift. "Just ask him what's buried in his precious factory," she wept as it arrived and Abbey stepped into it.

"You'll see," Rose cried out. "You'll find out. That'll wipe the—" but the elevator doors snapped shut and Abbey was left with nothing but the silent, sweeping cloak of her own remorse and shame.

CHAPTER TWELVE

"Once you've done your stirring and your waiting and your thinking and the time is right, there is a single moment, and I'm not messing with you here, there is one single moment when it all comes together and you realize that your milk has gone and your cheese is on its way."

JOSEPH FEEHAN, from *The Cheese Diaries*,
RTE Radio Archives

*B*y three o'clock Brian Clancy was once again hammered. He'd eschewed the sandwiches and replenished tea supplies that Avis had provided at lunchtime in favor of the contents of a hip flask of whisky. While his fellow interviewees debated world issues—such as tuna paste versus tuna flakes—he sat perfectly happy, sipping and snoozing. The same could not be said for Thomas Brennan. The poor man was positively itching for action and by midafternoon the pseudo business magnate's patience was stretched as far as it could go.

"This is ridiculous!" he snapped when the afternoon shadows grew so long the courtyard started to lose its sun and the hopefuls all had to lean up against the factory wall to catch its last rays. "Do they think we have nothing better to do all day than stand around here waiting for an audience with them?" Thomas demanded, looking up at the house for signs of life.

"Well, I think I speak for the lot of us, Thomas," Fergal drawled, "when I say we definitely don't have anything better to do."

Thomas tossed him a sour look. "Speak for yourself, Fergal," he said in a hoity-toity fashion. "But I for one have a business to run and every moment away from it is costing me money."

"So what is this business of yours exactly, Thomas?" Fergal asked, a dangerous glint in his eye. "We've been meaning to ask."

"That's it," Thomas seethed. "I've had enough." He strode over to the back door and started hammering on it with alacrity. "Miss O'Regan," he hollered. "Miss O'Regan! Open this door."

Inside, on hearing the racket, Fee propelled himself out of his chair and scrambled to the window. "Thomas Brennan's having a conniption!" he reported excitedly. "He's calling for you, Avis. Are you going to go?"

"Well, I have to go anyway," said Avis, looking up from her darning and checking her watch. "It's nearly milking time." She packed her mending away in an old-fashioned carpetbag and turned her attention to Corrie. He was not himself today and it weighed heavy on her heart, yet Fee seemed to be full of the joys of life which, in the circumstances, didn't seem to make much sense.

"Well, who says it has to?" Fee asked her cheekily. "Why does everybody always expect it all to make sense? Maybe it just doesn't. Maybe it's not supposed to. Have you ever thought of that?"

"Ah, stop doing that, Joseph, it's rude," she scolded.

"What's he doing?" Corrie said.

"Only reading my mind again and I don't like it," answered Avis. "I think it's bad manners."

"G'wan with you," Fee said sheepishly. "Is a man in my condition allowed no fun at all?"

Corrie and Avis looked at each other and weighed up the options. "No!" they replied in unison. He was ill, but clearly not that ill. When the mischievous glimmer had gone from his eye, then they'd let him have fun. In the meantime, it was safer not to.

"Do you want me to do something with them?" Avis asked, looking at Corrie over the top of her spectacles and nodding in the direction of the window. "Speed it all up a bit?"

"It might be an idea. We don't want them to get cold. What do you think, Joseph? Cheese-tasting time?"

Fee was jiggling with excitement at his watching post by the window and didn't even hear Corrie talking to him. Avis sighed. It was hard to get sense out of Fee at the best of times but it was a particularly hopeless task today.

"Brian Clancy's swigging out of a bottle again," he noted gleefully. "Constitution of an ox, God bless him." He ambled back to his chair and wriggled into it, his feet barely touching the ground by the time he was settled.

"What's got into you today, Joseph Feehan?" Avis asked. "Anyone would think you had won the lottery!"

"You never know what's just around the corner, Avis O'Regan," he said, his blue eyes twinkling.

Corrie looked over at him suspiciously. "Is there anything you're not telling us, Joseph? Is there a cheesemaker out there after all?"

Fee tried not to look too smug in case his funny feeling proved to be gas from last night's rhubarb crumble, but as his funny feeling had never let him down before, he had no reason to think it would today.

"I'm just saying that you never know what's around the corner."

Avis rolled her eyes at Corrie and headed for the sitting-room door. "Cheese test it is, then," she said, one hand on the open door as she turned to go out. "Just for fun. And you can mark it out the window."

Corrie and Fee both smiled and nodded their approval.

"Thomas," Avis said, opening the downstairs door just as the harried hopeful was about to batter it down. "How can I help you?"

The poor lad was purple with rage. "You can pass on to your employers," said Thomas spitting with fury, "that it is most unprofessional to keep applicants waiting in the baking hot sun for six hours just for an interview."

"Did you not get the morning tea?" Avis asked sweetly. "Or the lunch?"

"You can pass on to your employers," Thomas continued, ignoring her, "that this is not the way to conduct a search for the most appropriate person for the job and I for one cannot waste another minute of my valuable time standing here with these—these—"

"Other applicants?" Avis provided helpfully.

"These no-hopers," Thomas corrected emphatically. "And I deplore the lack of protocol demonstrated here today."

"Shall I pass on to my employers that you are not interested in the job, then?" Avis asked.

"That," Thomas said as he smoothed his hair down with the palm of his hand, "is right." And he turned on his heel and headed for the driveway.

"Well, who needs protocol," Fergal said, smiling winningly at Avis and watching Thomas's retreating back, "when you can have Avis O'Regan's baking? Weren't the rest of us all just complimenting you on your culinary skills?"

"You can save your silver tongue for stage two of today's proceedings," Avis said, giving Fergal the eye before retreating briefly to the kitchen and coming back with a large tray laden with different cheeses. She placed it on the foldout table and stood up again, rubbing her hands together as the hopefuls looked on—with the exception, of course, of Brian Clancy, who was busy taking a nap.

"Now, I have here a selection of cheeses from Corrie and Fee's private collection, some Coolarney and some from farther afield," Avis said. "I'm going to leave them here with you while I go to the dairy to start the girls off with milking, then I'm going to come back and ask you to identify which cheeses are which. Do you all understand?"

Brian snored; Fergal and Mickey looked worried; and Jamie was distracted, partly by worry that Avis had to handle the milking by herself, and partly by a strange noise he could hear coming from somewhere behind the house.

"First," said Avis. "I'm going to ask you a simple cheese-making question. The answer will go toward your final score."

"There's a score?" Mickey was getting nervous.

"That's right," said Avis. "Now, all Coolarney cheeses come in two sizes, kilo and dote."

Fergal and Mickey nodded.

"Well," asked Avis, "what is a dote?"

Mickey relaxed. He knew the answer.

"Shall we open the window, Joe?" Fee asked, looking down. "I want to hear what they say."

"It's the little cheese traditionally given to an Irish bride on her wedding day by the groom's grandmother," Mickey said proudly.

"What bollocks," said Fergal. "It's not at all. It's the

shape made in the ground by the first squirt if you milk a cow without a bucket."

"Why would you milk a cow without a bucket?" Mickey wanted to know.

"To see what size a dote should be, you eejit."

Avis raised her eyebrows at Jamie, who was looking mildly staggered. "Haven't a clue," he said. "I never really thought about it."

Avis smiled knowingly, then headed for the dairy, leaving the three men gathered close around the cheese tray. Finally, after a minute's silence, Mickey poked his pointy stump at a glorious green and gold rind.

"It looks disgusting," he said, his old face crinkled and cringing.

"Don't poke it, Mickey," scolded Fergal, "that stick's been halfway up Dermot McGrath's arse."

"Not this end of it, you eejit," countered Mickey. "I'd know if I'd got it that far up."

Jamie was distracted again by a noise coming from somewhere in the wild rhododendrons between the house and the factory and the dairymaids' cottage. "Did you hear that?" he asked, but the older men ignored him.

"It smells like rotten eggs," Mickey said, his face still scrunched with disdain.

"I can hear something," Jamie said, moving away from the cheese and toward the rose-covered archway. "Can you?"

"Jamie's making a run for it," Fee reported, even though Corrie was standing right next to him. "And Brian's asleep."

Just around the corner, Kit woke up to see a small, troll-like creature standing over him with a scowl on her face. She looked like the thing Niamh had put in his getting-fired box to bulk it up, only less green.

"Have you seen Jesus?" the troll asked.

Kit blinked and sat up. He must have been asleep for a while because the sun was sitting substantially lower in the sky than it had been when he first collapsed on the wooden bench, and his neck had a hell of a crick in it.

"Hello-o-o-o," the troll said again, quite sarcastically for a Christian, Kit thought. "I asked you had you seen Jesus?"

"I'm a Baptist," Kit answered, rubbing his sore neck. "Well, my folks are anyway, so I guess that means, yes, I have seen Jesus."

As if he didn't already have enough reasons to kill Niamh next time he saw her, he thought. The troll looked at him, confused, and then smiled a smile so radiant Kit wondered if perhaps he was still asleep and she was a dream.

"You've got me all wrong," the troll finally said, laughing. "Jesus is a cat. A fat ginger cat. I can find Mary and All The Saints but there's no sign of Himself and it's after four so the dear little dote'll be starving."

Kit looked at his watch in horror. The troll was right. It was nearly 4:30. He must have been asleep for more than three hours.

"I'm Lucy," said the troll, smiling again, and he saw at once that she wasn't a spooky creature at all. In fact, she was pretty cute in a punky little girl sort of a way, with a pile of dreadlocks scooped up on top of her head, too many layers of black clothes and runs in her tights.

"I'm Kit," he said, with a smile that was not lost on Lucy either. He held out his hand and took hers when she finally offered it, enjoying its smallness and warmth as he did.

"I'm waiting for Avis O'Regan," he explained.

"Out here?" laughed Lucy. "You'll be lucky. There's only one thing she hates more than the sun and that's the garden. She says flowers make her feel sad. Desperate, isn't it?" She looked at Kit's slightly crestfallen face. "You haven't been waiting long, have you?"

"I met some guy coming down the driveway when I arrived and he told me to wait here for Avis. Said she was in some fierce mood and I should keep out of her way."

"Avis in a fierce mood? I don't think so," said Lucy, thinking how handsome Kit looked when slightly crestfallen. "She hasn't a fierce bone in her body. In fact, she's so nice it makes you want to puke. She'll be up at the dairy now but you can wait inside the house. Corrie and Fee won't care. Well, they won't even know. They're interviewing for a new cheesemaker today and a bigger load of peckerheads you've never seen in all your life. In fact, it must have been one of the peckerheads who told you to wait for Avis out here." She rolled her eyes and looked contemptuous. "Was it a great big bollocks with a silly hat?"

Kit laughed at this apt description. "Yeah," he said. "Claimed he was covered in rat bites. Pretty strange, huh?"

"Come on," said Lucy. "I'll bring you inside."

Kit picked up his bags and followed her around to a glass and wood-framed conservatory on the opposite side of the house. Inside, a dark passage led to a big cozy kitchen, where Lucy indicated Kit should wait at the big wooden table pushed up close to the rear wall.

"I'd better go," she said, pulling her heavy leather jacket closer around herself. "I'll tell Avis you're waiting."

Outside, one of the cheesemaking applicants was asleep between two of the flower barrels lining the factory wall; two more were looking stupidly at a tray of rotten cheeses. Lucy ignored them as she had done all day and headed up the path to the cottage to get her milking gear. Halfway up she was disconcerted to see a blue-denimed rear poking out of the greenery.

"It's all right," the other end of the rear was saying into the ground. "It's okay. *Sccchhh. Scchhh.*"

The noise was frightening so before she could think much about it, Lucy gave the rear a boot.

"Owwwww," Jamie Joyce cried as he extricated himself from the foliage. He turned to see Lucy scowling at him. "What did you do that for?" he asked in a hurt voice.

Lucy took in his blushing sweet face and thought perhaps the kick in the arse might have been a bit premature.

"It was poking out," she said, nevertheless keeping her scowl in place. "And making the place look untidy."

Jamie decided to get over it. "There's a cat in here and I think it's having kittens," he said.

Lucy hardly had time to notice his speech impediment. "Is it ginger?" she asked, suddenly fearful. "Is it fat and ginger?"

Jamie nodded.

"Jesus! Show me where."

Jamie moved over to let Lucy into the foliage. "Right under the lowest branches of this rhododendron," he guided her. "There's a sort of a nest. Can you see?"

"Jesus," Lucy crooned. "Jesus!"

"It's okay," Jamie said, alarmed at Lucy's distress. "She's managing fine."

"No," said Lucy. "It's Jesus, the cat. Jesus is having kittens. God, I have to go. I have to milk. Could you stay here with Jesus until I get back? It'll only be an hour. Two at the most. Do you know about kittens?"

"They come from cats," smiled Jamie. "Yeah, I do."

Lucy looked at him suspiciously, then jumped up and

started to run for the cottage. "Oh, by the way," she said, stopping and turning back. "I thought you didn't speak?"

"I've usually got nothing to say," answered Jamie.

"Right," said Lucy, accepting his excuse without doubt. "See you in an hour. Don't let anything happen to Jesus." As she skipped up the path, Jamie settled back into the undergrowth.

Back in the kitchen, Kit was catching snippets of the most ridiculous conversation he had ever heard.

"Are you sure it's actually cheese?" Fergal was saying doubtfully.

"The square one in the plastic wrapper definitely is," said Mickey, giving it a poke with his stick. "But I'm fecked if I know what that purple thing is."

"Sure, smash a bit of the green one off with what's left of your stick, Mickey, and we'll give it to Brian. If he wakes up we'll ask him if he knows what it is and if he dies, well, would we even notice?"

The two men giggled like schoolgirls, then Mickey brought his stick down on the biggest cheese of them all. When he smashed through the rind, this released an odor not unlike that found in a busy men's urinal.

"Jaysus," cried Fergal, holding his nose. "Get it in his mouth, Mickey, before it eats away at your crutch!"

Mickey lurched over to where Brian was slumped and drooling, the near-empty bottle lying in the flower barrel. He brought his stick up to Brian's mouth and wiped the powerful cheese off on the slumbering drunk's lower teeth. Brian sputtered and coughed, then swallowed and suddenly sat bolt upright, his eyes flying open.

"Overripe Stanser Schafchas," he barked. "From Switzerland." Then he slumped back against the wall and started gently snoring.

Mickey and Fergal stared at him, open-mouthed.

"Did you hear that?" Mickey whispered.

"Has he caught Jamie Joyce's speech defect," Fergal wanted to know, "or was that the name of the cheese?"

"Fecked if I know," said Mickey. "Let's try another one." He limped back to the tray and squashed another wedge of cheese off onto the end of his stick, then turned back to Brian and repeated the tasting process. Again, Brian coughed and spluttered then noisily swallowed the cheese. Mickey and Fergal stared. Brian snored quietly and licked his lips.

"It must have been a sneeze we heard before, Mickey, do you think?"

Brian opened one eye but didn't bother to focus it. "Picodine Feuille Chabis," he said. "French."

Mickey and Fergal looked at each other. "Is he messing?" Mickey said suspiciously, giving Brian a vicious jab in the chest with his cheesy stick. Brian slept on.

"It's hard to know, really," said Fergal. "I think he did work at some fancy restaurant in Dublin once. I've heard him talk about it a bit at the pub, but did that sound like English to you, Mickey? Give him a bit of that blue one."

Again Mickey mashed off a splodge of vibrant blue cheese and hooked it into Brian's mouth.

"Gamonedo," the slumbering gourmet reared up and shouted. "Spain's finest." Again he slumped back into sleeping position.

"It's hard to know, really," Fergal said, scratching his head. "Being as I'm not much of an expert in the cheese department myself."

"That makes the two of us," Mickey said. "In fact, I don't really like the stuff."

"I'm with you there, Mickey," agreed Fergal. "Give me butter any day of the week but cheese, no thank you."

They looked at each other.

"Are you thinking what I'm thinking, Mickey?"

"Does what you're thinking involve a pint and a packet of pork scratchings?"

"It certainly does."

"Then I certainly am." Mickey looked at Brian. "What should we do with him?"

"I've seen him walk longer distances in worse states than this," said Fergal, moving to Brian and pulling at his arm. "And it'll rile us if he gets the job and finds the treasure without even being awake. You take the other side, Mickey, and if we give him a push at the top of the drive we can probably just pick him up at the bottom."

Fee monitored them incredulously from the top window. "They smashed the cheese with Mickey's stick, shoved it down the dead one's throat and now they're all leaving," he marveled.

Corrie looked up from his computer magazine. "That's how many for an interview then?"

"That's none," his friend answered cheerfully. "None at all."

Corrie put down his magazine. "I don't understand you, Joseph," he said. "We've lost it. We can't make it work. We don't know anyone who can—so why are you so cheerful?"

Fee shot him a strange look. "Oh, ye of little faith," he said. "Do the words 'don't worry' sound at all familiar to you, you miserable old hoor? Shift your arse and let's go down and have a nice slice of Brie, it should be ripe in about ten minutes. I suspect you've a little something Châteauneuf-du-Pape to go with it—Guigal, perhaps?"

"Right so," Corrie answered almost grumpily. "But what year?"

"Ninety-eight, of course," his friend answered. "And

stop trying to catch me out. You should know by now you never will."

The promise of imminent wine and cheese went halfway toward cheering Corrie and he rose to his feet and headed for the stairs. He supposed he shouldn't be disappointed by the day's proceedings. It was unlikely they would find somebody the first day. The first month. The first year, even. Not just anybody could be a cheesemaker, after all. Hardly anybody in fact. And even Corrie wasn't sure exactly who they were looking for. Just somebody with a certain sort of something. The curd would recognize him. So, probably, would Fee.

He walked into the kitchen and was surprised to see a sad-looking man of about thirty sitting at the table. Behind him, he heard Fee gasp.

"I hope you don't mind," the man said in an American accent, "but I made myself a cup of coffee. I think Avis O'Regan may have forgotten me."

In a moment Corrie took in the strong, smooth hands holding the coffee mug and the square kind face. He turned to Fee, who was beaming so hard his smile seemed to be doing laps of his head.

"I'm Kit Stephens," Kit said, standing and holding out his hand.

"Joseph Corrigan," said Corrie, offering his own, "and this is Joseph Feehan."

"You're the cheesemakers," said Kit.

"Well," said Fee, "we'd like to talk to you about that."

"To me?" said Kit.

"How long have you been waiting?"

Kit looked embarrassed. "Well, I arrived around lunchtime I think, but some guy with a funny little hat told me to wait in the garden and it wasn't until the girl with all the, you know, hair, looking for the cat, told me to come in here about three hours ago—"

Kit's rant was interrupted by a feeble knock at the kitchen door.

"Thanks all the same," Fee called out, his eyes still on Kit. "We've found someone."

"I know you've been interviewing for cheesemakers," Kit started, "and I think there's been some confusion . . ."

The knock on the door was back again, only louder.

"Position filled," Fee said again. "Thanks anyway. Maybe next time."

"I'm here to see Avis O'Regan," Kit was trying to explain. "I'm going to stay awhile. It's just that I—"

But the knock was back again, more persistent than ever.

Fee was about to say something when he froze, the only movement that of his eyes widening with the realization of what was happening. In a split second he slid wordlessly across the floor and opened the door, standing back to let the knocker in.

She was medium height with big brown eyes and long, rusty-colored hair and she looked tired and maybe even a little scared, thought Kit. But nice. As she stood in the kitchen, weighed down by her bag and whatever had brought her here, obviously unsure what to do or say, a strange noise like a cross between a gargle and a gasp emerged from Corrie's throat as he realized who it was. A single tear sprang to his eye and worked its way nimbly down the valley of his wrinkled cheek as the rest of him stood, frozen in an icy mixture of fear and hope.

"Abbey," he said quietly, as though speaking any louder would blow her away. "Abbey."

CHAPTER THIRTEEN

"Of course, you don't want to get too full of yourself after that one single moment because there's still a fair bit to be done."

JOSEPH FEEHAN, from *The Cheese Diaries*,
RTE Radio Archives

The kitchen smelled of sunshine and cinnamon, that was the first thing Abbey noticed. An ancient coal-burning oven built into a brick wall at the far end of the room was half-covered in dried lemon and orange skins, and she could sense the citrus lingering invisibly in the air. The floor was covered in big square black-and-white tiles, and the counters on either side of the sink in front of the kitchen window were groaning with fruit and vegetables, herbs and flowers, bottles of exotic-looking drink, loaves of bread, an obscene amount of cheese and many different-colored jars of fruit and pickles. Dried lavender hung from the walls around the kitchen, along with a collection of hats and feathered birds that she hoped weren't real (the birds, anyway). A rack hanging from the ceiling housed an enormous collection of copper pots and pans that caught the last of the evening sunlight shimmering through the window.

At a long table with bench seats on either side sat a clean-cut preppy-looking guy with bags under his eyes. The big tall man saying her name was her grandfather and the little fat one wasn't. That much Abbey knew. About everything else in the world, she remained in a state of total confusion.

"What's a dote?" the little fat man suddenly asked the preppy guy.

"I'm Kit," said Kit.

"I'm Abbey," said Abbey.

"What's a dote?" the little fat man asked again. "Have you any idea?"

"Fee," said Corrie, shaking himself out of his paralysis. "It's Abbey."

Fee looked as if he smiled any harder, his head would split in two. He put his hand in his pocket and stepped toward Abbey, pulling out of his indescribably awful corduroys a handful of rainbow-colored boiled sweets. She took one and slowly unwrapped it, then popped it in her mouth. Corrie looked on in awe. The old bollocks had stopped keeping sweets in his pocket more than twenty years ago. How had he known to have them in there today?

Kit watched the scene with growing unease. He didn't know these people but the air seemed thick with their secrets. Something private and painful was about to happen, he felt sure.

"Do you know, then?" Fee asked again, beaming at him. "About the dote?"

Common sense dictated that in the circumstances the question was an inappropriate one, but in the absence of anyone else saying anything else, Kit thought of the troll-girl in the garden looking for the cat.

"Is it something small and cute?" he suggested. "You know, like a little mite? A little dote?"

Fee seemed to flutter clear off the ground with delight. "This calls for a celebration!" he said delightedly. "I'm going to cook a roast."

"I've just seen Rose," Abbey said, rolling the sweet around in her mouth, "and it didn't go particularly well."

"Would I show you to your room, Abbey?" Corrie suggested, unfazed.

"Would you?" she asked, and she followed her grandfather out into the hall. The house was a maze of hallways and doors and landings and stairs. Dusty sunlight seemed to filter its way around the many corners and crannies, giving the whole place a golden dreamlike quality. At the end of a passage on the second (or perhaps the third, she'd lost track) level, Corrie stopped and opened a door, standing back to let Abbey step into the room.

It was enormous, with two sash windows, overgrown on the outside with ivy, looking out on to the house's riotous gardens. The double bed was high and puffy, with an old-fashioned patchwork quilt and white linen pillowcases and sheets. The yellow walls were splashed with faint red poppies and an antique dressing table sat against the wall. The curtains were the same shade of faded red as the poppies, hooked back with handmade swags that looked like braided straw. On a chest of drawers against the far wall sat a buttery-yellow washbowl and jug next to a similarly yellow vase of flowers filled with real poppies, purple ones. The recent hand of Joseph Feehan, Corrie realized.

"This was Rose's room," he said quietly, looking around and adding, "you were born in here."

He could remember the day as clearly as yesterday. Rose, scared stiff and lashing out, cursing and railing and blaming them all for her troubles, yet at the same time needing them desperately and hating herself for it. He'd thought his heart would burst that day, with anguish for his beautiful angry daughter and with fear for the life she was about to bring into the world. But from the moment Abbey arrived, everything changed. Even Rose appeared to fall in love with the little dark-haired, dark-eyed beauty who had given her young mother's soft bones barely a nudge as she made an easy entrance into the world.

Corrie had never felt closer to Rose than on that day, holding her as she held Abbey. He'd thought then that perhaps he could heal his daughter. That perhaps he and Fee and Avis could be enough of a family for her. But it hadn't been long before Rose was back to her old tricks, inflicting her own personal brand of pain and torture on those who loved her. And when Abbey was five she had hurt her father the best way she knew how, by taking his granddaughter far, far away and never bringing her back again.

Yet, here she was.

Abbey had moved over to the bed and was testing its springs. "I don't know what to call you," she said, looking at her grandfather with eyes so dark he couldn't begin to understand what was going on behind them.

"Sure, everybody else calls me Corrie," he said, realizing that anything more familial might seem strained at this early stage.

"I didn't have anywhere else to go," Abbey said, almost apologetically. "I hope you don't mind." She ran her fingers over the tiny valleys where the patches met each other on the quilt.

Mind? Corrie could barely contemplate that this lovely, lonely, lost little girl might not think she was welcome here. He wanted to hold his granddaughter in his arms and soak up all her sadness and fear and never, ever let her go. But how well he knew that healing wounds inflicted by Rose would not be a quick or an easy job.

"Ah sure, this is your home," he said as casually as he could. "You can stay for as long as you like."

At this fragile point he wanted to steer Abbey on a path less painful. There would be no talk of her heartbreak until she was ready for it. He made to leave the room. "I know he doesn't look it," he said turning at the doorway, "but Fee is poorly." Abbey looked at him quizzically.

"The curd has turned," he continued, "which probably doesn't mean much to you at this stage but it's something of a disaster."

Abbey sat on the bed, unsure what to say.

Corrie forged on. "We're too old for cheese—making it—anyway. The thing is, Abbey, Fee was only saying yesterday, would Abbey be a cheesemaker? Would Abbey come home and make the cheese? And here you are. After all these years. It seems . . ."

For the first time since leaving Ate'ate Abbey felt a happy little burr in her brain that she realized could be hope. "It seems . . . ?" she echoed.

"Well," said Corrie, trying not to overdo it. "It seems right. Somehow."

They looked at each other, a sea of unspoken questions and answers between them.

"I'll let you settle in," he said. Abbey was holding herself back, he knew, but if she would just stay here at the farm surely he, and time, and who knew what else, could help put her back together again. "You'll make a grand cheesemaker, I can tell," he said as he slipped out the door.

Abbey lay back on the bed and tried to stop her head from spinning. The escape from Ate'ate seemed like a dream, as did the days spent crying inconsolably into her pillows at Shirl's house. The long flight from Brisbane seemed more real but maybe that was because the distinct aroma of airplane food was still clinging to her. Then there was the shameful scene the previous day at her mother's house. And the ensuing journey to a dingy B & B at Heathrow, then the flight this morning to Cork, the bus to Schillies and the walk to Coolarney House. She'd come a long way in a short time, she thought tiredly. She supposed she should have asked about her grandmother. What had happened to her? What did Corrie have to do with it? But the effort involved in finding out seemed just beyond her reach. Besides, the idea of being a cheesemaker had created that little nugget of hope that was humming happily in her belly and she didn't want it to evaporate just yet. Wafts of unconsciousness drifted in and around the pockets in her thoughts until, lulled by the mouthwatering smell of roasting meat juices, she slept.

"Did she look like a vegetarian to you?" Fee asked in the emptiness that had stayed behind in the kitchen.

"I'm not sure," answered Kit. "What do vegetarians look like?"

"Never mind," said Fee.

Coolarney House probably wasn't the best place in the world to get a feel for what the average vegetarian looked like, now that he came to think about it, what with the gestation situation and all.

Kit stood up behind the table. "Look," he said, "I really should go find Avis O'Regan."

"Not at all," said Fee. "You've waited all day, you can wait a bit longer. Besides, I need help peeling the potatoes and I want to talk to you about cheese."

Nothing this guy said ever quite hung together, Kit had noticed. Yet strangely, it didn't seem to matter. Fee handed him some sheets of old newspaper, a bowl filled with dirty potatoes, and a small instrument with a rubber handle and a blade, which Kit presumed was a peeler of some sort. Where he came from, potatoes didn't have skins and were brought to you on a plate by a whippet-thin would-be actress with attitude. Since Jacey, he had not eaten a single meal in his own apartment, and even with her he'd only cooked a handful of times. He sighed at the thought of Jacey and concentrated instead on trying to operate the peeler without removing the top three layers of skin from his thumb.

Fee, watching Kit slyly out of the corner of his eye, was standing at the kitchen counter preparing a leg of beef. He knew he was right to feel the way he did about Kit. The poor devil had waited all day in the boiling sunshine but still had the brains to work out what a dote was. He'd arrived at Coolarney on the right day at the right time. And he had great long fingers on him. These were currently having trouble wrangling potatoes, true, but manual dexterity aside he bore all the signs of a natural cheesemaker.

"So, you've not done much with your hands, then?" Fee suggested, as another potato rolled away from Kit's grasp and onto the floor.

"Well, that would depend on what you call much, I suppose," said Kit, looking under the table for the escapee and locating it with his foot. "I work in finance, as an investment broker, so I'm on the phone and the computer a lot."

"Oh, like a secretary?" Fee said, without much interest.

"Kinda," admitted Kit, "I guess." Take away the zeroes and he supposed it was a bit like being a secretary. "So Abbey and Corrie haven't seen each other in a while, huh?" he asked, changing the subject, his face contorting with the concentration required by the petulant potatoes.

"That's right," said Fee. "She's been over in the Pacific Islands doing good works."

That figured, thought Kit. She did have that slightly bad-haircut Christian look about her. "And she's what? Like, his granddaughter?"

"That's right," said Fee again, bashing thyme, garlic and lemon rind together with olive oil using an ancient mortar and pestle.

"So where are her folks?" Kit asked, accidentally grating himself and watching ghoulishly as a trickle of blood seeped into his badly scarred spud.

"Well, we're her folks," Fee said, as a clatter of feet outside the kitchen door heralded the arrival of what sounded like at least a dozen chattering females. "Although she has a mother in London."

At that moment Lucy, hugely overexcited, burst through the door with Jamie and a string of cranky-looking pregnant women in tow.

"Hasn't Jesus only just gone and had six of the most gorgeous kittens," Lucy chattered, reaching across the sink to fill a glass with tap water. "You can fit two in your hand at once, although it's hardly advisable," she said, holding up a scratched wrist.

As her jacket fell open and he caught the curve of her exposed belly, it dawned on Kit that she too was pregnant.

"She looks totally knackered, poor cow. So who do you think the father is? And what will Mary and All The Saints make of it? Oh, hello," she said, suddenly noticing Kit and looking horrified. "Jaysus feck! I'm after forgetting to tell Avis you were here!"

"Hi," said Jack, sitting down next to Kit and taking the potato peeler away from him and pointing it at Lucy. "Ignore her. She's high on life. Who are you?"

"I'm Kit," said Kit, feeling awkward again. What was this place?

"I'm Jack, six months," said Jack, scooting over so the pregnant twins could fit in beside her and peeling potatoes at lightning speed, "this is Tessie and May, four-and-a-half, and that," she said, pointing to Wilhie, who was pushing her spine into the doorjamb and squealing with relief, "is Wilhie. Nearly eight. We are the pregnant singing vegetarian milkmaids."

Kit laughed but he laughed alone.

"It's not a joke," said Lucy from the sink. "We're like a new species."

"Yeah," said Wilhie, ferreting through the contents of the cupboards in an overcrowded wooden dresser by the side window, "the Pregnasaurs."

Again, Kit laughed. He was sure now that he had stepped through some magical looking glass and was in a parallel universe. Wilhie eventually found the large tin of biscuits she was looking for, at which point the commotion in the kitchen grew to a frightening level. Plates and glasses rattled and banged, cupboards opened and closed, the refrigerator door seemed to be permanently swinging and somebody had turned the radio to a jazz station, which was bebopping in the background.

Into this melee appeared the figure of what Kit instantly knew to be Avis O'Regan.

"He's here," he heard Fee say from somewhere across the clatter.

"You're here," Avis said. She bent down to where Kit was sitting and pressed her warm, smiling face to his cheek. She smelled of roses and dark chocolate, and for a moment Kit felt faint in her presence. He thought she whispered, "You're safe now," but before the words had even tripped over his ear, she seemed to be on the other side of the kitchen inspecting Fee's beef.

"Abbey's come home," Fee said. "I'm cooking a roast."

"Abbey's come home?" Avis stared at him in disbelief, a tremor of excitement jiggling her stays. So that's why he'd been so cool and calm all day, the old fox, she thought. Of course, he'd seen it coming. That's why he'd insisted on sprucing up Rose's room. A less lovely thought occurred.

"So she's seen Rose then?"

Fee nodded as he seasoned the meat. "She has."

Avis searched his wrinkly round face. "And is she all right?"

"I'd say not particularly, just at the moment," said Fee. "But I'd say she'll be right soon enough. With a little help from her friends. And perhaps one in particular." He grinned and nodded his head in Kit's direction.

"Oh no! Now you're not cooking things up that don't need cooking, are you, Joseph?" Avis warned. "We're not talking about people in tip-top condition after all. Wilhie—you should not be drinking that orange fizz at your stage," she said in a louder voice. "Have milk. God knows there's enough of it. Speaking of which"—she turned her attention back to Fee—"what are we going to do about a cheese-maker?"

Fee nodded again at Kit. "We're going to be all feckin' right for cheesemakers, Avis. We've got yer man and we've got yer woman. Who could believe such luck?"

Avis looked over as Kit tried unsuccessfully to open a jar of pickles Lucy had handed him.

"Give it here," said Jack, snatching it off him and opening it in half a twist.

"Are you sure, Joseph?" Avis said doubtfully, as Jack teasingly tried to goad Kit into an arm wrestle. "He doesn't look like a cheesemaker. He's not here for cheese-making."

"You can trust me on this the way you can trust me on everything else, Mrs. O'Regan," Fee said knowingly.

"Do you know about the wife?" Avis asked, worried.

"I know about the wife."

"And a man in his state is all right for cheesemaking?"

"In my experience there's not a state in the world," Fee said matter-of-factly, "that cannot be greatly improved by close proximity to cheese. Especially ours," he added.

Avis was distracted suddenly by an unfamiliar pair of legs. "And who's that?"

Fee hadn't really noticed Jamie up until that point, but it was hard to ignore him now, being as he was standing on a stool in the middle of the kitchen, fixing the chain that held the pot rack hanging from the ceiling. It had snapped about thirteen years ago and ever since the pots had been held up by one of Corrie's old ties. Jamie, though, had a pocketful of tools and was fixing the missing link.

"Oh, it's you," Avis smiled. "I didn't recognize you from that angle." She peered up and watched a blush creep up Jamie's neck to his chin, which was all she could see. It was the first time he had ever ventured into the house and she supposed standing on a stool in the middle of the kitchen must have somehow made him feel less conspicuous. She looked quizzically at Fee, who shrugged his shoulders and spread his hands out in a "search me" gesture.

"May!" Avis called, spotting the goings-on at the table. "Don't feed Kit biscuits if he doesn't want biscuits. You're scaring the poor man half to death!"

"Yer man and Abbey," Fee said, smiling again, "I'm telling you."

Avis thought about this for a moment. It worried her. But there was no point arguing with Fee. Now or ever. It was better just to wait and see. She thought instead about the thrill that had begun in her toenails and ended at the tips of her Danish pastry hairdo at the thought of Abbey once again being under their roof. After all these years. She and Kit arriving at the same time, just when Corrie and Fee needed a new cheesemaker. It did scream of the magic of coincidence, thought Avis. Her favorite kind.

"Girls, girls, girls!" she called in a bid to quiet the rabble. The noise was high-pitched and quite deafening, and it was hard to tell who was talking to whom. "Girls!" she shrilled again, finally getting everyone's attention. "A new and very special addition to the family arrived today."

Jack clapped Kit so hard on the back he nearly coughed up a lung as the girls cheered raucously around him.

"Shh," said Avis. "I'm sure Kit is special too but I am talking about Abbey Corrigan, Joseph's granddaughter."

The girls babbling bubbled to a stop.

"Abbey has come home today after a long time over-seas," continued Avis, "so we're going to make a bit of a splash on the dinner tonight. Fee is cooking meat for the carnivores"—she ignored the chorus of "oooohs" and "yucks"—"and I suggest you get back to the cottage and perhaps Jack could organize a bean casserole?"

She looked at her watch—it was after 7:30 already. The summer light always had her in a fix over the time. "Back here at nine, then?"

The girls got to their feet with an astonishing array of different groans and whines, then filed noisily out, leaving Jamie standing sheepishly under the pot rack and Kit sitting, totally shell-shocked, where he had been for the past three hours.

"I thought I could come back after the cows tomorrow," Jamie said to the room, looking studiously at his feet, "and help you with the factory roof. The iron's coming away on

the dairy side"—he cringed at his own noisy sibilants—
"and you'll lose three or four sheets if not the whole thing
in the next big easterly."

"Perfect," said Fee. "Would you be staying for a bite to
eat in the meantime?"

Jamie blushed again and grinned, then pulled a little
screwdriver out of his pocket. "I'll take the squeak out
of that cupboard door while I'm here, then?" He jumped
down and set to work immediately, as Avis gestured for
Kit to follow her over to Fee's cottage, where he would be
staying.

"Eight years!" Avis said, shaking her head as she
marched across the courtyard. "Eight years and barely a
peep out of the boy. What a day."

"He's not usually that chatty, huh?" Kit asked, making
conversation.

"He's been working the herd since he was twelve and
I've hardly heard a word," Avis said. "The poor thing is
so shy he can't even look a Maria in the eye. I must have
asked him a hundred times to come into the kitchen for a
cup of tea and he's never shown the slightest inclination,
but today . . . well, between the jigs and the reels it's a
strange one, all right."

"So Mr. Feehan lives here, too?" Kit asked.

"Ah, you'll hardly notice him," said Avis, opening the
door of the cottage. It was tucked behind a stand of
sycamores on the opposite side of the drive from the other
farm buildings and had the same red roof as the factory
and dairymaids' cottage, but was smooth stone painted
white, not the exposed gray slate of its neighbors. Kit, who
had to bend his head to get in the door, found himself in a
simple room with a fireplace at one end, another room off
to the right and a tiny stairway at the back.

"I'll leave you to make yourself at home," Avis said.

"You're upstairs. Mind your head. You should be all right without a fire but if you get cold, there's wood in the cupboard beside the hearth and there are extra blankets in your wardrobe upstairs. See you at nine over at the house."

She turned to go but Kit found himself suddenly desperate to ask her more.

"Avis," he said. "Do they all know why I'm here?"

She turned to look at him and he felt swamped again by her presence. "Why are you here?" she asked him, more directly than he expected.

"To straighten out?" he said, feeling stupid. "You know, to get back on my feet?"

"I'm sure you'll work it out eventually," Avis said cheerfully, as though he had answered the question incorrectly. "And in the meantime, perhaps a spot of cheesemaking could be considered therapeutic?" She stretched the last word out so long that it took Kit a while to recognize it.

"Cheesemaking?" he repeated doubtfully.

"That's settled, then," said Avis. "And in case you hadn't noticed, it's a bit of a madhouse here. Nobody really knows much about anybody else and it seems to work pretty well that way."

Kit looked uncertain.

"No one will judge you here, Kit," she said, her warm eyes soothing his doubts. "You are here to get away from it all and away from it all is exactly where you are—although away from what and for how long is your business and your business alone. You can do as much as you want here, or as little. We don't really care. It's gas, isn't it? We'll look after you, no matter what."

In the blink of an eye she left the cottage and Kit, exhausted yet at the same time strangely excited, climbed the narrow staircase to his tiny upstairs room.

CHAPTER FOURTEEN

"Of course, there is such a thing as a dead vat, which is when you have all the raw ingredients in the right place at the right time but the milk stays milk and the cheese never arrives. It hasn't happened to us but it does happen."

JOSEPH FEEHAN, from *The Cheese Diaries*,
RTE Radio Archives

*C*orrie and Fee had escaped to the quiet of the smoking room for a predinner snifter.

"Crack open the Coeur de Coolarney, would you, Joseph," Fee directed casually, as if he ordered such a thing every day of the week.

Corrie looked at him with surprise. "The Coeur de Coolarney?" he repeated. "What would we want with the Coeur de Coolarney?"

Fee looked vaguely uncomfortable. "Stop flootering around and get on with it, would you?" he commanded, rubbing his back for some diversionary sympathy.

"Well, I would if we hadn't given it to your woman from Goleen with the carbuncle on her face," Corrie said. "Unless . . ."

"Your woman with the carbuncle decided being single wasn't such a terrible thing, after all," Fee informed him. "And you can stop looking at me like that and just fetch the blessed thing." At which he waggled one of his fat little arms furiously in the direction of the bookcase.

Corrie, mostly out of curiosity, did as he was told and went to the C section of the bookcase. He hooked his finger into *Cheeses of the World* and opened a fake section of the library to reveal a small refrigerator-sized *fromagerie*. He and Fee had seen a similar fake bookcase in an old episode of *Get Smart* and had gotten one of their own installed immediately. It never failed to enthrall visitors who were keen to read *Cheeses of the World* but got to eat them instead. Corrie delved into this cheese supply on a daily basis and knew for a fact that the Coeur de Coolarney was long gone. Yet when he opened the door, there sat the heart-shaped brie, bold as brass and wrapped in cheesecloth, looking for all the world as though your woman with the carbuncle had taken a vow of chastity after all.

He carefully plucked it out and turned to his friend.

"That's for the new arrivals," Fee said, by way of an explanation. "You can bring some Gruyère out for us while you're over there."

Corrie plucked a wedge of the Swiss cheese from the back of the fridge and carried it with the Coeur over to the cheese altar. He was at a loss to understand what was happening. The Coeur de Coolarney was a secret and scarcely used weapon in the battle for love. They made one of the brie-style cheeses every year on the first of June, the day that Corrie's grandfather Joseph Corrigan had decided to propose to Corrie's grandmother Mary Roberts in 1893. As soon as he'd decided to plight his troth, Grandfather Corrigan had walked up the hill behind the house and cut a tender new branch from the magnificent oak that had stood there as long as anybody knew. He bent and shaped the wood into the shape of a heart, and with the milk of his favorite cow developed a soft curd, which he scooped into the mold and left in a dry box in the basement with two glasses of Spanish sherry. Every two days he turned it, and after a month it had developed into a firm, smooth heart-shaped custard covered in a white penicillin mold. Two weeks later, he met Mary under the oak tree, where they shared the cheese, drank the sherry and began a love affair that spanned another seventy years and was accepted as the happiest marriage in all the county.

Ever since then, the cheese had been sought after by the lovelorn, and while it couldn't keep people together, it could certainly bring them together. Corrie had used it to help lure his wife-to-be Maggie into his arms, and Fee had used it the following year to help persuade Mary-Therese McGrath into his.

Since then, it had been offered sparingly to those who heard of its powers, and the previous year bidding for a Coeur had reached an all-time high of $2,067 on eBay. That particular cheese had been given free of charge by Corrie and Fee to Maureen McCarthy's niece Sheila, who was thirty-nine and unmarried—and, as Fee pointed out when they heard the price the cheese had fetched, obviously not as silly as she looked.

Corrie looked at this year's version. He couldn't really understand how it was going to help them but then he couldn't really understand much right now. He had always thought that having Abbey back home would fill in all the gaps in his happiness, but it had been hours now and his heart felt more like Emmental than ever.

"It's all happening so fast, Joseph," he said in a shaky

and unfamiliar tone. "Your back, the curd turning, the boy from New York City, and now Abbey." His voice tripped uncertainly over her name. Fee said nothing and let him continue. "I've waited so long for this day, for Abbey to come home, but now that she has, I'm at a loss. She seems so far away from the little dote that lived here all those years ago. I don't know her at all, Joseph. And she seems all sort of broken. Who did that to her? Was it Rose? Am I somehow to blame? I just can't make sense of it."

Fee found it hard to watch his old friend in such distress. Corrie liked to make sense of things, always had; it was one of the big differences between them. Fee, who didn't care much for sense, trusted fate, perhaps because he usually knew where it was taking them. Most of the time, he could twist what he knew with what Corrie wanted to hear into some semblance of rationality and order, but tonight was different. He knew Corrie wanted to hear that time was a great healer and that if he left well alone it would work out all right in the end. That was Fee's stock advice and he was nearly always, in the end, proved right. But in this instance, Fee happened to know that leaving well alone was not the answer. Time was not on their side. It was of the essence. They couldn't waste it. There was none to spare. He thought carefully about how best to broach this.

"I think Abbey had a bad run on the husband front and the sooner she gets back in the saddle, the better for us all," he said, flooring his friend.

"Why does everything have to be about the one thing?" Corrie spluttered.

"I don't know," Fee answered agreeably. "Peculiar, isn't it?"

"No, no, no," Corrie shook his head, frustrated. "What I mean is that not everything is about the one thing."

"It is so."

"It is not."

"It is so."

Corrie knew better than to pursue this sort of conversation with Fee. He had more than seventy years' experience of getting nowhere. Still . . . "It is not," he repeated.

"It is so," Fee said robustly. "But it's also about our cheese and her salvation, so would you stop it with your bellyaching and open a bottle of wine. I'm dying of thirst over here. And you can take that face off you, too, Joseph Corrigan, I know what I'm talking about."

"And what's wrong with your own arms and legs that makes moving about the place such an impossibility?" Corrie wanted to know, moving nevertheless toward the wine rack.

"So you'd mock a man in constant pain," Fee said to Corrie's back, arching his own in dramatic fashion until he saw his friend's shoulders slump despondently as he stopped in front of their wine collection. "Not that I am in constant pain," he added almost guiltily.

"I've always felt that I could fix things," Corrie explained to the wine rack. "And up till now, apart from Rose, of course, and Maggie I suppose, I think I've done a pretty good job. But I'm not so sure about this, Joseph, and this is probably the most important thing that needs fixing of them all. What if I can't do it?"

It hurt Fee to hear his friend so rattled, and he considered reiterating the business about Abbey getting back in the saddle but thought better of it. "You're forgetting," he said instead, "that you are not on your own, Joseph. You never have been and you never will be." He watched Corrie as his hand reached out, trembling, and tinkered with the wine-bottle tops as if their touch was somehow reassuring.

"Abbey is going to be all right," Fee continued in a tone that suggested it was ridiculous that anyone would think otherwise. "Everything's going to be all right. It's business as usual, Joseph. She's like a fresh Coolarney Gold sitting in the cave. She's got to the right place at the right time, and given a good rub and the chance to let whatever's in the air do its bit, we'll get our result and it will be grand. Like it always is."

Corrie's hand lingered on a Californian red.

"Saintsbury Pinot Noir," Fee breathed enthusiastically before Corrie had even slid it out of the rack. "Perfect."

Corrie shuffled back to his chair with the wine in his hand and a pain in his heart. He envied Fee his certainty at a time when all he felt was doubt. Doubt that he had lived up to the promise he'd always assumed he had. Doubt that it had all been worthwhile. Doubt that he had done anything special in the world. He'd thought for a long time that the cheese was his major contribution. He knew that the cheese they made was better than anything with which the previous generations had trifled. That was thanks, mainly, to his thirst for ways to modernize and improve production, something his forefathers might have fought, and Fee's certainty about which direction was the right one. There was never any fiddling around with decision-making when Fee was involved. And to be sure, the cheese was special, but he knew that wasn't it. That there was more.

Then, when he met Maggie, he thought maybe she was the something special, or the woman with whom he could do something special. When it became clear that was probably not the case, he poured his hope into Rose. As she grew up, however, he had cause to doubt his confidence in himself, and when Maggie left he wondered what he had done wrong to invite so much heartache. And that was only the beginning of it.

"Would you stop fiddling with the wine and open it?" Fee demanded, snapping Corrie out of his reverie. "It's not communion wine, you don't have to pray over it. I'm dehydrating in front of your very eyes and the cork is still in the bottle."

Corrie wound in the corkscrew and felt his heart give a little jump at the happy "kloop" the cork sang as it popped out, letting the pinot vibes escape.

Fee sniffed the air like a dog at the beach and smiled. "And by the way," he said, "if you could stop wallowing in your misery over there for a minute you might like to remember the small matter of Avis O'Regan and the Coolarney milkmaids."

Could a man never be alone with his thoughts? Corrie wondered silently.

"No, he cannot, now pour the fecking stuff, would you?" Fee answered.

When Kit walked back into the rattle and hum of the country kitchen at nine, the table was heaving with food. The dairymaids were buzzing around like overstuffed honey bees, rearranging huge platters of food around the cheeses, jams, chutneys, mustards, pickles, loaves and dishes already on the table. Two heavy candelabra, one at each end, glowed with a dozen burning candles, and at their base bunches of fresh trailing rosemary and violets added to the evening's heavy scent. Avis was heaping more vegetables into a dish and Fee was carving the beef, while Jack was trying to decide which end of the table should be vegetarian.

Lucy, still ecstatic over Jesus's miracle of birth, grabbed Kit's hand and slid onto the bench seat behind the table, dragging him behind her. "So," she said, pointing her little pixie chin at him, "you're from New York."

Kit flinched. It had been bugging him—who did the little troll remind him of? But the fluttering eyelashes had just clinched it. It was Jacey. Not Jacey herself but perhaps Jacey's kid sister. Or even a young version of Jacey before the modeling and the big city and, well, everything.

"Yeah, I'm from New York," Kit said, conscious that everyone could hear him now that they were settling down around the table. "Just flew in yesterday."

He looked up to see Corrie walk in with Abbey, who looked bleary with sleep and in desperate need of a hairbrush. Her russet-colored locks were sticking out in all directions except on the left side of her head, where they remained stuck down flat, giving her a hopelessly lopsided look. She slipped in behind the table to the other side of Kit and slumped back against the wall as Avis did a quick round of introductions during which she just blushed and nodded.

She was a strange fish, thought Kit, almost out of place, despite being, as far as he knew, the only one truly entitled to be there. Fee brought the meat over and sat it at the carnivore end of the table where the smell of rich, juicy beefy gravy reminded Kit he hadn't eaten since Maureen McCarthy's that morning. He licked his lips and salivated; he couldn't remember the last time he had looked forward to food. Corrie sat at Kit and Abbey's end of the long table and Fee at the other, while Avis perched in the middle on the kitchen side between the twins and Jamie.

"Joseph," she said, looking at Corrie, "I think it should be you says grace tonight."

The dairymaids bowed their heads and Abbey and Kit followed suit.

"Bless us, Oh Lord," said Corrie, his voice clear and strong despite his earlier brush with doubt and depression, "bless this food and each and every one of us sitting here tonight. And thank you, Lord, for bringing Abbey back home and for looking after her all those years, and thanks too for sending us Kit, and also for giving us a closer look at Jamie Joyce, who could you remind me tomorrow, Lord, to ask would he mind giving us a hand with Old Fart Arse."

The girls tittered.

"Amen," said Corrie. A staggered collection of Amens spread around the table like a Mexican wave before food started being piled onto plates with alarming haste.

"So how long are you going to be staying with us, then?" Lucy asked Kit, as she put Brussels sprouts onto her plate.

"I'm really not sure. As long as you'll have me, I guess," Kit answered, taking the sprout bowl out of her hands.

"Oh, we'll have you for as long as you like, won't we, girls?" Lucy said saucily, and the Pregnasaurs fell into a group titter.

Kit looked up, embarrassed, and caught Avis's eye, which was rolling in the direction of Lucy. "I believe I am going to have an attempt at making some cheese," Kit said, to get the conversation back on an even keel.

Abbey felt a twinge of something that she thought could have been resentment. She had thought she was going to be making the cheese.

"Well, we'll be thinking of you tomorrow when we milk," Lucy said to Kit, making a slightly obscene pulling gesture that had Wilhie ramming a table napkin between her legs to keep from peeing herself.

"Ah, now come on," Avis said disappointedly. "Is this any way to behave in front of our new guests?"

"Don't worry on my account," Kit said, smiling at Lucy, "I've handled worse."

"I'll bet you bloody have," chipped in Jack, "and now's the time to raise your standards."

"Stop them will you, Joseph," Avis said looking at Fee. "I've seen all the *Carry On* movies I want to see."

He stopped carving his beef and looked at her. "You're a dark horse, Avis O'Regan," he said, then went back to his dinner. "Who's got the potatoes?"

Abbey picked the heavy bowl of spuds up from in front of her and handed it to Kit, for passing along. His little flirtation scene had permeated her armor of numbness and annoyed her. She supposed all good-looking husbands were the same. Shameless, the lot of them.

"So what do you know about cheese, then?" she asked Kit, trying for a casual tone but getting a slightly snarky one by mistake.

"Not a lot, I guess," Kit said, "although my mom was always a big cheese fan so we ate a lot of it when I was a kid. And I used to live around the corner from this great cheese shop in New York, called Murray's. You guys know that?"

Corrie and Fee nodded enthusiastically. Coolarney Gold and Blue sold like hotcakes at Murray's and he imported a healthy percentage of their Princess Graces as well. He also sent them a bottle of vintage champagne every Christmas. They liked Murray a lot.

"Your mother was a cheese fan, did you say?" Avis wanted to know, a sparkle suddenly glittering in her eye. "Where does your mother live, Kit?"

Kit swallowed and tried not to feel sick. "She's in Vermont," he said, wanting a drink.

"And your wife?" Abbey asked, again missing casual and getting snarky again instead.

"I'm sorry?"

"Your wife," Abbey said, pointing at the slim gold wedding ring on Kit's finger. "How does your wife feel about you being over here in Ireland making cheese for as long as you'll be had?"

The table's jovial feel disappeared as the milkmaids fell quiet and the sound of cutlery slowing on crockery scorched the air.

"My wife," Kit said, his voice suddenly husky. All eyes were on him, his knife and fork frozen and hovering just above his plate. "My wife," he started again, conscious of everybody's attention, as his cutlery clattered clumsily to his plate.

"Leave the poor bugger alone," Jack suddenly said, crossly. "It's okay, mate. You don't have to explain anything to anybody." She leaned across Lucy to glower meanly at Abbey.

"You're not gay, are you?" Lucy asked with thinly disguised horror. She couldn't believe she hadn't noticed the wedding ring herself.

"You can leave him alone and all," Wilhie said hotly. "Look at the poor sod."

"It's okay if you are gay," Jack said kindly. "A lot of people are."

"Yes, but not fecking everybody!" cried Lucy.

Jack shooshed her quiet. Kit tried to manage a smile and failed. He slowly pushed his knife and fork neatly together on his plate, intersecting the meal he no longer had the appetite for, then cleared his throat.

"I lost my wife three months ago," he said, without looking up.

Fee looked over at Avis, who was concentrating studiously on the contents of her own fork. Ah well, he thought to himself.

"Oh," said Abbey, retreating behind her numbness again. "Sorry." She sensed the dairymaids looking at her with contempt and didn't blame them, she was a horrible person. Kit seemed like a nice guy; she didn't know what rubbed her the wrong way about him—apart from the fact that he seemed perfect and everybody liked him.

"So, you're not gay," Lucy said, trying not to look too relieved.

"I'm married myself, you know," Abbey said loudly to the table, wishing as she mouthed the words that she wasn't. "But my husband has been sexing my neighbors."

Nobody spoke. For a start, no one was quite sure what sexing was. Jamie looked as though his eyes were about to pop out; Jack's mouth, full of food, was dumbly hanging open; Lucy looked thunderous. Abbey herself couldn't believe what she'd just said. She had meant to say screwing or bonking or shagging but sexing had popped out instead. She felt a frightening wave of dangerous emotion sweep over her.

"Leastways, he was getting biblical with them," she said, maniacally pushing a pile of beans around on her plate as she felt tears spring, cartoonlike, from her eyes. "And they were having his children." She abandoned her food and sat up, wiping at the tears on her cheeks and fighting to control herself. "In clumps, as it happens. Unlike me."

Corrie looked at her flushed face and felt tears prick the back of his own eyes. Such misery! What had happened to his beautiful little girl?

Avis looked across the table and did what she had to. "I had a husband once, too," she said cheerfully, "and a more miserable bollocks you never met in your whole entire life. Now Abbey, will you pass the greens up to Wilhie, please? She's a demon for skipping her spinach and God knows it's the only iron the girl's ever likely to get."

"Joseph," Fee called from the other end of the table, "would you be unwrapping the Coeur de Coolarney instead of sitting there gawking at the potatoes?"

"I thought we were going to have mashed as well," Corrie said, entering the spirit of changing the subject as knives and forks around the table were picked up again.

"Well, I didn't see your highness volunteering his services in the kitchen," Fee returned.

The hum of good-natured banter picked up and slowly buzzed once more around the kitchen, so that only Abbey and Kit were left silent and still at the table. Corrie unwrapped the heart-shaped cheese and, after translating a series of frightening facial expressions from his friend at the other end of the table, pushed it as surreptitiously as he could between them, both too steeped in misery to notice. The fumes of the Irish love cheese rose up and whispered invisibly between them.

"I really am sorry," Abbey finally said, "about your wife."

Kit, still unable to speak or look at her, just shook his head. "I'm sorry about your husband," he answered, in time.

The tentacles of the crafty Coeur were sensing resistance, but nevertheless wrapped themselves around him. Kit wanted to get up and leave but he couldn't. He felt frozen to the seat. Naked and exposed and more in need of a drink than ever.

Abbey too felt as heavy as lead and was suddenly desperate to undo the damage she'd done. She wasn't a mean person, she knew that, and now she wanted everyone else to know that, too. She tried to think of a witty way to get around bringing up Kit's recent bereavement but couldn't.

The love cheese tendrils waved and wafted around her.

"Shake?" she finally offered timidly, holding out her hand in Kit's direction as, unseen, ghostly coils of ardor essence slid over it like a glove.

Kit looked at her hand. She could stick it up her ass, as far as he was concerned, and he was about to tell her that when the Coeur lashed out and slapped him.

"Sure," he said instead. "Why not," and he took the hand she had offered in his own.

The *fromage d'amour* screamed with triumph and Kit felt a jolt, like an electric current, run up his arm, across his shoulders, and shoot down through his chest, via his groin, to the tips of his toes. He felt shocked, literally. He let go of Abbey's hand with a gasp and dazedly examined his palm, amazed to find there wasn't a raging red burn mark there. He swore he could still feel the tingle of her touch. He turned back to look at her and noticed, with another tremor, that her formerly flattened hair was now sticking out at right angles to her head. She was staring right back at him with a stunned look in her eyes, and he knew in an instant that she'd felt something too.

Corrie leaned forward and snatched the cheese away, snapping Abbey out of her trance. She looked at him questioningly.

"Smells delicious," he explained. "But tastes like shite."

It was true. Those who had actually eaten the love cheese were repelled by its overambitious flavor and its tendency to give lovebirds breath like the water left too long in the bottom of a vase. Once the thing had done its magic, one was better off by far to stick with Coolarney Gold.

CHAPTER FIFTEEN

"If you can see the magic in cheese, you can see the magic in everything."

JOSEPH FEEHAN, from *The Cheese Diaries*,
RTE Radio Archives

*K*it stood next to Avis, refusing to believe what he saw.

The morning air in the dairy was thick with the smell of effluent and milk and the sound of raindrops on rosebuds and whiskers on kittens. The Pregnasaurs were milking in time to the soundtrack of *The Sound of Music* and for a moment Kit thought the cows were actually dancing. On close inspection, they proved to be merely shuffling, but he couldn't be 100 percent sure that it wasn't in time to the beat.

On the other side of Avis, Abbey was equally astounded. She'd had a grim night's sleep, feeling ill at ease with all around her. In the middle of the night she had come to the conclusion that she was once again in the wrong place at the wrong time. Here she was, Corrie's own grand-daughter—and yet she felt less like part of the family than anybody else there. It didn't bother her that the place was full of unmarried mothers-to-be and other hangers-on. She felt quite comfortable with the aura of unusual. It was something else that irked her. Something she couldn't quite put her finger on. Something tall and handsome, perhaps, and just a tad goose-bumpy.

"What a sweet song." She smiled up at Avis as the milkmaids harmonized over their favorite things. "So when the dog bites or the bee stings, you're supposed to think of something happy. Sounds like that film *Pollyanna.*"

Kit peered behind Avis to see if Abbey was kidding.

"It's from *The Sound of Music,*" he said incredulously. "You know, the most successful movie musical of all time?"

Avis climbed aboard the tractor and started to drive toward the dairy.

"Oh, I never saw that," Abbey said.

"You never saw *The Sound of Music?*" Kit couldn't believe it. "I thought it was like, compulsory, for every kindergarten pupil."

"Hello," said Abbey, "look around you. How many kindergartens do you see? I lived here until I was five and then we moved to London where, excuse me, I never saw *The Sound of Music,* but *Les Mis* and *The Rocky Horror Picture Show?* Ask me anything."

"Oh, I never saw either of those," Kit said, moving to where Avis had backed the trailer to help load up the milk.

She watched the two of them converse uneasily and wondered where this was all going to lead. She knew Fee had high hopes for the two of them but if she had to put money on it, she wouldn't. They were coming from different directions those two, and there'd already been one collision. Her heart ached for Abbey, who she could see had inherited her mother's social awkwardness. Rose's way of dealing with it had been to make herself the center of attention, but Abbey seemed to lack the bravado required—for which, Avis supposed, they could all be truly thankful. She could already tell that the girl had more feeling in her little finger than Rose had in her entire body. It was just a matter of giving her the courage to handle it. Having the girl back, no matter what the state of her, had certainly given Fee a spring in his step, she thought with a smile, although she'd caught Corrie this morning, his tea gone cold in the cup, with such an expression on his face it nearly broke her already aching heart. Abbey being around was bound to dredge up memories of Rose, she supposed. She just hoped that the joy of one would help drown out the pain of the other.

Kit and Abbey sat on the back of the trailer, their legs dangling over the edge, as Avis drove the milk to the dairy.

"So you do know about Julia Roberts and Meg Ryan, then?" Kit was asking.

"What? Are they together?"

"No," he said. "About them being, you know, the world's biggest box-office stars. And you know about e-mail and cell phones?"

Abbey rolled her eyes. "I was in the Sulivan Islands, not—" She tried to think of somewhere more remote, coming up, lamely, with, "Iceland, you know. We had satellite television and DVDs before most of the rest of the world, including the United States of America." In fact, she wanted to point out, if he looked very closely he would see that she was currently sporting Julia Roberts's haircut, thanks to the latest *InStyle* and Imi's DIY hairdressing kit.

God but she was a hard nut to crack, thought Kit. Anyone would think he had asked about *her* dead wife in front of a roomful of people, not the other way around. Dead wife? He rolled the words over in his mind and wondered where on earth he could go to clear his head of Jacey. He was tired of the claim she had on his thoughts. Every time he started to appreciate where he was, she floated into his mind in a flimsy dress and brought him back down to earth with a dull ache in his stomach where he wanted a drink to be.

He squeezed his eyes shut as the trailer rattled and bumped over the crunchy turf. The morning sun was throwing the beginnings of the day's heat on the back of his neck, and it felt calm and soothing. He relaxed his shoulders and welcomed the warmth.

Abbey was watching him out of the corner of her eye. Something about him just made her want to swing out and give him a good slap. Was it because he was good-looking, she wondered? And well-dressed? And nicely spoken? And confident? And charming? And so at bloody ease with everything it made her want to scream? Or was it because of what had happened between them at the dinner table last night? Not the thing about the dead wife. No. He'd given her a shock, she was sure of it. Or she'd given him one. Either way the two of them had been zapped, and she didn't know what it meant but she didn't like it. They had sat there after it happened eating cheese and pretty much ignoring each other until her extreme tiredness, jet lag she supposed, had provided the excuse to sneak off to her room where she had hardly slept a wink.

Fee had informed them the night before that there was no time like the present and they were both expected to shape up for cheesemaking duties, but all the same, Abbey had been surprised to find Corrie gently knocking on her door at six o'clock.

"Have you ever—"

"Is this the first—"

She and Kit simultaneously tried to break the excruciating silence between them.

"Never mind."

"Doesn't matter."

They both laughed humorlessly, relieved to be almost at the factory.

"Holy Mary Mother of God," Fee prayed, watching the two of them coming toward him as Avis reversed the trailer up toward the east door and the milk tank. This was going to take more than Coeur de Coolarney, that was for sure. Wordlessly, Kit and Abbey helped pour the milk into the tank, then at Fee's behest entered the factory for the lowdown on Old Fart Arse. Inside Corrie hovered in the background, watching his granddaughter like a hawk.

"So the aim of this heap," Fee said, giving Old Fart Arse a thump, "is to heat the milk to 72 degrees Celsius for fifteen seconds, a process which kills off a lot of the allegedly harmful bacteria, thank you very much Louis fecking Pasteur, and does the same to most of the flavor."

"You think pasteurizing the milk is bad?" Abbey looked confused.

"Well, didn't we all survive perfectly well without it?" Fee glowered.

Kit opened his mouth to argue, but decided against it. Abbey forged blindly ahead.

"Has the cheese not always been pasteurized?"

"Most certainly not!" said Fee, while Corrie murmured, "Jaysus! Here we go," from behind him.

"It's a recent requirement of the Irish health authorities," Fee said with a forced smile, "in case one in a million people keels over with something that might or might not have come from an edible substance that might or might not have been cheese that might or might not have been made in this country. In France, of course—" He stopped, and smiled a calm, smoothing smile to himself.

"Happy thoughts," Corrie chipped in dryly from the background.

Abbey and Kit shared an uneasy glance.

"We can talk more about that later," Fee said, with forced serenity. "Now," he said, pointing to the outlet from the milk tank, "our lovely shorthorns' elixir comes out of this pipe here and is pumped directly over here."

They followed his finger to a collection of similar stainless-steel pipes that ran beneath the pasteurizer and turned corner after corner, like a huge French horn, eventually splitting in different directions around Old Fart Arse's barrel.

"Eventually the milk comes from here"—Fee was following a pipe on the other side of the pasteurizer now—"to the cheese vat. We call her Anneke."

"Hang on," said Kit, still looking at Old Fart Arse. "The milk goes from the tank through the pasteurizer and comes out here?"

"It comes into this vat here," Fee said again, patting Anneke on the side, "like I said the first time."

"But it goes from this pipe here?" Kit insisted. He was back by the tank, pointing to the first pipe.

"If you can't keep up I can go slower," Fee said nastily, but Corrie was smiling.

"Exactly what are you getting at?" Abbey asked impatiently.

"Oh, nothing really," Kit said. "It's just that if the milk comes out of this pipe and stays in this pipe"—he was tracing the pipe with his smooth, long fingers under and around Old Fart Arse—"ending up in this pipe—it is in fact all the same pipe."

Fee looked at the ground.

"And?" prompted Abbey.

"And," said Kit, "that would not at any stage involve actually going through the, um, pasteurization process."

There was a tiny silence.

"Well, if he's going to be picky," Fee said in a slightly whining tone to Corrie, "he can feck right off."

Kit chose not to take umbrage. His mother, actually, had always sworn by the locally made unpasteurized cheeses that were sold from farms around Vermont. He'd grown up with the strong earthy flavors of raw farmhouse cheese and didn't object in the slightest to Fee protecting Coolarney's original flavor, although he worried about the consequences of being caught.

"So you only pretend to pasteurize the cheese?" Abbey asked, agog.

"We pasteurize it when we have to," said Corrie. "Which tends to coincide with a visit from the local inspector."

"R. Swoole," Fee said bitterly.

"I'm sure they all are," agreed Kit. "But don't you have to keep records?"

"We certainly do and they're impeccable," Fee answered.

"You'd have to go a long way to find records tidier than ours," agreed Corrie.

"Avis does them on a Thursday night and I swear that woman has the neatest handwriting you ever saw. She could have been a nun with that handwriting."

Kit was not to be distracted. "But wouldn't you have to keep the records as you went? You know, times and temperatures and all of that?"

"Is he messing with me, Joseph?" Fee asked Corrie.

Corrie shook his head. "We have stringent hygiene measures, highly safe and sensitized curing procedures, exceptional packaging skills, and Fee, of course, knows when—" He stopped and changed tack. "Ah, sure, I wouldn't dwell on it if I were you."

"If we can continue," Fee said pointedly, opening the valve and letting the milk whoosh into the vat.

The smell as the warm milk hit the clean stainless steel was almost overwhelming. It reminded Kit of babies and homes and kitchens: things he pretty much never needed to think of.

Abbey too was soaking up the smell. She could remember now being here as a child, when she didn't even reach the top of the vat. The floor seemed familiar, as too did the slurping and gulping noises of so many gallons of milk starting their journey toward something much, much more interesting. The air in the dairy was warm and wet and yet somehow strangely refreshing. It felt like the beginning of something.

"Once the vat is filled we test the milk to see if it has reached thirty-five degrees like so," Fee said, sticking his elbow in the milk, closing one eye and poking his tongue out, "and Bob's your rudd!"

"For heaven's sake," called Avis through the east door. "Stop messing."

Fee looked sheepish and held up a thermometer tied with a chain to the side of the vat. "There's no getting away with the slightest thing with Herself hovering around in the background," he grumbled. "Okay, like so." He dipped the thermometer in the milk, where its digital reading showed them the temperature was in fact 35 degrees. "You're probably better off using the thermometer to begin with," he said. "Then, when you know the milk is the right temperature, you add the starter."

Corrie handed over a plastic cup, which contained what looked like tiny rice bubbles. Fee poured it into the milk and gave the stuff a stir with a long stainless-steel pole with a sort of potato masher on the end of it.

"Now, I don't want to go all technical on you because you're probably not able for it," Fee said, giving Kit a particular look as he did so, "but the bought-in stuff is basically a prescribed lactic bacillus. Good old-fashioned bacteria. We know exactly what's in it, where it's come from, everything about it. No surprises there, feck the lot of them. Put this in your fecking milk and you will get fecking cheese."

Kit looked from Fee to Corrie and back again. "And that's a problem?" Kit asked.

"Wouldn't no surprises be a good thing?" Abbey wanted to know. "Wouldn't always getting cheese be a good thing?"

"Are yis undercover agents for the government or wha'?" Fee said grumpily, his ears turning pink as he concentrated on stirring the milk.

"Very occasionally Joseph has trouble embracing change," Corrie said. "Just ignore him on that account."

"Embrace, me arse," Fee grumbled crossly.

"But why wouldn't you want the cheese to be the same every time you made it?" Abbey asked her grandfather.

Corrie answered quickly to head off Fee before he burst a gasket. "Well, the cheese is basically the same," he said, "although really it changes from day to day given the girls, the grass, the milk, and whatever you're having yourself. But the differences now are far milder than they once were and the purists"—he looked at Fee—"would say that a hundred years ago half the pleasure of a decent Coolarney would be not knowing exactly what to expect, just that you could expect it."

"I guess that doesn't fit into a modern marketing plan, huh?" Kit ventured. "The surprise factor's a bit harder to sell these days."

"Listen to him, with all his modern marketing," Fee mumbled grouchily under his breath, although privately he was begrudgingly pleased that the boy was on to it so quickly. "Now, if you could stop talking amongst your-selves for a moment and pay attention," he said impor-tantly, "you'll notice I am now adding the rennet, which is what makes the milk coagulate and form the curd."

"Where does that come from?" Abbey asked.

"Well it used to come from the stomachs of little baby calves," Fee said, "but now we buy that in, too."

"It's an enzyme," Corrie butted in, "that turns the liq-uid into solids. Some cheesemakers use a vegetarian one but Himself won't hear a word of it."

"Ah, you don't know how they molest that stuff," Fee exploded. "They feck around with DNA to get it, for feck's sake. Yeast DNA. Did you even know that yeast had DNA? Next thing they'll be growing cheese on a mouse's back."

"But what about the vegetarians?" Kit asked, thinking of the calf-stomach rennet's appeal to the Pregnasaurs.

"Well, they can buy vegetarian cheese if they want to," Fee replied. "I'm not stopping them."

Before Kit could respond, an almighty cacophony erupted from the factory office. "What the hell is that?" he asked, startled.

"That's Ruby and Marie," Corrie said. "They take the orders and deal with the office administration and they work very hard and we greatly appreciate them."

"Not that they'd ever stop their clattering long enough for us to tell them," Fee said.

An hour later Kit and Abbey were exhausted from attempting to translate Ruby and Marie's patchwork of instruction. Corrie and Fee had left them in the capable hands of the two workers, who had between them demon-strated the computer ordering system, the packing pro-cess, how to make four cups of tea with only one teabag and how to dance without using their arms—which came as a particular surprise to Abbey, who had never heard of *Riverdance*. When they emerged back into the factory, Corrie and Fee were smiling into the vat. By now, the curd had formed and was floating in the watery whey.

"How about that?" Kit said, impressed. He'd never really thought about the process of cheesemaking that much before. That it started out drinkable, and something made it edible.

"Now's the fun part," Fee said, smiling. He handed Abbey a blade paddle and demonstrated with his own one how to weave and cut through the curd.

"You'd think it's not stiff enough to stay put and be sliced," marveled Abbey as she started cutting through the solid curd. "But look at it!"

Fee handed Corrie's paddle to Kit and watched his strong, young shoulders maneuver the blade through the curd. In the morning light of the dairy, he looked, for a moment, just like Corrie had forty years before. Fee saw that Corrie had seen this too, and felt for his old friend. Of course it was grand to be delivered not one but two cheesemakers on a platter like this but on the other hand . . . Life would never be the same, and they both knew it.

The humidity in the dairy made cutting the curd hard, hot work, but Kit found it satisfying to sweep silently through the squeaky mass, breaking it down to smaller and smaller pieces. "Small enough for you?" he asked, taking a moment to wipe his brow with his forearm.

"Get on with you, you lazy article," scolded Fee. "You're not selling and marketing here, you know."

When the curd was broken down to crumb size, Fee pulled at a pluglike opening on Anneke's side and the whey started to course out onto the floor, flowing down a channel to a grill in the ground.

"Where does it go?" Abbey wanted to know.

"Back out to the farm usually," Corrie said. "It's just water and a bit of protein but it helps maintain our equilibrium."

"Besides, we can't find any other fecker that wants the stuff," added Fee.

He really can be quite grumpy, thought Abbey.

"By the way, Abbey," the old fox said, looking at her slyly, "did I mention how gorgeous you are looking this morning?"

Not grumpy exactly, she corrected herself. Just forthright, really.

When about a third of the whey was drained off, Fee looked at Corrie. This was an important moment for the future of Coolarney cheese and they both knew it. Everything rode on what was about to happen. Demeanor remaining casual while their hearts beat quickly in nervous anticipation, they entreated their apprentices to taste the curd. Kit scooped up a handful and held it to his nose.

"Smell's sweeter than I would have expected," he said. Fee felt excitement rising in his chest.

"God, it tastes delicious," Abbey added, curd spilling from her lips on to the floor.

"Incredible," agreed Kit. "It's fantastic."

Trying not to let them see his excitement, Fee dipped his arm into the vat. He lifted his hand slowly to his lips and closed his eyes to inhale its perfection. But before he even got it to his mouth, he knew something was wrong.

It was still there. Unmistakable. The taint of failure.

He shook his head ever so slightly as Corrie's face collapsed with calamity. He dipped his own hand in and swallowed a mouthful of Kit and Abbey's curd, willing it to sing and dance in his mouth, but it didn't. It sat in the audience. Maybe it even clapped politely, but it still sat in the audience. Ignoring his own disappointment, he nodded encouragingly at the apprentices then left Fee to show them how to heat the curd again then drain it and pack it into molds until each last crumb was spoken for.

When Fee found him sometime later he was sitting in the garden on the bench that had been home to Kit for so many hours the day before, looking old and gray.

"If you really thought they could get it first time around you're more of a simple old bollocks than I thought," Fee said.

Corrie just sighed. "And you didn't?" he asked his friend. "That's not what you were hoping for?" Fee simply shrugged his shoulders and sat down next to him.

"Is it him, Joseph?" Corrie asked. "Are you wrong about him?"

"Well, I don't think so, but shall we give it, oh, I don't know, at least another minute before we give up all hope and shoot ourselves in the head?"

Corrie sighed again. "I suppose you're right," he said. "We'll just wait and see. What else is there for it?" They sat there in silence, watching a gentle breeze run like a ripple through the poppies in the garden.

"Actually, I don't think we should wait for too long," Fee said eventually, sitting ramrod still on the bench. Corrie went to stand up but Fee pulled him back. "I don't mean now," he said, avoiding his friend's eyes.

Corrie sat back down. "Well, what do you mean?" he asked.

Fee kicked at the pebbles on the garden path with his filthy tennis shoe. "I mean generally. I mean there might not be a lot of time."

Corrie felt a pain rip through his chest as he processed what this meant. For the first time in his life, Fee, who believed in nothing much but time, didn't have any. Fee, who knew that it would heal all wounds. Who always waited, never rushed. Separated from time, Fee was not himself, Corrie thought. He was just a short, fat cranky cheesemaker with bad shoes. It wasn't possible. He felt the pain in his heart spread and push a lump up into his throat and hot tears to the back of his eyes. He took a moment to compose himself.

"Come on then," he said, with a shaky smile and a confidence he felt a million miles away from, "let's show them how it's done."

"No, no, no," Kit was saying to Abbey as they leaned against the benches packed with filled cheese molds, the factory heavy with the smell of settling curd, "she was training to be a nun but she got sent to teach the von Trapps instead."

"Well, who sent her?" Abbey asked.

"The mother superior or whatever they're called," Kit answered. "I don't know, but Maria wasn't making a very good nun because she kept running up into the Alps with her guitar and singing."

"You're clearly not up with what makes a good nun."

"Well, I know that handwriting is important," Kit said, but Abbey ignored him as Corrie and Fee appeared again. Kit wasn't sure if he imagined it or not but she seemed to stiffen ever so slightly at the sight of her grandfather. He supposed they hardly knew each other, but still . . .

Fee looked around with pleasure at the sight of all his cheese molds filled with curd, dripping happily onto the benches and the floor below. "A fine mess you've made while my back was turned," he beamed. "Tomorrow we'll soak these cheeses in that salty solution in the big stainless tub at the back there. In the meantime we'll need to turn the molds every hour to make sure the cheeses take on an even shape and also to squeeze out the last bits of whey.

"The face on you!" Fee said suddenly to Kit. "What's your problem?"

"Why do you have to salt it?" Kit asked. Years of nutrition advice at the gym he had frequented before Jacey used up all his time had steered him away from salt to the point where he no longer had a taste for it.

Fee huffed in an exasperated fashion. "Saints preserve us," he said. "What do you think is going on inside this contraption?" Fee rapped on the nearest mold, sending droplets of whey spinning into the air. "We've got something wet and warm to which we have added bacteria. It's alive," he whispered dramatically. "What we have in here is the result of our own specific equilibrium. Do you know about equilibrium, Kit?"

Kit nodded. He knew about equilibrium all right. Equilibrium, or lack of it, was why he was here.

"You take the amount of acreage out there," Fee said, nodding in the general direction of the farm, "the mood of the shorthorns, the nature of the grass, the amount of milk they give us, the time of year and whatever's in the air, you mix them together and what have you got?"

"Bibbity-bobbity-boo!" cried Abbey. "I did see that one!"

Corrie laughed but Fee rapped his knuckles sharply once more against the cheese molds, sending an angry message rattling down the bench. "If you're not going to take this seriously . . ." he warned.

"Okay, okay," said Kit. "I'm listening."

You great girlie swot, thought Abbey.

"Just feel the heat, the humidity, the smell, the plain Coolarniness of this place," Fee said, lifting his round red nose up to the air and waggling it. "The things that are going on in here . . ."

He closed his eyes and sniffed, Kit and Abbey with him.

"What's going on in these cheeses is dynamite," he said, snapping his head forward and opening his eyes to look at his apprentices. "If it keeps going on the way it is now we could be blown to kingdom come."

Kit felt the hair stand up on the back of his neck.

"What we do with the salt is cancel that bacterial life inside the cheese so we can gain control. The salt locks the flavor, freezes the equilibrium," he said, "so we can regroup for a moment."

Frozen equilibrium, Kit thought. Regrouping.

"We're using alchemy: turning liquid to solids courtesy of acidification, with the catalyst of rennet to trap the protein," he continued. "That much is chemistry. Anybody can do that. Monkeys, three-year-olds, investment brokers . . ."

He beckoned for Kit and Abbey to follow him to the back of the factory, where he headed down the stairs to the Gold room. He stopped reverentially and bowed his head (overkill, thought Corrie) at the door then slipped inside, entreating the others to follow. The smell was tantalizing. Nutty, sort of, Abbey thought, and grassy, but with a hint of tamarillo perhaps, or kiwi fruit. And there was a sourness to it, too: a Junior's shoes at the door on an especially hot day sort of a smell.

"So, science can get everybody some of the way," Fee said, "but the rest is up to us and this is where it happens." He looked proudly around the room at the neatly packed racks of cheese. "We bring Coolarney Gold down here and wipe it every two days with a yeasty smear that gives a bit of a turbocharge to the flavor and makes it this pale-yellow hue." He pointed at the racks closest to them. "It's not for wimps, Coolarney Gold. It's a cheese-lovers' cheese. Anyway, as the cheese develops and we keep washing it, it changes color, till it's golden or even orange," he said, pointing at the racks at the back of the room.

"No offense," said Kit bravely, "but it smells like old men's socks."

"None taken," Fee said delightedly, "it's supposed to. That's our older boys at the back there. Nothing like it anywhere else in the world. We've always had something different. Something you can't get anywhere else. Something unique," he said.

The four of them stood and soaked up the Coolarniness.

"So what we do," continued Fee, "is we bring our perfectly calculated cheese made at the right temperature with right ingredients at the right time—the stuff you made up there today—down into this room and we let something happen. That's always been the way, whether we made our own starter, our own rennet or not.

"We do what we can upstairs according to a fairly rigid set of calculations, then we stand back and let the farm, the air, the rain, the moon, the room we're feckin' standing in, make its mark and that becomes Coolarney Gold."

In the dim light of the curing room he smiled on the racks. "Can you believe it?" he said. "The magic of cheese."

Kit felt a shiver run down his spine. He was thirty-two years old and until recently a well-respected New York investment broker. He wore Prada shoes, Calvin Klein boxers and paid $100 every three weeks to get his hair cut. He had Louis Vuitton luggage, for chrissakes. But he'd screwed up his equilibrium, and as a result here he was standing in a dingy cellar in the arse end of Ireland regrouping. It's a strange old world, he thought to himself with a shudder.

Abbey too felt trembly and scared, but for a different reason. She wasn't sure if it was tiredness or stress or hope or fear but the intensity of the curing room was making her heart beat in time to the words her mother had hurled at her as she left the London flat.

"Just ask that old bastard what happened to your grandmother," she heard Rose sob. "Just ask him what's buried in his precious factory."

Corrie turned to say something to her, but at the sound of his feet moving in the underground room, panic gripped her. With a strangled cry, Abbey dodged the old man, wrenched open the door and stumbled up the stairs and through the factory. Outside, palms sweating and chest heaving, she leaned against the wall, threw back her head and gulped the fresh, clean country air.

"What am I doing here?" she begged the sky.

CHAPTER SIXTEEN

"If you think cheese is just food, you're an eejit, because it is so much more than that. It's poetry. It's passion. It's pathos. It's no coincidence that milk and human blood are almost the same temperature. Had you thought about that, now?"

JOSEPH FEEHAN, from *The Cheese Diaries*,
RTE Radio Archives

*J*esus, as it turned out, was a bad mother. When Lucy ran to check up on the kittens while Abbey and Kit were having their first cheesemaking lesson, it became clear that Jesus had succumbed to the lure of the night and abandoned her newborns. Two little corpses lay under the tree next to the old blanket Lucy and Jamie had put there the night before, and of the other four there was no sign. Jesus herself had been seen licking the cream off the dairy floor earlier on and had spent much of the morning yowling outside the kitchen door for food and attention. Apart from a slight bagginess about the undercarriage, she showed no recent signs of motherhood and didn't have the decency to exhibit so much as a glimmer of guilt over the whole affair.

Lucy was inconsolable. Nothing Avis nor the girls said could calm her down, and when Kit retreated to the garden after lunch for a bit of reflective peace and quiet, he found her hiccupping and grief-stricken on his bench.

After Abbey's abrupt departure from the curing room earlier on, Corrie had gone in search of his granddaughter while Fee and Kit stayed behind to smear the cheeses, an arduous yet comforting task that had worked up quite an appetite for the vegetarian pies Avis had made for lunch. Kit had gorged himself on Coolarney Blue and was feeling the need for a snooze in the sun, but Lucy's need for a shoulder to cry on was obviously greater—so he resigned himself to that duty.

"How could she leave them like that?" she wailed. "They were only tiny babies."

Kit was at a loss to explain. "Perhaps it just wasn't meant to be," he said. "Perhaps it just wasn't their time."

This only made Lucy cry harder. Her bony shoulders shook with grief, and when she lifted her little girl's face to Kit, it was blotchy and mottled and streaked with mascara. She looked about five years old, Kit thought, and his heart went out to her. All traces of the flirtatious minx from last night had been replaced by this tearful girl-child; he scooted closer on the bench and put his arm around her, squeezing her tight.

Lucy sobbed into his T-shirt, and Kit felt her tears wet and warm on his skin. He thought of Flynn and wondered how his own kid brother was doing. He'd sent him a check and a letter explaining that he was going away for a while, but hadn't quite had the balls to ring and tell him why. Flynn knew about Jacey of course, but not about Kit's problems since then. He sighed and held Lucy a bit tighter. It was hard to admit to himself that his life had spun out of control. How could he admit it to anyone else, especially Flynn, one of the few people left in the world who still thought the sun shone out his butt?

Lucy's sobbing subsided mildly but she kept her head on Kit's chest. He'd never seen dreadlocks up close, he realized.

"I just don't understand it," she said wetly. "Jesus is normally such a sweet little thing. Mary and All The Saints are the mean ones."

"Perhaps she just wasn't cut out for motherhood," Kit said, inspecting the tangle on her head and wondering how clean the matted locks actually were.

"That's what I'm afraid of," Lucy cried, anguished, pushing her face harder into Kit's T-shirt. "That's what's so scary." She wailed even louder and the penny, for Kit, finally dropped. It was sad about the kittens, sure, but her tears were out of proportion. The hysterics, when he thought about it, were unlikely to be truly about Jesus's maternal instincts.

"Lucy," he said, "is there anything else that's bothering you?" She seemed so innocent, he thought, looking at her round, blue eyes. So helpless and young.

She blinked away her tears and nodded her head.

"Is it about the baby?"

She sniffed. "Maybe," she said quietly.

Kit started to say something. Thought better of it. Then said it anyway. "Maybe," he said, "you're worried that you're not cut out for motherhood."

Lucy bit her quivering bottom lip.

"Do you want to talk about it?"

She took a deep breath and sat up straight so she could look at him more easily. "You're the only one who understands me," she said.

"I hardly know you," Kit answered with a brotherly smile. "I'm sure the others would understand you if you let them."

"I'm nothing like them," Lucy said. "I didn't even know I was pregnant until I got here. I could've been one of those girls that ends up on *Ricki Lake* having a baby in the toilets at a nightclub and not telling anyone."

"That happens?" Kit asked.

"All the time." Lucy sniffed again, her bravado making a brief return as she danced around the delicate subject of her condition. "And then their mothers go ballistic and their friends all turn against them and it's a total nightmare."

There was no correct response to that, Kit decided. "So how did you end up here, anyway?"

"I just went to the bus station and got a ticket for as far away as I could afford."

"Why?" asked Kit. "What were you getting away from?"

"A great stinking bollocks by the name of Eamon Casey is what," Lucy said with venom. "My so-called boyfriend back in Dublin."

"So-called?"

"Well, he was just my plain old boyfriend until, you know—" Lucy faltered.

"Until what?"

"Oh God, I can hardly bear to talk about it," Lucy said, screwing her face up again. They'd been going out for almost a year, she told Kit. Eamon played bass guitar in a Dublin grunge band called Oktober and she was in her first year of a music degree at Trinity College. They'd met at a mutual friend's party in a rambling student house in Dun Laighoaire and had declared themselves "exclusive" straightaway, or so Lucy had thought.

"Then a couple of months ago we were supposed to meet up one night and I got a message on the answering machine at home saying the band was having an extra practice and he wouldn't be able to make it. They had this huge big gig the next night down at Slane Castle, being the support act for the support act for the band before The Red Hot Chili Peppers, so it made sense. Except"— her lip trembled—"except that he was calling me from his cell phone and he must have hit the wrong button or not switched it off or something because the message on the answering machine didn't finish when he thought it did, when he said good-bye."

Kit said nothing. This was not going to be a story with a happy ending.

Lucy's bravado had disappeared again and Kit was reminded once more of what a perfect baby-sister she would have made for Jacey.

"He was with some girl, and he was telling her about me, calling me a groupie and a cling-on. He said I was a poor little rich girl with nothing better to do than spend my money on buying pints for him and the band." Her voice got very small. "They were laughing at me," she said. "And I think maybe they were in bed together. You know, bonking."

Eamon Casey sounded like a class act, thought Kit. "I am so sorry, Lucy," he said. "The guy sounds like a real asshole."

"Oh, but I loved him," Lucy answered with feeling. "I'd been with loads and loads and loads of guys before but I really loved him. He wrote a song for me," she said sadly, "called 'Crapcake.'"

It didn't seem appropriate to laugh.

"He told me that he loved me, too," Lucy continued,

"but I know that you would never say mean things about someone that you love."

Or sleep around with someone else, thought Kit. "So what did you do?"

"I went out that night, drank seven Red Bull and vodkas and then I shagged Gordy Wilde, Oktober's lead singer," Lucy answered. "I knew it would drive Eamon mad because he hates Gordy. Gordy's gorgeous-looking but he can't really sing and he doesn't write any of the songs or anything but the fans go ape-shit over him. He's gas. Anyway, he dumped me after the Chili Peppers for some seventeen-year-old knacker who said she was a cousin of the Corrs."

Jesus, thought Kit. My life may be in the crapper but thank God I'm not nineteen again.

"What happened with Eamon?" he asked.

"Gordy told him but he didn't even care," said Lucy. "He told Gordy he could have me. Then the band voted that I couldn't hang out with them anymore." She turned her face again to Kit. "I spent weeks phoning Eamon and trying to get him to see me but he wouldn't. He didn't want anything to do with me."

"Do you know whose baby it is?" Kit asked, although he supposed it didn't make much difference.

Lucy shook her head. "I think it's Gordy's," she sniffed. "We did it six times."

Okay, Kit thought, some aspects of being nineteen weren't so bad.

"But I don't really know," she cried, bursting into tears again. "All I know is that I don't want it but I don't want it to know that I don't want it."

She fell into Kit's T-shirt again and he let her, thinking of his own lost baby, which would have been due in a couple of months' time had Jacey not . . . Kit wondered what sort of a father he would have made. He'd never really thought about kids until Jacey came along. She was the first woman he had ever wanted to marry, to have a family with, to hold and never let go.

There'd been "significant others" before her, of course, two in particular. Ellen had been a friend of Ed's with whom he had very nearly moved in before her overbearing mother got the better of her and convinced her to go look-ing for a nice Jewish boy instead. Ellen was great fun, but the fact that he hadn't minded in the least when she broke it off suggested they were probably better off going their separate ways.

Sal had been more difficult to part with. A ferociously ambitious magazine editor working for a publishing com-pany specializing in rag-trade titles, they had taken on New York together. She was so upwardly mobile it was all he could do to keep in her jet stream, and for a while their dedication to their separate careers had bound them together so tightly he could not imagine life with anyone else. They'd shared an Upper West Side apartment for nearly two years before they took their first two-week vacation together, to Paris. It all came tumbling down around them among the bars and cafes of the Latin Quar-ter where they were staying. Without the stimulus of work and the buzz of Manhattan, he realized they didn't have a single thing to say to each other. Sal realized it, too.

"We're boring," she had sobbed into her *frites*. "How did that happen?"

But they weren't boring, they were bored. With each other. And when they got back to New York, Kit packed his bags and moved out. They'd stayed friends, though, and probably always would. Sal had gotten married, about the same time as Kit in fact, to the publisher of her magazine group. The wedding had been featured in all the right places and she had looked absolutely beautiful and happy beyond belief. He'd be surprised if she succumbed to the ticking of her biological clock any time soon, though. Too much work to be done. He sighed and felt Lucy nestle closer into his side.

"You're thinking about things a lot of the time, aren't you?" she asked.

"I suppose I am," answered Kit.

"Are you thinking about your wife?" Lucy asked.

"Mostly, I guess," he said uncomfortably.

"What did she look like? Was she pretty?"

Long blond hair down past her shoulder blades, a smile that could melt butter, legs like a thoroughbred racehorse.

"She was the most beautiful woman I ever saw in my entire life," he answered, pulling himself away from Lucy and standing up. He didn't want to talk about Jacey. He wanted peace and quiet. "I'm going to go take a nap now—I feel kind of whacked—but I want you to promise me that you will come and talk to me whenever you want to, Lucy. Whenever you need to. You know where to find me. Will you do that?"

Lucy looked at him with an adoration he failed to notice was far from little-sisterly.

"I will," she said. "Definitely."

Kit trudged up to Fee's cottage and flopped down on his bed, his belly full of cheese and his head spinning with images of Jacey and babies and Lucy. His eyelids drifted down toward his cheeks and, mercifully, he slept.

His dreams were not of his wife or the troubled Dublin teenager, though. They were of Abbey. No sooner had he closed his eyes than images of his fellow cheesemaker filled his head. In the dream, Abbey was riding a bicycle and laughing, her head thrown back in delight, her face radiating joy. Eventually he realized the bike had turned into a horse and her legs were bare underneath a see-through white dress, as she urged the stallion on with her thighs. His dream had all the makings of a crappy chocolate commercial and even in his sleep he was aware of trying to make it about someone other than Abbey, and less cheesy, but failing. Instead, Abbey lay on her side in long warm grass, spreading gooey Coolarney Blue on chunks of farmhouse bread and licking her glossy lips with anticipation. Her dress had ridden up to reveal the curve of her hip and she wasn't wearing any underwear.

He walked toward her and all of a sudden she rolled over and was lying on her back on the floor of the New York Stock Exchange. Kit knelt down in front of her, her big dark eyes pleading with him as he leaned toward her and bent his head, undoing with his teeth the buttons bursting over her breasts. She was wearing the sexiest bra he had ever seen in his whole entire life. It was pale green with pink roses embroidered on it and had tiny cups over which her breasts, blue and milky in the half-light of the abandoned Exchange, burst as the buttons popped open.

"Kit," she said in a voice that seemed to clash with her "come hither" body language.

"Kit," she said again, her clipped tone grating on his subconscious.

"Kit!"

His eyes flew open and he realized with alarm that the object of his dream was standing in his doorway calling his name.

"Are you awake?" Abbey asked stupidly.

"Yes," he replied equally stupidly, trying to squash the lust that had him in its grip. He was hot and sweating and throbbing in places that he didn't want Abbey to see. He didn't even like her. Not in that way. Not in any way. She was too small and sad and not at all his type. She was the opposite of his type. She had too-long hair and a woman's hips; no straight edges, just soft round curves and a full heavy bosom that seemed out of place on the rest of her.

"Can I help you?" he croaked out, realizing that his dream was still staking claim to part of his brain—and other body parts. Snapshots of Abbey, naked and writhing beneath his touch, crept into every crevice of his concentration.

"It's just that Fee wants to know . . ." Abbey was saying, but when Kit looked at her mouth he couldn't hear the words, he could only imagine those lips on his belly, his thigh, his— Suppressing a groan that was equal parts embarrassment and ardor, he sat up straighter in his bed and surreptitiously pulled a pillow onto his lap.

"He thought that maybe if you and I . . ." Abbey went on, but still Kit wasn't listening. He was transfixed instead by the way her T-shirt had ridden up just a couple of inches and was now exposing a slice of smooth firm stomach as it dipped to and from her belly button. He felt spellbound. Bewitched. Dumbfounded. He hadn't felt like this since, well obviously, Jacey, and even then—he stopped himself going further down that trail and squirmed on the bed.

"Well?" asked Abbey, stepping unsurely into the tiny room so that she was barely more than an arm's length away from him. "What do you think?"

"Yes, yes," Kit croaked, trying so hard not to think about his tongue on her skin that his face was contorted in pain. Jesus. He felt like some badly written character in a Harold Robbins novel.

Abbey faltered. "Are you okay, Kit?" she asked, worried for him. He looked ill.

"Fine," Kit gasped, pushing the pillow harder into his crotch and praying to God that she would leave. "I'm fine. Please. If you could just—" He was about to explode, he was sure. He pulled his knees toward his stomach and twisted away from her, to hide the humiliating throb in his chinos.

"Kit?" Abbey said, alarmed now as she moved even closer, so close he could smell her. He closed his eyes and breathed in through his nose. For just a moment he stopped fighting his lust and concentrated on her scent. She smelled of green grass and passion fruit and limes and it was utterly intoxicating. Vodka, thought Kit. I need vodka.

"Abbey," he heard himself whispering, and her sweet citrus smell loomed closer. He felt the weight of her on his bed and the damp warmth of her hand on his forehead. For a heartbeat, he did nothing. Then he turned slowly toward her and opened his eyes. Her lightly freckled nose was just inches away from his, her dark lashes ringing the inky pools of her dark, dark eyes.

"Abbey," he whispered again.

She looked at him.

The moment was there.

It hovered, tantalizingly.

It waited.

And then he took it. With his heart hammering in his ears, he strained forward and pressed his desperate mouth to Abbey's, a groan of knowing it wasn't the right thing to do escaping him as he did. His tongue slipped through her lips and sought out the ridges of her teeth as he felt her hand slip from his forehead to cup his cheek as she pushed her mouth hard against his.

She was kissing him back.

In one movement he pulled her toward him and tugged her onto the bed. Wordlessly he watched her eyes grow bigger and her lips wetter as he pushed one hand up under her T-shirt, under her clinging sports bra, so his thumb could toy with the nipple of his dreams. She closed her eyes and parted her lips with a sharp intake of breath that Kit halted with his own mouth as he felt the full beauty of her delicious breast in his hand. She pushed her pelvis toward him and he ground his own erection into her hip, feeling her buck underneath him. He lifted himself off her and moved his hand down her belly to the fastening of her cargo pants, which he undid with one deft movement, slipping his hand under her knickers and tracing the line of her hip, then her groin, to the warm, wet, juicy part of her abandoned for so long and crying now for attention.

He'd never noticed before but she had a perfect neck, and as his fingers worked their magic below, he dived gently into her nape and licked an outline with his tongue from her shoulder to her ear. Abbey's eyes were open but her look was far away. The feeling of hands on her body, in her body, was indescribable. It had been so long. She couldn't imagine it had ever felt this good before. Her breathing was getting quicker, she was sweating as Kit lifted her T-shirt and kissed his way down her cleavage, his tongue darting from breast to breast. She pushed herself into his hand, then felt him lift himself up on one arm and fumble with his zipper.

This is it, she thought. What am I doing? This is it. What am I doing? Oh, my God! This is it!

She felt Kit stiffen and gasp and closed her eyes in

anticipation of the climax. But instead of a host of heavenly angels singing a glorious chorus to her nerve endings, eighty-nine kilos of Kit collapsed heavily on top of her.

"Jesus," he said, looking at the doorway where Lucy was standing with a face like thunder. She spun around, her dreadlocks whipping around her face like tree branches in a twister, and raced down the stairs in a clomp of Doc Martens—but not before Abbey caught sight of her murderous face.

The moment that before had seemed so magical stopped hovering and suddenly packed up and went, taking Kit's erection with it, leaving him lying on top of Abbey wondering how the hell he was going to explain himself.

"Shit," he finally said, rolling off her and fumbling again with his zipper. "Shit." He closed his eyes and cursed himself for his stupidity.

Abbey, suddenly exposed in a trouserless fashion, felt the sheer lightweight happiness of the past few moments drain away to be replaced by humiliation. As it seeped into every pore, she wondered how the hell she had gotten from a polite inquiry at the doorway to lying underneath Kit with his hand down her knickers. With shaking hands she fastened her cargo pants and, without looking at Kit, sat up and swung her legs over the side of the bed.

"I'm so sorry," Kit said, reaching for her arm to slow her down. "I don't know what got into me. I shouldn't have—"

"Not at all," Abbey said quickly, with frightening politeness. "It's my fault. I—"

"No, no, it's not you," Kit said vehemently. "It's just—" He wanted to tell her why it was not right. Why it was too soon. Why he should really thank Lucy for stopping it. But he didn't want to hurt her.

"Let's just forget about it, shall we?" Abbey said, as Kit floundered on the bed. "I didn't realize that you and Lucy were—" She stood up and straightened her T-shirt. "Whatever."

"We're not," insisted Kit, wondering if the situation could be any worse. "I told her to come talk to me. She thinks she's going to be a bad mother like Jesus. Abbey, can we talk about this?"

Abbey didn't want to talk. She didn't want to think. She wanted to have sex. Not so badly that she would steal Kit Stephens away from the arms of a pregnant nineteen-year-old. But badly enough all the same. So, they really were all bastards. And she'd thought it was just the two she'd met so far. Well, if Kit Stephens thought she was going to be hurt by this rejection he could think again. There was a queue a mile long in front of him.

"I think all it's safe to say," she said, turning toward him but not meeting his gaze, which was anyway lingering on a spot on the bedspread, "is that it's too soon for both of us and we're hardly a perfect match, in the circumstances."

Kit tried not to look at her neck and nodded. He agreed. Completely. Wholeheartedly. Or at least his head did. His nether regions, inspired no doubt by mere thoughts of the neck, were not so easily convinced.

CHAPTER SEVENTEEN

"Of course, even a Coolarney Gold will taste like shite if you don't give it enough time to mature. Sure, it's only a matter of weeks but why drink vinegar when you can have Merlot?"

JOSEPH FEEHAN, from *The Cheese Diaries*,
RTE Radio Archives

*L*ucy was milking as fast as "So Long, Farewell" would let her.

The Marias were unimpressed by her ill humor and her fellow milkmaids were not far behind in that consensus although less inclined to kick the bucket. She'd been in a filthy mood for three days now, ever since discovering "that wrinkled old tart," as she called Abbey, fornicating with Kit.

"Well, why shouldn't she?" Wilhie had demanded when they had extracted the truth after the first day of her evil gloom. "It's a free country, innit?"

If Lucy had been capable of putting words to her feelings, she would have argued that she wanted Kit to be free to fornicate with her, given that he was the one human being on the planet on the same level as her and she needed him desperately. Instead, she said nothing, but her face spoke for her.

"You've got the hots for him, haven't you, you silly cow?" Jack had roared. "He's too old for you, Lucy. And why would he want a pregnant nineteen-year-old when he can have, um, anyone else?"

She hadn't meant her words to be hurtful but they seared Lucy like a red-hot barbecue grill plate. Jack was right. Who would want a pregnant nineteen-year-old? No one she knew, that was for sure, she thought, wrenching on Maria's udder.

"Lucy." She felt a tap on her shoulder and Avis's face was suddenly in hers. "How would you like it if someone pulled your teats like that?"

Lucy narrowed her eyes. "As long as *The Sound of* bleeding *Music* wasn't playing in the background it would be all feckin' right," she said.

"Well," said Avis, standing up and pulling her fawn-colored cardigan over her middle in a gesture of indignation, "such a rude and unfeeling young woman probably wouldn't want the sort of news I was about to deliver. So, I'll leave you to it. I just hope it's not me that has to come and pick bits of gray matter off the dairy floor when one of these fine expensive good-hearted animals of ours decides to trample your little head into the dust for being so bold." Avis turned on her heels and strode out of the dairy, leaving Lucy glowering at Maria's hind leg, trapped in her nastiness.

"Wait a moment," she called crankily, but Avis kept walking.

Lucy stood up and aimed an angry kick at her stool. It skittered underneath Maria, who gave it a swift left-hinder and sent it scooting under the bail in Jack's direction, where it took out her near-full pail of milk, splashing next-door Wilhie, who'd been having Braxton-Hicks all night and was nearly delirious with tiredness. The chain reaction of swearing drowned out Julie Andrews, the Captain, all the von Trapps, and most of the orchestra. Lucy turned her back on the din, extricated herself from her stall and stomped after Avis, who could move remarkably quickly for someone of her age and stature.

"I said, wait a moment!" she called, breaking into a run when it became obvious that Avis was not going to stop for her. "Didn't you hearing me calling you?" Lucy said crossly when she caught up, well clear of the dairy and in view of the factory.

Avis stopped and turned to her. "It's about time you snapped out of it and faced a few facts, young lady," she said, her smile and kindly face belying her crisp tone. "You might get away with this sort of behavior at home but in this family it is not tolerated. We will offer you all the help and support you need, Lucy, but in return we expect at the least a little kindness, at the most a little gratitude, neither of which you have displayed in the past three days to ourselves or the Marias, who have done nothing, as far as I know, to deserve the treatment you are meting out to them."

Lucy, in her embarrassment, took refuge back in her nastiness. "They're only stupid cows," she said sulkily.

"Well, around here, Lucy, we treat stupid cows with the same respect with which we treat everybody else," Avis said looking at her pointedly.

Lucy blushed at the inference but bit her tongue.

Avis appreciated this small concession and softened slightly. "Listen, Lucy," she said, "I don't know what is going on inside that pretty little head of yours but the

truth of the matter is that no one ends up here, as I think
Mr. Feehan has already told you, unless there's a shortage
of other places who will have them. You had better face
the fact that you're pregnant, Lucy. You are working as a
milkmaid. You are going to have a baby. You are going to be
a mother. Whether you stay a mother or not is up to you—
that's a big decision and one there's no rush to make.
However," she continued, "what you decide will affect the
rest of your life and the rest of your baby's life so you need
to do quite a bit of growing up between now and the day
you bring him or her into the world."

Lucy opened her mouth to protest but instead burst
into tears.

"But Kit's in love with Abbey," she sobbed. "I saw them
doing it and you can just tell by the way they're horrible to
each other."

Avis looked at her in surprise. You just never knew
which way the wind blew in these parts, she thought to
herself. "And what's wrong with Kit being in love with
Abbey?" she asked, in a kinder tone all the same.

"I want him to be in love with me," Lucy wept, seeming
younger than ever. "He's gorgeous." And she launched
herself, sobbing, at Avis's bosom. It was quite some time
before Avis eventually managed to deliver the good news
that one of Jesus's babies had been found alive and well in
Ruby O'Toole's knitting bag.

Fee, meanwhile, was sitting at the kitchen table belching up large chunks of Tessie's homemade marmalade. It
was nearly seven, Abbey and Kit were due any moment
now at the factory for their fourth attempt at cheesemaking and Corrie had just announced that today, for
the first time since the Greek flu of 1972, he wasn't
going to work. He was going to stay at home with a John

le Carré novel and a Camembert and wait for his morning tipple.

"You can't leave me alone over there with those miserable bollockses," Fee protested. "I'll freeze to death stuck between the two of them."

"It serves you right. You keep telling me everything will be all right," Corrie said, "but in the absence of any evidence—"

"All right, all right," Fee interrupted rudely, banging his mug of tea on the table. "Thank you for your input, Mr. Kavanagh QC. Evidence, me arse." He sat there looking grumpy. The truth was that the cheesemaking was not coming together as quickly as he needed it to. He already knew what today's curd would taste like. Like it had his grandmother's toenail clippings in it. And they hadn't called her The Old Crow for nothing. He looked across the table at his old friend and noticed his poor color. The past few days had taken their toll. Fee straightened up and stretched his aching back.

"You've trusted me before, Joseph," he said, "and you can trust me now, evidence or no evidence. They've got the chemistry, even you can see that, they just need the time. And in the absence of time, they need a bit of a shove."

"You talk about them like they're cheeses but they're not," Corrie said almost gruffly. "They're people. They're made of flesh and blood and we don't know what's gone into them so far. Chemistry or not, they don't seem to like each other and they're making cheese that tastes like toe jam."

And I'm the one supposed to know what people are thinking, thought Fee.

"Not to mention," Corrie was still going, "you said

there was no time to waste and that was three days ago, which means three days have been wasted."

Fee said nothing. He didn't make the rules, he just knew when they were going to be broken.

"It can't be Abbey," Corrie was saying. "She's family. She's one of us. Our flesh and blood. It must be Kit. We've been fools to think a boy from New York City with no ties to Coolarney at all could make cheese just because he turned up at the right time. I know you like him, Joseph, but don't you think his teeth are too straight? I think his teeth are too straight. There's been something bugging me about him since the moment I clapped eyes on him and I'm pretty sure now it's those great big teeth."

Fee looked at Corrie as though he were mad and shook his head in disgust. "Just because he turned up on time?" he repeated. "There's only one fool here and it's you, Joseph Corrigan, if you're doubting him on those grounds. Turning up on time is all that matters, as if I need to tell you. It's all about timing. Everything is about timing. I've told you this a million times and still you don't believe me. I'm disappointed in you, Joseph, I really am."

Corrie sighed. There had to be a reason why timing wasn't enough in this instance, but there was no point arguing this further with Fee now that he had pulled the disappointment card, which he only used when desperate.

"I still say it's the teeth," he muttered as Avis appeared from the hallway with a photo album under her arm and a smile a mile wide.

"Oh, it's the teeth, all right," she agreed, making much of bustling in between them and opening the 1970s album and pointing to a photo in the top right-hand corner of the page. It was of a beautiful dark-haired woman, about six months pregnant, smiling radiantly at the camera with a very tall, solemn-looking man, slightly balding, standing behind her. She was wearing a red-and-white gingham sleeveless shirt, flared out to accommodate her pregnancy, and red trousers.

"Greta," said Corrie, recognizing her immediately and running a finger over her face, then stopping, his eyes widening, as he realized the significance of her smile.

"It's the teeth!" Fee whistled.

"They're Kit's teeth," Avis said proudly. "I thought I'd seen them somewhere before. And then when he mentioned his mother being a cheese fan. Well, things like that don't happen around here without there being a reason."

"Greta?" Corrie asked her, in amazement.

"Kit's mother was a Coolarney girl," Fee said delightedly, clapping his chubby little hands with glee. Corrie looked at him for a split second then reached across and slapped him across the back of the head.

"Jaysus!" Fee was stunned. "What did you do that for?"

"Why didn't you tell me Kit's mammy was a Coolarney girl?" Corrie demanded.

"I just did," answered Fee indignantly, rubbing his ear.

"But Avis had already told me," shouted Corrie.

"Well, why do I always have to be first?" Fee retorted.

"Because you are the one who—"

Avis stepped back and reached around the outsides of the two men's heads, clapping one hand over each of their mouths as she did so.

"Gentlemen," she said, resting one head against each enormous bosom, "we have just made a very reassuring discovery that should be cause for celebration, not shouting at each other like common guttersnipes. I don't know what has gotten into everyone today. There's trouble in the air. No wonder the cheese tastes like a certain grandmother's toenail clippings. What would be the chance of a

Coolarney getting a bit of peace and quiet around here, I don't know."

She slowly took her hands away and Corrie and Fee remained silent.

"Tea anyone?" Avis asked, and they both nodded dumbly.

"A Coolarney mum, eh?" Corrie marveled eventually, the beginnings of a long-lost smile playing on his lips. "Next best thing to flesh and blood wouldn't it be, Joey?"

"Remind me about Greta, would you?" Fee asked Avis.

Avis sat down at the table, her hands clasping the teapot as a fond, dreamy look wandered over her face. "Oh, I remember the day she arrived like it was yesterday, don't you, Joseph?"

Corrie smiled and nodded. He did, as a matter of fact. Greta had been one of the best milkmaids they'd ever had and an excellent Scrabble player to boot. She'd been a favorite, inasmuch as he let himself have favorites.

"She came up the drive with her brother, Morris—they were twins, weren't they? Anyway, he was the most handsome young man you can imagine—gorgeous—and Greta sitting there beside him, glowing with health and what turned out to be little Christopher."

Greta, Avis reminded Corrie and Fee, had been on vacation in Europe with her brother when she had succumbed to the charms of a lanky French saxophone player after much cheap Chianti and a jam session at the 606 Club in London's Chelsea. She'd settled in beautifully at Coolarney House, but six months into her pregnancy was visited by an old school friend with whom she'd been corresponding who begged her to marry him and return home his wife.

"Do you remember him?" Avis asked Fee. "You must. We've not had that many rescued before. He was that nervous, the long streak of misery. Oh, my heart went out to the poor soul, and she was that happy to see him. Look at the smile on her." Avis turned to the photo again. "What a beautiful girl."

Avis wondered how long the smile had stayed on Greta Stephens's face. She knew that the girl had gone home, heavy with child, with Ben Stephens's ring on her finger, but that her father would not speak to her. She knew that Morris had gone on to study architecture even though it was his sister's dream, not his. She knew that Greta had given birth to a bouncing baby boy named Christopher but that was all. Greta had stopped writing when the baby was still small, each letter before then slightly sadder and more disappointed than the last one. Avis filled in the gaps in Greta's life, knowing where she was headed as a twenty-year-old, and where she had ended up, sitting now in a rest home, her head full of the adventures she'd never managed to have.

"She should have stayed here," she said to the two old men. "She should have had the baby here and gone on with her life."

"I'm sure her family would not agree with you there," Corrie said. "I'm sure her family think she did go on with her life. And she certainly seems to have done a fine job of bringing up Kit, more or less," he added, remembering the reason why Kit was here. "Anyway," he said to Avis, "you know as well as we all do that just because you don't end up leading the life you thought you would, it doesn't mean you've wasted your time." They had had this conversation many times before.

"You've got it all arse about face," interrupted Fee. "If she hadn't gone away, how would Kit have come back? We're one cheesemaker up on the whole deal so you can stop your bellyaching, the two of you."

"Do you think he knows?" Corrie asked suddenly.

"I'd say he definitely doesn't know," Avis answered vehemently.

"Can we tell him?" Fee asked excitedly. "It might speed the whole thing up a bit."

"No!" Avis and Corrie cried in unison. "You know our policy on that sort of thing," Avis scolded. "What happens on the farm stays on the farm and no exceptions."

"But doesn't he have the right to—"

"No!" Avis and Corrie closed him down again. "Don't you breathe a word, Joseph Feehan," Avis warned. "Not a word."

Fee finished his tea with a loud smack of his lips and stood up. "But if he knew about—"

"No!"

Fee lifted and then dropped his round little shoulders in an exaggerated huff. He knew they were right and he would not interfere, but it wasn't going to be easy.

"Still," he said to himself, shaking his head, as he went out the kitchen door, "a Coolarney girl all the same. Now, if that doesn't make sense I don't know what does." Warmed by this latest development, even if he did have to keep it to himself, he hurried over to the factory, where it came as a shock to find the temperature as frosty as it had been the day before, and the day before that. Kit and Abbey were silently cutting the curd, doing an excellent job, Fee had to admit, but he could just as easily have cut the air between them. The tension ricocheted around the well-scrubbed floors and counters and pinged off the vats and molds, rattling the whole room with its horrible silence.

Fee's back was killing him and he knew without even tasting it that the curd was plain but Ruby and Marie claimed the so-so cheese they had been producing was actually doing them a favor. They had months of back orders for cooking cheese that they had been unable to fill until now, so producing the stuff wasn't a total waste of time. With this in mind, he tried to put his bad temper and aching back behind him, and started to help Abbey and Kit pack the molds. Before long, though, the chilly atmosphere got to him. It was as clear as a bell that the two of them had what it took so why they didn't just get on with it he couldn't fathom.

"For feck's sake," he suddenly growled at the pair of them, as the last mold was packed and dripping its quick-time drip on the floor, "if the fecking curd wasn't sour already, it fecking would be now. Will the two of yis go downstairs and turn the Blues, I'm sick of the sound of you."

Like sulky schoolchildren, Abbey and Kit turned and headed for the stairs, entering the Blue room wordlessly. Kit washed his hands in the basin by the door as Abbey stood behind him waiting to do the same. He swore he could feel her breath on his shoulder blade and started to sweat slightly before heading to the opposite end of the room, leaving Abbey to start on the racks nearest the door.

This was the first time they had been alone in a small place since the near-sex episode of three days before, and he felt slightly panicked. His head and his body had totally different opinions about Abbey, and it made being close to her physically difficult, to say the least. He had tried to avoid her as much as possible over the past few days, outside their cheesemaking duties of course, but found his thoughts crowded with lustful apparitions of her when he was on his own. There was no doubt in his mind that a weird sort of chemistry existed between the two of them, but he hadn't the faintest clue what to do about it.

She didn't like him and he didn't like her, and the sooner his hormones got a grip on that, the better. Crouching to turn the cheeses on the lowest shelf, he glimpsed through the racks and saw Abbey's hands snake deftly around a perfect Coolarney Blue and flip it. She did have very nice hands, he tried not to notice. Practical and no-nonsense but still the hands of a woman.

His own hands sought out his next cheese and turned it. The rind felt cool and slightly damp to touch, and the sound it made as he dropped it back on the rack was a good sound. It was as though the cheese sighed a happy sigh when it got back on familiar territory. As though just a nanosecond out of its comfort zone was a nanosecond too long. You knew where you were with cheese, Kit thought. You knew what it needed and how to give it that. He sup-posed that was what Fee had been trying to tell them the first day they gathered down here, when Abbey had freaked out and run away. All you had to do was look after the stuff to a certain point and then you could rely on it finishing the job itself. He realized that he and Abbey were turning the cheeses in perfect time, the muffled "pflumpf" of the cheeses' overturned sides hitting the rack simultaneously, forming a fractured, almost funky, beat. He peered through the racks again as Abbey's hands, a rack higher now, worked their magic.

She had good wrists, too, Kit thought. He'd never noticed that before. Just the right size for her hands, with a sexy knobble of bone jutting out and rolling around as she lifted and turned. He lifted and turned some more himself and tried not to think about her. Instead, he found himself pondering her husband. What sort of a man would Abbey be married to? A bastard, surely, to be cheating on her when she was so incredibly—he checked himself. This was ridiculous. He wasn't some pimply teenager seething with testosterone; he was a grown man and could control himself. He thought for a moment he could smell her fresh passion-fruit smell but then realized that meant he wasn't controlling himself and so began instead to think of state capitals, starting with Alaska.

Abbey, too, could hardly ignore the uninvited tension that appeared between herself and Kit whenever they were in the same room and was also trying to quash it. Kit was a sexual predator hell bent on deflowering her, Lucy, most likely Jack, Wilhie and even Avis O'Regan, she tried to convince herself as her fingers sought the moist sides of the fresh Coolarneys and flipped them. He was a prick of the highest order and she should have reported him to the, um . . . she wondered who she should have reported him to. Her grandfather? Hmm. His mother? Hmm. And anyway, what would she report? She was the one who had gone to his bed and felt his head. But he seemed ill, she argued with herself. But you could have established that from the doorway, herself came back. But I tried that and it didn't work, she continued. And kissing him did? herself countered sarcastically.

It was hopeless trying to think of anything else, she realized. They should just turn all the cheeses and get the hell out of there before the whole place went up in smoke or melted or something. She'd spent the three days since the embarrassing close encounter trying to work out what to do with her life and where to do it. On one hand, it seemed pathetic that she was twenty-nine years old and had nowhere else to go apart from her grandfather's farm in the country. But on the other hand, the feeling that she constantly fought about being in the wrong place at the wrong time had diminished over the past few days to the point where she suspected that the funny little buzz she got in her belly when she woke up in the morning meant she was close to being home. Not to mention, she reminded herself as she moved a rack closer to the middle of the room, the way she felt about the cheese.

The swoosh of the milk into the vat first thing in the morning made her bones tingle. She swore the blood pulsed quicker through her veins at the very sight of it. After just four days she could feel muscles in her arms high-fiving each other with every slice of the curd-cutting paddle. And the feel of the sweet, squeaky stuff between her fingers? It made her want to scream, the same way the feel of the fat, soft, spongy arm of a happy milk-fed baby made her want to scream. In a good way.

She leaned in toward a cheese hiding at the back of the rack and found herself staring suddenly into Kit's troubled green eyes, peering at her from the other side. Abbey sucked in her breath and stood back. They had met in the middle of the room.

"Do you want to talk about this?" Kit said, mooching down slightly to look at her across the top of a tasty two-week-old.

"Talk?" she repeated, flustered, her heart beating a little too quickly for her liking. "About what?"

"About this whole thing," Kit said, absently turning another cheese. He hadn't meant to say anything at all, especially anything like that, but it had just popped out. "I mean I don't really know what's going on either but it seems to be bigger than both of us and I think we should talk about it."

"I'm not sure what you mean," Abbey said uncertainly, her hands reaching out for another Coolarney.

Kit sighed. He didn't want to be doing this. It was tough. His hands locked on a cheese, midtwist. "Abbey," he said, "please don't make this any harder than it is. I think you know as well as I do that ever since that first night there has been this great big scary sort of hot kind of thing between us and whether we like it or not it is there and as mature adults we should decide what we want to do about it."

Abbey was frightened by his honesty. In a thrilled sort of a way. Scary sort of hot?

"Corrie and Fee want us to make cheese together," she said lamely, her own hands tightly gripping an as yet unturned cheese.

"I'm not talking about cheese," said Kit, squeezing his own so hard in frustration that he rendered it unsaleable. "I'm talking about you and me and whatever the hell this zing is between us. Jesus, Abbey, I have spent three days trying to fight it but I just can't stop thinking about you. Every moment of the day you're either there right in front of me or inside my head. I can't explain it but it's driving me nuts and I want to talk about it."

"You Americans just want to talk about everything," Abbey said, attempting a lighter tone and failing. Kit said nothing, and it was her turn to sigh. He looked pretty done in, and she felt sorry for him. It had been brave to bring the whole humiliating subject up, and the least she could do was admit she knew what he was talking about.

"It's the same," she finally said, digging her thumbnails into the Coolarney she was still gripping. "It's the same for me. I don't know what to do about it, either. I don't know what to do about anything."

"You can't stop thinking about me?" Kit asked, looking at her, a bit of color creeping back into his cheeks, a light in his eye.

"You're not even my type," insisted Abbey, ignoring the question.

"Oh, that's okay," Kit added enthusiastically. "That's fine. That's great, in fact. You're not my type, either."

There was another silence.

"It's just that I haven't felt like this about anyone for a long, long time and I'm not sure that I want to now," Abbey said slowly, realizing as she spoke that it was true.

"Well, if it's any consolation, I definitely don't want to, but I still do," Kit said. "Does that make sense?"

They looked at each other across the cheeses. Kit had never noticed before how quiet the curing room was. Dead quiet. He could swear the Blues were listening.

"So," Abbey asked, "how would it work?"

"You mean us?" Kit answered. "I don't know. I guess we could decide that as long as we are both here making cheese then we should stop fighting whatever it is that's in the air that's making us so crazy for each other."

"You're crazy for me?" Abbey asked, smiling, releasing her grip, finally, on the poor mashed Coolarney Blue in her hands and starting to move slowly toward the end of the rack.

"Yeah." Kit smiled, dumping his own strangled cheese and moving in the same direction. "I am. You know, in a wanting-to-get-naked kind of way." They met, face to face, at the end of the rack and looked at each other.

"What about—" Abbey started to say but Kit put his finger to her lips. It tasted of honey and sunshine and blue mold and him.

"What about nothing," he said, and he took her in his arms and kissed her like he'd never kissed anybody before.

"What in the name of Jesus do you two think you are doing?"

Avis's loud hiss gave Corrie and Fee such a fright that they rose from their crouched positions outside the Blue door with great speed, bonking their heads together in the process.

"Jaysus feck," cried Fee, holding his temples with both hands. "You've broken it."

"What do you keep in there, you eejit, bowling balls?" Corrie moaned, rubbing the front of his own head where a medium-sized egg was already forming.

"You two should be ashamed of yourselves," Avis said, towering over them, hands on hips. "Grown men eavesdropping on two troubled young people. It's disgusting."

"We were not eavesdropping," said Corrie, wobbling on his feet. "I dropped something on the floor and Fee was helping me look for it."

"Oh, yes," said Avis, "and what would that be?"

"Something very, very small," said Fee, concentrating on his head still.

"Is that right?" Avis said, not letting up. "How small?"

The two men looked at each other. "So small it doesn't even have a name," Fee said proudly.

Corrie rolled his eyes, whimpering at the pain this caused in his head. "Is that the best you can come up with? So small it doesn't even have a name?"

"It's a terrible thing, concussion," Fee answered cheerfully, earning an extra headshake from Avis.

"Go away and leave them alone," she said, "before I take my broom to the pair of you."

"Go on," said Fee, a mischievous glint in his eye, "you want to know just as much as we do."

"Of course I do," said Avis, "but I'm not going to listen in on them. You should know better than to show such disrespect for other people's privacy, Joseph. Anyway, I only came to tell you that it's low-blood-sugar time so I've left a freshly baked raisin bread and a pot of tea in the smoking room. If you get over there now it'll still be hot."

*   *   *

Abbey was so hungry for Kit she couldn't think straight. Their kisses were desperate with unleashed passion and their hands were tracing hurried routes over each other's body as though scared they would never find their way to the good bits again. Abbey was pressed against the wall and had one leg wrapped around Kit's thigh, her groin pushed hard against his as his kisses devoured her. Her bottom half had long surrendered to his touch but her mind was still fighting something, not him, but something.

"I'm not sure," she whispered to the ceiling as his lips burned up her neck. "Perhaps we could . . ." she mumbled as his mouth found hers and nibbled at her lips, a helpless groan escaping him. "Oh," she tried again, as she smelled the clean freshness of his hair and he fitted his knee up between her thighs, lifting her higher against the wall.

"Kit," she cried, louder, suddenly sure what was wrong and pulling her head away from him in panic. "Not here!"

Her fear finally registered with him and he stepped back, panting. She was trembling, and not, he was certain, because of him.

"Not here," she said again.

"What is it, Abbey?" he asked as gently as a man knobbled in the throes of wild passion could. "What's the matter?"

"Not down here, that's all. Just not down here," she said, not meeting his eyes. Frustration wasn't a big enough word for what Kit was feeling. He knew she wanted him as much as he wanted her and he couldn't for the life of him work out why she was pulling the plug. She wasn't a tease, he was sure of that, but her flakiness was certainly confusing.

"Here, there, anywhere," he said. "Does it really matter?"

"It's not you," Abbey said. "It's here."

Kit thought again of her flight from the curing room on their first cheesemaking day. "Did something happen to you down here?" he asked. "Did something bad happen to you down here?"

Abbey felt hysteria nipping at her edges. She knew it was stupid, that she was stupid, but she couldn't fight the fear. "Not me," she said, as Kit put his hands on her shoulders and leaned down to make sure he was looking in her eyes.

"Then who? What happened? Tell me."

"My grandmother," Abbey whispered, tears gathering in pools at the bottom of her big brown eyes. "My mother told me . . . Oh my God, I can't believe I'm telling you this." She took a deep breath. "I think my grandmother is buried down here," she said. "I think Corrie buried her here."

Kit's eyes widened.

"You think Corrie buried your grandmother down here in the caves?" he asked.

Abbey nodded, an enormous weight lifting off her shoulders at the relief of having shared her terrible doubts about a man they were all convinced was so kind and sweet and helpful and dear.

"Why?" asked Kit. "What's wrong with the cemetery?"

"Oooh." Abbey shook her head and banged her clenched fists against the wall behind her in frustration. "You don't understand. I think he buried her—in secret—after, you know, doing away with her."

"Doing away with her?" Kit asked incredulously.

She nodded.

"With his own bare hands?"

She nodded again, although she hadn't actually thought about that.

"You think he did away with his wife with his own bare hands and then buried her down here with all this beautiful cheese under this stone floor that we're standing on right now?"

Abbey nodded, her tears spilling over her cheeks.

"This stone floor?" Kit asked again, stamping one of his feet on the ground. "This smooth, flat, unlined floor with no body-sized holes in it?"

Abbey nodded again. "I suppose," she said.

"What are you? Nuts?" Kit said, lifting his hands off her. "You think your own grandfather would do something like that? Jesus, Abbey, you have no idea how ridiculous that sounds. I mean does the guy really strike you as a murderer?"

It took a few moments for Abbey to realize that Kit was not agreeing with her. The weight came back and landed squarely on her shoulders again. Why had she told him?

"Well, what would you know?" she said, angry at having let down her guard. "You don't know anything about him."

"Yeah, well, you don't know anything about him either," Kit said, not unpleasantly exactly but with some frustration. "You've been gone since you were five and your mom has obviously been filling your head with garbage about the poor guy. But think about it, Abbey. Would your grandfather really want a rotting cadaver stinking up the very air that he relies on for the flavor of his precious cheese?"

"That's my grandmother you're talking about," Abbey said angrily, but Kit just laughed.

"Corrie, a murderer? Jesus, he must have laughed his head off when you put that to him. I mean, what did he say? Did he confess immediately and beg to be brought to justice?"

Abbey looked away and Kit knew then, for sure, that

she had not asked her grandfather about his wife, that that was the reason why she stiffened whenever he came into a room and seemed so uneasy in his presence.

"Oh, for Pete's sake, Abbey," he said. His heart, to his own surprise, was suddenly full of sympathy for her. She was so complicated it wasn't funny. It was very unfunny. She hung her head.

"It sounds silly, I know, now that I say it out loud," she said. "But why else would she run away and never come back? Why else would she keep me away from him all these years? You don't do that stuff for nothing, you know." She wiped her nose with the back of her hand and Kit pulled her toward him and took her in his arms.

"I don't know why she did what she did," he answered truthfully, "but I do know you need to talk to your grand-father about all this." He leaned back and pulled Abbey's chin up so he could look her in the eye. "And I promise that when he calls the Twinkie-mobile to come and drag you to the nearest nut farm, I will fight him with all the strength in my body."

If I have any left, he thought to himself, after all the effort of not throwing you to the ground and having you right here and now, dead murdered rotting cadaverous grandmother or not.

CHAPTER EIGHTEEN

"Your troubles are like germs, you can't bring them into the cheese factory. Cheese is sensitive, it can tell if something is weighing heavy on your heart, and in my experience, it doesn't give a shite. It wants you to feck right off and come back when you're able."

JOSEPH FEEHAN, from *The Cheese Diaries*,
RTE Radio Archives

*C*orrie and Fee were sitting in the smoking room with an aged cheddar Fee had filched out of the *fromagerie*. Avis's tea had gone cold, and anyway they both felt their separate headaches would be improved with a bit of a tipple.

Corrie had something he knew would be perfect for the match and was not even halfway to the wine rack when Fee crowed with delight.

"You're right," he said. "A Chilean Merlot. Who would have thought?"

"You won't know this one," said Corrie. "I got it sent over from London specially."

"Casa Lapostolle Clos Apalta, if that's how you say it," said Fee. "Well done yourself."

Corrie was torn between being highly impressed and

highly irritated. Was there nothing he could do to surprise the little toad? The little toad looked at him and shook his head, beaming from ear to ear as he watched the wine being opened.

"Is shitey a word, do you think?" he asked, changing the subject and stretching his fat little legs out in front of him.

"As in what?" Corrie asked.

"As in 'The day started quite well and then turned shitey,'" Fee answered.

"Did you really think it started well?" Corrie said.

"I'm not talking about today," said Fee, "I'm talking about shitey."

"Well, I think today started out shitey, got a bit less shitey, then a bit more shitey, and will hopefully not be so shitey again," said Corrie, rubbing the egg on his forehead as he let the Merlot breathe.

"So you do think it's a word, then." Fee grinned. "I thought as much. Well, now we have that settled do you think you could do us all a favor and cheer up a bit?"

The truth was, Corrie was scared to be happy. They thought they had overheard hopeful sounds coming from the curing room, but what say they were wrong?

"For the love of God!" cried Fee, reading his thoughts. "Would it kill you to look on the bright side for a bit? Abbey's come home, there's a fellow wants to make cheese and who knows what else with her, the sun is shining and everything is going to be all right."

"I'm not sure she likes him," said Corrie. "And I'm not sure she's wild about us either."

"She seems to like me all right," Fee said. "So what could she possibly have against you?"

Corrie sliced off a chunk of mature cheese and scooped it into his mouth, its zesty zing giving him a brief respite from his depression. "Well, I can't be absolutely sure," he said slowly, "but she seems to be scared of me, Joseph, and all I can think is that Rose has been telling her things that have frightened her."

Fee took a sip of wine and savored it, then swallowed. "So," he said eventually, "she knows they're not your own teeth?"

Corrie ignored the poor attempt at humor and pressed on. "It'll be to do with Maggie, like it always was. I think Rose might have been up to her old tricks again, Joseph, telling Abbey stories about Maggie. Her favorite stories."

"And what makes you think that?" Fee asked.

"Because why would anybody be scared of me? God knows I've made mistakes but I've always tried my best to do what is right—well, what Rose wanted and what is right and they weren't always one and the same but I tried my best. I just wonder . . ."

Fee swallowed and licked his lips. "You wonder what?"

"I wonder if perhaps my best wasn't good enough," said Corrie.

"Don't be so feckin' hard on yourself, Joseph," Fee answered. "You weren't a bad father at all—you just didn't have the ideal daughter. It happens. Sure, you're not the only one who's had a hard row to hoe as far as their children are concerned, you know."

"I do know but she's my only child and Abbey's her only child; they are all I have so I must have done something terrible to end up without either of them. I don't know, Joseph. I just don't know." For the first time in a long time, he felt his age. He felt old and achey and slightly confused and not sure what to do about any of it. He had thought having Abbey back home would be the best thing that could ever happen to him. He had waited for it for so long.

Yet, here she was and here he was. The two of them, miserable.

And the cheese, more miserable again. Fine for cooking no doubt, but where was the magic? And Fee. You wouldn't know to look at him, tucking into the crumbly cheddar, that his days were numbered, but the curd was never wrong. And did he seem even slightly bothered by the distressing turn events had taken? He did not, thought Corrie, sinking further into the mire.

Just then, Abbey burst in the door. It was the first Corrie had seen of her all day and she looked flushed and defiant yet anxious at the same time. He'd been right to think she was scared of him and it saddened his old heart more than anything else that had happened.

Fee's fat hand stretched out for another chunk of cheese and it was all he could do to keep a smile off his face. Perhaps, now, they were going to get somewhere.

"What happened to my grandmother?" Abbey demanded breathlessly, standing, legs apart, arms folded, in front of Corrie. "What did you do to her?"

Corrie put down his wine glass and looked at Fee in an I-told-you-so sort of a way. He couldn't help but notice how much Abbey looked like her mother, standing there in front of him, raging. Yet even in her fury there was a softness to Abbey that he realized at that moment Rose had never, ever had.

"I don't know what your mother has told you," he started.

"Don't give me that shite," Abbey interrupted rudely, shaking her head angrily. "I am sick of all that shite. I've had a lifetime of shite."

"It's shitey, wouldn't you say?" Fee interjected, earning a dark look from both of them.

"I've asked you a direct question," Abbey said, hands on her hips now, "and I want a direct answer. What happened to my grandmother?"

"There's nothing I can tell you about your grandmother that will make anybody feel any better," Corrie said calmly, but Fee could see his hands were trembling. "There's no good can come from it."

"Well, I can't stay here if I don't know," Abbey said, stamping her foot like a five-year-old. "I can't and I won't."

Good girl yourself, Fee thought from the sidelines. Perhaps she had balls after all.

"Well, I can't tell you," Corrie said sadly. "But I don't want you to go."

"Well, I think you should tell her," Fee piped up.

"And what would you know?" Corrie said crossly.

"More than the two of you put together," Fee answered.

"Excuse me," Abbey said, trying to steer the conversation back to herself. It was now or never, she knew. "What can't you tell me?"

"There you go," said Fee. "If you tell her what it is you can't tell her, then officially you haven't really told her."

"Don't be ridiculous," Corrie said to his friend. "You've been watching too much *Father Ted*. I keep telling you that real life's not like that."

"Don't be such a stick-in-the-mud," Fee said robustly. "Real life's what you make of it. Just put the poor girl out of her misery."

"Ah, Joseph." Corrie shook his head. "Didn't we always say . . . ?"

"Ah, Joseph, yourself," Fee scoffed. "Didn't we always say we didn't want the truth to hurt anybody but it's not knowing the truth that's hurting yer woman. I don't want to put any pressure on you, Joseph, but as she holds the future to the entire Coolarney empire right there in her hot little hands, why don't you just go ahead and tell her?"

Abbey turned and looked at Fee, who was filling his glass again. She swore for a moment she could actually see the aura of unusual emanating from his armchair.

"There's nothing to be gained from dredging up the past," Corrie insisted.

Abbey could not believe his callousness. "I'm not asking you to exhume her," she said incredulously. "I'm asking you to tell me what you did to her."

Exhume her? Fee mouthed across the room. So Rose had been up to her old tricks.

"Holy Mary, Mother of God," Corrie said. "Sit down, Abbey. It's really not what you think." There really was nothing else for it. He looked at Fee, took a deep breath and faced his granddaughter. "Your grandmother left me for another woman," he said.

Abbey was stunned. "For another woman?" she repeated stupidly. "Who?"

"Mary-Therese McGrath," Fee answered. "The one-time future Mrs. Joseph Feehan."

Corrie and Fee both reached for the cheese.

"Another couple of weeks," Fee said, holding up a wedge of the zingy cheddar, "and it would be eating us."

"My grandmother ran off with your girlfriend?" Abbey looked at Fee.

"Fiancée," Fee said nonchalantly, licking his lips, "and that's the truth of the matter."

Abbey's head was awhirl. Whatever she had expected Corrie to tell her, it wasn't that. Her defiance fizzled out, leaving confusion in its place. "So she's not dead, then?" she checked.

"Not according to the latest postcard," Corrie answered.

"Postcard?" echoed Abbey.

"Ah, sure we get a postcard once a year from the two of them. Alive and well and living it up in Portugal," said Corrie uncomfortably. "They're having a grand old time."

"Apparently they cook a very nice chicken in Portugal," Fee added. "And of course they have their own swimming pool."

Abbey was totally flummoxed. So her grandmother was living in Portugal with a woman, eating nice chicken and swimming in a pool. She was not underneath the curing room floor at all. Which left a flurry of questions to be answered.

"Why didn't Rose tell me that?" she asked Corrie. "Why would she tell me it was you? Why does she hate you so much?"

The question sent a shooting pain through Corrie's heart. He supposed Rose did hate him and for the millionth time in his life he wondered what he had done and to whom to invite such pain.

"Well," he said, trying not to let Abbey see how shaken he was, "there are a couple of reasons for that, the first being that no twelve-year-old girl wants to believe that her mother would abandon her."

"For a sunny climate and somebody else's fiancée especially," added Fee, slipping another slug of wine into his glass. "Although she had a great set of legs on her, Mary-Therese, you have to give her that. Much better than Maggie, beef to the heels and all that."

"No twelve-year-old girl wants to believe that her mother would abandon her for anything at all," Corrie continued, ignoring him. "And rightly so. I didn't want to believe it myself."

"Well, I can understand that," said Abbey, because she

did, "but why would she come up with such a horrible story? Why would she be so awful?"

"Ah now," said Corrie, "Rose wasn't so awful. Just confused and resentful on top of being a little bit difficult in the first place." He shifted uncomfortably in his chair. It wasn't territory he enjoyed going over but he realized now that if Abbey was going to move on in her life, in his, she needed to have all the family secrets laid bare in front of her.

"Before we got the postcard we didn't know for a fact that Maggie and Mary-Therese had run away together," he explained, "although the fact they both disappeared at the same time sort of pointed in that direction. And Fee, of course, had his suspicions, although for a few years there Mary-Therese had jammed his radar or whatever he likes to call it. Anyway, for the first few days I didn't know what to tell Rose so I just said her mother had gone away and I wasn't sure when she would be coming back."

"And that was the truth," Fee interjected, his mouth stuffed with the last of the cheese. "You were telling her the truth."

"But a couple of nights after your grandmother left me—Rose was very upset, Abbey, she was very angry—she saw something that she shouldn't have and the poor girl was in such a state she sort of put two and two together and came up with, well . . ." He petered out.

"Came up with what?" Abbey demanded.

"Well, it wasn't four," Fee added, not particularly helpfully.

"What did you do? What did she see?"

"It's hard to explain," said Corrie. "There was a bit of an incident here at the house—you wouldn't be helping me out at all would you, Joseph?—after Rose went to bed and we were sort of trying to clear all that up when . . ." He petered out again, much to Abbey's exasperation.

"When what?" she cried. "What did Rose see that was so terrible?"

"It was Mr. O'Regan," Avis pronounced from the doorway. "And may God rot his soul."

The three of them turned around in surprise.

"Colonel Mustard in the ballroom," Fee, a big time *Clue* fan, breathed, impressed.

"I couldn't stand back and let you face the music on your own," Avis said, moving to Fee's grubby armchair and standing behind him, her hand on his shoulder.

"Music?" Corrie said stupidly.

"It was the dead body of Owen O'Regan," Avis continued, addressing Abbey, "and your mother saw these two precious gentlemen lumping his useless lifeless corpse across the courtyard and into the factory where they buried him under the curing-room floor."

Fee choked on his Merlot while Corrie grew as pale as a Camembert.

"Your mother got up in the night," continued Avis, looking at Abbey, her chin trembling, "and saw them from the stairway landing and thought that what she had seen was her own poor mother being done away with."

"But why was Owen O'Regan dead in the first place?" Abbey asked. "Why was he even here?"

"He was here because he followed me here after giving me the hiding of a lifetime," Avis said, tears falling on her cherry-apple cheeks. "I was pregnant with his child and I ran here for help from a mile up the road and then I pushed him down the stairs because the drunken oaf had belted me for the very last time." She was fierce now. "And I would kill him all over again if I had the chance."

There was a stunned silence.

"Actually," Fee said, "you might well get it."

"He wasn't dead, Avis," said Corrie.

It was Avis's turn to change color.

"We gave him £200 and put him on the bus to Limerick," said Fee.

"Limerick?" whispered Avis.

"Sit down, Avis," said Corrie. Abbey stood up and helped the stunned woman into her chair then perched on the arm of Corrie's recliner, a tiny gesture that warmed the cockles of the old man's heart.

"I think a glass of wine might help sort your head out," Fee said, his own hand shaking as he poured more wine into his glass and gave it to Avis.

"All these years, you thought you had killed Owen?" Corrie asked her.

Avis nodded. "It was an accident," she said. "And I really didn't mind. In fact, I thought the world was an altogether better place without him."

"And you thought we got rid of his body?" Fee asked.

"I asked you what had happened and you said not to worry," Avis replied defensively. "You said he wouldn't be bothering anyone where he was going."

"Well, I was talking about Limerick, not the great hereafter," said Fee.

There was another bewildered silence as everyone took in what had just happened.

"So no one is dead, then?" Abbey asked, just to make sure.

"That's right," agreed Corrie. "No one that we know of, anyway."

"Slip a bit more wine in here would you, Joseph," Avis said, waggling her glass in front of Fee.

"Did you never get a funny feeling, with Avis thinking she was a murderer and we were accessories?" Corrie asked Fee in a slightly accusing fashion.

Fee blushed to the roots of what little hair he had. "Not about that, no."

"And yourself always claiming to know everything in advance," Corrie said in an exasperated fashion. "Why do you know what color knickers Patsy O'Connell wears to church but not that we're harboring a murderer?"

"What's Patsy O'Connell's knickers got to do with any of it?" asked Avis.

"She's not a murderer," insisted Abbey.

"But she *thought* she was," Corrie retorted. "And he could have saved her a lot of distress by telling her that she wasn't."

"I wasn't distressed," Avis interjected. "Although I am now. All these years with Himself only in Limerick and not so much as a postcard."

"Anyway, I was only messing about the knickers," Fee grumbled. "I saw her pegging them on the clothesline. They're all purple."

"There's not a lot to be said for postcards, Avis," Corrie said. "You're probably better off without them."

"And we may have banged his head a tiny little bit getting him down the stairs to the curing room," Fee confessed. "He may have been a bit confused when he came to."

"When he came to?" Abbey asked, dumbfounded.

"He hadn't quite slept it off by the morning, but he would have worked out it was Limerick eventually," Fee said crossly. "There are signposts there, you know."

"Avis," Corrie said. "You stayed here all these years thinking we had your dead husband's body buried under the cave floor? Whatever must you think of us?"

"I think you are two of the kindest, dearest, sweetest men in all of Ireland," Avis said, blushing to the roots of her bunlike arrangement. "I thank God for the day Owen O'Regan clipped me around the ears and brought me to the two of you. I lived because of it and my baby lived because of it and there's not a minute of the day goes by without me being grateful to the two of you. You're the best sort of men and I love you both." She sipped weepily at her wine.

"There was a baby?" Abbey asked.

"Yes, there was a baby," Avis answered, smiling at her with tear-filled eyes. "The first Coolarney baby. We've had dozens more since then but my Josephine was the first."

"And she was beautiful," crooned Corrie. "Wasn't she, Joseph?"

"Beautiful," the little man replied, misty-eyed himself.

"Where is she now?" Abbey wanted to know.

"She's living up in Galway, a nurse, with two grown-up children of her own. She was adopted by a lovely couple. They were, weren't they, Joseph? A doctor and his wife. She's had a fantastic life, Josephine, she really has. I see her once or twice a year and I write every week."

"Why didn't you keep her?" Abbey couldn't keep herself from asking.

"Oh, it wasn't done in those days," Avis answered, slurping at the bottom of her empty glass, her cheeks glowing but her eyes bright and clear. "There I was, a widow, or so I thought, with nothing to my name but a month of overdue rent and a baby on the way . . ." Her voice frittered away to nothing. "That's a point," she said dazedly. "I thought I was a widow."

Fee started to squirm uncomfortably in his chair.

"But you knew I was still married." She pointed one

stout-booted toe at Fee. "So all these years that's why you never . . ."

Fee's eyes were flicking from wall to wall as though searching for an escape.

"Never what?" Corrie and his granddaughter asked in unison.

Avis suddenly snapped out of her daze. "Never nothing," she said brightly, sitting up straight. "Never nothing at all."

Abbey looked suspiciously from Avis to Fee and back again. If she wasn't mistaken, there was something in the air. "You two!" she exclaimed.

Fee and Avis swapped looks of fear and delight and guilt and joy and the absolute horror of being discovered. Corrie felt his heart slow down to a languid, loud *ba-boomp* as he sat forward in his chair, his eyes near popping out of his head.

"You two?" he whispered.

Fee and Avis remained frozen, their eyes locked on each other.

"How long has this been going on for?" Corrie finally asked in a voice that didn't sound like his.

"Only since 1977," Avis whispered.

"We were going to tell you but then Rose took Abbey and it didn't seem the right time and I thought we were better off waiting," said Fee.

"You don't mind, do you?" Avis asked, worry crinkling her brow.

"Mind?" said Corrie. "Mind?" His best friend in the world had been snatched out from underneath his very nose by a woman he'd been harboring all these years. Did he mind? He thought about it, sitting there in his La-Z-Boy rocker recliner. Well, he hadn't even noticed—so what difference did it make?

"Of course I don't mind," he said, meaning it. "In fact, I'm delighted for you, Joseph. I couldn't be more delighted. All this time I've worried about you having no family, being lonely, you old bollocks, and here you were—"

"There's no need to forget we're in mixed company," Avis interrupted rather primly.

"I didn't think you'd mind," Fee said, rather cautiously, "but I can't always trust my funny feelings where Avis is concerned." He looked up at her and smiled as she squeezed his shoulder. "She jammers my radar too, you know."

"Is there any more of that wine?" Abbey asked. It was all a bit much, really.

"And you never talked between you about whether Owen was dead or in Limerick?" Corrie asked. Fee and Avis both shook their heads.

Please God don't let them say they've got better things to do than talk, Abbey silently pleaded.

"I heard that," said Fee, and winked at her.

At the end of the second bottle, Abbey joined Corrie for a walk. He liked to go down the lane to look at the sea, he told her, especially after such excitement. It soothed him. To his great joy, Abbey wanted to go, too. She was in the mood for a bit of soothing herself, it seemed. Despite the tying of so many loose ends, she had the oddest sensation that an itch she couldn't pinpoint was still in need of scratching.

"Why didn't Rose believe you about her mam going to Portugal with Mary-Therese and the pool and all that?" she asked Corrie as they strolled in the afternoon sun.

Corrie sighed. "She couldn't contemplate that option, Abbey. It was too hard for her. She didn't want to believe it. She told me she'd seen me with the body and I told her the truth about exactly whose body it was—and a perfectly healthy one at that. But it just didn't suit her to believe me."

Abbey took his hand and gave it a squeeze. She knew all about Rose twisting the truth to suit herself.

"It was easier for her to turn her heart against me than believe that her mother would leave her for another woman, of all things," Corrie went on. "I didn't realize until later that she'd told people at school and in the village her version of events, but the ones that counted knew the truth."

"What was she like?" Abbey ventured softly. "Before me?"

"Your mother?"

There was so much to say but he didn't want to say it. Corrie wanted to tell Abbey that her mother had loved her with all her heart and that she was a good and kind woman, but he knew that simply was not true. The pain of her mother's abandonment had settled in the already-selfish Rose's heart and hardened it when she was but a child herself. He had watched his only child grow wilder and harder with every year that passed.

"She was a complicated girl who grew into a complicated woman," Corrie answered his granddaughter. "And the best thing she ever did was have you."

It was his turn to squeeze her hand.

"What about—" she faltered. "I don't suppose you know . . ."

It would be unnatural for her not to want to know, Corrie supposed.

"About your father?" he prompted. "Not exactly, no."

"Not exactly?"

"Himself back there no doubt getting stuck into bottle

number three has the details but I gave up asking about them. Sure, I never cared how you got here, Abbey, just that you did."

Abbey bit her lip. It was hard to be this near, yet this far from the truth.

"Rose would have had us believe your father was a famous disc jockey from Dublin," Corrie continued, "but Fee says he came from a little closer to home. A lot closer, in fact. Schillies to be precise."

"He's local?"

Corrie shrugged his shoulders. "Fee says your man cottoned on to the fact that he was the daddy and had a go at Rose, who pretty much came home, packed her bags and was on the next boat across the Channel."

"But why would she leave and never come back? Why would she do that?"

If there was one thing that Rose was never going to be, Corrie thought to himself, it was an ordinary small-town girl bringing up the local barman's bastard. She had dreams far grander than that.

"She got a job," he said, "modeling in London. It was what she always wanted. And she never saw a reason to come home again."

"But what about me?" Abbey asked, trying not to sound wistful. "Did you never come looking for me?"

"Abbey, she broke my heart taking you away from me. I must have been to London two dozen times and rung a thousand more," said Corrie, "but your mother would never let me in or talk to me for any length of time. There was a part of Rose that enjoyed keeping you away from me."

"And that story about the curing-room floor was to make sure I stayed away from you," said Abbey slowly. "She's a one, is she not?"

The two of them looked at each other ruefully. Rose had created a world that focused solely on herself, and the miracle was that her father and her daughter had discovered each other again, despite her best efforts.

Abbey thought about her own unknown father. There would be time, she realized, and plenty of it, to smooth out the knots and tangles of her past. In the meantime, she was happy just to be who she was, where she was, with this warm, wonderful old man.

"I feel at home here, isn't that gas?" Abbey said, looking at Corrie, her face breaking into a smile he could remember from nearly twenty-five years before. They walked home in silence, swinging their arms and savoring the sweet sensation of whatever it was they were sharing.

"I thought I might take Kit for a picnic," Abbey said shyly as they walked up the driveway. "Do you think he'd like that?"

"I think he'd be mad not to," Corrie answered. "And he doesn't strike me as being mad, compared to most, anyway. We used to go for picnics when you were small, do you remember? In the field up behind the house, behind the dairy, on this side of the hill, under the old oak tree? It'll be beautiful up there now."

When they reached the courtyard at the top of the drive, they were surprised to see the tractor idling there.

"What are you doing?" Corrie asked as Fee bustled past him with a Thermos and a biscuit tin and jumped astride the rumbling machine.

"I'll be back later," Fee said, settling himself onto the tractor saddle and moving slowly forward, then turning down the drive. "Don't wait up!"

"Where is he going?" Abbey asked. Corrie shrugged his shoulders. Fee had never learned to drive a car and very occasionally took to the road on the tractor, but for what, on this occasion, he didn't know.

"Is it just me," Abbey asked, looking at Fee's fat round bottom jiggle down the driveway on top of the old machine, "or is he totally barmy?"

"It's not just you," Corrie said fondly, and went inside to find the picnic hamper.

CHAPTER NINETEEN

"Don't think just because you've got your cheese to the curing room that the hard work is over. It's not, you can still make a poxy whore's melt of it. Imagine what would happen if even a single blue mold spore got into the Gold room? Total disaster even at that late stage in the proceedings. Blue mold in the right place is a gift from God but in the wrong place it spreads like a cancer."

JOSEPH FEEHAN, from *The Cheese Diaries*,
RTE Radio Archives

*A*bbey and Kit were sitting on a tartan blanket under the oak tree on the hill behind the house, testing their dental work on May's nut toffee. It was delicious, but something of a challenge orthodontically speaking.

It was late afternoon, and they had pretty much picked over the basket Abbey had filled earlier with fruit and sweets and a Thermos flask of coffee before hunting down Kit and inviting him up the hill for a late lunch. Feeling a freedom and happiness that she hadn't known for years, Abbey had shared the events of the smoking room with her fellow cheesemaker, who had listened and laughed and listened some more.

"I can't believe I thought that Corrie would murder his own wife," Abbey said. "It seems so ridiculous when I think about it now."

Kit rubbed his jaw, aching now from the toffee. "Yes, but there's something about this place," he said, "that makes the ridiculous seem ordinary. Have you noticed that?"

Abbey closed her eyes and let the sun and her thoughts wash over her. The usual merged with the unusual a lot more at Coolarney House than anywhere else, she agreed. But she didn't mind that. She understood it. Just like she understood, perhaps always had, that her mother was a difficult woman, at times even dangerous, but she had survived her and she was going to be the woman that Rose never had been. She had goodness in her genes, thanks to Corrie, she knew that now. And she was going to stay here and make cheese because her heart did a little somersault when she thought about it and her nose was twitching now at the ghost of the warm, wet, yeasty factory smell.

Kit watched her face, wrinkling and beaming as she thought her happy thoughts, and felt an ache that he didn't recognize. He wanted to kiss her, and do more, desperately, right now, he knew that much. But there was more to his longing than that. He wanted to be old with her, he realized as the sun shifted and dropped the dappled shade of an oak branch's giant leafy fingertips over her cheek. He wanted to look across the milk vat in forty years' time and see her aged, wrinkled face break into a smile as she sucked the fresh curd from the palm of her crinkled hand. He wanted to slip up behind her as she packed it into a mold and encircle her with his own ancient arms, adding his strength to hers. He wanted their children, lots of them, to drive them crazy with their constant good-natured bickering and highfalutin labor-saving inventions.

The more he thought about it, the more he just plain wanted her.

Abbey opened her eyes and turned toward him, the leafy shadow sliding off her ear and onto the grass. "Can I help you?" she said, a mischievous glint in her eye.

Kit leaned forward and kissed her, long and hard, his soul soaring as he felt her body rise up to meet him. Her back arched and he slipped his hand behind it and hungrily pulled her closer, on top of himself as he lay back on the grass. She tasted like toffee and freedom. Freedom from his troubles, his bent and broken life, his inner ache. As he felt her heart beat against his he knew with a sudden monumental clarity that everything was going to be all right. He pulled away from her mouth, and her knees slid down either side of his hips as she sat up, straddling him, licking the taste of him off her lips as he slowly began to unbutton her shirt.

She moaned at the touch of his finger brushing her breast and realized with a shiver that of course it was the finger of her daydream in Ate'ate. Her shirt open now to her waist, she felt his strong, hard hands around her ribcage, and then his thumbs worked their way up and teased her nipples as a melting sensation ate up her entire body. Throwing her head back, she was distracted momentarily by the sound of a car speeding up the driveway, and in that moment passion subsided and reason took hold.

"Not here," she said, brushing away Kit's hands. "Not up here. Let's go back."

Kit groaned. "Don't tell me you have a sister you think is buried underneath this tree," he said. "I don't think I could stand it."

Abbey laughed. "I told you," she said, buttoning up her blouse, "no one is dead."

Kit groaned again but supposed that she did have a

point. Their picnic spot was clearly visible from the house and as their coitus had been twice interrupted already, it made sense to ensure they were really in private this time. He put his hands on Abbey's hips and pushed her down onto his thighs so he could sit up. Then he leaned forward to whisper into her perfect neck. "You're beautiful," she felt him say into her collarbone and she wanted him so badly, so immediately, she wondered how she was going to make it down the hill without imploding.

She stood up, smiling and wet with anticipation, and held out her hand to him. Kit took it, then brought it to his lips to kiss it with a tiny salty lick before he grabbed the picnic hamper and the blanket and they both started down the hill.

Abbey felt so happy it was all she could do to keep from skipping and jumping and screaming. Her body was humming with expectation and her heart was singing with joy. Who cared about anything else? The time was right and she could feel it right to the core of her skeleton. She sidled closer to Kit and kissed him on his arm just below his shoulder. He was such a good man, she thought. Such a good, good man.

Halfway down the hill she spotted the car that she'd heard earlier. It was a yellow convertible with its black roof down, which had swung into the courtyard between the house and the dairy.

"I wonder who that could be," she said, pointing at it. "Pretty fancy set of wheels for around these parts."

Kit looked at her, smiling a wicked smile, and shrugged his shoulders. "Who cares?" he said. "No one's going to stop us this time."

"It's not a Coolarney thing, you and I, is it?" asked Abbey, suddenly scared it was all too good to be true. "It's not one of those ridiculous things that seems ordinary just because of the 'Coolarniness' of it all, is it?"

Kit laughed again and swung her arm. "It doesn't feel ridiculous," he said, "and I don't know about you, but it doesn't feel ordinary either."

He was right, thought Abbey. Of course, he was right. It was right. She could be sure of that now. She couldn't wait to get naked. To be loved. To love.

They were at the bottom of the hill and Kit was helping her over the gate when an evil, dark cloud rolled over the horizon of their happiness. A voice calling to them from the top of the driveway seemed to freeze Kit to the spot. Abbey looked over his shoulder as he held her around the waist, ready to help her to the ground.

A tall, beautiful blond woman in a tiny flowery sun frock was walking toward them, teetering on the blacktop in a pair of red stiletto heels. She was almost painfully thin but deliberately so, her spaghetti straps showing off the skeletal bones in her neck and shoulders. Her legs were impossibly long—like a thoroughbred racehorse's—tanned and bare. She minced closer and shaded her eyes with her hands.

"Hello, y'all," she drawled, and Abbey saw the life drain from Kit's face as his hands dropped from her waist and he turned slowly toward whoever it was that was coming toward them.

"Well, don't look so surprised, darlin'," she called. "Y'all must have known I would come looking."

She started to pick her way across the dried mud track that led from the end of the sealed driveway to the gate where they were standing.

"Jesus Christ," Kit whispered, a loud buzzing like a jackhammer muffled with cotton wool vibrating the inside of his head.

"Who is she?" asked Abbey, confused. "Why has she come looking?"

"I said, hello y'all," the leggy blonde said again to Kit as she reached him. "What's the matter, honey? Deaf as well as disappeared?"

Close up Abbey could see the intruder was perfect. Her skin was golden and clear, her eyes brilliant blue and widely spaced, her mouth big and full and stretched into a smile that showed off two rows of impeccable teeth.

"Aren't you going to introduce me to your little friend?" she asked.

"Jesus Christ," whispered Kit again, still frozen, as the clear crisp landscape around him smeared and melted like a painting left out in the rain.

"You seem confused," the blonde said, ignoring him and holding out her hand to Abbey. "That's my name, honey. J.C. Jacey Stephens. Pleased to make your acquaintance, I'm sure."

Abbey stared at the hand being offered to her and then at Kit. He looked as though he were seeing a ghost.

"Jacey," he whimpered, his eyes black and disbelieving in his pale shocked face.

Abbey, feeling sick to her stomach, forced herself out of her frozen state and half jumped, half fell to the ground, steadying herself as she stood up straight with one hand on top of the fence post.

"I thought . . ." she started, then stopped.

"You thought what?" the blonde asked, her cold tone making a liar of her dazzling smile.

"I thought you were dead," Abbey said.

There was a split-second's silence, then Jacey threw back her long blond hair and laughed a deep sexy laugh lacking absolutely nothing but humor. "Dead?" she repeated. "Hell no, honey. I wasn't dead, I was in rehab." She turned her gaze again to her stunned husband. "What on earth have you been telling people, darlin'?"

Abbey looked at Kit for signs this was all part of some sophisticated prank but something in the look on his face told her it wasn't so. His shoulders were slumped, his eyes had sunk deeper into his head. His mouth was slightly open as though he were trying to scream but couldn't and a vein in his temple was throbbing so hard she could almost hear it. He bore almost no resemblance to the man she had been desperate to give herself to only moments before. He looked like a total stranger.

"Kit?" she ventured, a quiver in her voice. "Kit?"

"You're dead," Kit said hoarsely to Jacey, ignoring Abbey. "I thought you were dead."

"Just because you say I'm dead, honey, doesn't mean I am. It might be wishful thinking but it's still just thinking, sugar."

Kit closed his eyes and started to shake his head from side to side. He could not take it all in.

"You know what, pumpkin?" Jacey said, turning to Abbey. "My husband and I could really do with some time alone, so if you could just scram that would be great."

Abbey sought out Kit's eyes for confirmation this wasn't happening, but still they were closed.

"Kit?" she tried again, but he didn't seem to hear her.

"Run along now, honey." Jacey smiled with the warmth of a frozen Margarita. "I need to get reacquainted with my man."

"I have to go," Abbey said, as if she hadn't twice been asked to. She turned and started to walk, then run, toward the house.

Kit listened to the sound of her feet taking her away

from him yet was powerless to do or say anything to stop her. He'd been having a dream, he supposed, that had turned into a nightmare. He wanted to wake up and find himself walking down the hill again with the woman of his dreams. He opened his eyes. His dead wife was looking at him with interest.

"Snap out of it, baby," she said, clicking her fingers in front of his face. "A little harder to pretend I'm dead when I'm standing right in front of you, huh? Preferred it when I was tucked away in detox?"

"What are you doing here, Jacey?" Kit croaked, confused but becoming stomach-lurchingly less so. "I don't understand."

"Well, let me refresh your memory, honey. I had a little accident at home and wound up in the hospital. Then you dumped me, then I was ordered by the court to spend ninety days in rehab. Now the ninety days are up and I've come to get you, so can we please go? All this fresh air and countryside is getting to me."

Kit felt the panic that had left him alone these past few days start rising again in his chest. Visions of Jacey lying dead on their floor having lost their baby flickered through his head. Her pale face, her hair spread out like peacock feathers on the floorboards, blood. Paramedics bending over her, the hospital bed, the tubes, the oxygen, the doctor, vodka.

Kit started to tremble as he tried not to remember the doctor. He needed a drink so badly his toenails were thirsty, bent and clawing inside his shoes. The doctor.

"I thought you were dead," he said through lips that felt numb and wooden. "I really thought you were dead."

A real smile crawled across Jacey's beautiful face as she watched her husband's despair as he pieced together the puzzle of his fractured memories. She reached out and took both his hands in hers. "Don't think about that now, baby," she said in a soothing voice. "It's going to be okay. We're going to be okay."

Jacey was dead. Jacey was dead. Jacey was dead. The mantra bounced back at him from the recent past. Maybe if he said it enough, he remembered thinking in the days after Jacey's accident—when his wounds were open and raw—it would be true.

Standing there in that moment staring at his wife, Kit suddenly knew why he had been filling the hole deep inside himself with vodka. He had killed his wife. In his head, he had killed her. He had wished her dead and then he had wrapped himself in a shroud of alcoholic mist to keep the painful truth of her survival at bay.

"Jesus Christ," he said, fighting the urge to retch. "Jacey, what have I done?"

Jacey moved in, snaked her arms around his neck and reached up to kiss him on his jaw below the ear. "Let's not think about that now, darlin'," she whispered. "Let's just go and get your things. I want you to come back to New York with me. I want our life back, honey. You and me, the way it used to be."

She slithered away from him and held out one long, delicate arm. Kit stared at her hand. She was wearing her rings. The solitaire diamond engagement ring he had bought her and her wedding band. She was his wife.

"It was supposed to be for better or for worse, Christopher," she said, letting her smile be replaced by a tiny quiver as she sensed a pinprick of hesitation on his part. "That's what you said. I never in a million years dreamed that you would abandon me just when I really, really needed you. I never dreamed you were that sort of a guy."

Corrie watched aghast from the upstairs sitting room as the couple walked down to Fee's cottage, then Kit disappeared inside while Jacey waited impatiently at the door. He and Avis had bumped into a distraught Abbey flying through the kitchen minutes earlier on her way upstairs. Corrie had tried to find out what was wrong but his granddaughter had cried to be left alone and had run, sobbing, to her room. Corrie had wanted to go and find Kit but Avis had stopped him.

"What will be, will be, Joseph," she had said. "Leave them. He has to make up his own mind."

"Who is she?" Corrie asked as he watched Jacey scanning the courtyard for signs anybody was going to halt Kit's escape.

"His wife," Avis said.

"The dead one?"

"Not so dead, as it turns out," she said. "Though she's not the first one we know of in that category, now, is she?" They each looked out the window at her, thinking their private thoughts. "She's got a hold on him, all right," said Avis, "but Abbey's the one, Joseph. You have to trust that."

"Does Abbey know that?" Corrie asked, worry gnawing at him, making his arms tingle.

"She has to trust it too."

Corrie peered out again at Jacey. She reminded him of Maggie, although he knew Fee would say she had the legs of Mary-Therese. She had danger written all over her and if a seventy-three-year-old man with cataracts could see that, why couldn't Kit? He couldn't bear the thought of Abbey's heart being broken again. He was sure it would be too much for her, as it would be for him. "I wish Joseph would come back," he said. "When's Joseph coming back?"

Avis flicked at the curtain with a derisive "Pshaw.

Joseph Corrigan," she said, "have you ever gotten a straight answer out of yer man when it comes to matters of timing?"

Corrie, of course, never had.

"He'll be back when the time is right and it's up to us to trust that, too." She leaned closer to Corrie as Kit emerged from Fee's cottage with his bag and, seemingly in a daze, lowered himself into the passenger side of the top-less yellow sports car. In the roar of an engine and a billow of exhaust, he was gone.

As the car turned out of the leafy driveway and into the lane, Kit felt the wind ruffle his hair and blow the tears that were threatening to fall back into his eyes, for which he was grateful. The wild rhododendron that had lit up the countryside when he had first walked the lane to Coolarney House days before seemed faded now from the brilliant purple he remembered to a sad, dirty mauve.

Over the somber green of the rolling hills he could see the ocean, but even that had lost its sparkle, still now and slightly listless-looking. A filter of gloom seemed to dull everything he looked at and add to his confusion. He didn't know what he was doing, what he had been doing. Not an hour ago it had all seemed so clear and hopeful, and now here he was desperately bewildered again and going home with his wife. His wife. He looked across at Jacey and her beauty took his breath away. A little smile tripped across her glossy lips as she sensed his gaze, then turned to flash the smile even wider.

That smile. The doctor. The memories were trying to flood back.

Suddenly he remembered standing next to Jacey's hospital bed and telling her it was over, she was not the woman he married, she was dead to him, gone, forever.

Then he remembered leaving the hospital and going to the nearest bar where he had gotten so drunk that when he finally crawled home he didn't know what day it was, he didn't know anything except that he wanted to pretend his wife had never existed.

And in the weeks that followed, that was just what he had done. He had pretended that Jacey never existed, pretended that she had died, until he didn't need to pretend anymore because his anesthetized mind told him that she was gone, that he had lost her, that she was dead. Kit gripped the dashboard in front of him and sucked back a sob as real life hit him in the face. What sort of a monster was he that he could kill off his wife like that and not even know that's what he had done?

Jacey leaned over and put a hand on his knee. "Don't beat yourself up, baby," she said. "Most other guys probably would have done the same."

The wiring in Kit's brain was shorting. He felt as though all the details of his life had been cast high into the air on a windy day, then had landed on the ground too spread out and in the wrong order to ever come together again. Grappling to collect the scattered pieces, his memory took him back to the phone call he had got that awful, awful morning from Sasha Peterson, telling him that the super was trying to break down his apartment door because Sasha thought something had happened to Jacey inside.

As it transpired, Sasha had been wanting to talk to Jacey about smoking pot in the elevator in front of her daughters. After seeing her neighbor come in about eleven in the morning, she had had a cup of coffee to steel her nerves then gone and rapped on Jacey's door. As she'd done so, she'd heard a crash from inside the apartment, like someone falling and furniture moving, she told Kit, and sensing something was wrong, had called for help. When Kit reeled breathless and sweating into his own apartment twenty minutes after the phone call, Sasha and Benny were already inside and Jacey was lying on the blond polished floorboards between the coffee table and the sofa, looking as beautiful as she ever had, but for all the world dead. She was wearing a white spandex halter-neck top and white capri pants that were still slowly turning red from the groin outward. On the coffee table was a clear plastic bag of white powder and a small silver-backed mirror dusted with the same powder. Jacey, despite her narcotic coma, was still holding a rolled-up $100 note. The picture spoke a thousand words, every one of them dripping with tragedy.

Kit stood in his own doorway, stunned and unable to move until seconds—he supposed it was seconds—later, the paramedics arrived and pushed him out of their way as they attempted to revive Jacey with a ventilator and establish the severity of her condition.

Next thing Kit could remember was standing in the hospital corridor with a bald doctor wearing what looked like joke spectacles, who was telling him that his wife had snorted heroin and overdosed—mostly because of the amounts of Valium and alcohol already in her system—and had subsequently lost the eleven-week-old fetus she'd been carrying.

Heroin? Fetus? Kit had known nothing of either.

CHAPTER TWENTY

"Trust me. If you do everything right like I've told you, you'll eventually get your cheese."

JOSEPH FEEHAN, from *The Cheese Diaries*,
RTE Radio Archives

*I*n the bowels of Coolarney House, Lucy was discovering the woeful side of motherhood. In the bowels of Baby Jesus, Jesus's offspring, something had gone horribly wrong and was responsible for this discovery. The kitten, who in all other respects seemed to be enjoying perfectly good health, had been running amok for more than an hour, skittering from floor to floor, hallway to hallway, room to room, leaving foul-smelling piles that Lucy was trying to clean up before anybody caught him in the act and banished him.

On the third floor of the house, the kitten came to an exhausted halt and collapsed against a door.

"I should hope so too, you ungrateful little fecker," Lucy said, lunging at him before he could escape and do any more damage. As she picked the little creature up, though, she was distracted by a noise coming from the other side of the door. A crying sort of a noise. Without stopping to think, she opened the door and peered in. The room was very yellow and full of the sound of someone having a very miserable time, a sound to which Lucy was no stranger. She guessed that the lump lying with its back to her on the overstuffed bed was Abbey, and as she watched from the doorway she felt puzzled by an overwhelming sensation to make the back stop shuddering. She felt a warmth toward the back with which she was most unfamiliar. She felt sorry for it. She wanted to make it better.

She cleared her throat. "Baby Jesus has the squitters," she announced, stepping into the room. "He's after restaining the floors, the poor dote."

The back froze midshudder. "Go away," Abbey gurgled, her voice glutinous with crying.

"What's the matter?" Lucy asked, taking no notice of the order as she stepped closer toward the bed.

"I said go away," Abbey repeated thickly. "Leave me alone."

Lucy edged forward and after standing uselessly beside the bed for a moment or two, sprung up and perched on the side of it.

"Go away," Abbey said again.

Lucy took no notice; she was thinking. The unconnected jigsaw of the afternoon was starting to form a picture. She'd seen the yellow sports car arrive earlier but hadn't thought much of it. People came to visit the factory all the time, after all. Then Jamie had told her he'd seen a gorgeous supermodel stepping out of the car, but she'd assumed he was just saying that to make her jealous because he was so desperate for her. Now the car with the gorgeous supermodel was gone and Abbey was very, very sad. Her heart gave a jolt. It could mean only one thing. Well, it could mean a few things but she thought she knew which one.

"Where's Kit?" she asked boldly.

The back gave another big shudder.

"Did Kit leave? Did Kit bloody bollocking bastard leave?"

The back shuddered some more and Lucy let rip a string of expletives so heartfelt and disgusting she had to hiccup to get her breath back at the end of them. Her enthusiasm wrenched Abbey out of her snivel-fest. She cautiously turned over, then leaned up on her elbows. Her eyes were red and raw from crying and her tears had been soaked up by her hair, which was now stuck close to her face and neck.

As Lucy looked at her, the horror she felt at Kit's disappearance was swallowed by the same sensation she'd felt before. She truly, madly, deeply wanted Abbey to stop being sad. She knew exactly how it felt and it was too horrible to wish on anybody else.

"It was his wife," Abbey offered, fresh tears springing to her eyes and pouring wetly onto her cheeks. "His wife came and got him."

Lucy laughed. "But his wife is dead," she disputed matter-of-factly.

"Apparently not," Abbey answered, a catch in her voice. "At least she looked pretty bloody alive to me."

"That was her?" Lucy breathed. "The gorgeous supermodel?"

Abbey nodded.

"Back from the grave?"

"She was never in the grave," wailed Abbey, "she was in rehab. And she looked at me as though I were dirt. Kit just stood there, Lucy. He didn't do anything, he just stood there."

"That bastard," exhaled Lucy. "That complete and utter arsehole. How could he?"

"He just jumped in his car and took off with her," Abbey said, sitting up more, her forehead crumpled in uncomprehending misery, "without saying good-bye to anyone. Can you believe it?"

Lucy couldn't. "But I thought he was in love with you," she said bluntly.

"You did?" Abbey sniffed, recognizing the pathetic tinge to her voice too late to remove it.

"Only me and everyone else," Lucy said. "It wasn't half fecking obvious. And Avis said it was meant to be. And he could've had me," she added with the confidence only a pretty nineteen-year-old possesses, "but he didn't want to."

Abbey thought about this as she dried her eyes. "Then why has he gone back to his wife?" she questioned. "The wife he told us had died?"

Lucy didn't have an answer to that, but after thinking on it for a while, her face unexpectedly brightened. "Well, look at it this way," she said, "it would've been rude to have shagged him just after his wife popped her clogs, wouldn't it? At least you didn't do that." Abbey managed a weak smile. "Of course," Lucy added, "I suppose that means he was cheating on her with you."

"He never did anything with me," Abbey said after the smile departed. "We always seemed to get interrupted."

"Jaysus," gulped Lucy. "Sorry about that."

"Well, it wasn't so much you as the dead wife that really put a spanner in the works," reasoned Abbey. There was a momentary silence, and then she and Lucy looked each other in the eye and burst out laughing. It was nervous laughter, the sort that just as easily could have been crying, but it was laughter all the same.

"It's not funny," insisted Abbey between near-hysterical giggles. "It's really not funny."

"I know," Lucy kept saying. "I know, I know, I know."

"The man I'm madly in love with has left me forever," Abbey gasped between belly laughs.

"And I'm having a baby I don't want and haven't a clue who's the father," laughed Lucy, curled up on the bed now and clutching her own stomach.

"What a pair!" Abbey hooted.

"Twins!" roared Lucy.

They clutched each other and rolled around the bed, laughing uncontrollably, knowing that nothing about their separate situations was funny in the slightest.

"He might come back, you know," Lucy finally offered, wiping her eyes as her laughter subsided.

"I don't think so," said Abbey. "But I suppose you never know." She sighed and looked at Lucy. "What about you? Do you think you'll change your mind about the baby and keep it?"

"I don't think so," Lucy answered. "But I suppose you never know."

Distracted abruptly by a monumentally foul stench, Abbey lifted her nose up into the air and sniffed at it. "Phwoar," she said, grimacing. "What the hell is that?"

Lucy's blue eyes bulged in horror. "Baby Jesus!" she cried. "I forgot!"

Thirty miles away, contemplating the curves of the Irish countryside, Jacey was growing wary of Kit's silence. She'd had no inkling that luring him away with her would be so easy; she'd expected anger and recrimination and an embarrassing scene, but her husband had just seemed to collapse at the sight of her. It couldn't have gone more smoothly. He'd always been putty in her hands, powerless in her presence; most men were, but Kit especially so. And now it seemed that even after everything that had happened, she still had the same magnetic hold over him that she'd had since the moment they'd met. She was starting to feel uneasy about the silence though. He'd been in a world of his own since they left the farm.

Jacey leaned across and put her hand on his knee, ignoring his involuntary flinch, and with one eye on the road, she walked her fingers down his leg until she found the strap of her Prada shoulder bag, nestled at his feet. She scrabbled around inside until she found what she was looking for and pulled out a silver flask. Unscrewing it at the steering wheel, she flipped the lid and threw back her head, gulping at the contents before handing the flask to her husband, who looked at it dumbly.

"Go on." She smiled, looking at him and urging him to take it. "Have some. You know you want to. Besides, you could afford to loosen up a little, sugar. We're going to get back on top, Kit. We're going to start having fun again." She flicked her hair back over her bare shoulders and raised her face to the sun.

Kit took the flask and fingered it, relishing the cool smooth surface. He wanted a drink, of course he did. Now more than ever. Anything to calm the rising panic that was claiming him. Jacey had lost their baby after overdosing on heroin. He remembered every sad, sordid detail now, and her betrayal sickened him almost as much as his own weakness. He knew that the contents of the flask, vodka most likely, would help erase the repulsive truth the way vodka had done a thousand times before, but everything seemed different now, now that he'd had time to think.

He still couldn't quite fit all the pieces together and it was slowly occurring to him that perhaps the truth shouldn't be erased. Perhaps he should be feeling revulsion and shame. Maybe these sensations were trying to tell him something. The farther he got from Coolarney House, he realized, the more he liked the way he had felt there: vodka-free, clearheaded and connected to his thoughts. He didn't want to be sucked back down into the murkiness of drinking, despite its allure at this second. He fought his urge and screwed the top back on the flask.

"So, I see the rehab really took, huh, Jacey?" he said sadly, feeling half-disgusted, half-jealous of the buzz she was enjoying.

"Oh, come on." She grinned. "I only went because of the court order. I'm not the one with a drinking problem, darlin'. Y'all should know that." She reached for the flask and wrenched it back from him, fumbling with the top and swerving half off the road before correcting the steering with an unconcerned laugh.

"Jacey," Kit said anxiously, snatching the flask back after she'd swigged from it again. "You're going to get us killed. Jesus, pull yourself together, will you?" Jacey just laughed again, and held out her hand, waggling her fingers by way of requesting the drink.

"You can't say you don't have a problem, Jace," Kit said, holding the flask by the door away from her grasp, his voice slow and deliberate. "You overdosed on heroin, for chrissakes. You miscarried our baby on the floor of our apartment. You lied to me from the day I met you until the day you went into detox. Jesus Christ, Jacey, you've never even said you were sorry."

Jacey's smile faded and her face darkened but she fought the temptation to argue. She didn't want to mess things up now. "All right, sugar, if that's what y'all want to hear, I'm sorry. Is that better? I am real sorry."

"And you can cut the Southern crap," Kit said, his voice sounding tired and empty. "You're from Jersey, remember?

Please, you can drop the charade, Jacey. I've met your parents. I know where you're from. I know all about you. And there is nothing wrong with any of it."

Jacey's eyes hardened. She did not appreciate reality coming along and snapping her thong. Not one bit. But she was determined not to mess this up. "You're not still mad about that, are you?" she purred. "Jeez, honey, don't you think you could try and get over it?"

"Get over it?" Kit was aghast. "Get over it? Jacey, every single thing I knew about you, about my wife, every tiny detail, turned out to be a lie, do you really think I can just get over that?"

Obviously if he had been able to get over it, they would not be where they were now. They would have moved on from that terrible day at the hospital and got on with the rocket-fueled life they were living. Instead, Kit remembered with spine-chilling detail the devastation he felt as the truth about Jacey unfolded in the aftermath of her overdose.

Ed and his wife Mary had arrived at the hospital just as the bald bespectacled doctor had dropped his big bombshell, and Ed had launched a mortar attack of his own. Concerned at the downward spiraling direction of his friend's lifestyle under the influence of his gorgeous partygirl wife, Ed had been prompted to look into Jacey's background by a throwaway comment made by a bicycle courier. The courier had seen Jacey coming to pick up Kit for lunch one day, and commented to Pearl that she'd come a long way from Freehold Boro High School. Ed then attempted to locate the Louisiana newspaper baron Jacey claimed was her father, only, he told Kit, to find out no such man existed.

She was estranged from her family, Kit had protested in the sickly green light of the hospital corridor. She had

escaped a bad L.A. showbiz marriage and was hiding her
failure from her wealthy powerful New Orleans family.

Her family lived in New Jersey, Ed explained gently,
and were neither wealthy nor powerful. The courier still
knew one of her sisters, Cherie, and Ed had spoken to her.
Jacey's real name, he informed Kit, was Marlene Blundt.
She had run away to L.A. as a teenager and married the
owner of a suburban striptease bar who went bust and
wound up stealing cars for a living.

Jacey had been in contact with her family only once
in the past decade, Ed said, to ask for money about three
years ago when her husband went to jail. She was twenty-
nine, not twenty-six. She'd been dabbling with drugs
since she was twelve. Her much older boyfriend had given
her a boob job for her fifteenth birthday.

Turned out Kit didn't know anything about Jacey at all.

"You could try to get over it, couldn't you, honey?" Jacey
was smiling sweetly at him from the driver's seat. "For me?
For us? Y'all know y'all can do it if you try."

"Please, Jacey, drop it with the Southern stuff. It's crap
and you know it."

"Honey, I don't think you appreciate how much the
Southern thing works for me, professionally," Jacey as-
serted, ignoring the chill in his words. "I don't think the
folks at Ford would be too pleased if I changed right now."
Kit was not to know, after all, she reasoned, that the folks
at Ford wouldn't piss on her if she was on fire and neither
would anyone else of their ilk.

"But Jacey," Kit said bleakly, "it's not right to go around
pretending you're someone that you're not; that's basically
the root of all your problems. And you of all people—well,
there's nothing wrong with you the way you actually are."

"Well, honey, you might not like me the way I actually
am," she replied. "Had you ever thought of that?"

Kit sighed and shook his head. "Of course not," he said sadly. "You don't think I know the real you?"

"Nobody knows the real me, sugar," retorted Jacey. She seemed almost proud of the fact. "And that's just the way I like it."

"But I'm your husband, Jacey, and if I'm going to stay your husband then you have to drop all this bullshit and just be you. Otherwise, what's the point? I don't want to spend the rest of my life with a woman I'll never really know. What are you so afraid of? What's the big deal with being Marlene Blundt from Freehold, New Jersey?"

Jacey, furious at having her past dragged up again, was having trouble containing her irritation. "Well, I don't think you can rightly tell me who I should or shouldn't be, Mr. Burlington, Vermont," she declared with venomous sweetness. "You reinvented yourself too, you know. How come it's only a crime when I do it?"

"I never pretended to be anybody other than who I am," Kit argued. "I worked hard and it wasn't until you came along that I started getting messed up. Jesus, all that insane partying? The drinking? I was never into that shit before."

"Oh, so it's my fault you're an alcoholic," Jacey declared. "Of course. Heaven forbid you should ever blame yourself for anything."

"I'm not talking about that and of course I don't blame you," replied Kit earnestly. "I don't blame anybody but myself and I blame me for what happened to you as well, because I was obviously so messed up I didn't even notice what state you were in. What kind of a husband does that make me?"

"Oh, Chhheeerist," groaned Jacey. "Spare me the analysis. It's like being back in therapy. Really, honey, I have had enough of that shit to last me a lifetime. Truly, I do not, repeat not, need any more. Could you just be a babe and hand me the vodka instead?"

"What I'm trying to say," Kit said, ignoring her request, "is that I actually used to be pretty happy being exactly who I was, and I'd like to be that person again. I think maybe I even have been, these past few days."

Jacey tossed her head and blew through her lips in a gesture of derision. "That little bumpkin sure turned your head, didn't she?" she marveled. "What did she do—bake you an apple pie? Trust me, sweetie, two days back in the Manhattan swing and you will have forgotten her and this whole stupid country thing altogether."

"When did you get so hard?" Kit wanted to know. "I don't remember you being like this."

"Honey, you don't remember a half of it and you don't need to either. Now why don't you just sit back and relax, huh?"

"You know what?" Kit suggested. "I think I will. And you know what else? I'm going to do it without this," and with one swift right hook he threw Jacey's hip flask out of the car, up into the air and into the long grass at the side of the road.

Jacey's pretty face screwed up with anger as she slammed on the brakes and slid the car to a halt.

"Have you lost your fucking mind?" she raged, all Jersey now. "You get out and go back and get that. Go back and get my flask."

"I won't," said Kit, looking at her angry empty eyes and realizing that the scattered bits of his life were starting to rise up and rearrange themselves again. "I don't want our old life back, Jacey. We're better off without it."

"Don't make me laugh," Jacey bit back. "You were just a boring know-nothing bank boy before I met you. You never did anything but go to work and sit around watching TV. You thought Bang and Olufsen were Swedish magicians, for God's sake. Nobody even noticed you before you had me on your arm, honey. You were wallpaper. You want to go back to that?" Her eyes sparkled with fury as she watched him, knowing that no matter what his head told him, she still had the power to make him do what she wanted when it counted.

"I don't want to be noticed," Kit told her, quietly and calmly. "I want to be normal. I want a family. I want to stay in some nights and sit around in my sweatpants and watch TV. I want to invite friends over to play cards and have dinner."

Jacey threw back her head and laughed. Not her pretty Southern tinkle or her deep sexy chuckle but a hard mean laugh that came from somewhere deep and dark. "Give me a break," she said, "you've just described my idea of hell. You wouldn't last five minutes living like that, Kit, and neither would I. Maybe that's what your little show-pony girlfriend down there on the farm does for fun but ga-holly, cowboy, anywhere else? I don't think so. You want more than that, Kit, you know you do. You and I are the same like that, just admit it. We both want more and we are both going to get it. We'll both do whatever it takes. Now be a honey and go get me my fucking flask."

Kit felt sadness leach out of his heart and into the rest of his body as he realized that for Jacey this was true. But for him, it was not. In that moment, the staggering emotion he had thought he felt for his gorgeous, graceful, flawless wife and from which he had been running ever since her overdose and betrayal evaporated. He looked at her and for the first time didn't see the mesmerizing beauty who had kidnapped his soul and broken his heart, but instead a brittle shell containing nothing but a cold-blooded mass of manipulation. He had been wrong to abandon his wife and wish her dead, he knew that now. That had not been the right, not the brave thing to do, and it had led him down a path where escaping reality courtesy of Grey Goose was his best option. But in that moment, in that car, sitting there looking at her, Kit knew as clearly as he knew anything that even if he had stayed and been a brave understanding husband, he would have arrived at the very same conclusion he was arriving at now.

Jacey, bored with the resistance she was meeting and fearful of what it meant, lurched out of the car and slammed the door behind her. "You think you're so fucking special," she said as she teetered back down the road in search of her flask, "that you're so fucking righteous, throwing all our money at your stuck-up little brother and your crazy old mom, but you like to party with the big boys, too, Christopher. Admit it. You're not as 'holier than thou' as you think you are."

She stepped off the side of the road and got down onto her hands and knees to search for the flask. Kit watched her, horror mounting, as she desperately clawed at the long grass and wildflowers.

"Where is the fucking thing?" she mumbled under her breath. "Where the fuck is it?"

Kit slowly got out of the car and started to walk toward her as she groveled around at the side of the road, her hands searching like a blind woman's for the vodka.

"If you think I am going back to New York without you, you can think again, you selfish bastard," she said, her voice catching, as she continued scratching at the ground. "I will not go back to sharing one stuffy little room with three other catty bitches and schlepping around the city for pathetic little jobs that pay nothing." Her voice was stretched with the effort of controlling herself. "I will not be groped by one more fat ugly married asshole desperate to get into my pants because he thinks that's where buying me one lousy apple martini will get him," she railed. "I will not suck up to Ghislaine for her fucking castoffs or wear Violet's old shoes after she's already worn them everywhere I want to go." She seemed totally oblivious to a car flashing by, its occupants staring, their mouths hanging open, at the beautiful girl crawling on her hands and knees at the side of the road.

"I will not turn the cushions on some crappy sofa inside out looking for enough change to buy half an ounce of fucking talcum powder. I am Mrs. Kit Stephens and as of next Thursday I am worth a lot of money so screw the lot of them." She dropped her head down onto her arms, her butt in the air, and roared into the grass as she realized the hopelessness of trying to find the flask.

Next Thursday? Kit thought about the date. It would have been, he realized with another jolt, his tenth anniversary at Fitch, Wright and Ray, and the date on which his vested funds would mature. The final scales fell from his eyes just as Jacey, her head at grass-roots level, spied something glinting in the grass close to the fence and threw herself on it. "I found it," she cried, laughing as she grappled with the top, then throwing as much of the vodka as she could down her throat.

When she opened her eyes, her husband was gazing at her with a look she had not seen before but which she suspected was far from mesmerized. Her plan, she realized, had gone slightly awry. "Oh, cut the saintly routine," she said, wiping her sweating forehead with the back of one slightly dirty hand. "You'll be back in the swing of it before we touch the ground at JFK. Don't give me that happy-being-at-home-with-your-sweatpants shit, Kit. All this farm crap has messed with your mind."

"How did you find out where I was?" he asked her.

She looked up at him, squinting into the sun and shading her eyes with the flask. "That little swamp creature from your office knew."

"She told you? Niamh told you where I was?"

"Oh, what does it matter?" Jacey answered, getting clumsily to her feet and standing unsteadily for a moment before bending over to rub the dirt and grass from her knees.

"It matters to me," said Kit. "Did Niamh tell you herself or did you find out some other way?"

Jacey's face was red from exertion and stained where the dirt from her hand had mixed with her sweat and smeared across her forehead. She stepped out onto the road and started to walk toward him, and it was then that Kit realized how drunk, or stoned, or both, she was. She smiled lazily as she walked up to him, then kissed the tip of her index finger, and ran it across his lips as she passed him.

"Of course she didn't tell me," she said, over her shoulder, "she hates my fucking guts. Her new boyfriend told me. I bumped into him at our old apartment."

Kit turned and looked at her. "You bumped into him?"

"Well, I still had my keys, honey. I was a little surprised to find him there, I can tell you, but he was very kind and told me just where I could find you and then he gave me access to your personal effects."

So Tom wanted to sabotage Kit's chances of returning to his career and Jacey just wanted his money. This was what it all boiled down to.

"Come on, darlin'," Jacey drawled. "There's a big old jet

airliner down the road and it's got our names on it. Yours and mine, baby."

She pushed her hair back from her face, leaving another smudge on her cheek, and smiled at him, before slipping elegantly into her seat and starting the car. Kit walked deliberately toward her, thousands of cogs moving together in his head, finally synchronizing the machinery of his life as he knew it. He stopped at the passenger door. He looked at Jacey, taking a last slug from her now-empty flask, and he knew one thing, just then, and one thing only. He did not want to grow ten minutes older with this woman, let alone forty years. He could not imagine her wrinkled face smiling at him, nor see his own ancient arms adding strength to hers. He could not picture their children. He didn't want to.

"Jacey," he said, feeling safe and strong outside the car away from whatever it was that made his wife so mortally magnetic, "why didn't you tell me about our baby?"

She rolled her eyes, then when she saw the look on his face tried pouting at him. "You're not still pissed about that, are you, sugar?" she asked.

"Pissed?" Kit asked incredulously, gripping the car door, his knuckles white with the effort of not taking her scrawny neck and throttling her for her callousness. "You OD'd when you were pregnant with my child, a child I didn't even know I was having. Pissed is hardly the word to describe how I felt about that, how I feel. Can't you even see that?"

Jacey looked at him, calculating, wrongly, how to play it. "Oh honey," she said sweetly, "the truth is I didn't tell you about the baby because I wasn't planning on having the baby. I wasn't ready for babies. I was having too much fun and so were you." She smiled her sexiest smile, oblivious to her messy face and sticky hair. "It's only because I forgot about the Valium and the coke and tried that stupid shit of Violet's that you even knew about it. I was going to deal with it the very next day and you would never have had to worry about it."

She looked at him and assumed she'd hit her mark. "We can have all the babies you want when we're done with the good life, darlin'," she added. "There'll be plenty of time for that." She leaned over and patted the empty passenger seat. "Come on home, Christopher honey. I want to go home."

Kit's smile was sad but Jacey couldn't see that. "Jacey," he said, as softly as he could, opening the door and kneeling on the seat, then leaning over as if to kiss her. Her face softened with the glory of triumph as she realized she had won and that he was coming with her.

"I knew y'all'd come around eventually," she breathed, offering up her face.

But Kit, instead of kissing her, moved quickly past her newly resistible lips and pulled the keys out of the ignition, then jumped out of the car and threw them as hard as he could into the rhododendron bushes behind the stone fence at the side of the road. She would never find them.

"Our time is up," he said calmly as he turned, closed the car door and reached into the back, pulling out his bag. "I'm going to be a cheesemaker."

Jacey, her face contorted with shock and rage, bashed at the steering wheel with both hands. "Fuck you!" she screamed, shaking her head in fury. "Fuck you to hell! Go get my fucking car keys, you fucking asshole!"

"You might not be sorry, Jacey," he said quietly, "but I am. I am really sorry."

"I'm going for half of everything you have, you fucking

bastard, don't think I won't," Jacey shrieked at him, her features ugly in their bitterness.

"You're welcome to half of everything I have," Kit said, "you deserve it," and he threw his bag over his shoulder and started to walk back down the lane. He didn't care how long it took, he was going back to Coolarney House— if Coolarney House would have him.

"You can't do this to me," Jacey screamed at his back. "What am I going to do?"

"Hitch to the airport," Kit called over his shoulder. "Go home, Jace. Good luck."

Her insults became fainter and fainter as he walked away from her and back to the best thing that had happened to him in his whole entire life. As the road rose up to meet him, his shoulders squared and the emptiness that had swallowed him since Jacey came back into his life was replaced by excitement over his future.

He strode to the brow of a hill and again caught a glimpse of the sea that had earlier seemed so listless and dull. Now, although the light was fading and the sun was hanging lower in the sky, the blue water glimmered and twinkled, the green pastures shimmying at its edge. Kit was not a man to kiss away a marriage lightly, to kiss away anything lightly, but as he walked the winding country lanes of West Cork he knew without a shadow of a doubt that he and Jacey were not meant to be. It had been wrong to run away from her, from their marriage, from the truth, but it would be worse to go back—because he didn't love Jacey. He didn't even like her. He'd been bewitched by her and maybe he did like the way people looked at him when she was on his arm, but the man he was when he was with Jacey was not the man he wanted to be. He'd been tormented by guilt and anguish that his marriage had failed, he realized that now, yet with every step that brought him closer to Coolarney House and all it held, the torment became less consuming. There was room in his heart for strength and clarity and hope.

Jacey would be all right. He knew that. She would find what she needed with someone else. Someone who wanted what she did. Money. And to be noticed. Kit? He cared for neither of those. He wanted love and honesty and for the people he loved to trust him. He wanted Abbey to trust him. He wanted Abbey.

The steady chug-chug of a slow approaching motor intruded into his thoughts, getting louder and louder as he approached a bend in the road. Not a single car had passed him since he left Jacey at the side of the road and the only sound had been that of his own steady footsteps and, far away, the sea, splintered now and then by the caw of a seagull. The chug-chug got louder again as he reached the corner. As he rounded it, the road turned into a corridor of trees that met above the lane to form a canopy that cut out the light and made it hard for him to see. He could hear all right, though, and the chug-chug sounded an awful lot, he thought now that it was closer, like Avis's tractor.

"Jaysus feck," a familiar voice called above the clamor of the familiar old engine. "Don't tell me I'm late."

CHAPTER TWENTY-ONE

"In that fantastic explosive moment when you realize just how feckin' good it is, you know it's all been worth it."

JOSEPH FEEHAN, from *The Cheese Diaries*,
RTE Radio Archives

*O*ld Fart Arse was playing the maggot, knowing full well it was Kit and Abbey's first solo effort in the cheese factory. Baffled, the pair stood side by side and looked at the pasteurizer. They'd followed exactly the same procedure as they'd seen Fee do every single morning yet still the festering machine coughed and spluttered but refused to roar into life.

Abbey gawked uselessly at the wretched contraption, but it wasn't Old Fart Arse she was thinking about. It was the way her heart had jumped out of her chest and into her mouth when she had seen Kit lounging at the factory door as she'd arrived, bleary with spent tears and sleep, ten minutes earlier.

He had looked up when he heard her footsteps. She had caught his eye and in that moment, with the early morning sun dark and golden, he didn't look real. As she got closer, however, she realized that she wasn't dreaming, that it was him, that he'd come back, that perhaps all was not lost. And under his watchful gaze she had felt so naked she could barely breathe; not bereft of clothes, but of skin and flesh and bone as well, as though nothing but a weightless essence of Abbey wafted in the summer air.

"We were meant for each other, you know," he said softly as soon as she was close enough to hear. "I realize that now."

Abbey had looked at him uncomprehendingly and walked straight past, opening the factory door, pulling on her overalls and Wellingtons, dipping her feet in the bath, and patting Old Fart Arse in the rump like a faithful horse as she switched him on and checked the temperature gauge. Suddenly, Fee's irritating cheerfulness at the breakfast table made sense. Knowing that he knew Kit was back, his offer of cold cucumber slices to bring down the swelling in her raw red eyes didn't seem quite so unsympathetic. Her grandfather too had been smiling over his marmalade toast, but his good humor had not been quite as convincing. She could tell he was worried for her and she worried back, but had loved knowing how much he cared for her.

Now, here she was, eyes puffy and puce, her hair looking like a wig some wag would wear to a bad-taste party, and her heart beating so loudly in her chest she was thankful to Old Fart Arse for making such a commotion—otherwise Kit would have been deafened by her. She thought of the glorious weightlessness of just minutes ago and realized, with a slow understanding that gave her galloping goosebumps when it eventually registered, that without her usual accessories of fear and doubt and regret that was how she might feel all the time.

"Who is meant for each other?" she asked, turning to look at Kit.

He snapped out of his own reverie, confused. He'd been thinking that perhaps "We were meant for each other" hadn't been the right thing to say. That he should have said "Sorry," or "Please forgive me," or "About the whole wife thing . . ."

"We were meant for each other," he said again, spreading his hands out in a helpless gesture. It was what he meant. He'd never been so sure of the meaning of anything ever before.

Abbey seemed upsettingly unconvinced. "Do you mean you and your not-quite-as-dead-as-we-thought gorgeous blond supermodel wife were meant for each other, or do you mean you and . . . you and . . . ?" Her bluster blew. She was so scared of losing him that she had prepared a lot of anger just in case it was needed, and any hope she had been saving was battling inside her for space. "Because with all the being-quite-alive and the high heels and the going-away-without-even-saying-good-bye and then sneaking back for who knows how long, a person could get quite confused unless it was made perfectly clear to her," Abbey jabbered, her face blushing to match her eyes, which were now locked on the belching pasteurizer.

Kit nearly collapsed with relief as he reached out and took Abbey's face in both his hands, turning her toward him and stepping as close to her as he could, so he could feel her sweet breath on his neck, and smell her fresh citrusy smell. He tilted her glowing red eyes up to face him.

He'd been trying all night to rationalize what had happened, was happening, how he felt, but somehow words just didn't fit the picture. There were loose ends. There were problems. There were unlikelihoods. If it had been a Wall Street deal, he would have advised his clients against investing. But it wasn't. He didn't know what it was. But about four o'clock in the morning when his bones had finally stopped feeling the aftershock of Fee's tractor he came to the conclusion that it didn't matter. All he knew was that he wanted to be with Abbey and he wanted to be a cheesemaker. Simple as that. No argument.

"I just have this feeling," he said, "that if we could let it all go and just find ourselves somehow, I don't know, magically, in just the right place at just the right time, everything would work out. Do you know what I mean?"

"But your wife—" Abbey started to protest.

"If you could let that go," Kit said, his eyes not leaving hers.

"But a wife, a living wife, is a pretty big thing to let go," Abbey answered, with feeling. "You lied about her and then you ran off with her. You just abandoned me the instant she turned up. I felt invisible. I felt worse than invisible. Should I just forget about that?"

"I made a mistake with my wife," Kit said, his gaze so unswervingly sure that Abbey felt jealous, momentarily, of his certainty. "I made a lot of mistakes with my wife and when we've got time I will tell you all about them. I will tell you everything you want to know, Abbey. But the guy who deluded himself that his wife was dead? The guy who climbed into her car and drove off with her yesterday? That wasn't me, Abbey, you have to believe me. This is me, here with you, and this is where I want to be."

"How can I be sure?" Abbey whispered.

"Because I am telling you, Abbey, and I promise you, as sure as I am standing here now in front of this clapped-out excuse for a pasteurizer that we don't even need because we only pretend to use it, that I will never lie to you ever again as long as we both shall live. I will love you. I will look after you. I will help you make the best goddamned cheese in the universe. I will do anything for you if you will just let me."

"I'm scared," Abbey said, realizing that she was. "People loving me hasn't worked out the way I'd hoped so far."

"But you're here, Abbey, in this place, with me. That's the hard part done. All you have to do now is stand back and let the farm, the air, the rain, the moon, the room we're feckin' standing in, make its mark, and that's the magic of Coolarney." He smiled as the words of clever old Fee tripped off his tongue like they belonged there.

"Who are you?" Abbey breathed, her body feeling lighter and lighter with each passing moment.

"I'm just an ordinary guy from Burlington, Vermont, who for some reason I'll probably never know or understand ended up in this particular place at this particular moment with you, Abbey, you. You and I were meant for each other," he said. "You and I. Is that clear enough?" And he leaned down and kissed her with the long, languid, slow-burning passion of a man who knew he had a lifetime of this woman ahead of him.

Across in the kitchen, Fee was helping himself to another cup of tea and a fourth crumpet. "At fecking last," he sighed, raising his eyes to the heaven.

"At fecking last what?" Corrie said, looking up from the *Irish Times.*

"At fecking last that granddaughter of yours and the boy from New York City are getting on with things."

"What things?" Corrie said suspiciously, putting down the paper and eyeing his friend.

"All the things," Fee smiled, tipping his head in the direction of the factory and taking an enthusiastic bite of his crumpet. "And I mean all," he said, with his mouth full, spraying gobs of butter and honey across the table.

Corrie's face creased with worry. "Are you sure he's the

right one?" he asked again. "Are you one hundred percent sure?"

"Joseph, I was sure the moment I laid eyes on him. And after spending three and a half hours on a tractor with him, I'm doubly, triply, quadruply—what comes after quadruply?" he asked, not waiting for an answer, "I am as sure as I ever have been. He is the one."

"What happened out there?" Corrie wanted to know.

"His wife has a touch of the Maggie about her, Joseph; the pull, you know, the pull. But it only took him thirty miles to work out she was messing with his head and on the booze as well so he got her to stop the car, threw away the keys and turned back home to Coolarney."

"What sort of man leaves his wife in the middle of the countryside though?" Corrie worried.

"That's exactly where some wives should be left," Fee answered, "and twice as many husbands. It takes more strength to walk away from the wrong person than it does to stay, Joseph, and I'm not talking about you, I am talking about young Kit Stephens. But having said that, there's a lot of you in the boy and for that we can truly be thankful."

"But what makes you so sure they're right for each other?" Corrie asked.

Fee rolled his eyes. "What am I always telling you?" he demanded.

Corrie flailed about for an answer. Fee was always telling him so many things, after all, and half of them never made a jot of sense.

"I'm always telling you to trust me," Fee continued. "I'm always telling you not to worry, that everything will be all right."

Corrie must have looked doubtful because Fee sighed and put on his serious look, the impact of which was dented considerably by a large blob of honey on his chin.

"You worry too much, Joseph, did you know that?" he said. "And I wish you would stop it because you've absolutely nothing to worry about."

"There's you," said Corrie, "and Abbey and—"

"Worrying about myself and Abbey will get you nowhere," Fee said, his eyes gleaming, "and besides, as I say, there is absolutely nothing to worry about. You'd save yourself an awful lot of bother if you listened to me for once. That girl of yours and that boy over there with her are going to make the most beautiful cheese in the world, Joseph, and they are going to make a grand pair, a couple, into the bargain. It's not often two such good and honest souls meet, you know that. The last time was you and me, Joseph. There are not that many of us but as of right now there are two more. This is no ordinary day, my friend, and certainly no day to be sitting there with a face on you like a wet weekend."

"Is it any wonder I can't remember what you're always telling me when you're always telling me so much?" Corrie grumbled, but Fee's words had soothed his troubled heart. "You think she's going to stay then?"

"Forever and a day," Fee beamed, leaning across the table. "Do yourself a favor, Joseph. Trust me."

Corrie, tired of his doubts and worries, did himself a favor and trusted him. And as he watched his old friend find the blob of honey on his chin and proceed to lick it off, he even allowed himself the luxury of believing that all was right with the world. He felt better than he had all week.

Old Fart Arse lurched into action with such a thundering crack Kit and Abbey sprang away from each other in panic.

"That infernal machine!" Avis laughed as she popped her head around the door. "You'd swear it has eyes. Milk's in. Abbey, I don't know what you did to Lucy but she's a different girl this morning. She rang her mammy in Dublin last night, can you believe it? And she got up early and made tea and toast for the girls this morning. If it weren't for the dreadlocks and the earring on her tongue, I'd swear it was an imposter."

Abbey laughed. "Oh, it was nothing," she said. "Just girl talk. I don't think she realized what a thing it is to have a mother and a father both in the same family at the same time. She seems so grown up but she's only as clueless as most nineteen-year-olds."

Avis walked over and gripped Abbey on the arm. "You could have done with someone like you when you were nineteen," she said.

Embarrassed, Abbey shook her head. "I had Rose," she said.

Avis gave her a maternal squeeze. "Someone like you would have been better."

They worked side by side unloading the milk and then, after Avis had gone, Kit and Abbey beavered inside the factory getting the molds and counters ready for the curd, while the milk heated to the right temperature. After an hour, Kit flicked open the valve and the milk whooshed up and around Old Fart Arse and into the cheese vat. The noise made Abbey's blood bubble as she looked at Kit across the vat and wondered how it was possible to feel so happy, so at home, so how she had always imagined the lucky people felt. Kit was standing across from her with a huge grin on his face, mesmerized by the force of the milk as it shot into the vat, dancing droplets shimmying in a last solo appearance before they plunged into the chorus of milk below. When the time was right Kit added the starter, a funny secret smile playing across his lips as he did so.

"Did you ever wonder," he asked sometime later as he was stirring the rennet into the vat, "how Corrie and Fee make their money?"

"From the cheese, you eejit," Abbey laughed.

"Think about it," Kit said. "They make about a hundred and twenty kilos a day, five days a week. If they were selling that at a fiver a kilo, they would be making about £3,000 a week, all up, before tax and overheads—probably leaving them about £1,500 to play around with. They pay £750 to the Pregnasaurs, which leaves them another £750 to run the farm and the house and pay themselves and Ruby and Marie."

Abbey thought about it. When he put it like that, it didn't add up. "Please don't tell me they're drug runners," she pleaded. "I couldn't bear it."

Kit laughed. "They're not."

"Then what are they?"

"Two very canny old men, that's what they are. Lars and Peder Nielsen. The Nielsen brothers."

Abbey was confused. "I don't follow," she said.

Kit held up the rennet packet. *Brødrene Nielsen Mejeri*, it had stamped on the side. *Denmark*.

"Nielsen Brothers Dairy," Kit translated for her with a smile. "When Corrie and Fee realized commercial starters and rennets were the way of the future, they invested back in the sixties. Big time. Those guys are sitting on a gold mine over in Denmark. Fee told me they can't even keep track of the money that pours in. It's an international multimillion-dollar business—I remember when they listed it on the New York Stock Exchange. It went ballistic. And they own some Dutch vat-making company, too. They don't even need to make cheese, Abbey. How about that? Coolarney Gold is just a labor of love."

Abbey seemed stunned by the revelation. She stood there silently, fiddling with the well-worn handle of her paddle, and Kit was suddenly fearful he had exploded some childhood dream or something.

"Hey, I'm sorry," he said, coming over to give her a hug. "I didn't mean to—"

Abbey pushed him back so she could look at him. "No," she said, her eyes shining. "I love that. I love that it's a labor of love." She pulled herself together and held up her paddle, looking at it and tracing the dents her grandfather's fingers, and his grandfather's before that, had made on it over the decades. Somehow, the more ridiculous it got, the more it made sense. Her life, finally, was falling into place. But there would be time for celebration, lots of it, later. Right now, there was cheese to be made.

A tingle of excitement ran up her spine as she peered into the vat, the minutes ticking by without either of them noticing, as the thick creamy milk disappeared before their very eyes, leaving the sweet watery whey and shiny soft curd in its wake. Wordlessly, they picked up their blades and started the synchronized series of sweeping arcs that would bring them closer to their cheese. Almost instantly they fell into a compatible rhythm, each focusing on the different patterns their blades were slicing through the curd. The factory was silent but for the ever-present sound of dripping water, the friendly occasional clink of blade against steel and the slip-slop of the whey as the paddles sliced through it. When the curd was as small as it could be, Kit and Abbey looked at each other and grinned, both wet with effort and glowing with satisfaction.

"Bombs away?" Abbey queried. "Bombs away," answered Kit, and she pulled the plug on the vat, standing back as the whey hissed and spat its way onto the floor, finding the grate and slinking down it like an escaping snake. The factory never smelled better than at this moment, the whey departing, the curd settling and the air thick with promise, and it was at this moment Corrie and Fee, unable to stay away another second, fell in the door, each pushing the other out of the way and the little fat one, for once, winning.

"Gadzooks!" Fee said. "I think they've done it!"

"Gadzooks?" repeated Corrie. "When did you start saying gadzooks?" But he could feel it, too. It wasn't the look or the smell or the feel. It was all of those things and something else, something indefinable, something they had only ever been able to put down to Coolarniness. Kit grinned and invited them to taste the curd but at that moment the door flew open again and a wide-eyed and near-hysterical Lucy burst in, completely out of breath.

"Wilhie," she gasped. "Wilhie."

Abbey handed Kit her paddle and went to Lucy's side, urging her to calm down.

"Wilhie's gone into labor," Lucy panted. "I can't find Avis and I don't know what to do and it's happening pretty fecking quickly if you ask me."

"Where is she?" Abbey urged.

"In the big kitchen," Lucy said. "I thought with the boiling water and everything . . ."

"Kit," said Abbey, immediately taking control. "You go and find Avis. I'll go with Lucy and get Wilhie up to my room. Can you bring Avis up there when you find her? Are you two all right to pack the molds?" she asked, looking at Corrie and Fee. "I'm so sorry, I know today was supposed to be—"

"Go," said her grandfather, his heart nearly bursting with pride at his wise, warm, wonderful granddaughter. "Go."

She went, Kit and Lucy with her, and the two old men were alone in the factory.

"What did I do to deserve her?" Corrie asked in wonder, and his old friend clapped him on the back and said, "That you even need to ask, Joseph, makes you the man you are."

He took up his position on the opposite side of the vat. "Ready?" he asked. Corrie nodded.

"Are you sure?" Fee asked again. Corrie nodded again.

Fee bent down over the vat and lifted a handful of curd tentatively to his nose.

The curd smelled exquisite. Sweet and special. Warm and inviting. Pure and simple. Exquisite. He pulled his hand back just enough to let Corrie see his smile from across the vat and then brought the curd to his lips, sucked it onto his tongue, clapped his mouth shut, closed his eyes and savored the sensation.

Bliss.

It was perfect. Flawless. Faultless. But more than that, it was exceptional. Unique. Unsurpassed.

In a word, it was better.

It was the best.

There was absolutely no doubt about it whatsoever. Kit and Abbey's curd was the best Fee had ever tasted, and the thought of the cheese their curd would one day become made him shiver from the tips of the last few strands of hair on his head to the ends of the toenails he'd inherited from his grandmother.

His eyes flew open. "Jaysus feck, Joseph," he breathed. "They've only cracked it. They're only the best fecking cheesemakers in the whole of the world. They're only fecking cheeniuses! I knew it. I knew it!"

Corrie felt a warmth flood through his tired old bones and settle calmly on his skin as he cherished the look on his old friend's face. Blissfulness was a wonderful state. This was a grand moment to be relished and remembered.

He leaned in against the vat and stooped down, swinging his arm in a gesture so familiar he couldn't even feel he was doing it. He scooped up the curd and his skin tingled, seemed suddenly oversensitive, even, to the feel of the silky, warm pulp in his hand. For a moment he felt as though he could feel every molecule, every atom, every element that was being squeezed by his fingers into his palm. It felt like more than curd. It felt like everything. Everything he had ever done. Everyplace he had ever seen. Everybody he knew.

With a difficulty he didn't understand, he lifted the sweet soft mass to his lips. It exploded in his mouth with a buzz that was so overwhelming his brain could barely process the deep dark thrill as it quickly spread throughout his body, saturating every single cell.

Suddenly everything was happening in slow motion, flickering in front of him like an old home movie. He tasted. He swallowed. He realized that Fee was right. It was better than perfect. It was the best. His hand fell to grab the side of the vat. His other hand clutched at his chest, numb with the tingling that was taking over him. Still everything was happening in slow motion. Everything. Slow. Tasting. Swallowing. Realizing. His eyes widened in panic as he comprehended what was happening and with all his strength he lifted his head to look at his friend.

Fee was standing, stricken, on the other side of the vat, his mouth frozen open in a black, gaping *O* as tears spilled down his cheeks.

The world stopped moving. The sun stopped shining. The cheese didn't matter.

It's me, thought Corrie, his face paralyzed in an

expression that was half rapture over the glory of the cheese, half terror at what was happening to him. "It's me," he whispered as his legs gave way beneath him and he collapsed to the floor, his head bouncing off the smooth brown teak as the cold claw of death squeezed again at his heart.

"It's me," he whispered again as Fee appeared on the floor beside him and pulled the big man onto his lap, so that Fee was sitting against the vat, his faithful old friend lying, shocked and barely breathing in his arms, his head leaning back against Fee's chest.

"It wasn't you," Corrie said, looking in front of himself but finding nothing to focus on, "it was me."

Fee kissed the top of his old mate's head and let his tears fall wetly on that glorious mop of silvery hair. "Ah, sure, it was you," he whispered. "But what's a fellow to do?" He rocked Corrie, his short stocky arms looped underneath the big man's armpits, gently rubbing the chest beneath which scarcely pumped the heart that was killing him.

"I didn't want to tell you, Joseph," he confessed. "I didn't want you to worry. I wanted you to make the most of it."

"But I haven't . . ." Corrie's head was muddled.

"Ssshhhh," Fee soothed. "You have."

"But I haven't done it." Corrie labored over the words. "I never got there."

"Ah, Joseph, you did. You just don't know you did," Fee whispered. He hugged his friend closer to him and was quiet for a moment. He thought of all the things he'd told Corrie that meant nothing and knew these next words would have to be different.

"You always knew you were here to do something spe-

cial, Joseph," he whispered into his bewildered friend's
ear. "You always knew that you were different and that
there was a reason for it all and you were right, Joseph Corrigan, you were right, just not in the way you expected."
He felt Corrie shudder in his arms and his own heart con-
tracted with anguish.

"It wasn't the cheese," Fee said, extricating himself
momentarily to wipe at his eyes with his grubby sleeve.
"Ah, the cheese was good, the best even, up until now, but
that wasn't it, Joseph. And it wasn't Rose, although God
knows you deserve a medal for loving the little wagon after
everything she put you through." He pressed his lips to
the old man's bushy eyebrow and kissed him again, his
eyes closed and burning with grief.

"Abbey," Corrie said, or thought he said, but couldn't
tell.

"It wasn't even her," Fee whispered, "although she's a
credit to you, Joseph, and your Corrigan genes and she's
able for it just like you were. She'll do you proud, Joseph,
you know that. She got here in time."

Corrie smiled, or thought he smiled, until the pain in
his chest wrenched him away. "What was I here for then?"
he beseeched his friend, although he was well beyond
speaking. "What's it all been for?"

"There's a hundred seventy-four other babies born
happy and healthy here because of you, you silly feck,"
wept Fee, "and that's one hundred and sixty-nine girls no
one else wanted when they most needed someone to want
them. That's what you were here for, Joseph. It was happening right here under your nose all the time."

"That was nothing," Corrie imagined telling his dear
old friend. "It was a pleasure. It was nothing. Sure, anybody else would have done the same."

"That's why you're different," wept Fee, "because not everybody else would do the same."

"You would," Corrie felt. "You would do the same."

"Not without you," Fee whispered. "Not on my own." He felt Corrie stiffen himself against the monumental physical pain he was fighting and then relax as though the pain had gone away, or he had decided he couldn't fight it anymore.

In that moment Corrie thought of all the things he hadn't done. He hadn't made peace with his daughter. He hadn't finished this quarter's tax return. He hadn't talked to Ruby and Marie about the pay raise they'd been refusing to accept. He hadn't told the best friend a man could ever hope to have how much he loved him and how he didn't want to leave him alone in the world.

"You don't need to, old friend," Fee murmured into his ear. "I know."

A single huge fat teardrop leaked out of Corrie's left eye and trickled slowly down his cheek.

"Don't be afraid to let go, Joseph," Fee whispered into his ear, as a tear of his own fell and landed with a tiny splash on top of Corrie's, hurrying it down his face. "It won't be the same without you, it won't be perfect, but it will be all right. Trust me."

And Corrie, knowing that's what friends were for, trusted him. And feeling less than perfect but still lucky and loved and certain, for once, that the time was right, he let go.

EPILOGUE

*F*ee bounced Baby Corrie on his knee and studied the German lesbian.

"My girlfriend knows nothing," she said. "I am on safari in Africa and drinking with a young man from Australia when all of a sudden"—her eyes widened as if even being there hadn't been proof enough that it had happened—"I am in his sleeping bag."

Fee kissed Corrie on the head and marveled over the baby's soft blond hair at the breadth of the German lesbian's hands. She had big strong knuckles and no jewelry. Ideal.

"How do you feel about Austrian nuns?" he asked.

"It is a long while since I have thought about Austrian nuns," she answered, registering little surprise. "Why?"

"Oh, nothing really," Fee replied. "I did mention that you will need to sing to the cows, though, didn't I?"

"Yes," said the German lesbian. "You did mention that."

The door opened and Abbey came in, her face lighting up as she saw her baby jiggling on Grandy Fee's ancient purple tracksuit pants.

"There you are, you gorgeous girl," she said, reaching for Baby Corrie and lifting her into her arms to be smothered in kisses. "Oh, hello," she said, turning to the German lesbian. "I'm Abbey, the cheesemaker."

"Hello, I am Lili," said Lili. "You have a very beautiful baby. She doesn't look like you."

"No," laughed Abbey, kissing the little button nose between the bright blue eyes, "but she smells like me, that must count for something. Oh, that reminds me," she turned to Fee, "Lucy just rang, she's coming down this weekend to see Jamie and us, of course, and guess what, she's bringing her parents. Can you believe it? She said that meeting Rose has made her realize her own mother is practically a saint. Isn't that gas? Lucy is a Coolarney mum," Abbey explained to Lili, "and this one's birth mother."

She held Corrigan Lucy Stephens in the air and blew a raspberry into her fat little stomach.

"You keep all the babies?" Lili asked.

"I'd like to," laughed Abbey, "but my husband has other thoughts on the matter. No, most of them go home with their mothers, Lili, but don't panic just yet, there's plenty of time for you to decide what you want to do, as Avis will no doubt explain when she arrives. I think she's over in the cottage getting your room ready."

"But how could she be?" asked Lili. "She didn't know I was coming."

"Yes, well, you'll see," smiled Abbey. "Anyway, I'll leave you to it, as soon as I choose a cheese for lunch." She opened the *Cheeses of the World* section in the library and rustled around in the *fromagerie* while Fee explained to the newcomer the history of the Feehans and the Corrigans.

"The deal has always been," he said, "that the Corrigans would provide the cows, the cows would provide the milk, and the Feehans would provide the skills to make cheese—and that's the way we've been doing it for a long, long time now and doing very nicely as a result we are too, thank you for asking."

Abbey stopped what she was doing and turned around,

giving Fee a strange look as she adjusted Baby Corrie on her hip. "The Corrigans would provide the cows?" she asked. "And the Feehans would provide the skills to make cheese?"

Fee looked at her and nodded.

"The Corrigans weren't cheesemakers?"

"They helped make the cheese," he answered, "but they were mainly cow people. Until your grandfather, God rest his soul."

Abbey looked at him, aghast. "The Corrigans were cow people?"

"Before your grandfather, mostly, yes they were."

"So what happened?" she asked, as Lili looked on with passive interest.

"So turns out your grandfather didn't care for cows," Fee said. "Couldn't stand the creatures. Hated the look of them, the sound of them, the touch of them, the smell of them. They brought him out in boils. I think it was a phobia. He started selling cheese when he was twelve years old so he could afford to pay someone else to deal with the filthy things. That's sort of how we got going."

"But what about grand old tradition and it being in the blood and all those things you are always talking about?" Abbey asked, hitching Baby Corrie farther up on her hip.

"Ah, the secret's not in following tradition, it's in knowing when to change it," said Fee, making the baby laugh by poking out his tongue.

Abbey plucked out a chunk of Stilton, closed the refrigerator door and shook her head disbelievingly, a smile on her face all the same.

"You," she said, bending to kiss Fee's bald spot as she passed him on her way out the door, "just make it up as you go along."

"Did you hear that, Joseph?" Fee said to the clock. "Is she a chip off the old feckin' block or wha'?"

"You sing to the cows, you talk to the walls," said the German lesbian. "What kind of a place is this?"

ACKNOWLEDGMENTS

Being naturally nosy myself, I always wonder what other writers are acknowledging people for. In a bid to have no one wonder that about these acknowledgments, I've spelled it out so excuse me if I bang on . . .

Veronica and Norman Steele at Milleens in West Cork were the first artisan cheesemakers I met and I could not have asked for a better introduction. I had imagined that cheesemakers were different (in a good way, of course) from the rest of us, and Veronica and Norman backed this up wonderfully.

Similarly I am greatly indebted to the Ferguson family, especially Giana, at Gubbeen Cheese near Schull. Theirs is the warmest kitchen I've ever been in, and I don't mean temperature. It was the inspiration for the hub of Coolarney House. Before meeting Giana I knew that cheese was magical, I just didn't know how.

In New York City I'd like to thank Ed Needham and Bridget Freer for the unlimited use of their sofa bed with an extra hurrah for Bridget, who worked tirelessly helping me research "sissy boy" drinking and eating emporiums.

I would also like to give a big doff of the cap to Dale and Stuart Blunsome without whom I would not have received the benefit of being represented by the William Morris Agency and in particular Stephanie Cabot in London and Ginger Barber in New York. And what a loss that would have been! For me, I mean. Thanks too to Elyse Green, who gives such good e-mail, and to Jamie Raab, Colin Fox, and the heart-warmingly enthusiastic team at Warner Books.

I'd like also to thank the late Theresa Roberts, God rest her soul, for staying in Ireland, and Ratooragh in particular, when the rest of her family moved as far afield as New Zealand. Without having gone to find her, and the marvelous Mary and Connie Lucey who looked after her in recent years, I'd be two novels down.

Oh, and there's someone else. Someone who cooks and cleans and makes sure I'm sitting in an ergonomically correct fashion. Someone who thinks I can do anything. Someone by the name of Mark Robins, who I tricked into marrying me and trained so well he doesn't realize the doors aren't locked and he could escape at any time. Without him, what would be the point?

Last but not least, I would like to thank my dear, sweet lovely little friend Yetti Redmond for insisting, all those years ago, that I spend winter in Dublin instead of going to Turkey. So, I didn't get a tan but I did get to know and love her hometown and the surrounding country and for that, and for her eternal friendship, I am truly grateful.